A Time for Treason

Enjoy!

Anne N. Walther

ALSO BY ANNE NEWTON WALTHER

Divorce Hangover (Pocket Books, 1991)

A
TIME
for
TREASON

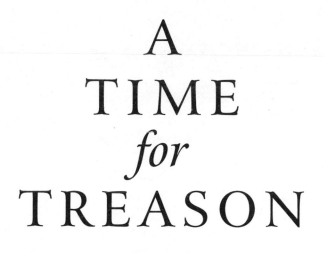

❧❧❧

a novel by

Anne Newton Walther

TAPESTRIES PUBLISHING
San Francisco

Copyright © 2000 by Anne Newton Walther

Published in the United States by
Tapestries Publishing
2006 Washington Street
San Francisco, CA 94109
800-270-9944

Jacket design: George Mattingly
Jacket map: *A New Map of the English Empire in America . . . revised by John Senex, 1710*. Collection of the Bermuda Archives.

Printed on acid-free paper
Printed in Canada

ISBN 0-9676703-0-6

5   4   3   2   1

To the men and women whose minds, spirits,
and sheer grit created one new brave nation
out of thirteen dependent colonies

Acknowledgments

Writing a book is a starkly lonesome business. Perhaps that is why the people who come and go during the process, lending their expertise, knowledge, and in some cases simple encouragement, are more deeply appreciated than is the case in other professions or endeavors.

I am indebted beyond words to the people of Bermuda who generously and graciously gave of their time and knowledge, without which my research would not have achieved its depth and scope; specifically: Frida Chappell and Dick Pearman (who together set me on the path), John Adams, Tom Butterfield, Aubrey Cox, John Cox, Harry Cox (raconteur extraordinaire), Michael L. Darling, Joyce Hall, William de V. Frith, Tony Palmer (offering his primary sources and prodigious knowledge of history), Andrew Trimingham, Hartley Watlington, and William S. Zuill.

The enthusiastic support of George and Claudia Wardman, my Bermudian godparents, is beyond measure.

I owe a great debt of gratitude to the precious number of you who helped build the three-legged stool, professionals who became friends: Zipporah Collins, how do I ever thank you; Alice Acheson, who saw the promise early on; and family and friends who lent their professionalism to the effort—Jad and Christina Dunning; Charlie and Nonie de Limur and André de Baubigny, my French connections, who helped me on so many levels; Anne Lawrence; Jim Holliday; Kathleen Bakula;

Paula Lucas; Gayle Grace; and a brand new friend, who came out of nowhere, Katherine Neville, a special angel.

To my dear friends Debbi and Eric Peniston: there is always someone—or in this case two people—who sets the compass at true north and aims the little craft at its destination; or, to say it in more prosaic terms, you set the deadline when you made me an offer I couldn't refuse.

As always, in all my endeavors, dear family, near and far, I couldn't have done it without you. To my husband, Roger, before, during, and forever, thank you for your staunch support, your enduring patience, and your love.

"If this be treason, make the most of it."

PATRICK HENRY

A
TIME
for
TREASON

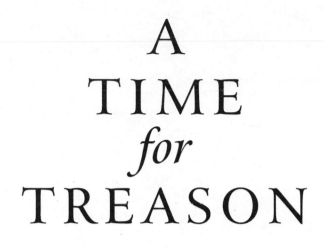

I

⚜ ⚜ ⚜

A lone figure on horseback stood poised at the far edge of the empty pasture. Early dawn light glanced off the glistening coat of the great roan stallion and highlighted the silver buttons on the rider's dark jacket. Suddenly, as one, horse and rider sprang forward. Hoofbeats shattered the morning's silence. Ground birds, flushed from their burrows, protested loudly and scattered in the rider's wake.

A second rider burst from a grove of trees, cutting across the roan's path. Wheeling sharply to avoid a collision, the roan responded to his rider's whip and leapt forward into a spine-crunching gallop. Neck and neck the two horses streaked across the meadow, each straining for advantage. So close were they that the plumes of breath from their flaring nostrils blended on the cool morning air. Only the fast-approaching riverbank brought an end to the headlong dash. Pulling hard on their reins, the riders wrenched the mounts back from the river's edge. Hooves danced, seeking purchase. The roan trumpeted loudly and reared high on his hind legs. The pursuer lunged to grab a maroon sleeve. Off balance, both riders crashed to the ground.

The maroon-clad rider jumped up, snatched off a tightly fitted cap, and flung it to the ground.

"*Mon Dieu!* Let me be!"

Still sprawled on the ground, the assailant stared up in shock as a riot of chestnut waves cascaded down.

"Eugénie—forgive me, Comtesse—is it you? God's blood! I could have killed you!"

Eugénie brushed back her hair and said with surprising composure, "Well, St. George, it appears you didn't." Flicking the mud and grass off her britches with one hand, she graciously extended the other to the young man, who scrambled to his feet. "As you can see, I'm little the worse for wear." She stared wide-eyed at the swollen rapids below. "*Jésus, Marie, et Joseph,* we both could have been killed."

Eugénie took a deep breath and looked up through thick, dark lashes at the young man standing awkwardly beside her. "You really gave me a fright. I had no idea you were my mad pursuer." She leaned over and picked up her hat, her eyes twinkling. "So, do I chastise you for intruding on my morning exercise, or do I give you a chance to explain yourself?"

"Eugénie . . . that is, Comtesse," St. George blurted out, "thank God you're unharmed. You may do with me what you will, as long as you allow me to bask in the radiance of your company."

Eugénie ignored the lavish compliment and gave him a long look. "I'm awkward in your language, St. George. Forgive me if I misunderstand or am misunderstood, but your escapade could have caused both of us serious harm."

"Escapade!" The word caught him by surprise. "Milady, uh, my pardon, Comtesse," St. George said, blushing. His usual sanguine nature deserted him as he continued to stumble over her title. "I beg you not to toy with me. I'm a simple man, the fourth son of a mercantile Bermudian, here in Williamsburg studying the law. Since I met you a fortnight ago and fell victim to your beauty, I've been in a state of confusion, a stranger to myself. You are like no lady of my acquaintance."

Eugénie smiled at his stilted speech but waved his declarations aside. "St. George, I really . . ."

"Comtesse Eugénie, please hear me out. This morning, even before the rooster's first crow, I was wandering out of doors, sleepless again. I saw a rider emerge from the stable on Mr. Whittington's prize stallion. I assumed thievery. There have been many reports of such lately. So, without a thought, I gave chase on the horse closest at hand, the great roan's own son. How could I have imagined that the furtive rider was you? Ladies of my acquaintance don't ride astride, dressed in clothes befitting a man. Nor do they exhibit horsemanship equal to that of any man in Virginia." Hitting his stride, St. George said, "And furthermore, Comtesse Eugénie, you carelessly risk your person riding unattended. Happily, I place myself at your service—a willing escort."

Eugénie laughed delightedly at the young man's earnestness. "St. George, call me Eugénie, *tout simple*. As to the other matters you mention, forgive me for shocking you with my unconventional dress. I'm so accustomed to exercising my own stable in the comfort of britches that I think nothing of it. The solitary nature of my ride . . ." She hesitated. With a Gallic shrug that charmed St. George, she said, "My dear mother and father, God rest their souls, knew that the responsibilities I would inherit would demand unique training. It may be scandalous to many, but my independence is my most prized legacy from my loving parents." Having said far more than she intended, Eugénie turned a bright smile on the thoroughly dumbfounded and besotted St. George and said abruptly, "I've been wondering about the merit of the great roan's issue. It would appear from our merry chase that the sire's bloodlines begat equal strength in his offspring."

"Aye," St. George agreed, "they are well matched. But for the star on the son, each could easily be taken for the other."

"Why has this magnificent beast never been named?" she asked, turning to stroke the roan standing quietly at her side.

"Some years past," St. George answered, "when this one's sire was a foal, Mr. Whittington claims to have received a message in a dream that predicted great strength and speed from the foal's line if the foal and his progeny remained nameless except for their color designation: Roan. The chosen foal from each generation has borne out the prediction. The might and swiftness of Roan I has been equaled by Roan II—and now Roan III."

"It seems an odd tradition, but I can't argue with the result," Eugénie said, looking skyward. "Now the sun's well up, and I'm eager to talk terms with my host. I've already received his hospitality one week short of a month. March is soon upon us, and I have done little with my time except discover the vastness of both land and bloodstock on this side of the ocean. There's much to do if I'm to return to France with my syndicate's mission accomplished."

In a graceful motion, Eugénie mounted the roan. Unruffled by the sudden movement, the stallion stood docilely awaiting her command. St. George mounted quickly, marveling again at her grace and sureness in the saddle. He muttered to himself, "How many men have shied from that fiery beast, yet he carries her with the meekness of a lamb."

Catching up with Eugénie, he said, "Your syndicate pursues an ambitious plan, bringing the sport of horseracing to France. It seems a long way to come to acquire your bloodstock, when England and Ireland's proven racers are so near at hand." It also seems strange, he thought, to entrust such a responsibility to a member of the gentler sex, great horsewoman though she might be. No telling with the French.

"St. George, the reasons are very clear. The English and Irish, as you well know, have never been friends of France, particularly now with the Seven Years' War, or the French and Indian War as you call it over here, so fresh in their minds. The English and the Irish have their own quarrels, but neither of them has any interest in furthering a French endeavor. Nor would we look to them for such assistance. My countrymen are still smarting from their recent defeat at the hands of the English. Perhaps one day such an exchange will be possible, but for now, *c'est impossible.*"

"There's still something that puzzles me," St. George began.

"And what might that be?"

Looking straight ahead, St. George missed her sharp look. "As you say, there's long-standing animosity between the French and the English. You're French. Don't you have similar feelings toward the American colonials who helped defeat your countrymen on this very soil?"

A look of relief swept over his companion's face. "*Au contraire,* the battles waged here were transported from across the ocean. They were inflicted on the colonials by their mother country. Neither I nor my countrymen hold the colonials responsible for the war or its outcome." Eugénie looked over at her companion. Seeing his discomfort, she lightened her tone. "It's quite simple, really. The American colonies, particularly Virginia, are known for unique breeding methods and superior racing stock, though the Irish and English are too arrogant to recognize it. Since horseracing in France is in its infancy, my syndicate can afford to introduce these new methods. I've been directed to return with both a good sample of strong bloodstock and a knowledge of the special methods used to produce it. Forgive me for going on so, but my enthusiasm for this project knows no bounds." The two rode in silence for a few minutes, lost in their own thoughts.

Glancing sideways at her companion, Eugénie said, "Certainly I know little of these matters, but it appears to me that there's a growing resentment here toward the British Crown, as well."

"Aye, 'tis true," St. George agreed. "I've heard many a discussion at day's end over a good pipe and strong brandy. The colonials are balking at the heavy burden King George places on them to pay for that war, though it seems they blame his ministers at Whitehall far more than the king. There is word that the Bostonians are taking things into their own hands more and more."

His words corroborated her information. Not wanting to arouse his suspicions by showing interest in his remarks, she tossed her head and replied airily, "Enough of such talk. It's no concern of mine. I leave it to wiser minds to wrestle with such weighty matters. Instead, I will tend to the far more delightful prospect of equestrian breeding and selecting the finest racing stock Virginia has to offer."

With that, she lightly flicked the roan with her reins. Needing little encouragement, the great horse set off across the meadow at a fast clip.

II

🙟🙟🙟

As they approached the Whittington stables, Eugénie was struck again by the beauty of the Virginia countryside. Situated between Richmond and Williamsburg, the seat of British government in the colony, the land belonging to her host, Mr. Whittington, stretched as far as the eye could see, interrupted only by whitewashed fencing.

John Whittington had learned much about farming from his father. But the knowledge he had acquired about new farming methods and animal husbandry while traveling as a young man in England, Italy, and France had helped him to create a plantation system unsurpassed throughout the Tidewater area of Virginia. His reputation as a generous host as well as an innovative planter drew people from the distant northern borders of Maryland to the deep southern regions of the Carolinas.

In any season, Oak Knoll bustled with the comings and goings of countless visitors who came to learn John Whittington's techniques or simply to enjoy the renowned Whittington hospitality. Eugénie had struggled since her arrival three weeks earlier to figure out who were members of the household and who were guests. Her efforts were further complicated by John's practice of housing students, such as St. George Tucker, from the nearby College of William and Mary. In addition, he extended his hospitality to the sons of neighboring planters who sought apprenticeships in his system. Eugénie's own status in the household was unique, based on the close friendship developed long ago between her host and her guardian when both were young students in Paris. Not since her parents' tragic deaths five years earlier had she enjoyed such a sense of family.

"I didn't know more guests were coming." St. George's words broke into Eugénie's reverie.

"Yes," Eugénie replied, "the dates for the livestock auctions have been moved up. Something to do with the activities up north. The first auction begins this afternoon, but only for those from the immediate vicinity. By midweek, they will include the whole eastern seaboard, with a ball at the Governor's Palace at week's end."

As they trotted into the stableyard, activity swirled around them. Horses, colts, fillies, and even foals pressed on all sides. Stableboys were running back and forth, and liveried servants stood by carriages, awaiting direction.

"Oh, dear," Eugénie cried in dismay. "We're much later than I had thought. Mary was counting on my help with tonight's dinner." Concern spread across her dirt-smudged face.

"Here, Eugénie, it is my fault you're tardy. I'll stable the roan as a small token of my appreciation for your company this morn."

St. George was rewarded with a relieved smile from his companion. Glancing at her dusty garb, Eugénie exclaimed, "What a sight I must be!" She whirled from the horse's back and raced out of the stableyard. Left holding the reins of the matched pair, St. George stared after her slender form.

Lost in thought, Eugénie rounded the corner of the stable and bumped solidly into a well-muscled body. The impact momentarily knocked the wind from her lungs.

"Hold there, lad. Is the Devil himself at your heels?" The rich voice and the strong hands that gripped her shoulders brought Eugénie up short. She looked up into a bright, blue gaze. Her breath caught again. She was aware of a height that dwarfed hers—no small feat—and sandy hair that framed a deeply tanned face. A chuckle died in the man's throat as he, too, was arrested by the vision before him. This was clearly no lad.

Eugénie drew herself up to her full height. "Let go of me, sir! How dare you grapple me! Lurking at corners, waylaying innocent people … I've a mind to report your impertinence to my host!"

The stranger not only ignored her words but also subjected her to a slow and thorough scrutiny. She felt her naturally high color deepen as his blue gaze traveled the length of her. A look of appreciation spread across his dark face as he savored her proud carriage, the disheveled chestnut beauty of her hair, even the silver challenge of her eyes.

Reluctantly he tore his gaze away from the full lips and bowed deeply. "Bridger Goodrich, at your service, ma'am. Forgive my grappling," he said, his eyes twinkling. With an exaggerated gesture, he clasped his hands behind his back. "However, had I not caught you, we both might have fallen into the dust. Certainly an unseemly experience for a lady, though from your appearance I might conclude that you've met with that fate already this morn."

Eugénie responded in cool tones, "Sir, I have not the slightest interest in your observations. Your behavior is repugnant and your manner worse. Step aside and let me pass." Mustering what dignity she could, Eugénie stepped around him and proceeded swiftly down the graveled path toward the main house.

Bridger watched her retreating figure with speculating eyes. "I look forward to our next meeting, my lovely," he murmured to himself.

At last, Eugénie arrived at her bedchamber. She took a deep breath, willing herself to dismiss the confrontation with the stranger. She entered the room and spotted her servant, Marie, embroidering a silk coverlet.

"Marie, thank God you are here! *Vitement,* my rose afternoon dress, *s'il vous plaît,* and a bath. *Vite! Vite!*"

"*Oui, mademoiselle.*" Marie moved quickly to do Eugénie's bidding.

Eugénie caught her reflection in the looking glass. I am a sight! she thought. No wonder he mistook me for a stableboy. Suddenly, appreciating the humor of the encounter, Eugénie burst out laughing. She felt again his strong hands and his intense gaze, and her breath quickened. With a shake of her head, she brought herself back to the moment.

"Wouldn't your green velvet riding costume be more appropriate for the auction?" Marie asked.

Ordinarily, such impertinence on the part of a servant would not be permitted, but theirs was a special relationship. Nothing in Marie's speech or appearance suggested that she had come from a long line of retainers in the de Beaumont household. Eugénie herself had been in the care of Marie's own mother since her earliest memory, long before the death of her parents. The two little girls had been raised side by side, as much friends as mistress and servant.

"Oh yes, of course, Marie. Whatever was I thinking?" Eugénie sat on the edge of the four-poster bed, absently smoothing the goose-down comforter. *Who was that arrogant stranger? How could I have overlooked one so uncommonly handsome?* Her teeth worried her full lower lip. *To carry out this mission and avoid mishap requires knowing by face, if not by name, everyone who has business at Oak Knoll. Who is he and what is his intent? Perhaps he's here simply to attend the livestock auction. Perhaps not.*

Marie pulled a small wooden tub into the center of the spacious room. Eugénie moved toward it, shedding men's shoes, hose, britches, jacket, and shirt as she went. Sinking into the warm, perfumed water, she let out a sigh of sheer contentment. When her bath was completed, she wrapped herself in a huge towel and sat down at the dressing table. Soon Marie's deft fingers had created a masterpiece of the glossy chestnut ringlets.

"Ah, once more a lady," Marie said, pleased with the result. In short order, Eugénie's toilette was complete. She looked at her reflection in the looking glass, nodding her approval at the tightly fitted bodice that accentuated high firm breasts and tiny waist. The flaring skirt, free of hoops, hung to the floor and showed just the tips of the matching green leather boots. Eugénie's slender frame disguised her unusual height and gave her form an almost delicate air. She clasped her signature gold bracelet to her wrist as Marie held out a confection of lace and bows. "Your parasol, Mistress."

"Marie, I ride all morning under the full sun and now, in the shade, I'm to carry a parasol? I hate such affectation!"

"But, milady, how else will you keep your complexion unmarred?" Marie, who had always taken an inordinate pride in Eugénie's ravishing beauty, chuckled, "You're already the envy of all the ladies. Let them believe it's the parasol and the special unguents and powders from the Continent that sustain your glowing complexion, rather than your health and high spirits."

Eugénie laughed. "Oh, very well, then, if you insist. Now, I must go. I fear I'm already too late to help Mrs. Whittington."

Eugénie hurried along the wide hall and down the broad mahogany stairway. She found her hostess still in the dining room, overseeing the preparations for the post-auction dinner.

"Ah, Eugénie," Mary said, greeting her warmly. "Don't you look fetching!" Although she was in her middle years, Mary Whittington's serene expression and slender figure belied her age. The delicate blue silk of the fashionably cut gown set off her blond coloring perfectly. Mary's kindness and gentle nature drew into her circle of warmth her four children, her doting husband, and all who met her.

"Come, dear Eugénie, and lend your special touch to these flowers." Relieved to be able to help her hostess, Eugénie went quickly to work. She sorted through the lush boughs of early spring fruit-blossoms and chose the vivid pink quince to blend with the deeper-toned redbud, and then, as a final touch, she added pale apple blooms. Their scent filled the handsome room, which gleamed with dark Chippendale furniture. Eugénie stepped back to admire her handiwork. The late morning sun highlighted the ornate silver flatware and large candelabra that graced the oversized dining table. Mary placed gold-bordered serving plates on the rich cream damask cloth that matched the swags and jabots framing the floor-to-ceiling windows. Over the sideboard, a heavily carved looking glass reflected the women's activity against the unusual peach wall pigment. As lovely a room as any in France, Eugénie thought with satisfaction.

"I believe we're just about finished, unless you can think of something I've missed," Mary said.

"*Non, non,*" Eugénie protested. "*C'est magnifique.* It's perfect just the way it is."

"Eugénie, I'm so pleased you like it." The grandfather clock in the hallway began to strike the hour and Mary exclaimed, "My, how the morning has flown! The auction is beginning. You must be off. I'll join you just as soon as I've checked the girls in the kitchen. Go quickly—there's nothing more to do here, and you don't want to miss your chance to bid for Roan II. He's early on the docket."

At Eugénie's surprised look, Mary laughed delightedly. "Dear child, there's not much I don't know that happens here at Oak Knoll. Your early morning rides and your love for that horse are the talk of the stableyard. If I may make a suggestion, there's word of a young bay gelding to be auctioned today. You might be interested in him, as well. Of course, he can't serve stud, but his strength and speed would be a great addition to any racing stable."

With a wave, Mary left by the side door that led to the separate kitchen buildings.

Now, how would she know that? Eugénie mused.

III

❧❧❧

Eugénie arrived at the stableyard just as Roan II was being led into the paddock. She was dismayed to see the great animal fighting his handler. With dancing hooves, the roan evaded the ramp leading to the auction block. He lifted his head suddenly, as if testing the wind, and then lunged to the left. Trumpeting his protest he reared high, forelegs pawing the air. The stablehand fought to keep his balance while grabbing at the harness. Ears laid back and eyes rolling, the mighty stallion reared again, his hooves climbing even higher in the air.

The crowd hushed, staring in horror. The voice of a man standing near Eugénie rang out in the silence. "Damn nag! A good beating would teach him his master." Eugénie gave the short, stout man a disdainful look and slipped through the crowd. As she approached the panicked horse, she placed two fingers to her lips and whistled softly. Roan II froze in midair and then settled quietly to earth. He shook his head as though coming out of a trance and turned toward the familiar sound.

"Ah, Eugénie, you have averted a catastrophe!" exclaimed John Whittington, stepping down from the block. "Name your price and the roan is yours. It's clear he will have no one but you."

Stroking the now-gentled stallion, Eugénie replied, "As you know, he is priceless to me. But let's not delay the auction. We can set our terms later. Can you move the bay gelding back on the schedule? I would hate to miss bidding on him while I'm stabling the roan."

"You've made an excellent beginning, Eugénie. The bay is another first-rate choice. I'll see that he's moved as far back on the docket as possible."

Smiling her thanks, Eugénie turned and led the proud animal out of the paddock, amidst the crowd's calls for the next entry. "So, you thought I'd abandoned you to that motley group?" she whispered to the roan. As if in answer, Roan II leaned down to nuzzle his new mistress. "You impostor, just a lamb beneath that brave front! I expect you to behave yourself when I leave you in Abraham's care. *Comprends-tu?*" As they entered the dim coolness of the stables, Eugénie could see the head trainer coming toward them.

"Ah, Abraham, the roan needs your attention. He's had a very trying morning."

"Yes, ma'am," Abraham said, his black face breaking into a wide grin, "Dat crowd done spooked dat po' hoss. Leave him to Abraham. He'll settle down in no time."

"Thank you, Abraham. I know he's in good hands, now," Eugénie replied as the trainer led Roan II away. She was nearly out of the stable when she heard a loud hiss.

"Psst! Psssst!"

Startled, Eugénie turned toward the sound. She looked around quickly and, satisfied that no one was watching, darted into the dark enclosure.

"Where have you been?" came the urgent whisper in French. "Early this morning I waited for you as planned. And again, when you returned to the stableyard. I've much to tell you about my trip north."

"Oh, Jacques, I'm so glad you've come back safely!" Eugénie whispered toward the dark shadow just inside the stall gate. "There's no time to go into everything now. I'll be missed if I stay much longer."

"*Oui, oui, c'est très dangereux ici.* At dusk, I'll meet you in the boxwood garden. It should be safe for us there. In the meantime, a man at the auction named Silas Deane bears watching. Until tonight!" The shadow separated from the dark wall and was gone.

Shaken by the suddenness of her countryman's appearance, Eugénie took a deep breath. For the first time since she had arrived in Virginia, she realized the grave danger of her undertaking.

It had seemed so simple when the cartel of France's intellectual aristocracy had approached her three months earlier. Her father's friends had come to her château on the Garonne and mapped out the political and economic reasons why they wanted to learn the extent of the Americans' dissatisfaction with the British Crown. It would be so simple, they claimed, for her to travel to Virginia and report back the colonials' discontent as a representative of the French thoroughbred racing syndicate. Then, if the situation warranted it, the cartel would assert its considerable influence to bring France in on the side of the Americans.

They listed the many reasons why she was perfect for the role. No one would ever suspect a French comtesse of doing such a thing. The long-standing friendship between her French guardian and the Whittingtons would ensure her a welcome into the colonials' inner circles, even to the British governor himself. As the racing syndicate's representative, she could move freely amongst the colonials without suspicion. Finally, she was unfettered by husband or family.

Yes, she thought, it had all seemed so simple then, looking out over the terraced vineyards of my château sipping my white Bordeaux with my fellow constituents. Oh, how eager I was to accept their plan that would finally give me a chance to avenge my parents' death. She flushed with anger, remembering again that day. The British frigate had no call to fire on my father's unarmed merchant ship, sinking it and drowning all aboard, including my beloved mother and father. I will have my revenge against the British. No matter what the risk, I will go forward.

Once more resolute in her purpose, Eugénie moved out into the bright sunshine and ran directly into Mary Whittington. Grabbing Eugénie's hand, Mary hurried her along the path to the paddock. "I heard about the commotion the roan made. He came to no harm, I trust?"

"Oh, no," Eugénie replied. "He's in Abraham's capable hands, no doubt even now nibbling undeserved sugar lumps for his mischief."

The bidding for the bay was well along when they arrived at the auction. Raising her hand, Eugénie entered her bid. A flurry of bids answered hers. The horse's price mounted. Soon, only Eugénie and one other bidder remained in the contest. Eugénie scanned the crowd to seek out her opponent. To her shock, her eyes locked with familiar blue ones. Bridger Goodrich raised an eyebrow at her and gestured to the auctioneer, topping Eugénie's last bid.

If it's a contest you want, Eugénie thought, then it's a contest you shall have! Lifting her chin, she held his eyes and raised Bridger's bid by a wide margin. As one, the hushed crowd turned to see if there would be a reply. The look of triumph froze on Eugénie's face when Bridger appeared to be ready to respond. He hesitated a moment, taking her measure, and then turned and gave the signal that he was withdrawing.

Eugénie wondered why the man unsettled her so. And why she felt he'd planned this outcome right from the start, merely to play with her.

Mary Whittington squeezed her arm. "Oh, I'm so glad the bay is yours. I thought for a moment that handsome Bridger Goodrich was going to top your bid, even though I can't imagine why he'd be interested in adding to his stables," she said, confirming Eugénie's earlier thought. "All the men in that family are at sea so much of the time, I'm amazed they even remember how to sit a horse. Actually, Bridger is as comfortable astride a horse as he is standing on the decks of a ship. There's little that he does that he doesn't do beautifully—now that I think of it. That's his younger brother, Edward, standing there next to him, and he has four other brothers who aren't here. Bridger is the one on whom all eligible ladies have their sights set—even some of the not-so-eligible, from what I've heard. Thank goodness my Bess is attracted to the milder sort," Mary said with a laugh. "Whatever the gossip, that young man can do no wrong in my eyes. He saved our lead foxhound from drowning, at great risk to his own life. Yes, I will always have a soft spot in my heart for Bridger."

While appearing to listen to Mary's running commentary, Eugénie watched the two brothers out of the corner of her eye.

"Now, who could that be?" Mary asked. "I thought I knew everyone at the auction today. Eugénie, do you know who that man is? See him? He's looking this way. There by the rail, the rather tall one with the severe expression. He certainly appears to be taking a particular interest in you." Eugénie followed Mary's gaze, but the crowd shifted and the man disappeared from view.

"I only caught a glimpse of him, but I can't say he looks familiar," Eugénie said lightly, trying to appear unconcerned. "I imagine my bidding war with Mr. Goodrich has attracted quite a bit of attention to both of us."

"John will know, I'm sure. Oh my, if John has included him for dinner, I'll have to add another place. Well, enough fun for now," Mary said briskly. "I must go back to the house and make sure everything's on schedule. I just wish I could stay to watch you keep all these men on their toes! I'll count on you to help me entertain our guests at dinner. Oak Knoll has never had so many illustrious guests under its roof at one time, including Mr. Jefferson and the young Lee boy. Now, there are two men who know their bloodstock. Until later, then." And she was gone.

As the afternoon wore on, the bidding became more intense. The heated contest between Eugénie and Bridger had opened some invisible floodgate. Eugénie made several more acquisitions but was outbid twice by the man who had made the offensive remarks about the roan. Pleased with what she had accomplished so far, Eugénie decided to pass on the last entry, a high-strung white filly. As she watched the final bidding of the day, her mind turned to Bridger Goodrich. In shipping, is he? On the surface, a good Virginian family that makes its fortunes at sea. But, should battle lines be drawn, what would bind their loyalty: their purse and a fair wind—or a higher calling? No matter. In my position, I must be wary.

Suddenly, the subject of her thoughts materialized at her side. "Fair lady, may I escort you to the main house? The auction appears over for the day."

Eugénie jumped as though stung. Against her better judgment, she let her eyes move slowly over sandy hair ruffled by a light breeze, then to shoulders broad beneath a dark waistcoat, and finally to a generous mouth tilted in a smile. She averted her eyes. "Ah, sir, you startled me."

Hoping to avoid his company without appearing rude, she continued, "Thank you, but I must forgo your kind offer. I'm on my way to the stables to assure myself that Roan II did not suffer from this morning's excitement. He was badly frightened by the crowd."

Undeterred by her obvious dismissal, Bridger fell in beside her, resting his hand lightly on her elbow. "I observed your bravery and was awed by your composure," he said warmly. "I'm certain an unfortunate accident would have marred this pleasant occasion had it not been for your quick wits."

Do I hear laughter beneath this elaborate courtesy? she wondered. " 'Tis not bravery when there's nothing to fear," she retorted. Pulling her arm from his grasp, she hastened her step down the path to the stables.

To her chagrin, Bridger moved right along beside her. "What reward will you give me for my generosity this day?"

"And just what generosity might that be?"

"Why, dear lady, your gelding acquisition, of course."

"On the contrary, sir, I owe a very large price for that horse, for which you are responsible, as you very well know. I owe you nothing but my ire for forcing me to bid so outrageously."

"Ah, but had I not driven the price up, who knows how long the other eager bidders might have continued to frustrate your efforts? I bow to your present time constraints and will collect my reward at a more opportune moment. Mark my words, fair lady, I am never closed out of anything that my heart desires. Had I desired the bay, he would this minute be mine."

Beneath his mild tone, Eugénie felt his iron will. She shivered, knowing that his words spoke to more than just the acquisition of the bay.

Seeing her tremble, Bridger quickly shed his jacket and draped it around her shoulders. "Madame, you are chilled. Forgive me for keeping you lingering in this cool afternoon air."

Is he laughing at me again? The feel of his hands on her shoulders was not the least bit unpleasant, yet she felt that for her own safety she must keep him at arm's length. "Mr. Goodrich, you haven't kept me lingering at all. I am seeing to my horse. I must ask you to remove your coat at once. I find the familiarity of such a gesture highly distasteful." Even as she spoke, she questioned the honesty of her words. Exasperated as much with herself as with him, she asked, "Isn't there something more pressing that needs your attention?"

"Please, call me Bridger. As to my attentions, I can imagine nothing more pressing for the moment than enjoying your fascinating company."

Eugénie attempted an indifferent shrug. She entered the stable and hurried to Roan II's stall, with Bridger still in tow. The roan pushed his head into her hands and then bent to nuzzle her neck. Eugénie crooned softly to him. Bridger, standing to the side, enjoyed watching the affectionate exchange between the delicate girl and the huge stallion.

"Rarely have I seen such a bond between a human being and an animal," Bridger remarked after a long silence. "He is truly fortunate in his mistress. He will serve you well."

Surprised at the tone in Bridger's voice, Eugénie turned to him. "Yes, he is a unique animal," she said softly, "but it is I who am the fortunate one." The roan moved toward Bridger and stood quietly under his stroking hands. Eugénie marveled at the horse's uncustomary behavior toward a stranger. In that minute, all three were caught in a skein of kinship.

"Brother!" called a loud male voice. Abruptly, the mood was broken. A young man came rushing toward them. "I've been looking everywhere for you. You must come at once."

Bridger turned sharply. "Edward, you forget yourself. My lady, I beg your pardon for my brother's boorish behavior. Comtesse Eugénie Devereux de Beaumont, may I present my brother, Edward Goodrich."

Thoroughly chastened, Edward stammered, "Comtesse, my haste makes me thoughtless. Please forgive me." Tearing his eyes from her face, he turned once again to his brother. "Nonetheless, Bridger, I do insist that you come with me. Immediately!"

"Comtesse, if you will excuse me, it appears my attention is needed elsewhere." Bridger took her hand and, bending over it, brushed his lips briefly across her fingers. After a lingering look, he turned and was gone.

Suddenly alone, she raised the hand to her mouth. She felt the heat from his touch and was again bemused by the effect he had on her.

"And what do you have to say for yourself, you fickle beast?" she murmured, absently stroking the roan's muzzle. "I feel unsafe with this man—and yet you befriend him." With a last look at the great horse, she made her way quickly from the stables.

IV

✤✤✤

The main house bustled with guests enjoying the Whittington hospitality. Many stopped Eugénie to offer their congratulations on her acquisitions that day or to ask her secret for controlling the great roan. A few expressed their surprise at her knowledge of horses and the complexities of bidding. All were astonished to discover that she was a Frenchwoman alone in Virginia.

Eugénie endeared herself to each person, inquiring politely about their families and where they lived. She elicited much information without appearing to do so.

She recognized Mr. Thomas Jefferson by his exceptional height and reddish sandy hair and made her way over to him. His initial awkwardness evaporated as he described to her the elaborate plantings at his home, Monticello. Warming to his subject, he began to pace back and forth on the veranda. "I've set aside one garden strictly for plant experimentation. During your stay, you must be my guest on the mountain. I think you'll find what I'm doing quite interesting. Yes, yes. And perhaps, with your knowledge and love of horses, my stables might provide an additional temptation for you."

"I'd love to see your gardens and planting, but it would be pure delight to visit your stables," Eugénie replied, somewhat breathlessly, struggling to keep up with his long stride. "I've heard they are renowned in the colony."

Jefferson's eyes lit up. "Miss Eugénie, they are one of the great joys of my life. If I may share a secret with you . . ." He leaned toward her. "I am far more at ease astride the four legs of a horse than on my own two feet."

They were still laughing when Jefferson's gaze was drawn to a young man moving toward them with great purpose. "Comtesse de Beaumont," Jefferson said, waving him forward, "may I present Mr. Henry Lee of the Virginia Lees, who is a great horseman in his own right."

"Sir, you flatter me," Henry Lee said, his respect for the older man apparent in his eyes. Then, turning to Eugénie with admiration of an entirely different sort, he bowed gracefully and said, "I'm charmed to make your acquaintance, milady. I envy you the roan and bay you purchased this day. And I have heard much of your horsemanship from St. George. If I'm not being too forward, I'd like to invite you to match your roan against my chestnut, should time and events allow."

"I accept with pleasure your invitation and eagerly anticipate the match," Eugénie replied, her eyes sparkling with the challenge. Her forthright manner raised both men's opinion of the French in general and Eugénie in particular.

Bowing again to Eugénie, Henry Lee turned to Jefferson and asked, "Do I hear rightly that my kinsman, Mr. Richard Henry Lee, is here? I'm amazed that so many of the illustrious of our colony are attending the auction, considering that the Philadelphia session is so close upon us."

"Perhaps for that very reason," Jefferson replied blandly. "Soon enough, the session will lay claim to the attention and efforts of all of us, not just those who go to Philadelphia. It's appropriate that we gather here at John and Mary's home. They've always offered hospitality to those of like interests and sympathies. It's a haven in more ways than one."

Half listening to the two men's conversation, Eugénie thought, Jefferson's openness surprises me. He must be very sure of his company. Clearly, there's little British support at Oak Knoll this day. It appears that the auction serves more than one purpose for others, as well as for me.

"Messages from the north suggest that events may soon dictate action," said Henry Lee. His words pulled Eugénie's attention back to the two men.

Jefferson's handsome face turned still. "Those are not words to be said lightly, Henry. Many things are at stake. Philadelphia will determine much, and the world will be watching."

Eugénie saw John Whittington making his way toward them. "Ah, I believe our host seeks your company, gentlemen," she said, seeing a chance to slip away. "I look forward to joining you later for the feast Mary has prepared for us. Until then?" With a polite curtsy, Eugénie hurried off.

"What a charming young lady your guest is, John," she heard Thomas Jefferson say as she moved through the crowd.

At last Eugénie gained her bedchamber to find Marie laying out her dress for the evening. "Oh, Marie, the peach-and-green silk! However did you find the time?"

Delighted at Eugénie's pleasure, Marie answered, "I learn much from the other servants as we all sit at our sewing." Carefully drawing the delicate fabric over Eugénie's elaborate undergarments, Marie said, "There's much talk of a city called Philadelphia where very shortly leaders from every colony, except Georgia, will be gathering. A man named Silas Deane, who arrived at Oak Knoll early this morning, seems to know much about the activities up north."

Eugénie turned sharply. "Again, that name. What have you heard of this man, Silas Deane? Jacques spoke of him just today. So far, I have yet to make his acquaintance."

"He seems little known hereabouts," answered Marie, "except that he is a delegate to the upcoming Continental Congress in Philadelphia and is of modest means, representing the colony called Connecticut. He seems of one mind with those who question the British authority, and he travels freely between the colonies carrying information. That's all I've heard. Oh, one last interesting note: he cast the winning bids on two horses you bid on. Not being a man of great means, I wonder if he acts as agent for another. Does that help you recognize him?"

"Indeed, it does," replied Eugénie. "He stood near me at the auction. He affects an affable nature, but his guard dropped at one point and I saw the cruel streak beneath. You've heard that he's one of the patriots. Hmmm, I'd better keep a close eye on him."

"Mistress, I fear for you. The stakes are high on both sides of this issue. You have a grave responsibility and no one to look to, should you be found out."

"Marie, Marie," Eugénie reassured her, "your devotion is my strength, and your concern is noted. What you say is true, but your risk is no less than my own. We came here on a mission that we must carry out. Yes, the stakes are indeed high for us as well as for them. But, dear Marie, we knew that from the outset. We must trust no one. Promise me that you'll be as vigilant for yourself as you are for me. We are alone in this—and the danger is ever-present."

"Mistress," Marie said, looking down at her hands, "I am not entirely alone. There is one whom I favor here whose company gives me much pleasure. His circumstances are such that our friendship cannot be out in the open at this time, but I think much of him and he of me. If, in my life, I have nothing more than your trust and his love, I will count myself amongst the truly fortunate."

Struck by the passion of her servant's words, Eugénie hesitated and then said, "I will not press you for the identity of this man. If he occasions such emotions from one so cautious as you, I will wait until you are ready to share his name with me. Pray, heed your own words, though, and go carefully. Do not let your emotions play you false and lay you open to . . ."

Marie interrupted before Eugénie could say more, "I would do nothing to endanger you, Mistress, even if I had to put myself at risk to protect you! I will be cautious and constant toward the purpose we both serve here. You must know that my devotion to your mother and father was not one whit less than my mother's."

Marie's agitation was clear. In an effort to lighten the moment,

Eugénie said, "Ah, and where is your devotion to my toilette? Come, come, we've dwelled enough on these weighty subjects. Enough said. I'd best hurry or I'll be late for Mary's dinner."

A short time later, Eugénie twirled before the glass, admiring the reflection of the peach-and-green vision before her. Then, regaining her dignity, she moved sedately to the door. Marie laughed at her mistress's playful manner.

"You needn't wait up for me, Marie. I meet with Jacques as soon as I can discreetly withdraw from the evening's events. I may return quite late." The moment of levity passed with the mention of the *rendez-vous*. Eugénie, already in the hallway, missed the look of concern that passed over Marie's face.

Eugénie arrived in the great center hall just as the guests were being ushered into the dining room, led by a radiant Mary Whittington.

"Comtesse Eugénie, may I?" An eager St. George stepped forward, extending his arm for her hand.

Stifling an urge to laugh at his formal manner, Eugénie said smoothly, "Why, St. George, how kind of you." Resting her fingers lightly on his arm, she allowed the beaming young man to lead her to the long table. Taking his assigned seat next to her, he entertained Eugénie with his light chatter. The first course was succulent brook trout dressed in its own juices with an oyster overglaze. Eugénie imagined that the delicious fish had come from one of the many streams and brooks at Oak Knoll. The next presentation was *faisan en croûte* served with tender spring vegetables and the renowned Virginia ham. Course followed course, each accompanied by a wine specifically chosen from John Whittington's vast cellars.

Eugénie nibbled sparingly, not exhibiting her usual healthy appetite. Beneath her surface calm, her mind worked frantically. Will this meal never end? How am I going to rid myself of dear St. George without arousing suspicion? While appearing to hang on St. George's every word, she listened carefully to other conversations. Discussions of the day's auction, the spring planting season, and other matters of local interest flowed around her. She felt a fine tension permeate the festive atmosphere and caught herself wondering at the *sang-froid* of these men and their women. If rumors were to be believed, these people were tied closely to others throughout the colonies who sought to change their relationship to Britain.

She had learned about many incidents over the past few years that had culminated in the dumping of 342 chests of tea into Boston's harbor by fed-up colonials dressed as Mohawk Indians. In retribution, London's House of Commons had passed the Port Act, which virtually closed the port of Boston and moved that colony's seat of government from Boston to Salem. Although it caused hardship for the colony, Virginia, acting out of sympathy for her sister colony, had decreed an end to all British imports as of November of the previous year. It was at about that time, November 1774, that Eugénie had been approached by her father's friends and had been persuaded to undertake her mission to the colonies. Only recently had she learned that one John Hancock was presiding over the newly formed Massachusetts Provincial Congress, in open defiance of British authority.

And on and on the acts of disobedience grow, Eugénie thought. *How much longer will it be before violence breaks out into the open? And will that violence drive the colonists back into the fold—or will it force them to take a stand and seek to separate from their mother country permanently? It's not up to me to unravel this—only to communicate back to France, once I learn which direction these patriots choose.*

"Eugénie, do you have a plan for transporting your stock to France?" St. George's question jolted her back.

"I've given it some consideration," she replied, "though not as much as it warrants, I daresay."

"Then perhaps my plan will solve your dilemma," St. George said, clearly pleased with himself. "My family has a fleet of trading ships that rivals any on the seas today. I know I speak for my father when I say that it would be our pleasure to put the skill of our captains and the speed of our ships at your disposal. A relative of mine, John Tucker, is, as we speak, off the coast not far from here. He can transport your stock to France at week's end when the auctions are over. Also, my father has been urging me to return to Bermuda. With the courts closed and, in my opinion, the American colonists on the brink of open hostilities, there is little reason to tarry here once my affairs are in order. I would like to invite you to accompany me to Bermuda. My family and I would be honored to extend our island's hospitality to you. Then, at your convenience, you can continue your journey home."

Eugénie thought quickly. This might be just the solution she had been seeking. Once she was finished in Virginia, what better way to familiarize herself with how the political winds blew on that island without arousing suspicion? How better than as the guest of one of its leading citizens?

"St. George, what a kind offer on both counts," Eugénie exclaimed. "I can think of no safer way to transport my racing stock than with a member of your family. Your family's reputation has reached even our French shores, as has word of your island's beauty and the graciousness of your people."

"Well then, that settles it," St. George said with obvious pleasure. "I'll write my father this evening. He and the family will be eager to meet the gracious French lady I've written about so often. Father will know best how to arrange for our passage. Our family stables can't boast the quantity of fine horses you find here in Virginia, but what we lack in number, we match in quality. You may even find some choice foals to add to your stock. We should arrive there in the middle of birthing season."

The dessert course interrupted their conversation. "Oh, my favorite, syllabub!" Eugénie cried, savoring the frothy bubbles. "Nowhere have I tasted its equal. I must find out Mary's secret." For the moment at least, Eugénie had nothing more on her mind than enjoying the airy delicacy before her. Scraping the last taste from the bottom of the fluted parfait crystal, she sighed with satisfaction. "What a fitting end to a delicious dinner!" At that moment, Mary gestured for the ladies to leave the gentlemen to their pipes and brandy. "Thank you, St. George, for your company and for your generous invitation," Eugénie said, rising from her chair.

"It's my pleasure, milady. If you'll excuse me, I'm off to the writing table." Eugénie watched St. George make his way to the doorway. As her eyes followed his departure, she caught Bridger Goodrich gazing at her. He raised his goblet toward her in a salute. She blushed at the intensity of his stare and began conversing with the woman nearest her. She joined the women leaving the room and made her escape.

V

✠ ✠ ✠

Eugénie shivered as she made her way quickly down the steps that fringed the broad veranda. Why didn't I think to bring a cape? she wondered. That Bridger Goodrich unsettles me so, I'm surprised I didn't make more of a fool of myself. Mistress Jackson must surely have noticed my sudden attention to her every word.

"Mistress! Mistress!" Marie's urgent whisper pierced the darkness. Eugénie turned to see Marie hurrying toward her holding a dark cape in her outstretched arms.

"Marie, *merci, merci!* At least one of us is thinking clearly. Now, quickly, back inside. It is too cold to tarry."

"Have a care, mistress," Marie said softly, slipping back into the shadows.

Eugénie settled the woolen cape around her shoulders as she hurried along the path that led to the gardens. She shivered again, this time not from the cold. The night was dark, and a chilling breeze brushed her cheek. Boughs above her creaked, and she could hear rustling in the hedges as she passed. Her footsteps on the gravel sounded loud to her ears. She began to fancy shadows where there were none.

Stop your imaginings, she chided herself. What use are you, frightening yourself like a small child? Why is it that distances always seem twice as far in the dark? She grumbled and tightened her cape around her, finally picking up the distinctive smell of the boxwood as she neared her destination. Much relieved, she slipped through an opening in the hedge.

Now, where might Jacques be? she wondered. As if in answer to her thought, she heard a night bird's call, low and close at hand, and answered back in kind. Immediately, Jacques was at her side. He took her arm and pulled her deeper into the garden.

"It's well you learned a more fitting call," Eugénie whispered, chuckling. "The woodcock's trill would surely be out of place in a formal setting such as this."

"This is no time for amusements, Eugénie," came the harsh reply. "It seems that the Whittington household and those who share its hospitality are in the camp of the patriots, but I have reason to believe that not everyone here is patriotically inclined. They hide themselves well, but on good authority I understand that the governor's coin has found its way into certain pockets. Both sides are in deadly earnest, with a lot at stake. Any stranger is suspect. Don't lose sight of the fact that either side, be they patriot or loyalist, could view you as a threat to their cause, should they surmise your true purpose here. You are expendable. Don't forget that! Beware and trust no one!"

His words sent a chill through her. "You confirm my thoughts," Eugénie replied, her tone now as sober as his. "I'll heed your warning, but what of you? Your protective coloring wears thin. I wish you had agreed to be a member of my household. But there's no point in fretting about that now. What news do you bring?"

"The Americans are gathering arms and gunpowder," Jacques responded. "Secret meetings are commonplace throughout the colonies, right under the British noses. I've learned that all the colonies are linked now by what they call Committees of Correspondence, a network of information and support. It began in Massachusetts in the spring of 1773 and was followed quickly by Virginia. More and more are following Massachusetts's lead and establishing their own Committees of Safety to coordinate and oversee the mustering up and training of special units within the militia. Sea trade is becoming increasingly difficult. Who trades with whom is a declaration of the parties' sympathies."

Eugénie, alarmed at Jacques's bald statement of the increased limits to sea trade, told him of St. George's plan.

"Excellent," he replied. "At all costs, your freedom of movement must be ensured. What have you learned since we last spoke?"

Eugénie quickly told him about the conversations she had been privy to or had overheard, and concluded by saying, "It's more than a feeling of overall disquiet. It's an alertness and a sense of keyed-up readiness. These Americans not only are close to defending their rights but are prepared to go the next step. Henry Lee may be called a hothead, but I've seen those around him nod when he speaks of action. Even Mr. Jefferson, a moderate, is beginning to speak in those terms. The leaders are no longer thinking only in terms of their own region or even their own colony but in terms of the whole family of colonies. I heard that the brilliant speaker Mr. Patrick Henry was the first to express that unity when he said, 'I am not a Virginian, but an American!'"

"Yes," Jacques replied, "I've heard of him. Next to Mr. Peyton Randolph, Jefferson's cousin, he's one of the most popular amongst the Virginians. I daresay, it's that, as much as his speaking ability, that Mr. Jefferson covets."

"How do you know these things? I marvel at you, Jacques."

"It's my business to know them—the nuances of expression, a casual remark. Mr. Jefferson may be well respected as a scholar and a scientist and is becoming known beyond the borders of his own colony. But he makes no effort toward the center and doesn't have the warmth or common touch that would draw others to him. He's one of the true aristocrats in this play, but, his brilliance notwithstanding, he'll make powerful enemies before it's done. He's already the target of jealous natures.

"But enough of that. We tempt discovery, staying here this long. I've some written messages that were entrusted to me for you." Pulling a packet from beneath his waistcoat, he continued, "You must destroy them as soon as you've read their contents. Should they fall into the wrong hands, they could compromise us both. Have you any messages you wish me to post?"

"Yes," she replied. "They're of great import to those we serve. Lastly,

I've singled out Silas Deane. He strikes a false note with me, though the patriots appear to hold him in high regard. Also, I may be imagining it, but there was a man at the auction today who seemed to take a particular interest in me. I'll see what I can find out about him and . . . What was that?"

Both had heard the sound of a twig snapping just beyond the boxwood wall. Placing his finger to his lips in warning, Jacques crept over to the thick hedge. He gestured to Eugénie that he heard nothing and then motioned for her to join him at the far end of the garden. In a quick, whispered exchange, they agreed on a place and time for their next meeting. Then Jacques left as silently as he had arrived.

Eugénie took a deep breath, placed Jacques's messages beneath her petticoats, and tiptoed along the hedge to the front of the garden. Only the usual night sounds met her ears. She hesitated for a moment and then forced herself to proceed at a normal pace back to the house.

Anyone wandering about at this time of night, she thought, is apt to be on the path that I used to go to the gardens. I'll return by the kitchen garden and pick some herbs for my cachepot. If I encounter anyone, I should look innocent enough.

She carefully avoided the gravel pathways. By the time she neared the herb garden, the late evening dewdrops had thoroughly soaked her green silk slippers.

"Merde," she hissed out loud, "the sacrifices I must make!" Just as she approached the buttery that stood at the edge of the tidy rows of herbs, an arm shot out, seizing her around the waist, and a hard hand clamped over her mouth, muffling her startled scream.

"Be silent!" A familiar whisper brought her up short. Her terror changed to outrage and her limp body erupted into action. "Be still!" At Bridger's command, Eugénie redoubled her struggles. She lifted her foot, bringing the sharp heel down hard on his instep. Caught off guard, Bridger loosened his grip on her mouth, giving Eugénie the chance she sought. Bridger swore and jumped back as she sank her teeth into the fleshy part of his hand.

"You!" she rasped, panting. Then, to his shock and her horror, she collapsed against him in a flood of tears.

"What in the . . . ?" Bridger began and then, without another thought, folded her into his arms. "There, there, shhh." He gently stroked her back and smoothed the hair away from her face, which was pressed against his chest.

Her weeping gradually subsided until finally, with a last shudder, she stood still in his arms.

"Now, what in the name of God could cause a lady brave enough to cross the Atlantic Ocean alone, stare down a wild stallion, and compete with the best horsemen in all Virginia to behave in this manner?" Bridger asked softly, offering her his linen handkerchief. She took it with a grateful smile and surprised both of them when she made no move to leave his arms. Eugénie dabbed at her tear-streaked face, quickly gathering her wits. *Sacré bleu!* I myself wonder! Where did all of that come from? Well, I might as well use it to my advantage and play the distressed demoiselle to its fullest. Even as these thoughts ran through her mind, she was aware of his scent, a pleasant mixture of tobacco and brandy mingling with his own natural maleness.

Marshaling her forces, she pulled back against his arms and looked for a long moment up into his face. Bridger caught his breath, struck by the naked openness of her beautiful face. He forced down the sudden physical rush that roared through him and felt an immediate need to protect her.

Eugénie took a deep breath and began, her voice low, "You scared me half to death." She shuddered, remembering that moment of overwhelming fear. Not knowing that her face had already completely disarmed him, she prayed that he would believe her mixture of truth and fiction. "After dinner, I decided to take a walk in the gardens before retiring for the night." Absently putting her hand to her forehead, she let the words tumble out. "This day has been full beyond measure. I sought the gardens' quiet to compose myself. I've found, since my parents' deaths, that if I go to sleep before reaching some peace of mind, I am prone to nightmares." Bridger was touched by such an admission from someone who seemed so self-possessed. He listened closely as she proceeded in a halting voice.

"I was startled from my thoughts by something that sounded like a twig snapping. I felt as though there were someone out there in the dark watching me, choosing not to be seen. I didn't stop to think, but headed back as quickly as I could toward the house. I went through the kitchen gardens—perhaps a circuitous route, but more out in the open. I don't know, maybe my imagination got the best of me, but I am quite certain that there was someone out there and that they were following me. When you suddenly grabbed me in such a violent fashion, it was all too much. I . . ."

Bridger's mild tone interrupted her. "I must beg your pardon for giving you such a fright. It appears there were several who sought the night's solitude. I, too, went out in search of my own company. Being used to a freshening sea breeze and horizons that stretch forever, I feel constricted when I'm ashore too long. I, too, had concerns that needed my attention and sought an escape from dear Mary's multitude. I'm as sure as you are that there were others roaming abroad, perhaps with less innocent purposes. When a dark figure emerged around the side of the buttery, my first instinct was to capture, not to question. Dear lady, you shudder!"

Without thinking, he closed his arms around her, nestling her head against his neck and nuzzling its soft curls with his chin. He shifted slightly and lowered his head to whisper to her just as she turned her head to speak to him. Their parted lips met. A shock coursed through them, leaving them both breathless. Eugénie's eyes flew to his face. His last thought before he clasped her to him and crushed his lips down on hers was of the remarkable quality of her silver eyes, which seemed to glow with a light of their own.

His hands moved instinctively, slipping beneath the folds of her cloak. He caressed her back and moved down to cup her buttocks, pressing her closer to him. Her hands reached up and grasped his thick hair. A moan escaped her mouth. He strained his body against hers, molding each curve. As if from a long way off, she felt his urgent strength calling forth her response. Deep within her, an ache began, then a pulse grew and spread through her limbs. Sensing her change, Bridger banked his intensity. He cradled her in one arm, leaving the other free to roam at will. Gently, he traced a line along her slender neck down to the tempting swell of breasts above her bodice. She lay back against him, as though in a sleep state. He tasted her swollen lips, sipping from their sweetness.

"Ah, the reward was well worth the wait. You are beyond the imaginings of any mortal man. You tempt me beyond reason." Before his last word was uttered, she snapped out of her trance and turned into a whirling dervish. Gone was the languor, gone the eyes at half-mast. In their place was a woman possessed.

"What in the world has come over me!" Eugénie cried. "What spell was I under to conduct myself in such a fashion? I must have taken leave of my senses. You disarmed me with your easy, comforting gestures and your beguiling concern. I despise you, but myself more. I intend never to be in your company again except under the most extreme duress!"

"On my word as a gentleman," Bridger began, only barely succeeding in containing his mirth, "I will take the memory of your unspeakable behavior to my grave. Your egregious secret is safe with me, for all eternity, mademoiselle. But the memory of it will warm me on many a cold night. And, may I add, should the same opportunity present itself in the future, you again have my word as a gentleman that I will avail myself of it with the greatest pleasure, now that I know the sweet taste of the fruit."

"This is no laughing matter, sir. And you are no gentleman." Eugénie whirled from him and raced through the garden, quickly disappearing from his sight. For many minutes, he stood looking after her, rubbing the tender spot on his hand left by her teeth.

When Eugénie finally reached her bedchamber, she tore off her garments, leaving them in a heap on the floor. She pulled her nightdress over her head and dove under the covers. But sleep was slow in coming that night and, when it did, it was crowded with the smell of box-wood, whispers, and snapping twigs . . . and the memory of gentle lips.

INTERLUDE

"Maman! Maman! Le pique-nique est ici!*" The young girl burst into the garden, white skirts flying, followed by a small white fuzzy bundle close at her heels. The tall, graceful woman dropped her clipping shears into the basket she carried. She placed the basket, overflowing with rose blossoms, on the bench beside her and turned, smiling, toward her daughter.*

"Ah, Eugénie, ma chère, *how beautiful you look! Come, let me see the dress Madame Henriette created for your birthday."*

Eugénie lifted her skirts and pirouetted gaily around the garden, her white slippers barely skimming the ground. In a swirl of white, the young girl and her loyal pup flung themselves into a spontaneous dance. Eugénie ended the im-promptu performance with an exaggerated curtsy at her mother's feet.

Clapping gaily, her mother exclaimed, "Très belle! Très belle! Mag-nifique, mon petit chou!*" Radiant with her exertion and basking in such praise, Eugénie threw herself into her mother's arms.*

"Maman, isn't it the most beautiful gown you have ever seen?" she asked breathlessly. "I didn't think Madame Henriette would ever finish, and she wouldn't let me have even a peek until it was all done. Now I'm so glad she made me wait. My very first gown with a long skirt! Now I must truly be grown."

"Yes, my darling, you are twelve years old today. You have crossed the thresh-old from childhood. Later I will show you how to dress your hair. As a young lady, you now may choose to wear it up for special occasions." Running her slender fingers through her daughter's glossy ringlets, she thought to herself, You, my precious child, have inherited your father's magnificent chestnut curls. You will never need curling irons or artifice to create the fashion of the day. The young girl leaned into the gentle touch, looking up at her mother's face with the same silver eyes that gazed down at her.

While mother and child talked, a host of servants transformed the garden into a festive picnic. Platters of food were arranged on brightly colored cloths. An array of plump pillows were scattered about for sitting or lounging in comfort on the grass. In the midst of it all, the little dog bounced back and forth between his mistress and each new exciting offering. Finally all was ready, including a mountain of colorfully wrapped and beribboned packages.

"Maman, where is Papa?" asked Eugénie impatiently. "It's time for me to present les cadeaux."

"Mes belles!" As if on cue, Étienne Devereux strode into the garden, his dark eyes alight at the beauty of the scene that spread before him. His gaze first sought his wife, and a look of great love passed between them. Eugénie sprang up from the bench she had been sharing with her mother and ran to her father's side. In one motion, he clasped her around the waist and lifted her high above his head in their time-honored ritual.

Eugénie shrieked with pleasure and then, remembering her new status, exclaimed, "Papa, Papa, put me down. I'm too old for such play. Maman says I am now a young lady."

"And so you are, my precious," her father laughed, setting her lightly on the ground. Hand in hand, they walked over to where the lavish feast and the expectant servants stood waiting.

"I see it is time for the presentation of the gifts. But first things first," her father said, leaning down to kiss his wife's upturned face. "Now, we can begin," he said, sitting down and tucking her hand through his arm.

Eugénie went over to the pile of presents and gifted each servant. A pretty shawl, a carved wooden bowl, a lace handkerchief, a favorite box of sweet-meats—all had been carefully chosen and wrapped by Eugénie with a specific person in mind. The pleasure that shone on the face of the retainers as they received the tokens of their young mistress's thoughtfulness made Eugénie's face light up with happiness. Finally, with feigned gravity, Eugénie picked up the last box and carried it over to a young girl very near her own age.

"Marie, I've saved the best for last." Accepting the gift, Marie curtsied gracefully and sat on the grass to open her package. She had barely removed the ribbon and wrapping when the lid popped up and a white curly ball exploded out of the box. Both girls clapped in delight as the little puppy jumped up to lick Marie's face, then darted over to Eugénie's dog and immediately began to nuzzle him. The two dogs cavorted around the garden.

"Oh, Mistress, thank you," Marie cried happily. *"I just love him."*

"I knew he was the perfect present for you," Eugénie exclaimed. *"You've always loved Puff so much. Now they'll be friends, just like we are."*

With the gifting ceremony completed, the servants collected the wrappings and ribbons. Then, with bows and curtsies to their young mistress, they withdrew, leaving the family to their picnic.

"Eugénie, what a wonderful idea to have a picnic as your birthday feast on this beautiful day!" her father remarked as he helped himself from the laden platter before him.

Nibbling on a slice of cold pigeon, Eugénie turned toward him. *"Papa, tell me again about how the birthday gift presentation began."*

"The ceremony goes back many, many generations in my family," her father answered. *"Our heritage of wealth and property began at the time of the first French kings. This tradition started on the birthday of my great-great-great-grandfather. His parents were overjoyed at his arrival so late in their marriage and presented gifts to everyone on their estate to celebrate his birth. Their son was a treasure far greater than all their land and wealth. The tradition has been carried on through the years by the firstborn in each generation. It serves as a yearly reminder to our family of two things: our family crest's motto, 'noblesse oblige,' and the fact that the lives of those who are served are closely intertwined with those who serve, and vice versa."*

"What does 'noblesse oblige' mean, Papa?" Eugénie asked. *"You haven't told me about that before."*

"My dear daughter, I think you're old enough now to understand a very important part of your legacy. 'Noblesse oblige' means to whom much is given, much is expected. Responsibility comes with good fortune. We know that we should not take good fortune for granted, but should realize that, having received an abundance of gifts, we as recipients must neither squander nor hoard them but rather use them to help others less fortunate. The gifts I speak of are not only wealth and property, but are even more important: the intangible gifts of character, intelligence, and beauty. Our lives, my dear daughter, are rich beyond measure. By dispensing those gifts wisely we find the real rewards in this life."

Feeling that he had given his beloved daughter enough food for thought for *one day, he lightened his tone, saying, "Ma Paulette chérie, haven't we something special for Eugénie to commemorate this day?"*

"Ah, oui, Étienne, the moment has come for our own presentation," said Paulette, plucking a particularly magnificent rose from her basket. "Voilà! Eugénie, may I present to you 'Eugénie.'"

In awe, Eugénie took the blossom from her mother. "Maman, Papa, a rose in my name? It's the most beautiful I've ever seen. Why, it has all the colors of the morning sky—crimson, apricot, peach, gold, cream, and coral. And look at the size. Mmmmm, and the fragrance." Beyond words, she flung herself into her parents' arms.

"Yes, my precious. Your father and I and Pierre have been developing it from the year of your birth. Just this spring it reached this splendor. We transplanted it into the garden this morning in time for your picnic. See it there on the west wall? It's facing east to reflect the beauty of the dawn sky, just as you described."
Eugénie jumped up and ran to her namesake. The tones of her glowing face blended perfectly with the shades of the glorious blossoms as she stooped to breathe in their scent.

"Eugénie," her father called her back, "we have one last presentation." With a flourish, he held out to her a long narrow box.

"What more can there be?" Eugénie exclaimed as she unwrapped the gift. Removing the lid, she carefully drew out a long gold band. The clasp was in the form of a shield on which was drawn a rose in full bloom surrounded by leaves that delicately traced her name and the motto "Noblesse oblige." Both sides of the clasp were attached to the band by a narrow link.

"The one link," said her father, "represents the day you were born, the twelfth of August; the other link, today, when you turned twelve. Each year hereafter, the band will be shortened to allow for the addition of another link. It's designed to include twenty-one links in all, which is the reverse of '12' and also the age that represents maturity. The clasp is your own unique seal."

"Oh, thank you, Maman and Papa, it's so beautiful! I will wear it always, remembering this day."

In her sleep, Eugénie smiled peacefully, as her hand rested quietly on her signature bracelet.

Eugénie looked around, unable to recognize her surroundings. She appeared to be in a glade amidst tall trees that looked unlike any she had seen before. Shafts of light penetrated the gloom and illuminated the mossy floor. She noticed a delicious fragrance that she couldn't place. The quality of the light was at once clearer than she'd ever seen and, at the same time, diffused. She had a sense of heightened awareness and utter calm.

Two figures emerged from the trees. She recognized her mother and father, but they looked younger than she ever remembered seeing them. She was struck by their tranquillity. When they held out their arms to her, she moved toward them and noticed, as she did, that she felt exceptionally light, as though she were hardly touching the ground. She reached out to them and saw her hands blend with theirs. There was no sensation of touching, only a surge of energy that radiated from them to her. Before she could speak, her parents intercepted her thoughts, and she realized that spoken words were not needed. They were communicating with each other through their thoughts.

"Maman, Papa . . ." Eugénie began.

"Grieve not for us, dear child. We've known your pain these past five years and have sorrowed for you." Eugénie noticed that their thoughts were conveyed to her in one voice. As close as she remembered them being in life, in death they had merged and become one soul. She knew, then, that theirs had been a perfect union and would be so throughout all eternity.

"We are very proud of the woman you are becoming. You have carried the responsibilities of the family holdings lightly on your shoulders. You have lent your courage and strength to those who would have lost their way during this time, were it not for you. We know also that your compassionate nature has lessened the hardships of those under your care.

"We applaud you for undertaking the mission to the colonies. Be firm in your resolve, Eugénie. Your belief in that young land and its people is well founded. They will prevail and build a mighty nation, but we have one grave concern. We know that the anger you carry for the British is a personal one. We understand that anger, but it's the anger of a hurt child. It will limit you and keep you from attaining your true stature. It can blind you and lead you into danger. If this anger is for our sake, put it behind you. The time for us on this earth was over. The British warship was simply the instrument of our destiny.

Relinquish your personal feud with the English. This time is of greater moment than the stuff of small vengeance. You will be crushed if you cling to your personal grievance. Instead, lift your eyes to a higher cause, and you will realize your own destiny, even as you contribute to a people who will prove to be friends to France in her time of need."

As Eugénie absorbed her parents' thoughts, the weight she had carried since their death began to lift. Her grief and anger dissolved, and a clear light flowed where before had been darkness.

"One last thing we convey to you." They spoke once more. "You have met a young man. Your mind resists him. He also has obligations and duties to others, which cause him much conflict. You tell yourself that you are wary of him because you think you and he are working at cross-purposes. That may well be true, but he will not betray you. You can rely on him should the need arise, even if it conflicts with his own aims. It is not he whom you distrust, but yourself. You are fearful of the passions he arouses in you. Whether you decide to share your passions with him or withhold them is your choice. Only you can choose the risks you will take, be they of the heart or otherwise. Remember, it is in the risks taken or not taken that you discover your full measure."

"Maman, Papa, I have missed you so and have needed your counsel."

"Dear child, we would not have gone from you when we did were you still in need of our guidance. We left only because you were ready to assume the role that was your destiny, not ours. Ours was over. We come to you now to relay a message that you are ready to receive. We are apart from you only on the physical plane. In every way that matters, we are with you and always will be."

Their last thought hung in the air as Eugénie watched their images fade and disappear.

VI

The warmth of the morning sun on her face drew Eugénie slowly from her deep slumber. As she awakened, her eyes fell on a shaft of sunlight that shone on her gold bracelet. She let her mind drift, remembering with sudden clarity the birthday when she had received the signature bracelet. She could almost smell the roses that bloomed so profusely that day and had a vivid recollection of the namesake rose her mother had handed to her from her basket that afternoon so long ago. She thought of the two dogs frolicking in the garden and of Marie's joy.

How simple life had been—picnics, presents, and puppies. She smiled, thinking of that young girl, so confident, so sure in her world. As she rested against the soft pillows, she allowed the memory of her parents' love to wash over her and realized with surprise that, for the first time since their deaths, she felt no accompanying pain, just a vast sense of peace. She mused over this change and wondered how it would affect her commitment to her mission. Again, she was caught by surprise. She realized with amazement that her resolve seemed tenfold stronger.

Choosing to prolong the moment, she let her mind wonder back over the events of the day before. She was pleased with the horses she had acquired and made a mental list of the gaps in her stable that she would need to fill by week's end.

Putting those thoughts aside, she turned her mind to the serious matters at hand. She felt that the false calm on the surface of the American colonies was swiftly coming to an end. The political tension was building at a rapid pace. It could be only a matter of days before the lid blew off and the colonies exploded into active rebellion. All the warning signs were there. The incidents were no longer isolated events. Each became tinder for the next. It was now only a matter of when, not if. What once had been conjecture was now a certainty.

The only question that remained was whether the action would be limited to a rebellion against the Crown's authority, or if it would be expanded into an all-out war for independence. Eugénie knew that there could be no official French sympathy, much less support, for a band of rebels who sought merely to undermine royal prerogative. As loose as the bonds were amongst the European princes, none could countenance such an attack on one of their own, for fear of suffering reprisals or falling victim to the same fate.

As she pondered the two possibilities, suddenly she knew that whatever the risk, whatever the cost, this brave, proud people would fight to the last to establish a true and independent state. The doubts she had suffered since she undertook this mission were gone. In their place surged a determination to do all in her power to help these people realize their destiny.

She felt goose bumps rise on her arms as she remembered the sound of the snapping twig in the darkness last evening. What manner of man, or woman for that matter, would remain concealed if his or her motives were pure? Her conviction of the night before remained. There had been someone out there. What was his purpose? What had he seen or heard? Was Jacques's identity compromised? Had he succeeded in getting away safely? Will my position in the household protect me against all but the most extreme contingencies? What of Jacques? And what of Marie? Can I protect them? I must, for all of our sakes, be even more watchful and avoid anything that doesn't serve my purpose here.

With that thought, suddenly Bridger Goodrich's face swam unbidden before her eyes. She felt her chest constrict. No one and nothing in her life had ever reduced her to such helplessness. Yet just the thought of him made her feel a life force that took her breath away. As she lay there, she yearned to feel his weight on her, to glory in his strength, his urgency. His presence was so real to her that she felt her body respond, open, and spread. She immersed herself in the memory of his mouth, his hands, his scent.

With a supreme effort, she wrenched her thoughts away from him and groaned out loud. Eugénie, *mon Dieu,* remember what you're doing here! This man is a distraction and possibly a dangerous one. You have so little knowledge of him. You don't know where his loyalties lie, but you suspect them. As if that would make any difference to you. He has ensnared you as surely as a hunter traps his prey. Even if we could reconcile whatever differences we have, is there a place for us now? Her mind ran in circles, her earlier contentment gone. Well, there's nothing to be gained lying here working myself into a state. I'll just put the whole thing aside for now. Oh, please, God, don't let me run into him until I have myself better in hand!

Stretching luxuriously, she said aloud, "I think a short ride. Yes, a ride would restore my peace of mind. Too bad it'll have to wait until the day's auction is over."

A light tap on the door announced Marie, followed by two stout servants lugging the wooden tub once more into the room. In no time, her toilette completed and dressed for the day, Eugénie was on her way to the stables.

"Abraham," she called out as she walked into the stableyard, "how does the roan seem to you this morning?"

"Miss Eugénie, he's right as rain," Abraham said, catching up with her. "All these folks stirrin' around makes him mighty jumpy, but don't you fret none; Abraham'll take good care of him."

"I know you will," Eugénie said as she reached the roan's stall. "Ah, there you are." She reached up to stroke the big horse. "We'll have our ride after today's auction. Here, I brought you a treat." The roan snorted his gratitude and, with the gentleness of a much smaller creature, carefully took the carrot from his mistress's hand.

The expanded auction took the best part of the day. The few disgruntled bidders, disappointed in their results, were quickly won over by the good humor that prevailed. Eugénie added two colts to her list of acquisitions, but found the rest of the entrants disappointing. With three days still to go in the auction, she felt no pressure to settle for anything but exactly what she needed to round out her bloodstock.

She scanned the crowd, watching to see who sought whose company. She was not surprised to see many unfamiliar faces, since the auction had been expanded beyond the narrow list of the day before, but she still made mental notes of every face. She watched Silas Deane making his way from one cluster to the next, apparently disinterested in the progress of the auction. He seemed well received, his words closely followed. She also had a good look at Mary's stranger and made a mental note to ask her his identity. She noticed that he seemed to have no particular constituency but instead floated from one group to the next without any apparent objective.

As she drifted through the crowd, she caught snatches of conversations. Other than horses, the only topic seemed to be the upcoming session of the Continental Congress in Philadelphia. She looked up at one point and caught Mary's stranger staring at her with a peculiar intensity. She quickly melted into the crowd. A short time later he reappeared. Again the watchful gaze. For the first time, she felt a shiver of fear. Was he following her, and to what purpose?

During the break at midmorning, Eugénie ran into Henry Lee, who regaled her with the local gossip. She found herself laughing in spite of herself. He was very proud of the Virginia delegates to the Congress, listing the six other men in order of their importance, according to him—his kin Richard Henry Lee, Peyton Randolph, Patrick Henry, George Washington, Benjamin Harrison, and Edmund Pendleton. He recited insights about each man and labeled each according to how he measured the individual's patriotic fervor.

"But what of Mr. Jefferson?" Eugénie asked. "I would have thought by his reputation alone that he would have been voted in by a large margin."

"On the contrary, his cousin Peyton Randolph drew the most votes, but he received only a paltry eighty-four. There are fifty-six delegates to the Congress," Lee added in an aside to Eugénie, "and twenty-two of them are lawyers! It'll be a wonder if they reach any consensus at all, seeing as how they are apt to argue over the simplest point. For myself, I'm for action. There's been talk enough. This time, I pray that the determined minds will prevail."

"What's this you say of lawyers?" St. George asked, joining them. "Patrick Henry's a lawyer, but, I vow, none in the colonies presses for action more than he. If it's action you want, take Mr. Washington. His bravery has been proven long since. Why, I heard that he volunteered to raise civil troops at his own cost and lead them to aid Boston!"

"My pardon, St. George," Henry Lee replied, for once calm in his demeanor. "I meant no harm by my words, but we'll all be harmed if some resolution to this stalemate is not soon forthcoming. The restricted trade alone is already causing hardship for some and, I warrant, there will be few who will fail to feel the pinch, if this situation persists."

Although he was a Bermudian, it was clear that St. George's sympathies lay firmly with the American colonists. He took up Henry's line of thought with a vengeance. As the two men launched into a discussion of coastal shipping and the availability of shipping lanes to the European ports, Eugénie became increasingly agitated.

I must carry out the arrangements for my horses without further delay, she thought.

"Gentlemen," she said, turning to the two young men in hot debate, "if you will excuse me, I have some matters I must attend to before the bidding resumes."

"Eugénie," St. George said, delaying her departure, "may I join you for a ride after the conclusion of today's auction?"

"By all means," Eugénie replied, and, thanking Henry for his pleasant company, she went in search of John Whittington.

———

49

It was some time later that Eugénie and St. George pulled their mounts up beside the riverbank. The late afternoon sun cast long shadows across the meadow and lent an intimacy to the setting. A flock of birds made their way lazily across the sky, in no hurry to seek their nests at day's end.

"The tranquillity of the countryside is a refreshing change from the auction," Eugénie remarked, stroking the roan's neck. A pleasant companionship settled over the two riders and their horses.

"I have grown used to the open spaces here in Virginia," St. George began. "'Twill be a change to be once more in Bermuda. I'm glad I got my letter off to Father with the early tide, for I received yet another correspondence from him just after noon. He's more eager with each day for my return. He speaks of the continuing conflict with Governor Bruère, who persists in holding Bermuda's customhouse at the end of the island in St. George's. Most of the merchants reside with their ships at the other end of the island. It's an ongoing game. My family and the other trading families grow tired of his stubbornness. Since they are the influential members of the Assembly, they can easily thwart the governor's demands—and then he tries to use his hand-picked Council to obstruct them in return. Meanwhile, trading continues."

"But what of Henry Lee's remarks this morning?" Eugénie asked him. "Should all-out war begin between the American colonies and Great Britain, where will that leave Bermuda and her trade?"

"Privately owned ships can always find a way around the hostilities, by one means or another. Even now, the customs men—the Searchers, as they are called—at Bruère's urging use any pretense to board Bermudian vessels. They search and seize cargo so that they can declare it illegal and pay themselves the fines. It's nothing new, this aiding and abetting those who work to defeat those efforts. Local pilots have always slipped ships into hidden inlets and safe harbors. The customs men don't have the knowledge of the shoals and reefs to navigate those waters. They're constantly thwarted in their efforts to catch their prey."

"Can't they go overland and catch them that way?" Eugénie asked.

"Ah," St. George replied, "there's much I haven't told you of Bermuda. There are few roads. The ones that do exist traverse the narrow dimension of the island, running north to south. They are called Tribe roads, and originally they divided the Bermuda Company shareholders' lands. These roads, such as they are, are very rough. No roads run the length of the island, so most travel is by boat. That's why the two ends of the island, even though they're only about twenty miles apart, are so remote from each other.

"Most of my family," he continued, "lives in Southampton and Somerset, the two westernmost parishes. My oldest brother, Harry, lives in St. George's, the seat of government at the eastern end of the island. He oversees our business right under the nose of the governor. In fact, he is married to Governor Bruère's daughter, Frances, whom everyone calls Fanny. Governor Bruère is quite fond of Harry. He even appointed him to the Council."

"It would appear that your brother is in quite a difficult spot."

"That he is, but he's a mild sort of fellow and well suited to it," St. George chuckled. "As long as he and Fanny keep producing lively grandsons, I daresay the two grandfathers will be too busy puffing out their chests to cause him much trouble."

And your name, St. George, thought Eugénie, is the name of the seat of the other camp. Now why would that be, I wonder? Changing the subject, she said, "St. George, I spoke to John Whittington this morning and he told me that he's already made arrangements to transport my horses back to France. I told him of your kind offer, but he would have none of it. He still feels indebted to my guardian for past favors and insists on undertaking their passage for me."

St. George looked crestfallen. "I hope," he said tentatively, "that you'll still accept my invitation to travel to Bermuda on your way back to France."

"It would be my pleasure," Eugénie said and watched his face crease once more into a happy smile. "Would it be too much to ask if the roan could come with me? I fear his behavior if I'm not near to calm him. Also I'd dearly love to try him out on the delightful terrain you describe."

St. George laughed, "It'll surely put him to the test. My family and I are at your service."

"It's agreed, then," Eugénie said, joining in his laughter. Pulling lightly on the roan's reins, she lifted his head from where he had been contentedly nibbling at the grasses on the river's edge, and said, "Well, can you meet the challenge, Roan II, or have you grown lazy on Abraham's treats?" As if in answer, the horse tossed his head and pawed impatiently at the ground. "He appears eager for a run. Shall we?"

"Ready when you are," came the answer. And the two horses took off at a clip across the meadow.

That evening, as Eugénie was preparing for bed, she said to Marie, "Mr. Goodrich's absence was well marked both at the auction and at dinner this evening."

"I understand," Marie said mildly, looking askance at her mistress, "that he received a message from his father calling him away on business for the rest of the week." As she folded away the coverlet in the chest-on-chest, she was puzzled by the expression of both disappointment and relief that swept over Eugénie's face.

"Marie," Eugénie smiled, "your knowledge of the comings and goings at Oak Knoll never ceases to amaze me. What else have you heard?"

"Only that there's great excitement about the ball at the Governor's Palace, which marks the conclusion of the auction," Marie replied.

"O, mon Dieu!" Eugénie exclaimed. "So much has happened these past few days, it completely slipped my mind. Dear Mary must be beside herself with preparations for that trip when she still has so much to do for the auction, not to mention all the guests she must look after."

"Mistress," Marie interrupted, "let me put your mind at rest. Madame Whittington asked me to let you know that all is in readiness for the trip to Williamsburg. She only wishes to know if you'd like to join her in her coach, or if you've made other arrangements."

"Oh, how kind of her to think of me, with all she has on her mind," Eugénie said. "I'd love to go with her. I'll be sure to tell her that and how much I appreciate her thoughtfulness, first thing in the morning."

How will I ever repay these dear people? Eugénie wondered as she blew out the candle by her bed and slid beneath the covers. Should the step toward independence be taken, perhaps my efforts on their behalf will compensate in some measure for all their kindnesses to me.

VII

❧❧❧

The last three days of the auction went smoothly. Almost too smoothly, Eugénie thought. The lighthearted, good-natured mood at the beginning of the week had shifted to a more somber atmosphere. There seemed to be an urgency to rush the days to conclusion without the banter and camaraderie that had marked the early days of the auction. Eugénie felt the tension mounting. The Continental Congress in Philadelphia was on every mind, and there was an unspoken understanding that this spring's auction marked the end of a time that would never be again. Some invisible line had been drawn separating what was past from what lay ahead. The colonies had come of age. There could be no return to childhood.

The earth herself seemed to share in this moment of exquisite suspension. Nature's forces were gathering for a new beginning. Later, some would recall those days that hung on the edge of that spring, when the birds' cries grew sharper, the sun shone brighter, and the smells of the earth were more pungent. The earth stood in readiness for Nature's might to propel her into the explosion of spring, on to summer and beyond.

Eugénie bid on the last few horses she needed to fill out her complement of racing stock, and then helped Mary Whittington prepare for the trip to Williamsburg and the governor's ball.

As she moved through those final days, her mind was divided between her need to circulate amongst the auction crowd, gleaning tidbits of information, and her wish to avoid the mysterious Mr. Darby, whose appearance on the first day of the auction had mystified the Whittingtons. He presented the usual reference letter, but Eugénie noticed that he seemed out of place amongst the other bidders, usually standing alone on the fringes of the crowd. And he continued to show more than a passing interest in her.

Mary Whittington, her composure unruffled, glided through the days, oblivious to the undercurrents that swirled around her. Eugénie tried unsuccessfully to match her hostess's self-possession. At the end of each day, she sought out the stables and the company of the roan. Only there did she find relief for her frayed nerves that were daily exacerbated by Darby's unsettling presence.

Finally, the day came when the last entrant on the auction ballot was presented, bid on, and sold. The auctioneer banged his gavel, bringing to a close the spring auction of 1775. Eugénie watched John Whittington as the last horse was led away. She saw his face sag with fatigue, only to revert to a smile as several of the participants came up to congratulate him on another successful auction week.

Only tonight, in the privacy of their bedchamber, will John and Mary share with each other the strain they've been under this week, she thought as she moved to his side.

"John, this has been one of the most memorable weeks of my life. I'm truly fortunate to have been a part of this event and to have had the chance to share in your generous hospitality," she said, the strength of her emotions taking her by surprise.

"Ah, Eugénie," John said tucking her arm through his as they walked out of the stableyard, "it has been our pleasure. Now that you've introduced riding astride to the ladies of the Tidewater, they, as well as the gentlemen hereabouts, will never be the same!" Eugénie laughed at his teasing, realizing with a pang how fond she had become of the Whittington family and how rare it was to have a second pair of people whose love she could count on, regardless of the circumstances. As if reading her thoughts, John Whittington continued in a different tone, "Eugénie, you've come to mean much to Mary and me. We want you to know that the doors of Oak Knoll will always be open to you. We think of you as a member of our own family." Looking up into his kindly face, Eugénie found tears springing to her eyes as she realized how long it had been since she had known a broad shoulder she could lean on.

He patted the delicate hand that rested on his arm and said, "Now I know without a doubt that you're a member of this family. The Whittington women can stare down a bobcat, but kind words are their undoing! I hear you're planning to visit the Tucker family in Bermuda before you set sail for home. We hope you're not going to cut short your stay here, now that the auction is over."

"I've come to feel so at home here with you," Eugénie said. "I'd truly love to extend my visit a few more weeks . . . if you're sure that I'm not taking advantage of your kindness."

"Dear child, you could never do that. Just the opposite is true. We will dearly miss you when you go." Lowering his voice, he went on, "Eugénie, I feel I must speak to you about a matter of a much more serious nature. Mary and I respect your privacy, so I hesitate to broach this subject."

The severity of his tone set off warning bells in her head. His next words increased her agitation. "I don't want to alarm you, but we know your purpose here goes far beyond acquiring a stable of magnificent bloodstock."

A deep apprehension swept over her, leaving her breathless. Her worst fears had been realized. Desperately trying to maintain an outer calm, she felt her body go cold and for one horrible moment thought she was going to faint. Her faltering steps came to a halt, and she bowed her head. Her first thought was of the Whittingtons and how their knowledge of her true reason for being in Virginia could put them in danger.

John immediately put his arm tightly around her and supported her with his strength. He spoke quickly to allay her fears and lessen the guilt he knew she felt. "Eugénie, forgive me for causing you such anxiety. We've known from the beginning. No action on your part has betrayed you. You've been faultless in your demeanor and behavior. No one has the least suspicion, as far as we know. We know only because my dear friend Gilbert, your guardian, informed us of your mission so that you would not be completely alone should the need arise. Your secret is safe with us.

"You must not burden yourself with concern for us," he continued, reassuring her. "These are times of treachery and intrigue with or without your presence. We've learned just recently that one of our own whom we all considered above reproach, Dr. Church of Massachusetts, is in league with those who oppose us. We know what you and your compatriots have set out to do, and why. Your courage is magnificent. If these colonies have but a few friends of your caliber, with your strength and ingenuity, then we need have no fear for what the future brings. I must offer a word of caution, though. For the most part, we're familiar with the guests at Oak Knoll. Williamsburg will be a different matter altogether. Guard yourself closely! Many would wish you well in your purpose, but just as many would not hesitate to do you ill. Mary will be relieved that we have spoken, for it was she whose concern for you overrode her respect for your privacy. Had I not overstepped a host's etiquette and intruded on it, I know full well that she would have taken the matter into her own hands. She wasn't going to let you attend the ball without that knowledge."

John Whittington paused. "Now, enough of such talk. Eugénie, I'm going to let you in on a small secret of my own. Unless I miss my guess, the last of our guests' carriages should be pulling away from the stableyard just about the time we sit down for supper. And I say, thank God! Never have I felt such relief as when the final gavel rang out this day."

Eugénie poked him in the ribs, causing him to break out in a broad grin. Laughing, he said, "Mary and I have been laboring all week to keep up our own subterfuge, all the while marveling at your stamina!" Her soft laughter and the smile she turned toward him were just the rewards he sought. Good, he thought; for the time being I have sent her demons away.

As Eugénie and John crossed the veranda and entered the center hall, Mary stood at the doorway of the small sitting room.

"Quick," she scolded them, "attend to your toilette and join us in here for a family supper. No formality tonight." She smiled at the relief she saw in her husband's eyes. She also read the message she sought in his slight nod as he passed down the hall to do her bidding.

To Eugénie's surprise and for the first time in many days, she discovered that she was famished. The supper was a quiet affair. The long week had worn everyone's nerves to a frazzle, and, as if by common consent, the conversation covered topics no weightier than the approach of the spring rains, the barnyard cat's new litter of kittens, and which of the assorted sweetmeats went best with which after-dinner cordial. The idle chatter turned to the coming of spring to the Virginia countryside.

"The first sign of spring for me," said Bess, the elder of the two Whittington daughters, "is when I see the first redbud blooming in the forest."

"I don't know if you'd call it a sign of spring," St. George Tucker said, "but my favorite part of spring in Bermuda is when the loquat fruit ripens."

"When is that?" asked Bess, hanging on his every word.

"After March first, just about now," he replied, "like clockwork, the loquats are ready to eat. I imagine Mother is out picking them right as we speak for her famous loquat jam."

"I'm not familiar with loquats," John Whittington said. "Were they in Bermuda originally?"

"No," St. George answered. "The first plants were brought to the island by ship captains. In fact, most of the shrubbery and trees on Bermuda came that way. There are very few plants that are native or indigenous to the island. Once there, though, everything seems to flourish. The loquats grow wild all over Bermuda. I'll make sure I bring back some of Mother's preserves when I return. There's nothing like them, and especially nothing like her loquat jam."

Lulled by the full meal and the relaxing company, Eugénie tried unsuccessfully to stifle a yawn. Ever attentive to those around her, Mary noted Eugénie's futile effort, rose from her chair, and announced, "Tomorrow will be an early day, so I, for one, am retiring. I'm not so vain that I can't admit to needing my full dose of beauty sleep, considering this year's flock of young beauties who will be attending the ball tomorrow night."

"Not so quickly, my lovely wife," said John, hastening to join her at the doorway. "You've been running circles around me since the day we first met. As to beauty, madam, you know full well that your reputation as one of the great Virginia beauties has yet to be challenged."

Beaming at him, Mary retorted, "I'm certainly not going to touch that! As for gallantry, dear husband, you have no peer in all the American colonies!" She put her arm around his waist and leaned her golden head on his shoulder as they walked together from the room.

Eugénie barely remembered getting undressed and sliding into bed. She was sound asleep the minute her head hit the pillow.

When Marie came in the next morning with a breakfast tray, Eugénie was just beginning to stir. "Mmmmm, pancakes and homegrown maple syrup: my favorites!" she exclaimed. "Marie, we've learned many new receipts since we arrived here. We mustn't forget to take them home with us. For us, no more of mademoiselle's stingy, delicate crepes—only these big, fat, spongy pancakes will do! *Magnifique!* And apple cider, too! Marie, how did you ever sneak this out of the kitchen? Our mission has taught you things a proper young Frenchwoman should never know. Whatever would your mother think?" The two young women giggled at the thought of how Marie's mother would respond if she learned that her daughter, so carefully trained in the arts of domestic service, was stooping to sneaking treats for her mistress.

"Maman could never say no to you either," Marie responded, "if she saw that it was within her power to do something to make you happy. She taught me well. The only difference is that she would've marched into the kitchen and demanded the cider!"

"Clearly, the last few days have stretched our nerves to the breaking point if we laugh at such foolish things," Eugénie said. "Or perhaps we laugh to relieve the strain we've been living with."

Making short work of her meal, Eugénie dressed and began stuffing more clothes into her trunk, which looked about to burst. "Marie, you'd think we were going for a week, instead of overnight. How is it that women seem to need to take everything they own wherever they go? We must have descended from the turtle!" In spite of her words, she went back to her wardrobe and brought out another cloak and walking dress. "You never know. Better to be prepared," she muttered to herself. At the last moment she crammed in a pair of britches, a waistcoat, and a jacket.

As the two young women walked out to the waiting coach, Marie asked, "Will you want me to powder your hair for the ball tonight?"

"No," Eugénie replied, "I don't think so. I've never liked that fashion. It makes my scalp itch. If it were the custom to bathe more often, such an artifice would not be necessary. I think I'll enjoy a departure from convention that being French affords me and wear my hair in the simplest of styles, which in some circles is considered quite the mode."

Mary Whittington, joining them at that moment, heard the last of the conversation and said, "Oh, I'm so pleased to hear you say that, Eugénie. I so detest powdering. Perhaps I will be forgiven for flouting custom if you set the example." Turning to look toward the drive, she said with relief, "Ah, the last of the baggage is in place. Now we may go. Come, Eugénie, girls, Marie." Just as Mary began to climb into the coach, she spied her daughter attempting to restrain the wild movements of a small brown dog. "No, Kate. The puppy does not go. We're overcrowded as it is." As her daughter started to protest, she continued, "Put the dog down, immediately. We must be under way, at once."

Grudgingly, Kate, who shared her mother's blond beauty, handed the dog to the footman standing nearby and climbed into the coach, settling herself next to her older sister. "And don't you look so smug," she whispered to Bess.

Indulgently, Mary looked over at her two daughters, each so different from the other. "Kate, you have the kindest heart for animals of anyone I know. I just hope that the fortunate young man who wins your heart has room in his for your menagerie."

Lost in her own thoughts, Eugénie gazed out at the beautiful countryside. She barely noticed the March sunshine pouring down on the early-spring tobacco crop. Sounds of chattering birds blending with the horses' hoofbeats and the sway of the coach gentled her into a half-sleep. She mused over the appointment that she and Jacques had scheduled for that afternoon as she slipped off to sleep.

She was riding over a familiar countryside and saw Bridger, St. George, Jacques, and Silas Deane approaching up ahead in hunting dress. Their attention was riveted on something in the distance, beyond Eugénie's vision.

What could have brought these four men together? What is it they see? Only Bridger turned as she drew nearer. He looked at her sharply, and she saw his features tighten. Then, wrenching his mount's reins, he swerved and galloped away. The other men, still unaware of her, turned their horses and rode off in the opposite direction. As suddenly as they had appeared, they were gone, leaving Eugénie alone.

VIII

꙳ ꙳ ꙳

The sudden lurch of the coach jolted Eugénie awake. Mary laughed at her startled face.

"Yes, we've arrived in Williamsburg. Weren't you clever to sleep away this dreary journey? We'll be staying here," she continued, pointing through the window at a multichimneyed residence set back from the street. "It was originally owned by John Custis." Eugénie looked out at the brick house beyond which she could see a breathtaking sculpted yew garden.

"Wasn't one of his relatives married to George Washington's present wife, Martha?" she asked, trying to clear the cobwebs from her head.

"Yes, his son, Daniel Parke Custis," Mary answered, collecting her skirts and carefully climbing down from the coach. Eugénie quickly joined her, and both women turned to watch John and the other men, still on horseback, milling around in the graveled courtyard that fronted on the main road and the house.

St. George and Jack, the Whittingtons' oldest child, dismounted and struggled with the straps that secured the baggage. Several liveried servants appeared and hurried to the aid of the weary travelers. In short order, the horses and coach were led away and the guests were shown into the main hall, where refreshments awaited them.

As they sipped the strong tea and helped themselves to the selection of sweets, Mary continued where she'd left off.

"As the story goes, John Custis held his son's wife's family, the Dandridges, in such low esteem that in his will he stated that his son, Daniel Parke Custis, and his wife, Martha, couldn't reside in this house."

Chuckling, John Whittington took up the story. "But his efforts were in vain. When Daniel died, Martha became a very wealthy widow, and this property reverted to her. So John Custis, whom many thought a strange man at best, had his wishes soundly thwarted in the end. Since then, Martha and George have let out the house over the years. I'm not sure Martha has ever actually lived in it."

"It's rented now to Peter Hardy, the coach maker," Mary went on, "who has kindly offered it to us for our stay since he and his wife are visiting her family on the James River. We thought it would be more pleasant to stay here on the edge of town than to be in the middle of the hubbub nearer the Governor's Palace." Placing her teacup on the exquisite Queen Anne lowboy that stood beneath the portrait of the original owner, she turned to Kate and Bess.

"Will you please help the servants sort out the baggage and then join me upstairs? Eugénie, come with me. I'll show you to your room. It's very charming. John and I stayed in it the last time we were here. Once we're all settled, I'm going to retire and take the opportunity to get a little rest before it's time to prepare for this evening's activities."

Eugénie was delighted with the room Mary had chosen for her. The two large windows that flanked the spacious four-poster bed looked out on extensive gardens at the back of the house. Sinking down on one of the window seats, she looked about her at the simple but pleasant furnishings. The blue and white pattern of the coverlet on the bed was repeated both on the window seats and on the homespun curtains that adorned the windows. A trundle bed, in the small alcove to the left of the doorway, provided a second sleeping space. A multicolored rag rug decorated the gleaming, wide-planked floor. Flames danced merrily in the fireplace, and two spooled rocking chairs were positioned invitingly on either side of the hearth.

As Eugénie completed her study of the room, Marie came through the doorway, followed by two servants carrying the baggage.

"Marie, let's get unpacked and go for a walk. I've heard much about the orderly design of Williamsburg." Both women immediately began to unclasp the fittings of the trunk that the men had set on the sturdy bench at the foot of the bed. As the door closed behind the departing servants, Marie reached into her apron pocket and withdrew a small sheet of paper sealed with a bit of plain wax.

"Mistress, a young lad delivered this," she said, handing it to Eugénie. "He waits below for your answer." Eugénie quickly opened the note and scanned its contents and then tossed it into the fire. The edges of the note darkened and disappeared into the flames.

"It's from Jacques. I'm to meet him in the cluster of trees behind Chowning's Tavern on the Duke of Gloucester Street." Marie left the room to carry her mistress's reply to the young messenger and was back before Eugénie could quell the feelings of apprehension that gripped her at the prospect of the meeting. Eugénie glanced up at Marie as she entered the room and was alarmed at her pale countenance.

"Marie, what is it? Are you ill?"

"It will pass," Marie mumbled. "The coach travel didn't sit well with me." As she spoke, she turned even paler, and she grasped the edge of the bed.

"What is it?" Eugénie asked again, rushing to support her. Lowering Marie carefully to the bed, she commanded, "Stay right there." She went to the bedside table, dunked a cloth in the water bowl, wrung it out, and placed it gently on Marie's clammy forehead as she eased her back against the headboard pillows. Eugénie rummaged in her toilette bag, withdrew a bag of lavender, and held it to Marie's nose.

"Marie, Marie, we've traveled through storms at sea and suffered carriage rides countless times. No mere two-hour coach journey could bring you this low. You're my dearest friend. Speak to me."

In answer, Marie groaned and lurched to her feet. Clutching her arms across her stomach, she rushed to the waste vessel and retched. Eugénie retrieved the cloth, dipped it in the cool water again, and held it to Marie's face and neck. Weakly, she took the cloth from Eugénie's hand and turned away from the concern on her mistress's face.

"I'd hoped I'd mistaken the cause of my lingering malaise, but I fear I am with child."

"Oh, dear, no!" Eugénie gasped.

In a resigned voice, Marie said, "I won't embarrass you by remaining here. I'll leave on the first ship to France." Eugénie sprang from the window seat and clasped Marie's dejected form in her arms.

"What are you saying? You'll stay right here with me where I can look after you. For you, whom I've known all my life, whom I've loved as a sister . . . for you, who has such an unbending honesty and sense of propriety . . . for you to be *enceinte* can mean only one thing. You must love this man beyond measure." Tears slipping down their cheeks, the women embraced each other. After a long moment, Eugénie drew back and looked into Marie's face.

"Are you a little better?"

"Yes, the feeling has passsed," Marie said shakily.

"You must promise me, Marie," Eugénie said sternly, taking Marie's hands in her own, "that you will never, never again keep something of such importance from me because of some misplaced concern you may have for my feelings. We're alone here and have only each other." Having extracted a nod from Marie sealing the promise, Eugénie brusquely changed the subject, sensitive to her servant's fragile state of mind. "First, I'll change into clothing less apt to attract attention. Then, we must go out and find an apothecary." Quickly donning the drab britches and jacket she had packed that morning, Eugénie continued, "No one will look twice at a servant and her lackey." Pulling a floppy cap well down over her face, she turned to Marie, "Well, how do I look?" Her words and impish grin brought a reluctant smile from Marie.

Bustling around the room collecting their cloaks and her *porte-monnaie,* Eugénie spoke sternly. "Marie, there will be no argument. Once we've made our purchases, you'll return here and rest while I keep my appointment with Jacques."

"Dear Mistress . . ." Marie began, filled with remorse.

"No," Eugénie's voice was firm, "not another word. Later we'll dis-

cuss the remarkable fellow who has won your heart and decide how
we can best handle this situation. For now, we must get the herbs I
need to make a remedy for you and the babe you carry. Come, we
must be off."

Shortly after leaving the quiet seclusion of the John Custis home, they
found themselves caught up in the bustle of the colonial capital. The
streets were wide and cobbled, causing a distinctive clicking sound as
carriages and horsemen hurried in every direction. They passed cottages with early spring flowers blooming in tidy gardens bordered by
white picket fences. They heard children's voices ringing out in a boisterous game of blindman's bluff and stopped to watch a young boy
trundling his hoop, with a small dog nipping at his heels.

They made their way along Duke of Gloucester Street, admiring
the craft shops that sported signs advertising their wares. Eugénie
noticed clusters of red-coated British soldiers standing on the street
corners. They appeared oblivious to those who passed by, but she
noticed that they often cast a look of disdain in the direction of a passing colonial once his back was turned. Apart from that disquieting
note, the carefree scenes that spread before her gave her spirits a lift.
She could almost forget why she was there and the afternoon's errand
that lay ahead of her.

"Ah, there's the apothecary shop, Marie," Eugénie said, pointing out
the mortar-and-pestle sign just ahead of them. "Oh, and look, there
just beyond is Chowning's Tavern." Under her breath, she listed off the
herbs to Marie and handed her the purse of coins. Heady smells of
herbs and soaps assailed them as they entered the tiny shop. As was
appropriate to her assumed role, Eugénie hung back and browsed
about the dimly lit interior as Marie made the necessary purchases.
Then, carrying her head forward and slightly down in the posture of
the station she was affecting, Eugénie followed her servant out of the
shop.

As they emerged into the bright sunlight, Eugénie mimicked the
broad colonial accent, saying, "Madame asked me to go by the black-

smith's and report his progress. It shouldn't take long, but you'd best hasten back all the same. You know her impatience if you tarry." With a nod and a wink, she left Marie and darted between two shops.

As she neared the stand of trees behind Chowning's Tavern, Jacques stepped out and beckoned to her, saying quickly, "I'll be gone for several days, perhaps a matter of weeks, on a trip north to test the climate again in Massachusetts. If what you tell me is confirmed in the northern colonies, our mission here will soon be over."

"Oh, Jacques, I pray that it's true. Tell me what you've heard about the Philadelphia Congress."

"The time has come when the moderates can no longer hold sway over the radicals, who are winning numbers to their side daily. The word is that when the Congress convenes, matters will come to a head. The political fires that have already started in the leading colonies, Virginia and Massachusetts, will ignite the others. I've no doubt that it won't be long before all the colonies follow suit and explode into flame." With those words still hanging in the air, they urged each other to take care, bid each other adieu, and parted company.

Eugénie made her way back the way she had come. She had just gained the street when a group of rowdies burst through the door of the tavern in front of her. They had clearly partaken generously of their host's brew. To her horror, Eugénie glimpsed Bridger's tall form in the midst of their number. Lowering her head further, she hastened to get by unnoticed. Before she could slip past, a hand shot out and grasped her wrist. She found herself looking up into a grinning, red face.

"And what have we here?" her captor barked, drawing the attention of the group. "Why, 'tis a young laddie. Such a pretty youth! I warrant he could almost pass for a lass. I see a chance for a bit of sport here. What say you, my good fellows?"

Bridger, who'd been looking on with an amused grin, caught the turn of the young lad's cheek and a silver glint before the young boy quickly lowered his eyes. Suddenly suspicious, he moved toward the two and clapped his hand on the huge man's shoulder.

"What use is this skinny lad when there's still good drink and willing wenches down the street yonder?" he drawled, aptly assessing the appetites of his comrades.

"Aye, let the lad be, Davey, and off to the Shield Tavern with us," yelled out another in the group.

To Eugénie's relief, Davey released her and shoved her aside. Taking the arm of the one closest to him, he staggered down the street after his ragtag fellows. Her relief was short-lived, however.

"Ah, Mademoiselle Devereux, we meet again!" Bridger chuckled, blocking her escape. "How fortunate for me. I held little hope of a *rendez-vous* after your sharp words and sudden departure at our last, shall we say, more intimate meeting. Come, tell me, what causes you to be wandering abroad in such fetching attire? Why, for a minute there, you even had me fooled. Unlike my less discerning comrades, I shall never be deceived by such disguises for long, knowing as I do what treasures lie beneath."

"Oh, please. I have no time for your insults," Eugénie snapped, shaking his hand from her arm. "What kind of man are you to remind a lady of an unfortunate moment of weakness? Furthermore, I owe you no explanations!"

"Insults? No, dear lady. I was simply paying homage to your fair person that shines through even the lowliest garb. And if we're discussing slights and manners unworthy of a lady, what thanks did I receive for gallantly rescuing you from the hands of that motley crew and who knows what fate? For shame!"

"How ungallant of you to demean your companions in such a fashion," she retorted, but she couldn't resist smiling. She was only too glad that he had not pressed her further about her appearance and her being unescorted in the middle of Williamsburg. As she looked at him more closely, she noticed that Bridger's dress was only slightly better than hers.

Seeing her glance, he replied enigmatically, "When flying with the flock, 'tis best to blend with its colors." She had little time to assess the meaning of his words, for with an abrupt shift of mood he said, "Come, I'll escort you to your residence."

She bridled at his words and patronizing manner, and wondered what she could do to dissuade him. Just then she saw Darby, the man from the Whittington auction, rounding the corner down the street. Fearing that standing there arguing would attract his attention, she immediately changed her tactics. Bridger was surprised and pleased when she suddenly acquiesced. "Oh, all right. As you wish."

She turned on her heel and marched briskly down Queen's Street. Bridger caught up with her, chuckling under his breath. "Upon my word, there's no guessing your next move. Fair lady, I do believe I have met my match, and I rise happily to the challenge."

As the pair walked along the streets of Williamsburg, Bridger showed her points of local interest and amused her with stories about growing up as one of six rambunctious brothers. As they turned onto Francis Street, Eugénie finally gave up trying to resist his charm and found herself laughing in spite of herself. By the time they arrived at their destination, his delightful company had completely won her over.

On delivering her safely to the Custis house, Bridger took her hands in his and gently turned her to face him. He, too, had felt the change between them.

"Mademoiselle, I've enjoyed this chance meeting and the pleasure of your company more than you know." His words and the expression in his eyes moved her, but before she could speak he said softly, "I look forward to our next time." Torn between anticipation and dismay, she watched him move off down the street whistling a merry tune.

Gripped by the conflicting emotions he never failed to arouse in her, Eugénie stood looking after him long after he had disappeared from sight. Then, pulling herself together, she slipped into the quiet house and up the stairs unnoticed. As she crept into her bedchamber, she was pleased to see that all was in order and that Marie was fast asleep on her bed in the alcove.

IX

❧❧❧

The Whittington coach joined the others lined up in front of the Governor's Palace. The imposing structure stood in its walled court-yard, ablaze with light. As their coach awaited its turn to approach the entrance, the occupants stared out at the glittering array of guests alighting from the coaches ahead of them.

"I warrant," John said, "except for the seven in Philadelphia, all of Virginia is in attendance!"

"There's Martha Washington in the company of Thomas Jefferson's wife, Martha," Mary said delightedly. "I'm so glad she came, even though George is in Philadelphia. No one gives a finer party than Martha Washington, and there's no kinder hostess in all Virginia."

"Except for you, my dear," her husband said, eliciting a tender smile.

"Oh, and there's Tom," Mary cried, pointing out Thomas Jefferson striding toward his wife. "With his height, there's no missing him, even in this crowd." As Mary continued to name the guests for Eugénie's benefit, the coach crawled forward. Finally the door swung open and a liveried servant extended a gloved hand to assist the ladies. Before descending from the coach, Eugénie remembered to collect the carry-ing case of rare vintage Bordeaux that she had brought from her estate for the colonial governor of Virginia, Lord Dunmore. As the Whitting-ton party joined the flow of guests, John remarked, "That's extremely thoughtful of you, Eugénie, considering the strained relations between France and Great Britain."

"Ah, but perhaps this small token will soften whatever displeasure he may feel at having to entertain me, one of the loathed French," she replied with a mischievous twinkle in her eye. "After all, one might say that it's the fault of my countrymen that the English have been denied the pleasure of tasting our great French wines lo these many years!"

At her words, the Whittingtons burst out laughing, and heads around them turned to discover the source of such mirth. What they saw produced even more interest, for few in the room matched the beauty of Eugénie, Mary Whittington, and her two daughters. The women suddenly felt elaborate in their wigs and overpowdered hair, while the men envied John, Jack, and St. George for being in such lovely company.

Unaware of the stir they had caused, the Whittington party moved forward in the receiving line, conversing with those around them and enjoying the beauty of the reception hall, which had all the trimmings of its British counterpart in London. The long, graceful room glowed with the flames of hundreds of beeswax candles set in wall sconces and in the multitiered brass candelabra hanging from the ceiling. Silver candlesticks had been placed randomly on brocaded cloths bedecking the Chippendale sideboards that ran the length of the room. Each sideboard boasted an array of platters laden with foods from throughout the colony. Clusters of highly polished tables and chairs stood at inviting intervals along the opposite wall. Reflecting the entire colorful scene were rare, gilt-framed looking glasses spaced along the mint-green walls above the elaborately carved wainscoting.

Attentive servants offered refreshments to the guests, making the interminable wait more pleasant as they bided their time in the governor's receiving line. Eugénie occupied herself scanning the guests, who either lingered chatting in the reception hall or moved through to the ballroom beyond. She could just barely pick up the strains of one of her favorite Vivaldi pieces. She smiled to herself, imagining that later in the evening, the same instruments would launch into a minuet or the local favorite, the Virginia reel, or perhaps a French quadrille.

"Comtesse de Beaumont! It is indeed a pleasure to welcome you to Williamsburg." The governor's voice cut through her thoughts. As she arose from her deep curtsy, Eugénie extended her hand.

"Lord Dunmore, the pleasure of your kind invitation is mine." Dipping once more to retrieve her carrying case, she presented her gift to the governor. "May I offer a small token of my appreciation?"

His curiosity piqued, Lord Dunmore unclasped the casings and drew out a bottle of Eugénie's estate-bottled Bordeaux. His eyes opened wide and his face broke into a pleased smile as he recognized the extravagance of the gift. Then he paid her the ultimate compliment by speaking in her own language.

"Ah, Comtesse, I'm deeply touched by this generous present. I've thirsted for the sight of feminine beauty unique to the French and for the taste of the finest wines, also unique to your country. I humbly thank you. You've quenched my thirst on both counts. Were you aware that, to try to fill the void left by the absence of your country's wine, the Crown has required a specific number of acres to be planted in grapevines here in the colonies? To our continuing sorrow, our best efforts still fall far short of what only your country seems able to produce." Eugénie was disarmed by his candor and his elaborate praise. She felt she had been given a rare insight into the man hidden beneath the polished diplomatic facade. He seemed to sincerely regret the strained relations between their two countries.

Bestowing a brilliant smile on the governor, she demurred, saying, "*Merci, monsieur*. It is I who am gifted by your kind words and your willingness to touch on what the loss of goodwill can cost us, even in small ways." They looked at each other with new understanding, realizing the deeper meaning that lay behind their words. As she turned and moved away from the governor, Eugénie saw the ever-present Darby. He was across the room, listening attentively to two men. Ah, here he is again, she thought. This may be my chance to learn his purpose.

Watching her blend into the crowd, the governor, Lord Dunmore, thought, What a remarkable woman. Had there been more of her kind on both sides of the English Channel, I daresay our histories might have turned out quite differently.

Bridger saw her the minute she entered the room. Impatient for her arrival, he had come early to the reception to position himself. He watched her as she moved gracefully along the hall toward Lord Dunmore, the hue of her gown shifting from the palest blue to a shimmering silver that captured the shade of her eyes. The lace at her bodice and sleeves was so finely wrought, it appeared to be transparent. Her radiance reached out and held him.

As she rose from her deep curtsy, he saw the candlelight reflected in the highlights of her artlessly dressed hair. His fingers tingled, remembering the silkiness of it. He watched the exchange between her and Lord Dunmore and observed the governor, a seasoned veteran of women's charms, falling under her spell. Bridger felt an irrational urge to grab Dunmore by the throat and haul him to the floor when the governor's lips lingered on Eugénie's hand. He watched intently as her rosy complexion deepened in response to the governor's words. His eyes devoured the classic profile she turned toward Lord Dunmore before she moved away. He noticed, too, that Lord Dunmore's gaze followed her as she melted into the crowd.

"Bridger, what's come over you?" Edward Goodrich asked. "You haven't heard a word I've said. Come back here, dammit." But Bridger, oblivious to his brother's words, had already disappeared into the throng.

Never losing sight of Darby, Eugénie moved toward him, stopping here and there to converse with people she had met at the auction. As she chatted with Rebecca Bland, one of the Whittingtons' neighbors, out of the corner of her eye she noticed a slight movement. She turned and found herself suddenly face to face with her afternoon's companion. Staring into his deep blue eyes, her words caught in her throat.

"And how did you find the governor's company?" Bridger fairly barked at her.

"I beg your pardon?" Eugénie said, taken aback by his harsh tone. What in the world has come over him? she wondered. Oh, how bothersome! Looking over Bridger's shoulder, she saw Darby exiting through the door into the main hall with the other two men.

"It certainly appeared that you and the governor conversed with exemplary ease, considering your adversarial positions!" Bridger stormed on.

Resigned for the moment to let her target slip away, Eugénie responded coolly, "I found the governor every bit as charming as I'd heard, and our discourse was anything but adversarial. In fact, quite the opposite." She wondered again what had caused his churlish manner. Then, shrugging it off, she made an effort to turn his distracting stare away from her. "Rebecca, may I introduce Mr. Bridger Goodrich? Mr. Goodrich, Mistress Rebecca Bland." Rebecca blushed, and her stammering reply was drowned out by Bridger's next impatient words.

"Yes, yes. Rebecca and I grew up together." His eyes never wavered from Eugénie's face. "I daresay by now even our resolute mothers have given up their fruitless, tho' heartfelt, wish to see us wed. Rebecca, if you'll pardon us, there's something of great importance that I must discuss with Miss Eugénie, in private." Rebecca, by now thoroughly undone, was only too glad to watch Bridger place his hand possessively on Eugénie's elbow and steer her swiftly away.

His senses reeled at her physical closeness after the nights he'd spent dreaming of her. Had it been only a week? Over and over he had replayed in his mind the feel of her, her taste, her smell. Now he found himself consumed with the smell of her. What was it? It made him think of summer rain, fresh-cut grass, the scent of roses, twilight. He felt aroused and strangely stirred.

"Am I boring you, sir?" He snapped out of his reverie, her words cutting through his thoughts.

"Ah, twilight, elusive, soft, suspended between." For a moment, he thought he saw an expression of wariness touch her eyes. Then it was gone, and a cool reserve returned to her face.

"Twilight! Mr. Goodrich, indeed you flatter me. I've often been told that I'm made of much more substantial stuff—too predictable, too direct, not enough artifice to be *de rigueur*."

"Oh," said Bridger, "but your critics have missed your subtleties, the complexities that lie beneath the surface of that calm, like a quiet lake whose reflection belies the depth below."

"Sir, I have heard much about you, but poet . . . ?" Her words faded as his eyes moved to her mouth. He couldn't remember looking at, nor could he recall being so completely mesmerized by, lips before. Soft, he remembered their softness. Sculpted, even when they moved. He noticed the natural smile that lifted the corners, even in repose, and the upper lip, full, almost swollen.

"Ouch!" His eyes shot up to clash with hers. "What was that for?" His shin throbbed. How could such a small velvet slipper inflict such pain?

"Mr. Goodrich! I'm glad I finally have your full attention. Listen, and listen carefully. In my country, only a certain sort of man treats a lady as you've been treating me—invading my privacy, making suggestive remarks, not to mention taking outrageous liberties with my person. Then accosting me in a public place, monopolizing me and cornering me so that there is no way that I can gracefully escape your attentions. Rudely dragging me away from the company I was enjoying, with some feeble excuse. Finally, appearing first bored, and then staring with intensity at my mouth in the most vulgar fashion. As I said before, sir, you are no gentleman!"

"Dear Comtesse, my apologies," Bridger replied, bowing. "You find me, again, quite without defense. I agree to a certain lack of deportment on my part in our encounters. However, at times your dress and manner have been quite misleading, even extraordinary. But to see you as you are tonight has left me breathless. You mesmerize me. You knock me off guard. I am at your mercy."

His heartfelt words and beguiling smile were her undoing. His eyes raked over her, leaving her raw and exposed. She was jangled by his intensity. Every time he was near her, she felt drawn by an irresistible force, as though he were spinning an invisible web around her. Her mind screamed to keep her distance.

"Oh, Bridger, honey! Now where have you been all evening?" Amelia Stanton's sharp voice broke through Eugénie's thoughts. Tossing her carefully styled blond curls that just missed being fashionable, Amelia looked up at Bridger through her pale lashes. She wedged herself between them, drawing attention to her voluptuous breasts by fiddling with the ruffles that edged her gown's plunging neckline. She had used every artifice at her command to enhance her more attractive features and to diminish her large nose and short neck. The effect was quite striking and entirely lost on Bridger.

"Bridger, darlin', you must not monopolize dear Eugénie," she purred, plucking at his sleeve with short, clawlike fingers. "She's the guest of honor, after all. Why, it's all the talk that she has just wound that poor old governor right around her itty-bitty finger!" Preening under the appreciative male stares cast in her direction, she went on, "Now, Bridger, sugah, you come along with me. I just know that you are simply dyin' for some of that delicious fruit punch. Eugénie, honey, don't you worry your little head about little ol' Bridger, you heah? I'll take good care of him while you tend to all those folks who are just clamorin' to meet you. Why, there's Mister Jefferson practically plowin' people down tryin' to get over here." With that, Amelia thrust her arm through Bridger's and fairly dragged him away, but not before his parting glance promised Eugénie a continuation.

Amelia's words proved true. Before Eugénie could slip away to seek out Darby, Tom Jefferson was at her side. He lost no time sweeping up Eugénie and leading her onto the floor for the first minuet. He was a strenuous dancer, if not a graceful one. He regaled her with more stories about his childhood in Albemarle County, his early love for horses, and the unending tribulations of designing and building his show-place, Monticello. Eugénie thoroughly enjoyed his company and was genuinely sorry when the dance came to an end.

Each dance was barely over before Eugénie's next partner appeared to claim her. Her pursuit of Darby had to be put aside for the time being. During the evening, she noticed members of the two political factions mingling easily with each other. It appeared that they had set aside their differences for the evening and were committed to relishing the festivities. Bridger, she noticed, was less happily occupied, monopolized as he was by Amelia Stanton, who clung to his arm and refused to let him out of her sight. Eugénie almost laughed out loud at the look of discomfort on his face.

Nor did Bridger fail to notice that Eugénie was claimed for every dance by one of the young bucks of the county. His face darkened as he watched her laugh up into the faces of her partners. It took all of his willpower not to fling the cloying Amelia aside, confront Eugénie's partners, snatch their hands off her, and claim her as his own.

At one point, Eugénie looked around the ballroom for St. George, realizing that she hadn't spoken to him all evening. She saw him across the room, apparently infected by the spirit of the evening, chatting amiably with several British officers in scarlet jackets.

Later, during another minuet, Eugénie was happy to see Bess partnered with St. George. Eugénie smiled, knowing that Bess secretly longed for his attentions. As Eugénie watched Bess's lovely face laughing up at St. George, she thought how striking their dark looks were together.

Perhaps Bess's gentle nature will finally break through his indifference, and St. George will discover the treasure that has been within his reach all this time. Wouldn't Mary be pleased? She's always been so fond of him. Eugénie mused over this possibility just as the last chord of the minuet was struck. She gave a deep curtsy to her partner and begged off the next dance, pleading the need to retire to the powder room. Before anyone could detain her, she left the ballroom and made her way in the direction Darby and the two men had taken. She worked her way down the hall, glancing through open doorways and listening at closed ones.

"After all this time, no doubt they've completed their business and left altogether," she muttered crossly. She was about to return to the ballroom when she heard lowered voices. She crept forward. Deeply engrossed in conversation, the three men failed to see her as she peeked around the corner. She quickly pulled back and slipped into a curtained alcove, hiding behind the cloaks and capes. Although muffled, their voices carried clearly to her.

"Well, I think that about sums up our strategy over the next few weeks. It's essential that we ferret out the enemies of the Crown," one was saying in a clipped accent. "You've done well, Darby. The auction week paid off handsomely, but keep an eye on the Frenchwoman. I've heard rumors of French interference in our little quarrel. If she poses a threat, you know what to do." In her hiding place Eugénie shuddered, alarmed by the implication of the man's words.

"That I do," came the answer. "You can count on it. It won't be as easy without the auction crowd, but I'll find a way." Darby's thick local drawl imprinted his voice on Eugénie's mind.

"Well then, enough said. I bid you good night and happy hunting," said the first. All three were still chuckling as they passed Eugénie's hiding place and moved down the hallway.

Eugénie waited for her breathing to return to normal and then peered around the curtain. Seeing no one, she hurried back to the reception. She had just melted into the crowd when Henry Lee placed himself squarely in front of her.

"Ah, Mistress Eugénie, here you are! I've come to claim the dance you promised me." Eugénie couldn't help but laugh at the brash young man. She enjoyed his refreshing directness and had developed a great respect both for his knowledge of horses and for his exceptional horsemanship.

"Why, Henry, I've been wondering where you've been all evening. I thought maybe you were avoiding me, since the great roan beat your stallion by two lengths." Henry began to sputter his protest when he noticed Eugénie was struggling to keep a straight face.

"I see, milady, you are toying with me. The deep devotion and respect that I've laid at your feet from the moment we met is only heightened by the purse you won from me. I must keep you in my sights if I expect to reclaim my losses." They were still laughing as they joined the two rows forming for the Virginia reel.

Eugénie was soon caught up in the lighthearted spirit of the dance. Laughing, she whirled to meet her next partner and found her arm hooked by Bridger's. They moved naturally together, following the couple ahead of them and ducking beneath the arched arms made by the two lines of dancers.

At the end of the dance, her heart pounding from more than the rigors of the lively step, Eugénie curtsied to her last partner and went to stand in the open doorway that led out to the grassy terrace beyond.

She stared up into the black sky, feeling the night air cooling her hot cheeks. Without thought, she responded to the darkness that beckoned her and moved out into the night.

Even before Bridger spoke, she felt him beside her, in step with her pace and mood. When his long fingers clasped her own, she felt his heat radiate up her arm. "We'll waste no more of the little time we have left in senseless banter. Come," he said, leading her down the slope away from prying eyes. Without hesitation, her steps matched his as he guided her into the shadows. They turned toward each other as though the moment were preordained and moved into each other's arms. With infinite care, they gave themselves up to explore the feel, the taste, the scent and sounds of the other as the night closed around them.

Later, holding her close to his heart, he murmured, "I can give you nothing, no promises, no tomorrows. Where I go, I must go alone." His voice roughened, "But now that I know you, how can I imagine a day without you in it?" At his words, her passion evaporated and she fell back to earth.

"Everything has moved so quickly," she breathed. "I'm over-whelmed. In your presence I can't think or make sense of anything. I'm breathless, as weak as a newborn babe. Your words are my thoughts as well. I, too, know that the future is a luxury we do not possess."

As he began to speak, she laid a delicate finger on his lips. "This night your hands, your lips and body have breached the kingdom of my heart. But we need time to think, to understand what's happened between us and what it means beyond a few snatched moments in the dark."

He had no words to combat her wisdom. He bowed his head and rested his forehead against hers. He sought her lips once more and took them urgently. Then, hand in hand, they walked slowly back to the Governor's Palace.

X

❧❧❧

Mary Whittington watched the steady stream of traffic passing by the Custis house. Our decision to stay on the outskirts of town has proven to be wise in more ways than one, she reflected. She had planned an early start that day but didn't have the heart to rouse the household after their late return from the ball. The quiet early-morning hours before the household awoke had always been her favorite time of day.

Earlier she and John had indulged in the rare luxury of staying in bed and sipping their coffee, which they both preferred to tea. They had chatted about the activities on the plantation and planned and dreamed about the future, but it was clear that John was upset.

"The upcoming meeting about Sam Brown worries you," Mary said as she refilled her husband's cup.

"Yes, it does. I just want to get this damn thing settled once and for all. My own fault, I guess."

"Don't blame yourself. It was a kind thing you did. How could you know how he would repay that kindness?"

"I only hope Tom Sidley is as good as Peyton Randolph says he is. When you have one of the best lawyers in Virginia, it's hard to settle for someone else. Well, my dear, I'd best get dressed and be off."

Mary thought about that conversation, as she walked into the sunlit morning room. With all that's on John's mind right now, she thought, this Samuel Brown matter is such a nuisance. And it's all because of John's kind heart. I wish we'd never heard of the man!

Putting the unpleasant subject out of her mind, Mary settled herself on the settee and picked up her embroidery. One by one, the other members of the household began to make their appearance. As they helped themselves to the breakfast laid out on the broad oak table at the end of the room, they chatted about the ball. Little had occurred during the evening that went unobserved by at least one member of their group, so the chitchat during breakfast was rich with anecdotes and gossip. Bess's color was especially high, and her spirits were quite lively.

"Oh, and then the British lieutenant was fairly knocked down by Mistress Stone, as she bore down on him and snatched poor Sarah off his arm," Bess said with a giggle.

"Yes, poor thing, it was her first dance all evening," Kate continued. "Her mother is such a monster. She dresses Sarah in the ugliest things and then watches her like a hawk. She'd scare off any young man who might be the slightest bit interested in Sarah. Marry Sarah, get Mistress Stone. There's not a man in all the colonies brave enough for that!" Both girls laughed, imagining Mistress Stone, whose girth and apoplectic rages were legendary, glaring at the hapless lieutenant.

"Girls, girls, how unkind," Mary chided her daughters, even though the corners of her mouth twitched and her eyes twinkled at the picture they had drawn of the redoubtable Mistress Stone. "Since her husband died and her other daughter, Betsy, ran off with that young man from Maryland, she's had a hard time of it. She's just determined to protect Sarah."

"Died with relief, no doubt," Kate retorted, "and can you blame Betsy? I just bet poor Sarah prays every day of her life that some young man from anywhere would come along and whisk her away from her mother's clutches."

"Kate, really, that's enough," her mother admonished her, but Kate was already on to the next juicy tidbit.

"And then, did you see Amelia Stanton flouncing around as if she were the belle of the ball, making such a fool of herself over Bridger

Goodrich?" Kate asked no one in particular. "Why, she was hanging on him all evening. She really thinks she's God's gift! She was whispering to anyone who'd listen that she was just sure any day now that Bridger was going to ask her father for her hand. Can you imagine! She's so stuck on herself she can't see the nose in front of her face—and, considering the size of hers, that's saying something! Anyone with eyes can see that Bridger is so taken with Eugénie that he can barely see straight. Now, isn't that so, Eugénie?" Startled to suddenly be the target of the conversation and for that conversation to be about Bridger, Eugénie almost dropped the cup she was holding.

"Oh, Kate, you know Amelia," her mother said, unwittingly coming to Eugénie's rescue. "She's always been that way. She doesn't mean any harm by it. It's just the way she is."

"Oh, Mother, there you go again, standing up for everybody. And I'm not so sure she's so harmless. I, for one, wouldn't want to turn my back on her. No, indeed! And another thing, she's such a flirt," Kate said firmly. "One of these days she's going to get herself into trouble. She already has the worst reputation."

"Kate's right, Mother," Bess agreed. "Her father has spoiled her half-rotten. Why, there's nothing he won't let her have or do. And she's just plain nasty to her mother, who's the only one in her life who's ever tried to say no to her. Her father just lets her act any way she pleases and doesn't say one thing." The usually mild-tempered Bess gave weight to Kate's remarks. The sisters looked at each other knowingly, but, catching their mother's stern expression, they decided it was probably a good idea to drop the subject.

"Well, if everyone's finished eating, I think we'd better finish our packing so that we'll be ready when your father gets back," Mary said, bringing that conversation to a close. "Oh," she continued, "I didn't realize that you weren't through, St. George. Don't let me hurry you." Seeing an opportunity, Bess swooped over to the tea service.

"May I pour you some more tea, St. George?" she offered, dimpling prettily when he smiled at her and nodded. "Mother, I'm all packed and ready to go. I'll just stay here and keep St. George company while he finishes," she said, as she sat down beside him and filled both of their cups.

"That's fine, dear," Mary replied, following Kate and Eugénie out of the room. "Oh, I hope those clouds can hold off until we get home," she murmured, looking out of the window at the dark sky. "The roads were completely unpassable during the last storm."

It was not long before John Whittington returned. Soon everyone was assembled out front by the coach.

"Oh, dear," Eugénie said in dismay, "I think I left my bracelet upstairs." Just as she spoke, Bridger Goodrich turned into the square riding a large bay and leading another mount. When his eyes found Eugénie, his face lit up in a broad smile. At first Eugénie appeared uncharacteristically flustered, but then an answering look of pleasure spread over her face. Kate nudged Bess.

"See, I told you," she whispered to her sister. Bridger dismounted and tied both horses' reins to the hitching post. As he strode toward the group, he doffed his tricornered hat and saluted the ladies, singling out Eugénie.

"Miss Eugénie, I was hoping to arrive before your party set off. Oh, pardon me for forgetting my manners, Mistress Whittington," he said taking Mary's hand and bowing over it.

"Bridger, how nice to see you," she said, smiling. "You know you can do no wrong in my eyes." While this exchange was going on, Marie took the opportunity to slip upstairs. She returned with the missing bracelet as Eugénie moved over to the young horse.

Stroking the filly's gleaming coat, she said, "Oh, Bridger, she's lovely. Is she the one you spoke of?"

"Yes, she is." Bridger answered, inordinately pleased that Eugénie had remembered. "I met her owner's price this morning. I was hoping you'd be willing to ride with me part of the way back to Oak Knoll, that is, with the Whittingtons' permission, of course." He and Eugénie both turned to Mary. She hesitated for a moment, considering the unconventional nature of the request. Then, seeing the expression on Eugénie's face, she put aside her concerns.

"Why, I think that's a fine idea. I just wonder about those storm clouds overhead."

"They've been threatening the last few days. The young people will just have to risk it. Knowing Eugénie," John chuckled, "they'll probably outrun the storm even if it does come."

"Wonderful!" Eugénie exclaimed happily. "It's settled, then." Anticipating her next thought, John directed the coachman to lower her trunk down onto the gravel.

In no time, Eugénie had picked out the clothing she needed, disappeared into the house, and returned dressed in a riding costume of her own design. Looking down, trying to clasp her signature bracelet on her wrist, she missed seeing Bridger's admiring eyes sweep over her. Her skirt was slit down the center, exposing trousers beneath, which allowed the wearer to ride astride or sidesaddle. Eugénie had noticed that Bridger had saddled the filly without the sidesaddle trappings.

"May I help you with that?" Bridger was suddenly at her side, his strong fingers making short work of the complicated clasp. "What an unusual design. Is that crest also a seal?"

At Eugénie's nod, he continued, "My family trades with goldsmiths throughout Europe. I have never seen such a remarkable piece." Aware of her nearness, he placed his hands on her waist and said huskily, "May I?"

Reading several meanings into his words, Eugénie felt her cheeks flame. She looked pointedly at the saddle and said, "That would be very kind of you, sir." Bridger heard her cool tone but watched the pulse at the base of her neck quicken. His smile deepened.

"It's my pleasure," he said. He lifted her effortlessly and swung her up into the saddle. Then, with a quick movement, he mounted his own horse. The filly began to dance in place, kicking up puffs of dust. In answer, the bay began snorting and pawing the ground. Little of this was lost on John Whittington.

"It looks as though we'll be a little while, yet," he said. "Why don't all of you who are ready now ride on? We'll catch up with you later." Since St. George had already decided to ride in the coach with the ladies for the first part of the journey and Jack was still busy helping with the baggage, Eugénie and Bridger discovered to their delight that they would be on their own for a few precious moments.

The dark clouds loomed overhead and the March wind picked up as they left the tidy streets of Williamsburg behind them and broke out into the open country. They started off down the road at an easy canter. Eugénie matched her seat to the filly's rhythmic motion. Used to the size and strength of the roan, she felt the delicateness of the young horse and enjoyed the contrast.

"How does she respond?" Bridger asked, admiring the beauty of the horse and rider beside him.

"She's wonderful! Her mouth is so soft, it's as though she knows my wishes even before I do."

"She comes from two strong bloodlines," Bridger said. "She isn't as fragile as she appears."

Am I imagining it, Eugénie asked herself, or does everything he says to me today have a double meaning?

Bridger's next words left her no time to mull over her thoughts. "Let's see what she can do."

Feeling the light tap of Eugénie's heels against her flanks, the filly leapt forward into a gallop. Both riders flew down the road. Eugénie laughed out loud at the sheer joy of the moment, the crisp wind, the exhilaration of the ride, and Bridger beside her. Bridger's horse began to edge past, testing the filly's stamina and will. She needed no urging. Eugénie felt the filly lift her performance to the next level, as she lengthened her stride and surged forward. Neck and neck the two horses opened up into a full run, their hooves hardly touching the ground.

Then at the same moment, as if on signal, Eugénie and Bridger began to slow their mounts down.

After riding steadily at a slower pace for a few minutes, Bridger said, "We've run them hard. Perhaps we should give them a rest and rub them down. I have some cloths and currycombs in my saddlebags."

Eugénie nodded in answer, slid down from the saddle, and led the filly over to the side of the road. Still exhilarated from the ride, she looked up at Bridger, her eyes dancing.

"It's a good thing she wasn't included in the auction or I would have snapped her up."

"You would, would you?" Bridger chuckled. "Now, that would have been a mighty difficult thing to do, since I had an inside track with her owner." As he handed her a currycomb, he was unable to resist resting a hand lightly on her small waist.

"Oh?" Eugénie raised an arched brow, at both his words and the intimacy of his touch.

"I would've skinned Edward alive if he had reneged on our wager," Bridger said.

"Edward? You mean your brother? And what might that wager have been, pray tell?" Eugénie paused in her currying motion to turn and put her hands on her hips.

"Oh, just a little thing, like getting a certain beautiful comtesse to refrain from looking down her imperious little nose at me and to return the deep affection that I've felt for her with all my heart from the first moment I laid eyes on her."

"Of all the . . ." Eugénie's voice stalled as she looked into his eyes twinkling with devilment. She saw their depths darken, and his carefree grin disappeared. With a groan, he clasped her to him. He held her for a long moment, then gently tilted her face up to his and kissed her parted lips.

"Eugénie, I wrestled the long night with thoughts of you, and I ended where I began. It's not convenient for me, this passion. But I'm trapped by the very game I started, with no wish to be set free. This morning, I fought with myself to keep from coming to see you. You are a distraction that I can ill afford. But I had no choice. I came to you, today, because I could do naught else. I feared when I awoke this morning that last night had only been a dream. I had to know, even if it meant learning that the worst of my imaginings were true."

She lifted her eyes to his, and in their shining depths he saw the answer he sought.

"I need no other words than the ones your eyes have spoken," he said quietly. He took her hands and drew them to his heart. "I don't know where we go from here. We'll have to take the moments as they are given to us. Know that wherever I am, whatever course I follow, your sweet face will always be there before me. I'll be true to us, no matter what should befall me in the other circumstances of my life."

Eugénie felt he was preparing her for something, but she couldn't figure out what. She also felt he was setting them apart and insulating them from the rest of the world.

"Bridger, we both have obligations that will carry us away from each other if we let them. I, too, want to protect and preserve what we found in each other," she murmured.

He pulled her to him and kissed her deeply. Then, setting her away from him, he said urgently, "Eugénie, there are things that I must do for my family's business that may be misinterpreted. Do not trust any words that you hear about me until you have heard them from my own lips. These are capricious times, and deeds will be done . . ." Eugénie placed her fingers lightly on his lips, saying, "Bridger, I expect no explanations. You ask none of me. Something very rare has occurred between us. That's all we need to know. Our world is a universe of two. What exists outside of that is of no consequence. The other worlds cannot intrude or lay claim. This is ours and ours alone."

They came together then, leaving the world behind. In their embrace, each opened up a world to the other and closed out all that did not exist within their two hearts, minds, and bodies.

Too soon, they heard the clatter of coach wheels and the steady clopping of horses' hooves. They turned as one toward the sound. Their precious moment had come to an end.

"The other worlds await us," Bridger said softly. With gentle fingers, he brushed back the wisps of hair at her temple. "I must feel this silkiness one last time and memorize it for all the days and nights that stretch out before me." Eugénie turned her head and kissed the palm that tenderly caressed her.

By the time the coach and the Whittington party rounded the bend, Eugénie and Bridger were once more settled on their mounts. Seeing the two riders, the coachman reined in the horses. John and Jack rode over to where Eugénie and Bridger were waiting.

"How did the filly perform?" Jack asked, admiring the lines of the young horse.

"Oh, you should have seen her run! She's truly magnificent!" Eugénie exclaimed. "Had I not already lost my heart to the roan, I wouldn't be able to part with her."

"Mistress Eugénie overlooks an insurmountable obstacle to her heart's desire," said Bridger. Eugénie noticed that in the presence of the others, Bridger thoughtfully took on a formal tone. "The young lady is in my possession, and I do not part easily with my possessions."

Eugénie heard and understood Bridger's meaning, and a warmth flowed through her. "Well," John said innocently, "you'll have to see that you and the filly make frequent trips to Oak Knoll. Which reminds me, Mary asked me to extend an invitation to you to sup with us tonight."

"I'd eagerly accept your kind invitation," Bridger answered, "but I fear I must postpone the pleasure. Even now my father and brother Edward await me at port. We must sail on the evening's tide if we're to enjoy the favorable winds. But if I'm not being too presumptuous, John, I see a possible solution to a dilemma I have. I didn't consider that I'd be aboard ship so soon when I purchased the filly. Would you be willing to take her with you to Oak Knoll while I'm away?"

Turning to Eugénie, he asked, "And Mistress Eugénie, would you be willing to care for her until such time as I return to reclaim her?"

Eugénie replied immediately, "If John agrees, I'd be more than happy to do my part." To herself she thought, He tells me much, while appearing only to carry on a casual conversation. He'll come to me at Oak Knoll when he returns.

"We'd be happy to stable the filly," John replied warmly, "and we look forward to seeing you at your journey's end. May you have fair winds and good fortune." The two men clasped hands, and John and Jack rode back to the coach to convey Bridger's regrets to Mary.

Looking long into Eugénie's face, Bridger said softly, "Until we meet again, may God go with you."

"And with you," Eugénie answered. She watched as he turned his horse back the way they had come. With one last backward glance and a wave, he set his horse at a gallop and disappeared from sight.

Some time later, the family and their two guests were gathered in the small breakfast room. It was situated on the east side of the house to catch the morning sun. Its dimness at the end of the day created a restful atmosphere that suited the quiet mood of the weary travelers. They all seemed absorbed in their own thoughts as they shared the simple fare. St. George excused himself early to write a letter to his father, leaving the others sipping the after-dinner wine and finishing the last of their desserts.

"What came of your visit with Tom Sidley this morning, John?" Mary asked, scooping up a spoonful of her rice pudding.

"I've been mulling over what he said all day, trying to make a decision," John replied. "I hadn't realized that Tom's been handling this, and handling it well, since the Randolphs left for the Continental Congress. He's right, I never should have lent Sam Brown acreage on our property without a binding contract."

"He was in no position to sign one at the time, and you couldn't just send him away," Mary replied, placing her hand over his. "He'd lost his property and then his wife died, leaving him with those three little children. What else could you do?"

"That's true. But I should've done something when he first started making trouble. Actually, he's been trouble from the beginning. He's never lived up to his side of the bargain—what bargain we did have. He hasn't kept up the cottage on that property, and the little ones are left on their own while he disappears for days at a time. I should have done something as soon as I heard how he was treating our people when they were working the land next to his, not to mention the other rumors that I can't confirm. He's bad business. I agree with Tom. I have no choice but to put him off the land. Thank goodness we can count on Hank Oldfield. He's the best overseer in the county. Tomorrow I'll send him to speak to Sam, and that will be the end of it."

"Oh, John," Mary said, "I know how hard this is on you. Those poor children."

"They're the reason that I've waited this long," John said. "But I realize after talking to Tom this morning that I have no means of holding him accountable, so the longer I wait, the worse it will be. I don't like turning him out because of the children, but I can't have him around here upsetting our people and letting our property deteriorate, not to mention some of the other things I've heard. He'll land on his feet. That sort of baggage always does. He's a good farmer when he chooses to be, and his crops have shown a profit the last three years. He'll go from here better than he arrived. Tomorrow will be the end, once and for all. Forgive me for burdening you all with this unpleasant situation."

"My dear," Mary intervened, "I believe it was I who introduced the subject, and I think it's best that we all know your decision, and why you made it." Looking around the table, she said, "If you'll excuse us, it's been a long day. Whoever is last to retire, please put out the candles."

XI

❦ ❦ ❦

The storm that had been threatening for the past few days broke with a vengeance during the night. Eugénie awoke with a start. Sitting bolt upright, she stared about her, at first confused by her surroundings. A flash of lightning illuminated the room. Thunder broke over the roof, its might shaking the house to its foundations. Two more flashes of light and rolls of deafening sound in quick succession brought Eugénie to her feet.

The horses! she thought. They'll be terrified. I must get to the stables. She scrambled quickly into the clothes she'd carelessly discarded the night before, grabbed her woolen cloak, and dashed for the door. Wrenching it back on its hinges, she almost collided with Marie, who was dressed similarly to her mistress.

"Come," Eugénie cried, "We must get to the stables!" The two raced down the hall and out of the front door just as the first deluge poured down from the sky.

The dark night was a scene of mass confusion, lit by frequent slashes of lightning and filled with roaring thunder. Branches were hurled through the air by the gale-force winds that accompanied the storm. Dislodged planking and pieces of slate whirled to the ground, causing further damage where they fell. Eugénie saw that some fencing had blown over. Shrubbery bent to the wind or lay smashed on the ground.

Lifting her skirts to speed her steps, she called to Marie to hurry, but her words were snatched from her lips and blown away. For an instant, she thought of Bridger aboard ship, and her heart slammed against her chest. With an effort, she put aside the thought and concentrated on getting to the stables and to the great roan.

Thank God, the rest of the stock set sail two days ago and are now well beyond the reaches of this storm, she thought, as she rounded the corner and burst through the stable doors.

"Has there been great damage?" Eugénie called to John Whittington, Jack, and St. George, who were laboring to batten down the shutters.

Yelling above the roar of the storm, John shouted back, "The storm's strength is slamming against the north end of the building. The men are sandbagging those walls, but I worry for the safety of the stalls. We're moving all the horses into the stalls at the south end."

"*Mon Dieu!* The roan is in the north end!" Eugénie ran in that direction, oblivious to the stablehands moving back and forth in her path, lugging great sacks of sand to fortify the building. She heard the trumpet of the roan's fear and the crashing of his hooves against the walls of his stall, frantic to escape.

"I'm here, my great horse," she called. Hearing the whistle that he'd learned meant safety, he pricked up his ears and ceased slamming against his stall. She swung open the gate and moved close to him, leaning against his side to give him the comfort of her physical nearness. Her breath caught in her throat when she saw the size of the welts he had inflicted on himself in his fear. Her heart ached as she realized the terror he must have felt.

"There, there," she crooned, stroking his side. "I'm here. I won't let anything happen to you. You're safe, now." Just then, a flash of lightning and a clap of thunder broke above them. Instantly, Eugénie smelled smoke. "Oh, my God! Fire!"

Hearing the screams of "Fire!" nearby confirmed her fears. The roan threw his head back, and his eyes rolled white in their sockets. Fighting her own fear, she continued stroking him as she slipped the bridle over his head. Calmed by her touch, the great horse overcame his instinctive fear of fire and placed his trust in his mistress's hands.

Eugénie drew him with her and moved back out into the main part of the stable building. What met her eyes made the earlier chaos seem like nothing. Horses were everywhere. Already panicked by the storm, they now were driven to madness by the smell of the smoke, their rearing bodies and flailing hooves endangering both themselves and everyone and everything in their path. Eugénie kept close to the wall, avoiding the pandemonium in the center of the room.

Once she had settled the roan safely in a large stall at the south end of the building and moved Bridger's filly into one next to him, Eugénie ran outside to see the extent of the fire. She stood in the downpour, staring at the wisps of smoke and the blackened roof.

This is nothing, she thought, compared to the disaster that would have occurred in dry weather. But, in dry weather, there wouldn't have been lightning to start the blaze in the first place, she reminded herself, and hurried back into the stable.

Eugénie sent Marie back to the house to help Mary and turned her attention to helping John relocate the rest of the horses.

Finally satisfied that the makeshift supports he had constructed would hold the stable walls until morning, John visited each stall, assuring himself that all the horses were settled in their new locations. Then he turned wearily to Jack, Eugénie, and St. George, who were leaning against a nearby wall.

"We've been fortunate, this night," he said, wiping his hand across his brow. "The lightning and thunder are passed. We've seen the worst of it." Listening to the storm raging overhead, Eugénie wondered about the truth of those words. As if in answer to her thoughts, John continued, "I feel a change in the energy. That means the winds and rain will pass soon. There's nothing more we can do for now." Raising his voice so that all in the large building could hear him, he said, "Get what rest you can in the night that's left. We'll assemble at first light to see the damage and get the repairs under way." John turned to Jack, Eugénie, and St. George and said in a more normal voice, "Thank you all for your help. Your quick wits and steady work helped to avoid what could have been a catastrophe. Take as much rest as you need."

Exhausted, Eugénie nodded her response and said, "Don't wait for me. I'll be right along after I've checked on the roan and the filly."

Reassured by the horses' calm demeanor, Eugénie pulled her cloak more tightly around her and stepped out into the storm. For a moment, she thought she had caught a furtive movement out of the corner of her eye.

'Tis nothing but your imagination, she scolded herself. You can brave lightning, thunder, fire, and storms, but darkness will always be your downfall! With that, she hastened her steps and finally gained the shelter of the main house, where Marie awaited her with some warm gruel and a large drying cloth that she had heated by the fire.

Eugénie awoke the next day to a morning sent straight from heaven. Sunlight streamed through the windows, playing with the dust motes that danced in its brightness. The chirping of birds mingled with the sounds of chopping axes and whining saws. The heavy air that had heralded the storm for the past few days had lifted, replaced by a sweet freshness that drew her out of bed. She embraced the day, stretching luxuriously. Marie, already up and dressed, turned from her tasks to smile at her mistress's radiant face.

"'Tis a day the Lord made," she said, capturing Eugénie's very thought. "I've been downstairs, and there's little for you to do. The main house held firm but for one or two shutters here and there. The stable is where the greatest damage was done." At Eugénie's look of alarm, Marie hastened to reassure her, "The roan, the filly, and all the other horses survived the night with nary a problem. Mistress Whittington has already assembled a legion to repair the gardens and fencing, so you might as well enjoy your breakfast and tend to your two charges when you're ready."

Eugénie sipped her tea and then turned her thoughts to planning the next few weeks. "Marie, we'll remain here for the time being, but I don't think it'll be for long. The results of this session of the Continental Congress and Jacques's reports from up north will determine our course of action." She went on to describe Darby in detail and what she had overheard at the Governor's Palace. "Keep an eye out for him," she warned. "If you should see him, report him at once to me or the Whittingtons. He and his cohorts are dangerous to the patriots and anyone who is sympathetic to them. Under no circumstances risk approaching him yourself. Promise me." When Marie nodded, Eugénie abruptly shifted to a new subject, asking, "What of you? How are you feeling? Has there been a return of your sickness?"

"Your remedies have set me right," Marie answered, smiling at her mistress. "Were it not for the increasing bulk I carry, I'd never know I was with child." To distract Eugénie from her concern about her condition, the mission, and Darby, Marie continued, "Perhaps you'd enjoy a ride on this beautiful morning?"

Appreciating Marie's efforts to allay her worries, Eugénie said, "That's a fine idea. It'll give me a chance to see if the roan's injuries caused any real damage."

As Eugénie approached the stables, the sights and sounds of repairs were well under way. "My, my, Marie didn't exaggerate the beauty of this day," Eugénie said aloud, putting aside the thoughts that weighed on her mind. The roan saw her and whinnied. She saddled him quickly, and they set off at a fast clip down the drive.

Curious to see the effect of the storm on the countryside, Eugénie directed the roan out onto the high road. Here and there, small trees were down and branches from ancient oaks and linden trees lay twisted along the roadway. Crops and pasture grasses lay flattened on the ground. But the sun shone warm above her, and a breeze, now gentle, brushed her cheek. She was glad to be out on such a day to witness the permanence and strength of the earth and its ability to withstand and endure.

She came upon a path leading off the main road that was new to her and decided to take it, thinking that it would eventually lead her back to the main house. As she made her way along the lane, she passed planting gone to seed and an abandoned field that had not seen a till or a hoe in at least one season. When she saw a cottage in the distance, it occurred to her that perhaps she had happened on the land that John

Whittington had lent to Samuel Brown, the topic of last night's conversation. She remembered both Mary and John's concern for the three small children. Putting aside a sense of foreboding, she continued down the lane.

I'll just stop by long enough to see that they've come to no harm from last night's storm and then be on my way, she thought. She tied the roan to what was left of a post-and-rail fence and hurried up the weed-choked path, already eager to be gone. On closer inspection, the dwelling was little more than a shack, showing nothing of what once might have been a charming cottage. As she approached the door, she saw no sign of life. No smoke showed above the chimney, and there was an eerie silence about the place.

Eugénie raised her hand to knock just as the door burst open, revealing a rusty musket aimed directly at her chest. Eugénie jumped back. Staring at the firing piece, she saw that the hands gripping it were none too steady. She reluctantly raised her eyes from the gun barrel and found herself looking into a pair of bloodshot eyes and a face so filthy and vile that she recoiled in spite of herself.

"Explain yourself, woman!" came the hoarse command.

Eugénie tried to speak but her voice caught in her throat. Taking a deep breath, she began again, "I was out riding and just happened on this lane."

"Happened! Happened, you say!" The hoarse voice broke into a shriek. "And what, pray tell, would a hoity-toity lady such as you be doing 'happening' by here except to spy on me and mine?"

Eugénie realized with horror that the creature before her was teetering on the brink of madness. She still had seen no sign of the children and now genuinely feared for their safety. She instinctively pitched her voice low in an attempt to draw the venom from the wild beast that faced her. "Sir, I mean you no harm. Only to see if the inhabitants of this house had survived the storm of the night past without injury."

A look of confusion passed over the man's face, causing it for the moment to appear more human. Her show of kindness and gentle ways had struck a chord somewhere in the recesses of his mind. Lowering his weapon, he shook his head from side to side as if to clear the mists away.

Seeing an opening, Eugénie continued in her quiet tone, "Are you alone? Do you have little ones who need help?"

As if stung, his head shot back up. A look of suspicion settled on his face and once again he pointed the gun at her chest. "Little ones? What do you know of little ones?" he shouted at her, spraying spittle in her face. Then, his tone changed and a note of craftiness crept into his voice. "But, I know of you. Aye, my grand lady, I know of you. I have watched you riding that great horse of yours. I've seen you crooning to him in the stableyard." At his words, Eugénie felt her skin crawl and her blood run cold. For the first time, a genuine fear gripped her. "He matters much to you, does he not?" He leaned closer, the threat clear in his voice. "If you know what's good for you, Mistress High-and-Mighty, you'll watch your step. Take this message back to that fine gentleman, Mr. John Whittington," he said with a sneer. "Tell him, I and mine are gone from here this day, and good riddance to him. I have friends who appreciate my talents. I've no need for his paltry handouts after today. Tell him that!" With these last words, his voice rose to a screech, and he lurched back into the cabin, slamming the door in her face.

It took all the courage Eugénie could muster to turn and walk unhurriedly back down the path to the roan. She could feel Sam Brown's eyes boring into her back, and a chill ran through her. As she galloped away down the lane, she thought she heard a high, piercing cackle.

Her agitation communicated itself to the great horse, and he set a pace that brought her safely back into the stableyard in no time at all. She dismounted and leaned her head for a moment against his neck. With an effort, she collected her shattered nerves and allowed the calming sights and sounds of the stableyard to seep into her.

Even the soothing routine of unsaddling and rubbing down Roan II was not enough to dispel the sense of foreboding that she had felt from the moment that she had first seen Samuel Brown's cottage. She wasted no time finding John and Mary and telling them what she had seen.

"There is madness in him, John," Eugénie shivered, remembering his wild eyes. "Whether it's from drink or a mind that has finally snapped under the burden of bad fortune and real or imagined slights, I know not. But there's no doubt that he wishes you and your family harm."

The curiosity that both John and Mary had shown when Eugénie began her story turned to concern. Her concluding words brought a look of horror to both of their faces.

"I hadn't realized that he'd become so deranged," John said. "He was once a hardworking, God-fearing man who loved his wife and took pride in his work and his family. What could bring a man so low?" Shaking his head, he went on, "This evening, I'll send Hank and two stout men to make good and certain that he's gone. If he hasn't departed, they'll escort him to the sheriff. For the deeds that he's already committed, as well as his act of physically threatening you today, the sheriff will have the authority to ban him permanently from this county and place the children with a family for their own safekeeping." Mary and Eugénie looked at each other and then back at John.

"I hope he'll still be there," Mary said grimly. "Then we'll know that the right steps will be taken to rid us of him once and for all and place those poor children in good, loving hands."

"You said, Eugénie, that he mentioned friends?" John asked. "What sort would have dealings with such as he?"

"He gave no indication of who they were," Eugénie replied, glad to have the whole incident off her shoulders. "Only that 'they,' as he put it, 'appreciated his talents.' John, over the last few weeks there've been occasions when I've felt the presence of someone lurking about in the dark. The most recent time was last night when I was leaving the stable. I wrote it off to my imagination, but now I'm not so sure. He certainly was familiar with me and the roan, and he knows things he could've known only if he were here to see them with his own eyes."

"Well, after this evening he'll be gone, one way or the other," John said in a relieved voice. "I suspect it'll be the last we hear of the unfortunate fellow."

After supper, when the family, Eugénie, and St. George were sitting out on the veranda enjoying the first balmy spring evening, Hank Oldfield and the two men who'd accompanied him to Sam Brown's cottage rode slowly up the way. Their faces were set in grim lines as they dismounted and doffed their hats.

"Mr. Whittington, sir, Samuel Brown is gone," Hank said. But the relief on everyone's face disappeared with his next words. "He left nothing behind. He burned the cottage, the fencing, everything to the ground. Not even the chimney was left standing." He shifted on his feet, his honest gaze focused on John Whittington's face. "I wish I'd gone sooner and had been there to see what he was doing. I would've torn him apart, limb from limb!"

"Don't waste another thought on such scum," John said with uncharacteristic harshness. Then he lightened his tone in an effort to lessen his overseer's frustration. "'Tis far better that you weren't there. It is done. Even as deranged as he is, he won't dare show his face around here after the deeds he's done this day. He'll get as far away from here as possible. The best thing we can do now is put him and this unhappy episode behind us and out of our minds."

XII

❧❧❧

Sam Brown was soon forgotten in the days that followed, as spring planting and Mary's annual cleaning of the main house and the dependencies got under way. Any time not devoted to these activities was spent wondering what was happening in Philadelphia.

Information had begun to trickle in, and everyone was pleased that the Virginia delegates were building enviable reputations. Peyton Randolph's stature as president of the Continental Congress increased daily. Rumor had it that, should it become necessary to take military action, a standing army would be drawn from the individual colonial militias. George Washington had the most support for Commander-in-Chief, not only from the Virginia contingent but also, unexpectedly, from both Samuel and John Adams of Massachusetts.

Eugénie spent the days helping Mary, Bess, and Kate bring the plantation out of winter into spring. She could not help but compare the running of her holdings in France with the Whittingtons' plantation. Her properties were run like clockwork by a retinue of servants who had inherited their positions down through the generations. Each knew his or her role and responsibilities. If an occasion called for additional servants or a particular skill not readily available amongst their ranks, the word was put out, and promptly a relative or an acquaintance was found to fill the need.

Life on the Whittington plantation had a clearly defined structure, though it was neither as rigid nor as formal. Each person on the plantation was defined by his or her job, but the demands of the young colonies rewarded ingenuity and performance. This created a fluidity that did not exist in the older established structures in the mother countries. This system applied to the slaves on most plantations, with a few glaring exceptions. The African population had been introduced into the colonies by the mother country as a cash crop for England and as a labor force for the colonists.

Another way that life at Oak Knoll differed from Eugénie's experience was John and Mary's close involvement in and attention to every aspect of the plantation. There was never a task so menial or mundane that one or the other wasn't there to oversee it or take part in it. They began each day in their separate offices, going over in minute detail the accounts and reports of everything that happened on the plantation. Their lieutenants—for lieutenants they were—were selected to oversee and manage each phase of the work on the plantation and then to make reports to either John or Mary. The qualities for these positions were intelligence, ingenuity, resourcefulness, stamina, and an overall concern for the success of the plantation.

This style of management took place on plantations throughout Virginia and the other agricultural colonies. John had the final word on all that occurred outside the house while Mary's domain was the main house, the dependency buildings on the plantation, and the areas that supported their smooth running. They each had a thorough knowledge of the whole plantation, owing to their natural curiosity and to the full hour that they set aside each evening before supper to bring each other up to date on the day's happenings.

Guests and special occasions at Oak Knoll rarely interrupted the well-oiled system. On the contrary, Eugénie noticed that, more often than not, the guests were folded right in, giving them a more personal experience with the family and the plantation than would have been possible otherwise. Her participation in the everyday activities had allowed her to develop a closeness with the Whittington family that was very precious to her. She enjoyed her late-night chats with Bess and Kate, sharing the knowledge and intimacies common to young women of their age.

With each day, the sun shone warmer and the evenings grew longer. Eugénie was too busy keeping up with Mary to dwell on her mission or on Bridger's whereabouts. The full days saved her from fretting overlong about her lack of news on both counts. She was confident of Bridger's welfare, since news of shipping accidents and shipwrecks traveled quickly along the coast and no such reports had come in. Even the threat of Darby had slipped from her mind, since she had not seen him nor heard of him since the governor's ball.

Finally, the morning arrived when Mary gave her stamp of approval to the indoor cleaning. Every wall had been scrubbed, every surface dusted and polished, every window washed, every floor waxed and buffed, every chandelier and sconce polished, every mattress beaten and turned, every hanging fabric and floor covering taken outside, beaten with straw brooms, and hung to freshen in the March breezes. Every cabinet and cupboard had been turned inside out, every room aired. Every surface glistened and shone, from the combined efforts of Mary's troops.

Next, Mary moved her army outside to the kitchen and herb gardens to repair the winter damage and the wreckage caused by the storm. Mary lent Eugénie one of the wide-brimmed, plaited palmetto hats that St. George had brought back from his last trip to Bermuda.

Straightening up to relieve the strain on her back after a morning of hoeing and weeding, Eugénie looked over at the girls and Mary working steadily in the rosemary patch. Watching their heads with the large floppy hats bobbing up and down, she began to laugh. Soon tears were streaming down her face. Mary looked up, hearing the strangled sound, and saw Eugénie bent over double leaning on her hoe. Dropping her own, she ran over to Eugénie's side. She placed her hand on the young woman's back to comfort her.

"Eugénie, Eugénie," Mary said with alarm, "What is the matter?" Eugénie looked up, her eyes dancing with merriment.

"Oh, Mary," Eugénie gasped, "I just looked over and saw the three large hats flapping up and down and then I pictured myself and what I must look like and I . . ." She broke out laughing again, unable to continue. Mary, caught up in the picture and Eugénie's infectious laugh, collapsed against her, laughing heartily. By this time, Bess and Kate became aware of Eugénie's and their mother's odd behavior and looked over, puzzled.

"What's so funny?" Bess asked Kate, who shrugged her shoulders and called out to her mother.

"Mother, what are you laughing at?" Eugénie and Mary, unable to speak, pointed in the direction of Kate's and Bess's heads and then grabbed the brims of their own hats and waggled them up and down. Finally understanding the pantomime, Bess and Kate joined in the laughter, pointing at each other and to their mother and Eugénie. This was the happy scene that greeted John Whittington as he strolled into the herb garden.

"Well, nothing like a little levity to lighten the labor, I always say." He stopped to admire the beauty of his wife, who stood with her palmetto hat askew on her tousled golden curls, her cheeks flushed and her eyes brimming with laughter. "Whatever this method is, Mary, could you teach the men in the fields? We could use some merriment to lighten that backbreaking work."

"The secret," Mary said, trying to pull herself together, "is in the palmetto hats, but I don't think there are enough to go around." Imagining all the men in the fields with palmetto hats bobbing up and down was more than the four women could stand, and they went into gales of laughter again.

"Well, palmetto hats or not, I want to join this party. It looks to be considerably more fun than what I've been doing," John said with a chuckle.

"Come," Mary said putting her arm around his waist, "let's go in and attend to our toilettes. Bess and Kate can finish up here and then join us for the picnic I've planned for the beginning of the spring season." Appreciating her ability to read his feelings, he leaned down and kissed her lightly on her temple.

"A picnic! What a wonderful idea! It's past the vernal equinox already. Where did the time go? Just yesterday it was the end of February!"

It wasn't long before everyone had arrived at the side lawn where the picnic had been spread out on a large, colorful cloth under the shade of the huge oak trees that gave the plantation its name.

"Why, thank you, St. George," Mary replied, as the young man helped her settle on the grass. "You boys have a seat and help yourselves to the feast Opa has prepared for us. She really outdid herself today."

Jack watched St. George settle himself between Eugénie and Bess. "Mother, that's because she's 'tryin' to put some meat on Mr. St. George's bones,'" Jack said, capturing Opa's lilting singsong speech perfectly. "You know she's taken 'quite a shine' to him, and to her, fat is a sign of great beauty. Not that St. George can get any better in her eyes!" He stopped suddenly as the target of his teasing reached around Bess and poked him in the ribs.

"Opa's always had an eye for the men," Mary said, laughing at Jack's accurate assessment of the magnificent woman who had been the cook at Oak Knoll since the children were small. "I've had to watch her like a hawk to keep her from plumping up your father all these years. You don't remember, Jack, but when I wasn't looking, she used to feed you so many sweets that I thought you'd never outgrow your baby fat. But look at you now. Whatever she did, you certainly turned out just fine." Mary smiled fondly at her handsome son, who had inherited his father's height and dark good looks.

Soon everyone was relishing the crisp fried chicken with thin slices of Virginia ham and steaming biscuits that Opa called her specialty. The baked meat pie did not go unappreciated, nor did the slices of red apples still crisp from the root cellar and the homemade, sharp-flavored yellow and white cheeses.

"Will anyone have the last helping of cobbler?" Mary asked, looking around the circle of satisfied diners.

"One more bite, Mother, and I swear I'll burst," Kate exclaimed.

"Mistress Whittington, I don't want to disappoint Opa by leaving even a crumb of her delicious feast," St. George said. "But Jack's going to have to roll me back to the house as it is."

"Opa's picnic could feed an army, but I think we've all done a yeoman's service to her efforts," John agreed. He turned his head as the sound of a rider coming up the lane at a fast pace reached their ears. "Who could that be, coming at such a clip?" he mused out loud. "Maybe it's the messenger from Richmond that I've been expecting." At her host's words, Eugénie's eyes flew to his face. She felt a shiver pass through her. Somehow she knew the long wait was over.

"Jack, go and greet our guest. Bring him out here so that we all can hear what news he brings." While Jack left to welcome the visitor, the rest of the party put the remains of the picnic in baskets. They were just settling themselves on benches beneath the trees when Jack and a young man strode toward them.

"Mother, Father, may I present Robert Downing?" Jack's introduction was brief, as he knew his parents were eager to hear the young man's message. The Whittingtons rose to make him welcome and gestured toward a bench. Robert Downing shook his head.

"Thank you, but I prefer to remain standing after the long ride from Richmond." He took a moment to position himself and then began, "Mr. and Mistress Whittington, I come with news from Philadelphia and Richmond. At this last session of the Continental Congress, the delegates once again agreed to send appeals to England—but this time with teeth: the threat of a trade embargo. Just four days past, on March twenty-third, Virginia's Revolutionary Convention met at St. John's Church in Richmond to decide whether or not to approve the actions in Philadelphia. Opinion was divided over what to expect from the most recent communications sent to England, but Mr. Patrick Henry had no such doubts. He gave the most stirring speech that the world has ever heard!"

John and Mary glanced at each other briefly, smiling at the young man's fervor.

"I and other messengers have been sent to carry the word out to the countryside. I've brought with me a copy of the speech. If you would like to read it, sir?" Robert held out a sheaf of papers to John Whittington.

Skimming the first sheet, John knew an auspicious moment had arrived. He returned to the beginning and began to read aloud the powerful words before him.

"It says here that Mr. Patrick Henry put forth a proposal to prepare the Virginia militia in case of war with Great Britain and that on the twenty-third of March in the year of our Lord, 1775, he stood before the Revolutionary Convention to defend his proposal. 'Mr. President...'" John turned to Robert Downing, "I imagine the 'Mr. President' whom he is addressing is Peyton Randolph, who is presiding?"

At the young man's nod, John continued reading:

"No man thinks more highly than I do of the patriotism, as well as abilities, of the very worthy gentlemen who have just addressed the house. But different men often see the same subject in different lights; and, therefore, I hope it will not be thought disrespectful to those gentlemen, if, entertaining as I do opinions of a character very opposite to theirs, I shall speak forth my sentiments freely and without reserve. This is no time for ceremony. The question before the house is one of awful moment to this country. For my part, I consider it as nothing less than a question of freedom or slavery; and in proportion to the magnitude of the subject ought to be the freedom of the debate. It is only in this way that we can hope to arrive at truth, and fulfill the great responsibility which we hold to God and our country. Should I keep back my opinions at such a time, through fear of giving offence, I should consider myself as guilty of treason toward my country, and of an act of disloyalty toward the Majesty of Heaven, which I revere above all earthly kings.

"Mr. President, it is natural to man to indulge in the illusions of hope. We are apt to shut our eyes against a painful truth, and listen to the song of that siren, till she transforms us into beasts. Is this the part of wise men, engaged in a great and arduous struggle for liberty? Are we disposed to be of the number of those, who, having eyes, see not, and having ears, hear not, the things which so nearly concern their temporal salvation? For my part, whatever anguish of spirit it may cost, I am willing to know the whole truth; to know the worst, and to provide for it."

John Whittington paused, his face grave, and then continued:

"I have but one lamp by which my feet are guided, and that is the lamp of experience. I know of no way of judging of the future but by the past. And judging by the past, I wish to know what there has been in the conduct of the British Ministry for the last ten years to justify those hopes with which gentlemen have been pleased to solace themselves and the house. Is it that insidious smile with which our petition has been lately received? Trust it not, sir; it will prove a snare to your feet. Suffer not yourselves to be betrayed with a kiss. Ask yourselves how this gracious reception of our petition comports with those warlike preparations which cover our waters and darken our land. Are fleets and armies necessary to a work of love and reconciliation? Have we shown ourselves so unwilling to be reconciled, that force must be called in to win back our love? Let us not deceive ourselves, sir. These are the implements of war and subjugation; the last arguments to which kings resort. I ask gentlemen, sir, What means this martial array, if its purpose be not to force us to submission? Can gentlemen assign any other possible motive for it? Has Great Britain any enemy, in this quarter of the world, to call for all this accumulation of navies and armies? No, sir, she has none. They are meant for us: they can be meant for no other. They are sent over to bind and rivet upon us those chains which the British Ministry have been so long forging. And what have we to oppose them? Shall we try argument? Sir, we have been trying that for the last ten years. Have we anything new to offer upon the subject? Nothing. We have held the subject up in every light of which it is capable; but it has been all in vain. Shall we resort to entreaty and humble supplication? What terms shall we find, which have not been already exhausted? Let us not, I beseech you, sir, deceive our selves longer. Sir, we have done everything that could be done, to avert the storm which is now coming on. We have petitioned; we have remonstrated; we have supplicated; we have prostrated ourselves before the throne, and have implored its interposition to arrest the tyrannical hands of the Ministry and Parliament. Our petitions have been slighted; our remonstrances have produced additional violence and insult; our supplications have been disregarded; and we have been spurned, with contempt, from the foot of the throne! In vain, after these things, may we indulge the fond hope of peace and reconciliation. There is no longer any room for hope. If we wish to be free—if we mean to preserve inviolate those inestimable privileges for which we have been so long contending—if we mean not basely to abandon the noble struggle in which we have been so long engaged, and which we have pledged ourselves never to abandon, until the glorious object of our contest shall be obtained—we must fight! I repeat it, sir, we must fight! An appeal to arms and to the God of Hosts is all that is left us."

John looked up, his eyes shining, and then continued reading.

"They tell us, sir, that we are weak unable to cope with so formidable an adversary. But when shall we be stronger? Will it be next week, or next year? Will it be when we are totally disarmed, and when a British guard shall be stationed in every house? Shall we gather strength by irresolution and inaction? Shall we acquire the means of effectual resistance by lying supinely on our backs and hugging the delusive phantom of hope, until our enemies shall have bound us hand and foot? Sir, we are not weak, if we make a proper use of those means which the God of nature hath placed in our power. Three millions of people armed in the holy cause of liberty, and in such a country as that which we possess, are invincible by any force which our enemy can send against us. Besides, sir, we shall not fight our battles alone. There is a just God who presides over the destinies of nations, and who will raise up friends to fight our battles for us. The battle, sir, is not to the strong alone; it is to the vigilant, the active, the brave. Besides, sir, we have no election. If we were base enough to desire it, it is now too late to retire from the contest. There is no retreat, but in submission and slavery! Our chains are forged! Their clanking may be heard on the plains of Boston! The war is inevitable—and let it come! I repeat it, sir, let it come.

"It is vain, sir, to extenuate the matter. Gentlemen may cry, Peace, Peace—but there is no peace. The war is actually begun! The next gale that sweeps from the north will bring to our ears the clash of resounding arms! Our brethren are already in the field! Why should we here idle? What is it that gentlemen wish? What would they have? Is life so dear, or peace so sweet, as to be purchased at the price of chains and slavery? Forbid it, Almighty God! I know not what course others may take; but as for me, give me liberty or give me death!"

As the last words faded away, the silence that had gripped the group at the beginning of the reading continued to exert its hold over the people sitting there. Then, as if a dam burst, everyone began speaking at once.

"It is done, then," John said, knowing that the floodgates would hold no longer.

"Father, what will happen now?" Bess asked, her heart still thumping from the power of Patrick Henry's words.

"My own father has been saying that a trade embargo was imminent," St. George said, in low tones. "It will mean hardship for Bermuda."

I've been beguiled by the soothing routine of the past few days, Eugénie thought. I must remember my purpose here! Thank God, I'll meet with Jacques soon.

"Come," Mary said, her calm voice rising above the others. "Let us go to the house and offer Mr. Downing some refreshment. He has ridden hard this day." Kate simply stared at Robert Downing and wished with all her heart that she, not he, had been in St. John's Church to hear the stirring words with her own ears.

Oak Knoll, always a center of information during the unsettled times of the past several years, was inundated with visitors throughout the afternoon and into the evening. A steady stream of people came and went, seeking and dispensing news. Mary could see that the talking would continue well into the night, so she had banquet tables set up along the verandas and in the dining room to accommodate refreshments.

In the late evening, Eugénie quietly slipped away from the throng, seeking a restful place to think. She knew that her purpose for being at

Oak Knoll was fast coming to an end. She was deeply saddened at the thought of leaving these people. Would Patrick Henry's thrilling words sustain the brave men and their families through the long, hard months—perhaps years—ahead? Would his words provide them with the courage to make the sacrifices that would inevitably come? And what of Bridger? His family's livelihood, like that of many of the other American colonists, depended on the trade Britain provided. Would that livelihood determine his and their loyalties? And what of St. George? His loyalties were clear. He stood firmly on the side of the patriots. But would Bermuda, herself a British colony and highly valued by the Crown for her lucrative trade and strategic military position, desert her mother country as well and join forces with the Americans?

These and other questions ripped through Eugénie's mind. But she had an answer to nary a one when she finally turned back toward the beckoning lights of what had been her home for the past several weeks.

XIII

❧❧❧

People continued to congregate at Oak Knoll during the days that followed Robert Downing's news. The plantation's location on the road between Williamsburg and Richmond made it a convenient place to stop for a short rest and some refreshment.

Each day, fresh news arrived reporting skirmishes between British soldiers and patriotic colonials as well as between colonials loyal to the Crown and those who were not. Fighting erupted in taverns, on street corners, between neighbors. On the veranda at Oak Knoll, tempers even flared over the intent of Patrick Henry's words and what course of action the colonials should follow.

Several days after Robert Downing's arrival, the family had just sat down for a quiet dinner when one of the servants burst into the room.

"Master Whittington, Master Carter's boy just come by to warn us that they's been some mischief here'bouts." The man was in such a state of agitation that his words ran together, their meaning incomprehensible. John Whittington rose quickly to his feet.

"Come, come, Alexander, calm yourself. What is it you're trying to say?" Alexander took a deep breath and rubbed his palms down the sides of his britches, trying hard to collect himself.

"Master Carter sent his boy round here and to all the neighbor places to tell them that they's been some men goin' round causin' trouble and we's to keep our eyes peeled lessen they come this way. They been makin' trouble, stealin', fightin' with folks, scarin' the lady folk. Tha's all he say, Master Whittington."

"Is he still here, Alexander?" John Whittington asked, intending to question the messenger further himself.

"No, suh. He say he got to get goin' cause he got to get to all the other plantations, here'round." Alexander's head drooped as though he felt responsible for letting the man get away when Mr. Whittington still had questions for him.

"Alexander, you've done a good job coming to tell us right away. Will you go and tell Isaac and Mr. Oldfield that I'd like to speak to them and to come here as quickly as they can?"

Alexander's face brightened at John Whittington's praise. His chest puffed out and his head went up as he took pride in being the bearer of the important message. Bobbing his head several times in his eagerness, he answered, "Yessuh, yessuh!" and dashed out of the room.

"It's come to this," John said soberly, returning to his chair. "Malcontents and marauders on both sides will start to take license. We must watch for any incident or any unfamiliar person abroad for no apparent purpose and keep each other informed, as John Carter is doing this night."

"Oh, John," Mary said, "what have we come to?" Before he could answer, Hank Oldfield and Isaac, the head field hand, arrived in the doorway.

"Come in, men, and have a seat," John said, motioning them toward the table. Eugénie had learned from the first day of her arrival that the Whittington plantation operated on a far more egalitarian basis than most of the other plantations in the colony. John and Mary often asked leaders amongst their people to make suggestions or to keep them informed about life on the plantation. The respect and loyalty that flowed amongst the family and the field hands and house staff were unique.

"You men have probably heard about the lawlessness that has broken out recently. It's time we took steps to make sure we at Oak Knoll remain safe. I've called you here to help me develop a plan that will protect Oak Knoll and its people from harm. I'll count on the two of you to carry out whatever plan we come up with this night."

As the two men expressed their concerns and discussed the methods they thought would work to protect the plantation, Eugénie sat quietly, observing the interaction amongst the plantation owner and his two leaders. Hank Oldfield's proposals bespoke the man of action that he was. He was quick to formulate a plan based on a team of men and women who would be responsible for selecting their own subteam. Each subteam would be obliged to keep watch over its section of the vast plantation and report to each other and to the Whittingtons.

While Hank spoke, Isaac listened impassively, his handsome face a blend of his Iroquois and African heritage. In spite of his great size and physical strength, he was known for his wisdom and gentleness. All the servants on the plantation deferred to his judgment and sought him out to settle the inevitable disputes that arose from time to time. He and Hank were a formidable pair that inspired loyalty and obedience on the part of all the Oak Knoll people. Isaac made a few additional suggestions that simplified and strengthened the overall plan.

"Good," John said finally. "We will put the plan into action this night, and then we can all rest easier." He stood up, signaling that the meeting was at an end. Excusing himself from the others, he walked outside with the two men. As Eugénie fell asleep that night, she wondered if perhaps Darby's hand had been behind these disturbances.

The next morning, looking out of the window, Kate exclaimed, "Amelia Stanton, as I live and breathe! What in the world could she want? It's not like her to be up, much less dressed and making calls, before high noon at the very earliest!" Bess joined her sister at the window to see Amelia alighting from her carriage. They watched as she closed her parasol with a snap and flounced up to the front door.

"Girls, girls! Really. Where are your manners?" their mother chided. "Go and invite Amelia in." As Kate and Bess left to do her bidding, Mary turned to Eugénie, raising an eyebrow and shaking her head. Almost immediately, they could hear Amelia's piercing voice coming down the hallway.

"No, not a word! I'm not sayin' one word till I see your mama! It's a scandal and an outrage! Why, it's the talk of the whole county, probably all Virginia, by now!"

"What's the talk of the county, Amelia?" Mary asked, meeting the highly excited young woman at the doorway and ushering her into the room. Plopping herself onto the overstuffed, brocaded gentleman's chair, Amelia fluffed her hair and smoothed her skirts, plainly enjoying everyone's undivided attention.

"Why, I'm just shocked and amazed that word of this outrage hasn't reached you all yet," Amelia purred, prolonging the moment. "Oooh, I do so love Opa's lace cookies. May I?" The question was clearly rhetorical since she had already plucked a handful of the cookies from the platter in front of her and was cramming one into her mouth as she spoke. "Mmmmm! Just as good as ever!"

"Would you like some tea, Amelia?" Bess asked her, dryly.

"Why, how sweet of you. I don't mind if I . . ."

"Oh, stop all the fuss!" Kate interrupted, impatiently. "I know you're dying to tell us your news, Amelia. So just stop fiddling and tell us!"

"Well," Amelia said, drawing out the word for dramatic effect, as she daintily blotted her lips with a lace-edged napkin. "The entire Goodrich family has been run out of Virginia!"

"What!" Even Mary's composure slipped.

"Yes, the whole kit and caboodle of them—lock, stock, and barrel!"

"Why in the world!?" Bess's stunned tone reflected everyone's reaction.

Eugénie, who had taken little notice of Amelia other than to nod at her politely when the young woman had entered the room, sat up abruptly in her chair, her eyes wide with shock. Could this be what he meant when Bridger had said, "Trust no words that you may hear of me except those from my own lips?" Her mind raced. What in the world could have happened? Are he and his family part of what's been happening in the county? *O, mon Dieu, non!* Is he hurt? Will I ever see him again?

"Dear Amelia," Mary said, "what in heaven's name are you talking about? The Goodriches are an upstanding family. There could be no call for such an action against them. You must be mistaken in what you heard."

"I certainly am not mistaken! I know exactly what I heard!" Amelia retorted sharply. Her pouting lips narrowed into a straight line and her eyes turned to slits. "And when you hear what I have to say, you'll know I'm not mistaken." Then, sitting up ramrod straight as though she were a child reciting to her teacher, she launched into the explanation.

"Well, you know how our colonial merchant ships just run around all over the place, picking up something here and picking up something there and you know how sometimes they just happen on another, say, French or Spanish merchant ship, and our captain will just take over that other little ol' ship and, in the blink of an eye, all that lovely cargo is just snapped right up and lands in the hold of one of our nice little ships?"

By this time, Bess and Kate were rolling their eyes. "Amelia, Amelia," Bess burst out, unable to control herself another moment, "we know all that. What in the world does it have to do with the Goodriches?"

"I am gettin' to that!" Amelia snapped. "Just hold your horses! Anyway, as I was sayin', we all know that this kind of thing has been goin' on forever and as long as customs get their little ol' share of the pie, they don't ask any questions and everyone gets what they want and goes on their merry way. Well, it appears that some months past, the Goodriches brought in a big, shall we say, requisitioned cargo that included a whole pile of gunpowder and guns. Somehow they snuck it by the British customs agents. The Goodriches were just pleased pink and were about to divide it up amongst themselves when along came a group of colonials of the patriots' persuasion who raided their warehouse and took everything. Now, who knows what those naughty Goodriches had planned to do with all that stuff, but you can be sure it wasn't to just hand it over to the colonials. And since they'd pulled the wool over the customs agents' eyes, they couldn't just turn around and petition the British courts here to help them get their stuff back, now could they? So every one of those six boys and their daddy crossed over to the other side and started sailing as agents for the British against us. Can you imagine?"

The horror on the faces of her audience was answer enough. "Since then, they've been sneaking around snaring our Virginia-owned ships, taking the ships' cargoes, and setting the ships adrift. Remember all those mysterious disappearances of our merchant ships?" As the four women nodded, she continued, "And you know about the ship own- ers' getting together for all those special meetings to try and find the culprits? Well, they finally caught those boys and their daddy red- handed. They had placed an informer on one of the Goodrich crews. And once they had the evidence, that was that. They confronted the whole bunch of them and gave them forty-eight hours to get them- selves and their families out of Virginia once and for all. Now see what I told you? I certainly was not mistaken one bit! They've been run out of the colony, and that's the God's honest truth! I always knew they were up to no good, and I say good riddance!"

Considering your unbecoming behavior, panting after Bridger all these years, you sure could have fooled me! Kate thought, but held her tongue.

"When were they given the ultimatum?" asked John Whittington, who had quietly entered the room and overheard the last part of Amelia's story.

"Yesterday, midday." Amelia was very pleased to be the bearer of such shocking news. "So by noontime tomorrow—that would be April fourth—if they're not gone from the colony of Virginia, we law- abidin' citizens will take steps to remove them."

"What a sad state of affairs!" John said, commiserating with the Goodriches' lot.

"Well I never, Mr. Whittington!" Amelia exclaimed self-righteously. "How can you say such a thing? Why, they are vile, vile, vile! Cheats, liars, thieves! A young lady such as myself wouldn't feel safe knowing they were prowling around the countryside. But now I can sleep safe in my bed, knowing they've been run out of this colony!" Rising on that dramatic note, Amelia made a great show of collecting her things and assuming a posture of importance. "Well, I must be getting along now. I have so much, so much to do, and it's already almost noontime. Lord above, where has this day gone to?"

"Thank you for bringing us the news, Amelia," Mary said, her voice composed once more. "We appreciate your coming all this way to tell us. Bess, would you please see Amelia to her carriage?" Amelia, her face set in a smug expression, looked through her lashes at Bess and then curtsied to Mary Whittington, saying, "Why, you are more than welcome, I'm sure. Just doin' my civic duty." On that note, the two women departed. Soon they heard the front door close, shutting out Amelia's shrill voice.

"I swear, Mother," Kate said, "how can you be so nice to that girl? I declare, her voice could crack glass. My ears are still ringing. Doesn't she notice that nobody else carries on a normal conversation at the top of their lungs? It's the only way she can get anyone's attention."

"That's enough, Kate," her mother said firmly. "Oh dear, oh dear, what a turn for that poor family."

Eugénie's face had grown paler and paler as she listened to Amelia's damning words. Even if Amelia Stanton's tale was exaggerated, she thought, the fact remains that the Goodrich family are turncoats. They've thrown in their lot with the British! They've made enemies of the patriots, which makes them now my enemy, as well. I fear for you and your family, but most of all I feel heartsick for us. Oh, Bridger, what have you done? Her limbs felt heavy, and she heard the conversation around her as if from a great distance. The room darkened before her eyes.

"Eugénie, dear!"

Mary's cry of alarm pulled her back, and she was amazed to hear herself answer in a normal voice. "I felt light-headed for a moment, but I'm quite recovered now."

The older woman moved to Eugénie's side and put her arm around her shoulders. "Events are moving so rapidly. It's a wonder any of us can keep our heads at all," Mary said gently. "John, Amelia, bless her soul, may have exaggerated somewhat. Perhaps we should seek out someone less excitable to make sure of the story."

"My thought, exactly," John said. "I'll ride over to the Lee plantation. They were part of the group investigating the lost ships. They'll know where the truth lies in all of this."

"Please take Jack and St. George with you. It's not safe to ride out alone these days," Mary said, concern in her voice. "And arm yourselves."

"I will do just that if it will give you peace of mind, my dear," John said, smiling at her indulgently.

Needing to unburden her heart to her good friend, Eugénie wasted no time slipping from the room and going in search of Marie.

After relaying the news about Bridger, Eugénie fell into her servant's arms. "I know that my best course of action is to close my heart and mind against him, but I can't," Eugénie's voice choked as she lifted her head from Marie's shoulder.

"If only I knew the words to comfort you," Marie said, gazing sadly at Eugénie's distraught face.

"Dear Marie, what would I ever do without you? I'm afraid there's nothing anyone can do. It's a nightmare! I won't rest until I hear from his own lips what's happened! But should such an occasion arise, how can I be with him without betraying the trust of my countrymen and the patriots! *Mon Dieu,* what have they done and, in God's name, why? By his own actions he's made us adversaries. Why does my heart still reach out to him? I feel torn apart! Oh, what am I to do?" she exclaimed. Unable to sit still, she paced around the room, her movements jerky, tears streaming down her face.

Finally, she stood at the window, staring out at nothing. After a few minutes, she turned abruptly. "There's no point in continuing to torture myself. I must stop it at once. We have a purpose here that must come above all else. I'm meeting Jacques late this afternoon. Before then, I must put on paper all that's occurred these past weeks since he left." Her words continued in a disjointed fashion. "It's been so long since I've seen him. I've been terribly concerned about his safety. Once my report is in his hands, there's little to keep us here, Marie, now that it's clear that the American colonies have set their course for independence. We must make ready to accompany St. George to Bermuda. His father's last correspondence was quite insistent that he stay here no longer. Once there, we'll determine the Bermudians' loyalties, and then we'll set sail for France." A small sigh escaped her. "Ah, Marie, I do so miss the sight of my beloved Garonne."

Knowing how seldom her mistress allowed herself to pine for her homeland, Marie realized how deeply she had been shaken by the Goodrich family's betrayal of the American cause—and what Eugénie would perceive as Bridger's betrayal of her. Marie knew how much her mistress needed to return home to restore her strength. The stress of the mission over the past months had taken its toll, but the cost to Eugénie's spirit caused by this morning's news was beyond measure.

"I'll begin to prepare our trunks," said Marie. "St. George's servant knows his master's mind, and he told me that Mr. John Tucker's ship is due by week's end. No doubt his master will return to Bermuda on the first favorable tide."

Sitting down at her writing desk, Eugénie spoke over her shoulder. "It won't take long for me to recount all we've learned. When I'm finished, I'll tell Mary of our plans and then go and wait for Jacques at the appointed place."

The late afternoon shadows had begun to stretch across the lawn as Eugénie made her way once more into the boxwood garden.

How many times have we met here, Jacques and I? she wondered. Today surely must be the last. She settled herself on a bench and gazed at the water lilies bobbing serenely on the small fishpond. As she watched the small silver-and-gold bodies darting amongst the lily pads, her thoughts drifted back over the shocking events of the morning. She watched a long-legged mayfly skitter across the pond's surface just out of reach of a plump frog that rested on a large, heart-shaped pad. So engrossed was she in her thoughts that Jacques was almost at her side before Eugénie became aware of his presence. She sat up with a start.

The two friends, bound by long friendship and the mission they shared, grasped each other's hands, enjoying the sweet moment of reunion.

"Oh, Jacques, my dear friend, how I have missed you and worried for your safety these long weeks," Eugénie cried. Jacques was alarmed at the emotion in her voice and the tears that shimmered in her eyes.

"Eugénie, what is it? What has happened to affect you so?" Jacques sat down beside her on the bench and looked at her with concern.

Eugénie handed him her letter and quickly related all the events of the weeks past. Then, taking a deep breath, she took Jacques slowly through Amelia Stanton's story, pausing frequently to regain her composure.

"Eugénie, the Goodrich family has made enemies amongst the patriots, and they have long memories," Jacques said quietly. "Their foolish acts may have filled their coffers and satisfied their bloodlust for revenge, but they will never again be able to set foot on these shores. I've learned up north that these colonies will forge a single nation in the weeks to come, and they will drive the English and all loyal to them from these shores—or die trying."

His eyes softened at the stricken expression on her face. He took both her hands in his own and said gently, "I've heard of your attachment to Bridger Goodrich and his to you. His poor judgment and the choices he's made have cost him dearly. 'Tis best to put all thought of him behind you. He is lost to you. Move away from your heart and think with your head. We have a mission to carry out, and danger lurks around every corner. If your heart makes you careless . . ."

"Oh, Jacques, dear friend, I know your words are wise. They mirror my own. I'm torn in two, for I cannot so easily put aside my feelings about this man. I know not what lies ahead, but I do know that he will always be a part of me."

Seeing nothing to be gained by pursuing the subject, Jacques abruptly moved on. "I will see your missive and myself on the next ship to France. I'm glad to see your rose seal in place. There can be no question that these words come from you. I'll also tell our constituency that you plan to travel to Bermuda to complete the mission and that you'll inform them in person of your findings there when you return to France."

With great effort, Eugénie forced her mind to follow Jacques's words. "Yes," she said gravely, "we've completed our mission here in the American colonies. Once I return from Bermuda, we can lend our knowledge and support to those who'll speak to the Ministry on behalf of the colonial patriots."

"As we speak," Jacques said, lowering his voice, "plans are afoot to send a contingent of Americans to France to seek French support and allegiance. They will travel separately. According to my information, Mr. Silas Deane may well be on John Tucker's ship, which sails for Bermuda on his way to France. Also, word has reached me that the young Lafayette, impatient for action and enamored of the Americans' cause, has resigned his French commission and is even now preparing to set sail for these shores to offer his aid to the young army. History is on the march." Rising from the bench, Jacques continued, "I've lingered too long. Dusk is upon us, and I have far to go before I rest my head this night."

His words sent a shiver through Eugénie, and she whispered urgently to her friend, "Take special care. When we meet again, it will be on our own beloved French soil."

"Till then, my friend," Jacques said, smiling warmly at her. "May God go with you and keep you safe." They embraced. Then, taking the path in opposite directions, they stopped for one last wave of farewell, slipped through the hedge, and were gone.

XIV

❧❧❧

Eugénie lay staring into the darkness, trying to settle her mind for sleep. But try as she might, sleep alluded her. Her thoughts jumped from one thing to another. She kept returning again and again to the news about the Goodrich family. She could understand how they might question the wisdom of siding with a few untrained, under-armed patriots against the British might. Thinking about it in those terms and setting aside philosophy, fervor, and will, only a fool would take up arms against the greatest army and navy in the modern world.

She knew that many would remain loyal to the Crown. But the Goodriches' actions were neither loyal to the Crown nor patriotic. The whole incident began when they cheated the British customs, probably not for the first time, and then continued when they plundered the colonial ships. Their actions seemed motivated simply by expediency and opportunity rather than philosophical resolve. By their foolhardy acts, they had hung their fate in the middle, neither beholden to nor protected by either side. A family without cause or country, only clan.

Oh, Bridger, Bridger, her heart cried, How can I love you so deeply when our creeds lie so far apart? Is petty revenge, as they tell it, your God? Can it shield you from harm and inspire you to great deeds of glory? Now, your actions have made me look more closely at mine. After all, I undertook this mission driven by my need for revenge. How easy it would have been to cling to my anger, to seek to repay the people who for sport took my parents' lives and my childhood. What seemingly inconsequential acts shape the course of an individual's history or the history of a nation?

I don't know your brothers or your father, but I know you to the depths of your soul. The Whittingtons' fondness and respect for you is great as well. Could we have assessed you so wrongly? Are you the black scoundrel described in these tales? Whether it's revenge, opportunity, or the need to carry out the dictates of your family that drives you, I don't know. I do know, God help me, that what I feel for you is enduring and is blind to your motives. You must live your destiny, as I must live mine. But will that be enough?

Knowing that she could go no further with these thoughts for the time being, she turned her mind to other things. In a few days, she would leave this Virginia and these people she'd come to love and would continue on to Bermuda to carry out her final obligations to the mission. What would she find there? What manner of people were the Bermudians? Her last thoughts before drifting off to sleep were of the Whittingtons' kindness and the beauty and bravery of this young land.

She felt Bridger's hand touching her lightly, caressing her back. She moaned, turning toward his hand.

"Mistress! Mistress! Wake up!" Caught between her dream and Marie's demanding voice, Eugénie slowly emerged from her deep slumber. She opened her eyes to see Marie's anxious face hovering above her. In her confusion, she spoke sharply. "Marie, why do you disturb my sleep?"

"The stables, mistress," Marie cried with alarm. "The stables are burning!"

"*Mon Dieu!* Again! But I hear no storm!" Eugénie leapt from her bed, shaking her head to clear away the cobwebs.

"It was no storm of nature that caused this fire." At Marie's words, a sense of dread swept over Eugénie, and she redoubled her efforts to throw on whatever apparel was close at hand. "There's no reason to rush. The harm's been done. Dress and prepare yourself, for the devastation is great. I'll go with you when you're ready." Disregarding Marie's words, Eugénie dressed with haste. Pulling her cloak closely about her shoulders, she hurried with Marie to the stableyard.

The sight that met her eyes was worse than any nightmare she could imagine. Fire had consumed the whole north end of the buildings. Blackened hulks loomed menacingly against the night sky. The flames had moved southward and were still leaping from the south wing, illuminating the wholesale slaughter that had taken place. Everywhere she looked she saw mangled bodies of horses and stablehands, some burned beyond recognition, others lying where they had been struck down, necks slashed, heads smashed in, blood and gore mingling with ash and fallen timbers.

"*Mon Dieu! Mon Dieu!*" Eugénie cried, falling to her knees, hands stretched out as though in supplication. "The roan, the roan," she repeated over and over. What horrible death had stalked and slaughtered that mighty spirit? She wept, feeling his pain and fear.

She felt a gentle touch and turned her streaming eyes to see John's face, colored a ghastly hue by the wall of fire behind him.

"Come, Eugénie. This is no place for you." Taking her arm, he gently raised her to her feet.

"John, I can't leave. I must find the roan and Abraham who loved him so. Oh, and the filly, too." Overcome, she cried out, her voice thick from smoke, soot, and emotion, "Who, who could have done this thing? This evilness, this cruelty. Oh, John, your beautiful, beautiful horses and your devoted people. Why?" The sobs came, choking her, and she collapsed against his chest.

John looked down at her and tears slipped down his weathered cheeks as he wept for all of it—all the pain, all the loss, all the suffering of that night. They stood sharing an infinite sorrow, seeking to understand beyond the ken of the human mind.

After a few minutes, John took Eugénie by the shoulders and gently set her back from him. "Dear child, I insist that you return to the house." The face that turned up to him was no longer that of the grieving young woman he knew. The tears had dried, the gentle mouth was set in a grim line, and the eyes glowed like flint in the flame-light. Her voice sent a chill through him.

"Those who did this deed will not live to see the next sunset. You and yours are beloved in this county. This great wrong done you will not go unpunished. The blow against your household will reverberate from plantation to plantation. As others protect you, they protect themselves. As they avenge this night's work, they will strike fear into those who would spread wanton destruction. Now, let us go from carcass to carcass, corpse to corpse, and determine the extent of this carnage." Picking up her skirts, without a backward glance, Eugénie plowed into the center of the mutilated bodies.

She was heedless of the efficient waterline that worked tirelessly along the south and east walls to contain and put out the last of the fire. Soon she had organized every able-bodied man, including several neighbors who had come to help when they saw the flames leaping into the night sky. Meticulously, each fallen man and horse was inspected for signs of life and for identification. It was a tedious and nauseating task. Eugénie saw hardened men turn away at the sight of a particularly mangled body, or start to weep shamelessly at the sight of a suckling foal, who, with neck slashed, had sought its mother's side even in death.

Eugénie made her way through it all, never flinching even when she came upon Bridger's filly, her throat slashed, her eyes staring. Eugénie knelt down beside her and smoothed back her forelock.

"You are safe now," she whispered. "They can hurt you no more." She rose to her feet and continued on. Finally, she arrived at a stall at the far end of the stable, which, at first glance, appeared to have escaped the death and violence that surrounded it. As her eyes adjusted to the dim light, she beheld a form dangling from an iron hook on the far wall of the stall. When her torch's beam illuminated the figure, she staggered back, her scream piercing the bedlam in the stableyard. In an instant, men crowded in to see what had caused this woman to cry out, this woman whose unwavering courage had inspired others throughout the long night.

"*O, mon Dieu! Mon Dieu!*" She clasped her arms around the limp, broken legs. "Jacques, Jacques, what have they done to you?" But Jacques's ears could no longer hear the cries of his compatriot. Mumbling French endearments, she gently touched the wounds the dead man could no longer feel. He had been slit from throat to chest to abdomen. Bone, sinew, and organs lay exposed in the path of the gash. His had been a slow death, rendered silent by the filthy cloth she pulled from between his clenched teeth. The rag had been rammed in with such force that it was lodged well down his throat.

She noticed a discarded piece of parchment lying in the corner behind the dangling body. Picking it up, she recognized the letter she had given Jacques that afternoon, with its telltale seal broken. She knew in that moment that Jacques had tried to protect the contents of that letter at the price of his life. Eugénie bowed her head, holding the folded sheet to her cheek. Then, turning to two strong men beside her, she said in a deathly still voice, "Please help him down. He's far from home and has far to go before he may rest his head."

The two men did her bidding, even though they thought the poor woman had taken leave of her senses.

During the confusion that had ensued, Marie, who had followed her mistress into the stall, had a few precious minutes to recover from her own shock. Now she hastened to catch up with the small procession and spoke in undertones to her mistress, "I'll see that his wounds are bathed and that he's prepared for burial. You're still needed here."

Eugénie turned with blank eyes to her servant and was about to resist her suggestion when she saw in the depths of Marie's eyes a truth that gave Marie the right above all others to administer to Jacques's last earthly needs. Eugénie reached out blindly to her childhood friend and held her close. She slipped a crest ring from her baby finger and showed it to Marie, speaking softly, "This is the French cartel's membership ring. All of us wore it as a sign of commitment to the mission. Jacques's was stolen from his hand this night. He served with honor and he will wear again the token of his courage on the long journey that lies before him. We'll find my ring's match and when we do, we'll know the monsters who perpetrated these crimes. Their ignorance of its significance will be their downfall." Eugénie put the ring once more on her finger and watched Marie and the two men bearing Jacques's body until they disappeared beyond the stableyard. When she could see them no more, she turned once again to her task.

"Eugénie! Eugénie!" St. George was suddenly at her side. "What is this I hear of a Frenchman gored and hung in the far stall? Did you know him?"

Eugénie flinched at his words but responded in a calm voice, "St. George, there's no time for discussion now. We must count the losses of the men and horses. Please help me. I'm desperate to find what remains of Roan II." Not waiting for his response, she moved quickly along the tidy lines that had been laid out along the paddock fencing.

Hurrying to catch up with her, St. George exclaimed, "That's why I've been looking for you. I've been searching everywhere for the roan. He's not here."

"What? But that's impossible!" Finally, something in Eugénie snapped. She rushed at him, slamming at him with her fists.

"You are mistaken!" she screamed. "You are lying! How can you be so cruel? He is here! He is here and I must find him!"

When St. George grabbed her flailing wrists to ward off her blows, she lost her last vestiges of control. "Let go of me! Let me go! I must find him!"

Only John Whittington's voice behind her could pierce the red cloud that threatened to engulf her and send her over the edge into madness. "Eugénie, St. George speaks the truth. We've all searched for the roan. He's not here."

With a wail, she sank to the ground, all fight gone. Seeking the strength of the earth, mindless of the bloodied dirt beneath her, she stretched out full length, her face on her arms, and wept. "My great roan, my beautiful spirit: better that I found you here in death than to imagine you in the hands of those monsters."

Crouching down, both men gently lifted her up until she stood swaying unsteadily between them. "You cannot subject yourself to any more, Eugénie. Let St. George take you back to the house. There will be no sleep this night. We'll repair ourselves as best we can and meet in the sitting room. Messages have already been sent out, calling forth all the leaders of the county, and I've questioned the patrols here at Oak Knoll. Their leaders will join us as well. Before the night is out, we'll mount a manhunt of such magnitude that the smallest gnat will not slip through our net."

Finally accepting that her beloved roan was gone, Eugénie leaned heavily on St. George's arm and allowed him to guide her back to the main house. As they entered the center hall she nodded her thanks to St. George and slowly made her way up the stairs to her room. "Oh, my dear Marie!" All thought of her own sorrow vanished as she looked at Marie standing quietly at the window, stroking a silk scarf that she recognized as Jacques's.

"There will be time enough for grieving later." Marie's emotionless voice sent a chill through Eugénie. "For now, we must ready ourselves. Let me help you disrobe. The bath is prepared, and we can refresh ourselves with the tea and biscuits Mistress Kate so kindly brought up for us."

Eugénie knew that Marie's stoic manner spoke to a grief far deeper than any outward show of lamenting and weeping could express, and that her childhood friend would not rest until Jacques's killers had been caught and brought to justice. Then, and only then, in her own private manner, would Marie allow herself to give vent to the full measure of her grief for the man she had loved and the father of her child.

Later, Eugénie sat quietly in the packed sitting room absorbing all that had happened over the last few hours and listening intently to what John Whittington's hand-chosen group from the plantation and the county leaders had to say. Unbeknownst to many in the room and long before most were even aware of the massacre and burning of the stables, a band from Oak Knoll led by Isaac had set out to track the outlaws. They had left word for John Whittington that they would not return until they had captured them.

The men in the room were discussing the identity of the French-man who was found in the stableyard. Eugénie knew, although no word was said, that they had made a connection between her and the dead man. She was aware of questioning looks cast in her direction, but she kept her face empty of expression and her eyes averted. They spoke, too, of increasing the protection around each plantation and practicing with firearms and formations. They also set up a schedule to help rebuild the Whittington stables.

Their conversation was suddenly interrupted by loud voices com-ing from the front of the house. John Whittington and several of his neighbors sprang to their feet and walked quickly into the hallway. Through the front door came Isaac, carrying a trussed-up, squirming body over his broad shoulder. Behind him came the other Oak Knoll men leading a disheveled group of ruffians, tied together by a length of rope. All had their hands bound behind their backs. Their bedraggled appearance was not improved by numerous black eyes, bruises, and angry welts on their sullen faces.

"Who's their leader?" John Whittington asked, advancing toward them down the hall.

"This one, Master Whittington," Isaac answered grimly as he uncer-emoniously dumped his burden on the polished floor. With a quick slash of his knife, he cut the rope that had wrapped his prisoner from head to toe. Once freed, the man leapt to his feet, hampered only by his bound hands.

"Sam Brown!" John said in a shocked voice. Before anyone could move, Brown closed the distance between them and spewed a wad of brown spit at John Whittington's face.

"I'm a free man!" Brown screamed, his wild eyes bulging, his mouth stretched back over yellowed teeth. "I'll see you and your darkies hung for this. Me and my men were minding our own business when these cutthroats grabbed us and dragged us back here. You've not heard the last of this damnable act against God-fearing, law-abiding folks such as we. The Brits take care of their own." Seeing their leader's show of courage, the rest of the band began to mutter in agreement.

John Whittington slowly wiped the filth from his face and shirtfront and spoke in a calm tone. "Neighbors, keep a close eye on them while I speak to Isaac alone." With that, he and Isaac moved down the hall and conversed in low tones. The prisoners, faced with the barrels of several pistols, quieted down and moved back against the wall.

After a few minutes John walked back to stand in front of the prisoners. "Isaac, you stay with me. The rest of my people may go. I thank you for your work this night."

Facing the slovenly group before him, he spoke in a low, ominous voice, his rage barely held in check. "I accuse you of the willful slaughter of seven good men and fifteen horses, and the willful destruction by fire of private property. These acts are punishable by hanging by the neck until dead."

One of their number began to blubber incoherently.

"Shut up!" Brown's voice rang out. "Don't listen to him! There's no evidence. It's his word against ours!" Eugénie moved quietly to John Whittington's side and whispered urgently to him as she surreptitiously drew his attention to the crest ring on her finger. John nodded his understanding and again addressed the group.

"Each man is to be thoroughly searched. No harm will come to you if you remain perfectly still. Anyone who makes an untoward move will be pistol-whipped. Is that clear?" All cockiness drained from the faces before him, replaced by the first signs of fear.

One by one, each man was separated from the line and methodically searched by one of the planters. The stink of fear combined with the stench of overripe bodies and foul breath. As John Whittington approached Sam Brown, Brown's foot suddenly lashed out with surprising speed. Isaac, even quicker, stepped in front of his master and absorbed the blow. He brought his giant fist down on Sam Brown's shoulder with such force that the sound of splintering bone cracked through the room. Without a sound, Brown's eyes rolled back in his head and he slumped to the floor.

"Revive him," John said harshly. "He must witness his own indictment." Immediately, a bucket of ice-cold water appeared and was dumped on the prostrate man. Slowly, Brown began to stir. Grasping him under the arms, Isaac wrenched him up onto his feet and held him there.

"Harrison, come stand by my shoulder to act as witness to this search," John said to his neighbor as he began to search the man. When he reached toward the pocket of Brown's soiled waistcoat, Sam Brown's eyes widened in horror. Too late, he realized the incriminating evidence secreted there. As John drew forth the twin of Eugénie's crest ring, Brown let out a long howl and crumpled to his knees at John Whittington's feet. With a superhuman effort, Brown wrenched his hands free of the bonds and wrapped his arms around the startled planter's legs.

"I didn't mean to do it! I didn't mean to do it!" he slobbered. "Have mercy! Have mercy! For the sake of my poor children, have mercy!" Isaac dragged the wasted creature off his master as John stepped back, holding the gold ring aloft.

"This ring was stolen by the hand of Samuel Brown from the man tortured and slain in the stables this night. It proves that Brown and his confederates did slaughter both men and animals and did set fire to the stables. For these, their many heinous acts against God and man, I pronounce them guilty, and with the authority vested in me as a magistrate of the county, I sentence them one and all to hanging by the neck until dead. The sentence shall be carried out with utmost speed, that all others of their ilk shall know that justice is true and swift in this county! I hereby deputize you, Harrison Tyler. Get them from my sight, before I tear them apart limb from limb with my bare hands!"

Resting his hand on his friend's shoulder, Harrison replied, "Yes, my friend. I'll see that the sentence is carried out and their bodies thrown into unmarked graves. Justice will be done before the first cock crows."

"John, John," Eugénie touched him lightly on the sleeve. "What of the roan?"

"Ah, Eugénie, Isaac saw no sign of the great horse when he caught up with that bad lot." Hearing his words, Eugénie ran after the prisoners, who were being herded down the hallway.

"Please, please," she cried, clutching Sam Brown's arm. "What have you done with the roan? Please tell me." Brown turned on her with such force that she lost her footing and fell to the floor.

"Get off me, woman," he snarled. "I'll see you in hell first." His eyes glittered with evil. "Since my boys and I finished with him, he won't be much use to you. Your fine stallion's not the arrogant horse he once was. He's learned to mind his betters."

Hearing Sam Brown's cruel words, Marie hurried to her mistress's side, gathered her in her arms, and led her up the broad staircase away from the man's parting taunts. Before Eugénie was out of earshot, she heard Sam Brown shout with false bravado, "And speakin' of betters, our leader's better than all you high-brows here. And where might he be, I asks you? You don't see him here, do you? No, he's too smart for the likes of you. Hah! He's long gone from here. Safe and sound to play another day. Hah! So chew on that bit, mates, and choke on it!"

XV

Over the next few days, the members of the household withdrew into themselves, each coming to terms in his or her own way with the magnitude of what had become known as "the massacre." Neighbors stopped by to offer their sympathy and their help, staying for only a short while since there was little anyone could say or do until the wounds began to heal.

The morning after the massacre, the family joined Eugénie and Marie in the small family plot to bury the courageous Frenchman. In the late evening, the whole plantation gathered to bury its own in the large cemetery on the gentle rise behind the gardens. Opa, the recognized leader amongst the women and the mother of one of the slain stablehands, spoke first, raising her voice to exhort the spirits to carry their sons' souls through the darkness safely back to their homeland. When she had finished, tears were streaming down her face and she was led by two sisters back to her seat.

Isaac rose to his feet and strode to the pine coffins lined up beside the open graves. After placing his hands on each one, he turned facing out over the assembled. He stood before them adorned in the full ceremonial dress of both of his people. He spoke first in the Iroquois tongue and then in the African, bringing to life once more each of the slain men. As he spoke, members of their families chanted in unison with his words. When he had finished, he stretched his arms upward toward the darkening sky and, raising his eyes to the heavens, pronounced their spirits free to follow their path home. At that moment a single voice soared above the chanting in a song of such beauty and sadness that all who listened needed no translation to understand the meaning of the words.

As the last notes faded in the air, the coffins were lowered into the graves. Before the soil was shoveled over them, returning their physical bodies to the earth, a procession formed, and tokens of love and gifts to speed them on their journey were laid on each. John Whittington then placed the first shovel of dirt on each lid and the ceremony was over.

All but the families of the dead departed quietly, leaving them to finish mounding the graves and to mourn in privacy. Before leaving, Eugénie placed the roan's bridle on Abraham's coffin and knelt at the side of his grave to offer one last prayer for the man who had shared her love for the great horse. St. George raised her gently to her feet and, with his arm around her waist, guided her footsteps after the departing Whittingtons.

"Eugénie," John said when the family had gathered in the drawing room after supper. "We can't delay your departure for Bermuda any longer. By offering the proof of Sam Brown's crimes, you exposed your link to Jacques, whose identity and purpose are well known now. This makes both of you heroes to many, but enemies to just as many others. We know now that Darby was directly responsible for stirring up the local riffraff. In Williamsburg, you yourself heard him told to keep the French here in the colonies under close watch and to take whatever steps he felt necessary. And now Jacques is dead. The significance of that can't be lost on you. You're no longer safe here."

Eugénie shivered, acknowledging the truth of his words.

"My cousin John Tucker is in port, ready to set sail with the first favorable wind," St. George said. "There may be those who know of this and would do you harm, Eugénie, but I'll protect you with my life."

"Thank you, St. George," Eugénie replied, smiling at him. "But I can't allow you to endanger yourself for my sake."

"Eugénie . . ." St. George began to protest.

"St. George, you're right," John interrupted. "'Tis far better that Eugénie travel under your protection than to await passage with some unknown captain and crew. Eugénie, you're artful at disguise. No one need know that you've left Oak Knoll until well after you've gone."

At that moment, Marie appeared in the doorway and said, "Mistress, a letter has just arrived for you from Lord Dunmore."

"The governor?" Eugénie asked with surprise. She rose from her chair and took the letter from Marie. She broke the seal and quickly scanned its contents. "For my past kindness and as a gesture of good faith to me as a representative of France visiting here under his protection, he offers a company of British soldiers to escort me to the harbor and safe passage on any ship bearing the British flag. From this letter, it seems that he knows all—the massacre, Jacques's death, and my involvement in these events. Clearly, he is directing me to leave, and leave at once," she said in a shocked voice. "He also includes a letter of introduction for me to Mr. George Bruère, the governor of Bermuda."

"That's all well and good," St. George spoke sharply. "But in the name of the British Crown, those scoundrels slaughtered men and animals and burned property. Who's to say others of the same persuasion won't use Eugénie's identity as reason enough to breach Lord Dunmore's protection and do her harm?"

"St. George, your words make good sense," John agreed. "It's late and we're all weary. Let's sleep on this and discuss it again in the morning. One thing is certain: delay poses grave danger for you, Eugénie. The longer you stay here, the more time those who wish you harm have to devise their own plan."

The next morning, St. George announced that he was going down to the harbor to confer with his cousin and also to see what other ships were in port. Eugénie and Marie spent the day packing their trunks so that all would be in readiness to leave at a moment's notice. The quiet task gave both women the opportunity to be alone with their thoughts and at the same time to take comfort in each other's company.

By late afternoon Eugénie felt her things were well enough in hand to take a few minutes to rest and compose her thoughts. She sat down on the window seat in her bedchamber and gazed out over the back lawn of the plantation. From her vantage point, she could look down at the garden in which they had worked so diligently that spring, now boasting a profusion of colorful blossoms. She could see beyond to the elaborate boxwood garden, which brought back so many poignant memories of Jacques.

Then, as she lifted her gaze to the stand of trees that stretched along the back of the property, she saw a tall, bent figure emerge from the woods leading a horse that walked with an uneven gait, favoring one of its forelegs. The late afternoon sun glanced off its distinctive coat, and Eugénie's breath caught in her throat.

"Marie! It's the roan! Look there. It's the roan!" Eugénie cried. As she spoke, she grabbed the shawl in her lap and raced to the door. The two women rounded the side of the house to discover that others also had seen the approach of the bedraggled man and horse. Mary and John were already talking excitedly to the man, who was handing the horse's bridle to Jack. Eugénie was confused by their familiar attitude toward the stranger who, with his unkempt appearance and torn clothing, appeared to be nothing more than one of the many tramps often seen wandering the roads, seeking work during planting season.

As she drew nearer, she saw that his clothes, now little better than rags, had once been finely made and that his left arm hung limply at his side. At her approach, startling blue eyes fastened on hers, causing her to stumble and almost fall.

"*O, mon Dieu!* Bridger, is it you? How in the name of God . . ." was all she had time to say before the now-familiar stranger was before her, clasping her to him. She threw her arms around him. All the fear, heartbreak, and anguish of the past weeks were forgotten as she pressed him to her.

Realizing the impropriety of his action, he stepped back and with a crooked grin said under his breath, "Ma'am, didn't I say I'd return for my filly?"

Blushing hotly, Eugénie plucked mindlessly at bits of grass and straw that clung to his shirt, as words tumbled out of her mouth. "Oh, Bridger, what's happened to you? I've been frantic. You're in danger being here. Come, we must tend to your arm at once. You look like you haven't slept or eaten in days." Almost as an afterthought she added, "Where did you find the roan?" Suddenly a dark suspicion crept into her mind. She stopped abruptly, looking up at him with horrified eyes. "Surely, you didn't . . ."

Before she could finish, the warm smile on his face turned cold. "Nay, my lady, I did not," he interrupted her. Turning his back on her, he walked over to the Whittingtons. "The roan is in great need of better attention than I've been able to give him." Mustering a light tone, he continued, "Being persona non grata has forced me to avoid all commerce with my former Virginian comrades. We've had only each other for company and spring berries to sustain us. We'd both appreciate some refreshment and some attention to our wounds. Then, I'll gladly make a clean breast of our adventure to you."

His last words were almost inaudible as he staggered, and he would have fallen had not John and Jack braced him between them and half dragged, half carried him toward the house.

Eugénie reached out to him and said softly, her eyes shimmering with tears, "Please, forgive me." Watching his retreating figure, she thought she saw a slight nod before she turned to comfort the roan. "My beautiful roan, I thought you were gone from me forever. What have they done to you?" she said, stroking his neck. She touched a deep gash on the horse's forehead that had festered, causing one of his eyes to swell shut. She traced the welts that covered his withers and flanks, but her greatest concerns were his damaged foreleg, which seemed to have difficulty bearing weight, and his broken spirit.

At her touch, he lifted his head and pricked up his ears in a sad imitation of his former playfulness.

"Come, we'll get you to the stables and Andrew can take a look at you. We'll have you right in no time." He nuzzled against her and whinnied softly. Then he gamely hobbled along at her side toward the stable. As they approached the paddock, he pulled back on his lead.

"I won't take you into danger," Eugénie said, speaking softly to him. "That night is over, and those monsters will never hurt you again." His hardships had not diminished his trust in his mistress, and again he plodded forward at her bidding.

When they reached the yard, Andrew, one of the stablehands who had not been in the stables the night of the massacre, rushed over. He could hardly believe his eyes.

"Miss Eugénie, is dis de roan? I never did think to see him agin. He's gwine to miss his Abraham, but de boys and I will see him right as rain in no time. I sees his po' leg's frettin' him. Let ol' Andrew take a look." Kneeling down beside the great horse, Andrew gently inspected the swollen leg. After several minutes of probing and manipulating, he looked up at Eugénie, a broad smile creasing his face.

"Dey's no permanent harm. Dis horse's too strong for dem rascals. 'Tis only a bad sprain. We just use some wormroot poultice to draw out de evil and keep a salt compress on it, and he be runnin' in no time."

"Oh, Andrew, you really think he will heal from this beating?"

"Now, Miss Eugénie," Andrew scolded her. "You is in worse shape den he is. Don't go lettin' him see you worryin' yo'self or else he gwine to think they's somethin' to worry about. He be just fine, long as he don' have to worry 'bout you. Now, git on back to the house and let ol' Andrew git to work here."

Placing her hand on the roan's side, Eugénie said, "You do exactly as Andrew says and I'll be back to check on you later."

She found the family sitting on the veranda enjoying the tranquillity of the late afternoon.

"Bridger should be down shortly," Mary said to Eugénie. "I set his broken arm. Other than needing some good food and a night's sleep, he should be just fine. I must say, even his dear mother wouldn't have recognized him this afternoon. Thank God, he and Roan II come from strong stock. I can't wait to hear how he found that poor horse."

At that very moment, the subject of the conversation appeared in the doorway.

"Here, Bridger, take a seat," John said. "Jack, go get the young man a good stiff drink."

"Thank you, sir," Bridger said. Except for a certain gauntness, he looked little the worse for wear now that he had bathed, shaved, and availed himself of a fresh suit of Jack's clothing. Even the bandage and sling on his left arm gave him a jaunty air. "I could've used several stiff drinks these past days. Ah, Opa, you angel!" His eyes lit up as Opa and two of her girls came through the doorway carrying heaping platters. "Just the sight to delight a starving man's eyes."

Everyone helped themselves and settled down to enjoy the feast. Bridger waited to see which chair Eugénie chose before taking a seat beside her. A look passed between them, and the tight knot that had gripped her insides all afternoon relaxed.

After savoring two big bites, Bridger launched into his story. "Let's see, it was the night before my family and I were to leave port in accordance with the ultimatum that I'm sure you've all heard about. Before I go on, I must tell you that the decision my family and I made to side with the British in this quarrel was made strictly in terms of what is in the best interest of our family. I will not apologize for that decision or explain further. I hold every one of you in the highest regard. I would sacrifice my life for each of you if it meant keeping you from harm. That is my bond, a far stronger one for me than the stuff of petty politics."

He took a deep breath. "I was staying out of sight in one of the low-life taverns down on the waterfront, awaiting the last of our family ships, which was expected that day from the West Indies. I overheard some men talking about a wholesale slaughter up at the Whittington plantation. With the help of a little liquor and a few encouraging words, they were only too eager to tell me the whole story about Sam Brown and his rascals and a man named Darby, known hereabouts for inciting this kind of rabble to carry out misdeeds of the worst sort. According to their story, Brown and his miscreants, mistakenly hoping to ingratiate themselves to the British authorities and to work off some steam at your expense, sneaked onto the plantation that night and killed and burned everything in sight. Apparently, Brown had some special reason for wanting to steal the roan and 'teach that horse and his mistress a lesson.' He must have finally tired of torturing the poor beast and abandoned him shortly before your men captured him and the others.

"As soon as I'd learned everything they had to tell, I took off to come back here and see what I could do to help. For all I knew, the whole plantation had been burned to the ground and everyone in it killed. I was on my way here when I stumbled on what I thought was a stray horse. When I realized it was the roan—for he was barely recognizable—I put him on a lead and brought him along. Leading him slowed me down considerably and made me easy prey for a band of rascals who beat me up, stole my own horse, and left me for dead. If the roan hadn't been in such a sorry state, no doubt they would have stolen him, too. When I regained consciousness, he and I took to the woods and made our way here as fast as our wounds allowed us. I feared for what I'd find when I got here. Thank God, it wasn't nearly as bad as I thought it would be."

"Bridger, you saved the roan," Eugénie said softly. "I'll never be able to thank you for what you've done. Nor can I forgive myself for my ugly doubts about you concerning that awful night."

"Having you in my debt is well worth any pain, dear lady," he said, his eyes gleaming at her. "As to the other, were I in your shoes, I would have had grave doubts myself."

She thanked him with her eyes for his generous words and then hurried on. That hurdle was over, but there was still much that stood between them. "If it becomes known that you're still in Virginia, you'll be in terrible danger," she said. "You must leave immediately!"

"My only concern is the danger that I place this family in, with each minute that I remain," Bridger answered gravely. "I'll be on my way once the dark settles in."

"You'll do no such thing," Mary said stoutly. "You'll stay right here until you regain your strength. I will hear no more about it. The plantation is in mourning. No one will seek our hospitality during the prescribed grieving period."

"You are generous beyond measure, madam, and a true friend. I'll never forget this kindness." Bridger's voice was rough with emotion.

"Good," Mary said smiling at the young man. "Now that that's settled, we must make plans to ensure your safety, Eugénie."

"I can't leave until the roan is well enough to travel," Eugénie said adamantly. At that moment St. George arrived.

"The roan? The roan is back?" he asked. His eyes swept the group and saw Bridger Goodrich sitting calmly, making short shrift of Opa's vanilla flan. "My God, man! What are you doing here? Are you mad?" When the others had filled him in on Bridger's rescue of the roan, he looked with concern at Eugénie.

"What I've heard and seen down at the harbor bodes ill for you, Eugénie. You must leave without delay. My cousin's ship is prepared to depart on the morning tide, and you and I will be on it," he said firmly.

"That's foolishness," Eugénie said. "Everyone knows that I was planning to leave with you. If there are those who court British favor, it will be a simple thing to intercept us on the way to the ship. And as I just said before you came, I'm not going anywhere without the roan. A far better plan would be to send a messenger to the governor this evening, accepting his offer of an armed escort, and then have Marie go disguised, in my stead. She's about my size, and with a few adjustments she could easily pass for me."

"Eugénie, that's a splendid idea," John agreed. "The British guards wouldn't know one of you from the other, and no one would dare interfere with them. Then, when Bridger and the roan have healed enough to travel, you can dress yourself as a member of the crew and easily slip onto his ship, no one the wiser."

"Sounds a solid plan to me," Bridger agreed. Unseen by the others, he grinned meaningfully at Eugénie, who quickly dipped her head to hide the high color mounting on her cheeks. With a big yawn, he rose, saying, "Even the pleasure of this company isn't enough to compete with the charms of a feather bed. If you will excuse me, I'll seek its comfort while I can still climb the stairs."

"Sleep well, Bridger," Mary said, embracing him warmly. "Come to me in the morning and I'll check your dressing. Now, the rest of us had best get busy if we're to be ready on the morrow." A messenger was quickly dispatched to Williamsburg. St. George retired to his room to finish his packing, and Eugénie went to find Marie to tell her the plan.

The household was up early the next morning. The company of soldiers had arrived shortly after dawn and was helping St. George lash the trunks to the top of the coach when Mary and John came down to oversee the departure. Upstairs, Eugénie was making some last-minute changes to Marie's costume.

"Mistress, I'm concerned for your welfare. These times are dangerous. Even Oak Knoll can't protect you from the lawlessness."

"Fear not for me, dear Marie, but look to your own safety and the safety of the child you carry. I promise that I'll be with you before you have a chance to get used to being without me. When I arrive, you'll be able to tell me all about this island, Bermuda, and the Bermudians. Let me take a look at you and make sure everything is just right. Yes, perfect. Were I not myself, I'd swear that you were Eugénie Devereux! Now, it's time for you to go."

Their brave words fooled neither of the young women. Holding each other tightly, they murmured more encouraging words to each other. Then Eugénie stepped back and ushered her servant and friend to the door. Marie braced herself and, with one last backward glance and a trembling smile, hurried along the hall and down the stairs.

The family put the word out that their houseguests had set sail and breathed a sigh of relief when word came back from the port that the party had embarked without incident and that the ship had been seen making its way out of the harbor on schedule.

Eugénie spent the next few days rarely away from Roan II's side, applying her own herbal preparations and assuring herself that the great horse was indeed on the mend. It was there that Bridger found her late one morning. Eugénie looked up from her work and was startled to see him leaning casually against the paddock fence, observing her with an unfathomable expression. Their eyes caught and held.

The silence stretched out between them. Finally, unable to endure the awkwardness any longer, Eugénie turned from his relentless stare and rose to her feet.

"That's enough of that," she said, speaking as much about the tension between them as about the salve she had been applying to the roan's back.

"Your efforts are showing results. He looks greatly improved," Bridger said easily.

"Yes. Andrew was right. He'll recover from his injuries as good as new," she answered in a distant tone, without looking up. "I still can't forget how he looked limping so pitifully across the lawn." She paused and added softly, ". . . and you, how broken and wretched you looked." Two pairs of eyes watched Eugénie as she finished putting salve on the roan's foreleg.

When the roan was once more in his stall, Bridger took Eugénie's arm and turned her to face him. He loosely laced his fingers behind her, expecting her to pull away. When she didn't, to his surprise and pleasure, he leaned back to look into her face, causing the small of her back to fit snugly in his hands.

"The time is near when we must discuss the things that stand between us," he said quietly. She raised her eyes to meet his.

"Yes," she nodded, "but the concerns go far beyond just you and me. Much has changed that will never be the same for any of us. There's no going back, I know, but both of us must find a way to understand all that has happened. Only then will each of us know how to go forward." They had not bridged the abyss that lay between them, though they had taken the first steps. He drew her against him, and she laid her head on his shoulder, absorbing the warm comfort of him. She felt him take a deep breath and release it slowly.

"Mary and John await us at the house. There's news from the north."

He said no more, but picked up her basket of herbs and vials and, taking her arm in his, turned their steps toward the house.

As they approached the veranda, John, Mary, and Jack walked quickly down the steps to meet them. "Messengers have been sent throughout the colonies telling of the fighting in the Massachusetts towns of Lexington and Concord," John said, his voice grave. "The lines have been drawn once and for all. We're at war with the British. George Washington has already left for Princeton, in New Jersey, to take command of the colonial forces. Jack and I will be leaving soon."

"Lord Dunmore has been driven out of Williamsburg and is circulating his empty proclamations from a ship offshore," Jack added, his eyes dancing.

"Eugénie, you and Bridger can delay no longer," Mary said with alarm.

Eugénie, who had been listening quietly during the discussion, spoke for the first time. "The roan is mending well. He's ready to travel."

"My ship is hidden in a nearby inlet, awaiting my arrival," said Bridger. "If I leave immediately, I'll be able to bring it up river to your wharf by dusk. We can board the roan and what few belongings remain and be off before nightfall."

"I'll saddle two mounts and go with you, Bridger," said Jack.

Eugénie stood looking after Jack, for several moments. She turned around and reached out to the Whittingtons. Her face was pale in the bright sunlight. "Mary and John, I worry that we've put you at risk remaining here as long as we have."

"We wouldn't have allowed you to do otherwise, dear child," Mary replied, embracing her. At that moment Jack rode up, leading another horse. Bridger sprang into the saddle, clapped Jack on the shoulder, and the two men cantered off.

The long hours of the afternoon seemed to stretch out endlessly for Eugénie and the Whittingtons, and then suddenly dusk was upon them. Mary went upstairs with Eugénie to collect her few remaining possessions.

"I had hoped there would be more time to prepare to leave you," Eugénie said, her voice trembling.

"There's never enough time to say good-bye to those we love. We'll dearly miss you, Eugénie." Mary put her arms around the younger woman and held her close. "The British ships have already blockaded the coast. I thank God that you're in Bridger's care. His British colors will safeguard your passage to Bermuda, and his skill will ensure your safety. We'd better go down and join the others at the dock. It's time. Andrew should have Roan II there by now."

As the two women arrived at the deepwater dock, they could see Bridger at the helm of his ship, making his way up the river in the darkness. All too soon, he had heaved to and drawn the ship up to the pier. When the roan was safely boarded in the hold, their departure could be delayed no longer. The time for the last tearful promises and farewells had come.

"I'll send word of my safe arrival by return ship," Eugénie said, clasping Mary in her arms for one last embrace. "When this time is over, and you can travel safely, please know that my home will always be open to you and yours. You'll have to come to see the great racers that the roan will sire."

"That we will, and you'll finally have the chance to meet our fourth child, Edmund, who's been studying on the Continent," John assured her as he gave her a last embrace. "Now, you must be off. Your captain grows impatient."

Eugénie stood at the rail and wondered when she would see their dear faces again, and who of them would survive to meet again in happier times. She watched their torches waving bravely from the bank until the bend of the river cut them off and they disappeared from sight.

XVI

❧❧❧

Eugénie remained standing at the rail as dusk deepened into darkness. The barking of the first mate's orders, the creaking of the ship's planking, and the halyards and shrouds slapping in the wind were strangely soothing to her ragged spirit. A lifetime had passed since she first set foot on Virginia soil only three months earlier.

Watching the river slip by, she thought of the extraordinary people she had met who now wore the mantle of history on their shoulders. Had they, with bold spirit, gone forth to grasp history to their breasts, or had they instead been plucked reluctantly from the commonplace by history's own hand and cast in the role of her architects? she wondered. Whatever has brought them to this moment, their acts will frame the future for generations to come. The magnitude of their responsibility sent a shiver through her, and she pulled her cloak more tightly around her.

Her mind tumbled on. What of her own role? What role had she played and would she play in the events of these people's lives? Once back in France, was she prepared to shed the cloak of witness and assume the garb of advocate for the Americans' cause? These thoughts and others so absorbed her that when he spoke in the darkness she started.

"Milady, 'tis late to be standing watch." Bridger's voice seemed a natural part of the night. "There are others assigned the task," he added, chuckling. His voice took on a more sober tone. "The past cannot be changed, and even the keenest eyes cannot pierce the veil that shrouds the future."

How had he crept so easily inside her mind and read what lay concealed there? Without thought, she turned to him and he folded her into his arms, holding her without words, seeking nothing, offering only comfort. She was held so closely that she could feel the drumming of his heart, and its steady rhythm calmed her.

Sensing that her agitation had passed, he turned and drew her with him along the deck toward his cabin.

"I've seen that your things were placed in my quarters. It shall be yours for the duration of the voyage. I've had my own trunk moved in with my officers."

"*Mon Dieu!* I've lost all track of time!" she exclaimed. Still feeling awkward around him, she said in a stilted fashion, "How remiss I've been in expressing my gratitude to you for your hospitality and your willingness to place yourself, your crew, and your ship in peril to transport me to Bermuda. Before I can seek my own comfort, I must go to the roan and see to his needs."

"I am happily and completely at your service, Eugénie. And please, don't for a moment worry yourself about peril where I and my crew are concerned." A chuckle rumbled deep in his chest. "Peril is as familiar to us as the tang of the sea air and the roll of the ocean's waves beneath our feet. As for the roan, he's well and safely bedded down. I saw to that myself. His leg pains him little now, and he's taken to the ship as naturally as a fish to water. I've never seen the like of it. Tomorrow will be soon enough for you to attend to him. For now, you're in far greater need of your own attention than the roan."

"I'm doubly indebted to you, then," Eugénie said as they arrived at his cabin. Bridger swung the door open and stepped aside to let Eugénie enter the spacious room. Flickering candles lit the rich furnishings that transformed the ship's cabin into an elegant drawing room. Her few belongings had been placed on a massive inlaid chest that stood at the foot of a four-poster bed that filled one end of the long room. Maps and papers were piled in careful order on the broad, elaborately carved desk that stood against the opposite wall. Through the open portholes, the fresh breeze that bore the ship down river and the sounds of lapping water filled the cabin.

As Eugénie stood riveted in the center of the room, Bridger moved to the sideboard and poured two generous portions of tawny port from one of the finely etched crystal decanters. He turned and offered one to Eugénie.

"Oh, it's so beautiful," she breathed. "It was clear to me from the first minute that this was a fine ship, but now I see that it's cared for by very loving hands. I've never seen a room aboard ship that was so large and luxurious, for surely this is no cabin!"

"Dear lady," he answered, deeply touched by her words, "the ship is a great joy to me. Not a day passes that I'm not grateful for her. It pleases me no end to have you aboard to share her beauty. There are many ships in my family's fleet, but none finer than she. In addition to her other attributes, *The White Heather* was the first craft awarded to me in Prize Court."

"How can you tear yourself away from this beautiful ship?"

"Ah," he replied, taking a long swallow of port, "I never leave her decks without the greatest regret. But I, like she, am in the service of my family, and we both must obey when duty calls." He paused to give his words weight. "She's Bermuda-built, which places her in the ranks of the finest crafts that sail the seas. I'm impatient to show her to you, but there's little enough left of the night, so I'll leave you to get what rest you can." He tossed back the last of his port, and Eugénie followed his example, closing her eyes to savor the feel and taste of it.

Suddenly she was aware of his nearness. Her breath caught as she lifted her gaze to meet his. He gently took the empty goblet from her and placed both glasses on the sideboard before drawing her into his arms and holding her close against him.

"Eugénie . . ." She heard the question in his voice and felt the hesitancy in his embrace. In answer, she took his face in her hands and kissed him softly on the lips, crossing the barrier that had separated them since his family's dishonor and the fire and slaughter at Oak Knoll.

"Until tomorrow," she whispered. He held her gaze as he opened the door. Then he turned, closing it quietly behind him.

Eugénie absently touched her mouth, still tasting the sweetness of his lips. Shaking herself out of her reverie, she lost no time shedding her clothes. With a sigh, she crawled gratefully between the cool linens. Aided by the port and the ship's gentle rocking motion, she was soon fast asleep.

She awoke to an insistent knocking on the cabin door. At once she was aware that the ship's rhythm had changed. We must have reached the mouth of the river during the night, she thought, and now we're sailing on the open sea.

The knock came again. "Yes, yes, one moment," she called out. Leaping from the bed, she hastily donned the cloak that lay draped over the chest where she'd tossed it the night before. She unbolted and threw open the door to see a giant of a man standing there, awkwardly bearing in his huge hands a silver platter of covered dishes that gave off the most mouthwatering aromas. Eugénie suddenly realized that she was ravenously hungry. Only by sheer will was she able to resist grabbing the tray out of the giant's grasp and falling upon it. Instead, with a nod, she beckoned him into the cabin.

"Please come in," she said sweetly, her eyes glued to the tray. "You may place it there on the table." With surprising grace for a man of his size, he followed her instruction.

"My name is James Mackenzie. I'm Captain Goodrich's man," he said simply, taking a soldier's stance as though awaiting further orders. The charming lilt of his voice and his vivid blue eyes, not to mention his noble clan's name, identified him as a Scot.

"I haven't often had the pleasure of being in the company of your countrymen," Eugénie said, "but the ones I've met have been unfailingly gallant and brave. I thank you for attending to my needs when no doubt you have many more pressing duties to perform."

Her beauty had struck the first blow to his romantic heart. Now, her pretty speech hopelessly enthralled him. Were it not for the discipline of a lifetime of soldier's training, he would have flung himself at her feet and sworn his eternal fealty. Only his mother, now dead and buried in the Scottish soil at Culloden Fields, and his captain, Bridger Goodrich, held such sway over this giant's heart.

Oblivious to the emotions that she had aroused, Eugénie placed her hand lightly on James's arm and ushered him to the door.

"Please, thank your captain for his thoughtfulness and tell him I will join him on deck shortly." No sooner had the door closed than Eugénie fell upon the offerings before her. Never had sliced capon and river trout tasted so sublime. The chilled ale struck just the right refreshing note. She was just dabbing up the last crumbs of a blueberry muffin when a second loud knocking jarred her solitude.

Is there no peace and quiet on this ship? she thought crossly as she yanked open the door. If the sight of the food had sent her into raptures, what she beheld as the door swung open left her speechless with joy. There before her was James directing four sturdy men laboring under the weight of a huge brass bathtub, followed by a line of crewmen carrying buckets of steaming water. Later, Eugénie would wonder how they had wrought this miracle aboard ship and how the ship could continue along her way when it appeared that every available hand had been commandeered to carry out this task.

"Careful there, mates," James barked, "and no slopping the water in the captain's, er, the mistress's cabin." In the blink of an eye, the tub was carefully placed in the center of the room, lashed down, and filled to the brim. Then the men turned and were gone as quickly as they had come.

Delighted with this miracle at sea, Eugénie rummaged in her satchel until she found her favorite scented oils and milled soap. Chemise followed cloak to the floor as she pulled the pins from her hair and lowered herself into the steaming water. She eased back against the tub's curved side and let the warm, scented water release the last knots of tension from her body. She lay there, luxuriating in the exquisite physical pleasure of it, rousing herself reluctantly to bathe only when she felt the water begin to cool. Refreshed and invigorated, she hopped from the tub and padded over to the chest in search of some means to dry herself.

"Oh, dear," she giggled, noticing the path of wet footprints on the priceless carpet. "Dear James would be most displeased with me." She opened the chest to find linens as rich and fine as any at her château. She also came upon long, rectangular cloths of an unusual texture and exclaimed, "Why, these must be the Turkish towels I have heard so much about at Court. How lovely!" She wrapped one around her hair and set to briskly rubbing herself down with another. The texture seemed to absorb moisture better than the bath cloths she was accustomed to, and also left her skin tingling and rosy.

Her stomach comfortably full and her toilette completed, she returned to her luggage to look for some suitable garments to wear aboard ship.

"What they lack in style, they make up for in comfort," she muttered to herself as she raked a comb through her tangled curls.

"Oh, Marie, I do miss you!" she exclaimed as she struggled to bring some order to her unruly mane. Soon weary of wrestling with it, she grabbed the first ribbon she could find and tied the chestnut mass back at the nape of her neck. Slipping a light woolen shawl around her shoulders, she left the cabin. She went first to assure herself that the roan was faring well on his first day at sea and then hastened above decks in search of the ship's captain.

It was not long before she found him standing at the helm, his wide stance braced to accommodate the ship's soft, rolling motion. His hands rested lightly on the wheel as he stared off across the water, lost in thought.

"You rested well, milady?" he asked, aware of her presence even though she was still well behind him.

"I know never to try to take you by surprise," Eugénie spoke, laughter just below the surface of her voice. "I've seen too often the extraordinary alertness you have to your surroundings. Yes, I slept last night as I haven't slept in many weeks, in no small part due to your careful attention to my comforts. I thank you, sir. In fact, I find myself now so deeply in your debt that I can think of no means to ever repay you."

Bridger gave her a searching look, the hint of a quirky smile tugging at his lips. His voice deepened. "Your company is payment enough, Eugénie, but if you think additional reward is due, I'm quite sure my fertile imagination can devise some means to accommodate you."

She had forgotten how the sound of her name on his lips sent shivers through her. The implication in his words reminded her of moments she had shared with this man. She felt her bones melt and her face turn hot.

"First things first," he murmured to himself, his eyes reading her clearly. "Come," he said brusquely, his manner shifting again, "stand in front of me and take the wheel. I intend to make a sailor of you before we reach Bermuda. I guarantee you'll need nautical skills on that island."

Eugénie was grateful for any distraction. Matching his mood, she laughed and slipped in front of him, placing her hands on either side of his. Neither had anticipated that the other's nearness would strike them both like a physical blow. Eugénie resisted the inclination to sink back against his strength, and he, with an equal effort, refused his body's command to take her in his arms and crush her to him. Bridger recovered first. Clearing his throat, he spoke close to her ear. His breath grazed her cheek, causing her to shiver again.

"Your touch on the wheel must be as gentle as if you cradled a new babe in your hands, and as firm as if you held the reins of a shying colt. Now, ease the wheel a bit to starboard until you feel her resist. Now back to port. That's enough. The wind is off starboard, and she's riding close to the wind, so you'll feel resistance to starboard almost immediately. If I take her off the wind to a reach, that'll give you greater play to starboard, but the wind will still be coming off the starboard bow."

They fell into an easy camaraderie as Bridger continued his instruction. He spent the morning teaching her how to point the bow, luff the sails, and take the ship through the wind. Although neither lost their acute awareness of the other, both student and master directed their attention to the task at hand. The ship flew through the waves, carrying them farther and farther away from the dangers and demands that had plagued Eugénie's mind night and day in Virginia.

The crew surreptitiously watched their captain take the beautiful young woman through the ship's paces. They marveled at his patience and his willingness to answer even the most foolish questions. They nudged each other and snickered at how their usually taciturn, domineering captain was rendered almost giddy by this female. They mimicked the scene before them, simpering at each other and batting their eyes until Bridger, well aware of his crew's antics, decided it was time to restore decorum on deck. He barked out several orders, which caused Eugénie to jump at his side but also had the desired effect on the crew.

Morning turned into afternoon, and afternoon waned into evening as Eugénie and Bridger discovered again the pleasure of each other's company and the joy of sharing the ship. He basked in her easy laughter and threw himself into outrageous antics to make her laugh, smiling to himself each time he succeeded. She watched him out of the corner of her eye and caught herself envying the steady breeze that played with his sun-streaked hair. She longed to feel the texture of it and draw it through her fingers. He, in turn, felt a strange, proprietary pride as he watched the sun touch her cheeks with a rosy blush. They laughed together at the fish leaping and dancing amidst the waves and the sea birds hurtling themselves after their elusive prey, often with little more than wet feathers to show for their efforts.

Below decks, the ship's cook, a French expatriate, was enjoying the chance to prepare a meal for the captain and his captivating guest. Given the nature of life aboard a working privateer, the opportunity to demonstrate his expertise seldom arose. He had noticed the baleful expressions cast his way during the midday mess and took pity on the crew, who had been subjected all day to the delicious smells wafting from the ship's galley, and expanded the portions, when possible, for the general mess hall as well.

Eugénie returned to her cabin, reborn after spending the day under the warmth of the sun's rays and breathing the invigorating sea air. Staring dreamily out of the porthole, she felt a warmth spread through her as his face swam unbidden before her eyes. She turned reluctantly from the evening sky that still blazed with the vivid streaks of the setting sun and set about selecting a gown that would set off to advantage the fresh glow of her skin. She hummed a bawdy French tavern tune she had learned at her father's knee, while she added final touches to her toilette and eagerly awaited the arrival of Bridger and the promised feast.

From the moment he arrived in the cabin, Bridger's eyes never left Eugénie's face. They conversed about this and that, enjoying the chef's delicacies and the pleasant intimacy of the captain's quarters, away from the prying eyes of the crew. During a lull in the conversation, a feeling of self-consciousness stole over Eugénie. Bridger had been listening intently to an episode of her childhood, holding her eyes with an unwavering gaze. She stopped in midsentence, barely noticing the taste of the lush claret as she took several quick gulps. To cover her sudden nervousness, she changed the subject abruptly.

"Um, you were speaking of the unique qualities of *The White Heather*. And what might they be, pray tell?" she asked, as though there had been no break in the conversation.

"Ah," Bridger said, taking a moment to pick up Eugénie's new train of thought, and smiling at her need to seek a less personal subject. "I mentioned that the ship is Bermuda-built. Her birthplace gives her a great advantage over her less-fortunate sisters. Like all Bermuda-built ships, she's made of a particular cedar, native only to Bermuda. It's denser and more buoyant than pine and other timbers traditionally used in shipbuilding, including cedar indigenous to locations other than Bermuda. This cedar hull is impregnable to the creatures that gnaw and pit other woods, which allows these crafts to be seaworthy without the encumbrance and additional weight of encasing their hulls in the conventional way with metal. This makes *The White Heather* and all ships built in Bermuda lighter and therefore faster than their sisters.

"In addition," he went on, "the Bermudians have developed a rigging that is triangular instead of the traditional square-rigging. This 'Bermuda rig,' so called, has revolutionized sailing methods, allowing ships greater maneuverability and the ability to sail close to the wind. The combined effect of cedar hulls and triangular sails makes these ships far faster and maneuverable than the cumbersome square-rigged, heavy-hulled vessels. The Bermudians have outstripped even the Dutch as the foremost traders on the seven seas. Taking some pride in my own skills, it pains me to admit that there are few who can outsail a Bermudian in a Bermuda-built ship." He laughed, holding her gaze over the brim of his goblet.

"There are few pleasures that I know of that are greater than being at the helm of *The White Heather.*" He raised his brow and stared meaningfully into her eyes, then allowed his gaze to drift to her lips. He was rewarded with a blush that deepened her already high color. Before his eyes could descend lower, Eugénie broke in, her voice strangely husky even to her own ears.

"Her name, *The White Heather* . . . is there some special significance to it?" she blurted out. "And James Mackenzie, he's a Scotsman. How came he, a Scot, to place himself under your command? Also, unless my eyes deceive me, there are others of the crew also from Scotland?"

His laughter boomed out as he held up his hands to ward off the barrage of questions. "Mercy!" he exclaimed. "Even the inquisitors of England's infamous Star Chamber allowed their victims respite between questions." Eugénie joined in his laughter.

"I'm afraid your delicious claret has gone right to my head and has rendered me a babbling *badaude,*" Eugénie said, coloring.

Ah, dear lady, he thought to himself, were it only so, and I not the gentleman my sweet mother raised me to be. Aloud, his voice took on a serious note.

"To answer your questions—white heather is the symbol of luck in Scotland. Even though that bonny flower flourishes in every crag of her hillsides, Scotland has seen precious little luck. You also ask about James Mackenzie. Ah, Jamie. The enormity of the man is matched only by the size of his brave heart. There are few people to whom I would trust my life. He is one. You questioned how he came to be in my command. Jamie is under no man's command but his own. His grandfather and many of his clan were slaughtered in the service of Bonnie Prince Charlie, waging battle against the English in his ill-conceived efforts to take the British throne. The massacres by the English that followed those defeats wiped out many more. By degrees, those left alive in the clan made their escape and joined others who had fled their homeland to seek safety and fortune in the New World.

"I learned all this from Jamie some years past when I came upon his family's ship that was being attacked by a Spanish galleon. Jamie and his brothers were some of the lucky few who'd been able to make a life at sea. Having no love for the Spanish, I threw my ship into the fray to even the odds, and we finally drove off the Spaniards. But the damage was done. His brothers had died in the fight, as had most of the crew. There was little of the ship worth salvaging, but what there was left, Jamie forced upon me, throwing himself and what remained of the crew into the bargain. It was the luckiest day of my life, and to honor that moment and to salute the courage of Jamie and his men, I rechristened the ship *The White Heather*. Rarely does a day go by that I don't rejoice in the happy conclusion of that afternoon's chance meeting."

Eugénie was touched by the depth of his feeling. This man had seen much of death and destruction. Now, along with his family, he was a man cut adrift from the land he had called home and was shunned by the people of his childhood. He had much in common with that brave giant. She may have lost her beloved mother and father, but she still had the precious treasure of home and homeland. For the first time since she had heard about his family's betrayal of the patriots' cause, she questioned her quick censure of this man's actions. Her heart went out to him, even as her hand reached across the table to cover his.

Her touch pulled him back to the present. He looked at her, his face open and unguarded, vulnerable. He turned the hand that lay softly on his, exposing her palm, and lightly traced the delicate lines and long fingers. Her chest constricted as an ache spread out from her center. His thumb stroked the plump Venus mound, and her slender hand closed reflexively around his finger as her eyes sprang to his face. A moan escaped his lips. No longer willing or able to resist his hunger for her, he rose in one fluid motion, drew her up from her chair, molded her body to his, and brought his mouth down on hers.

Her body melted against his hardness as she gave herself to him. He kissed the pulse that beat erratically at the base of her neck, smelling roses and sweet womanness. Her hands found his hair. She buried her fingers in its thickness, straining him against her. She arched to him, exposing the rise of her breast. His head bent in pursuit of that softness and tasted nectar. Together they shed the layers of doubt and hurt that had separated them and let those impostors slip away. There were no questions, only the answers found in the feel, taste, and scent of the other. He took her hand and led her over to the four-poster bed. She turned to him, and he was transfixed by the silver of her eyes. Just as he lost himself in the richness of her, an old Scottish prophecy swept through his mind: "Those who walk the Highlands in moonlight when the white heather turns to silver are amongst the truly blessed of this earth." At that moment, the moon path flowed through the porthole and bathed the oblivious pair in her gentle light.

XVII

※·※·※

The winds held true and sped *The White Heather* on her way at a break-neck pace. Late one afternoon, as had become her habit, Eugénie stood at the rail, admiring the way the light danced on the crest of the waves and then turned to shadow in the troughs. She felt the surge of the ship beneath her feet and tasted the salt spray on her face. She thought again about how much she had changed since she and Marie had arrived in Virginia. It seemed a lifetime ago. She wondered what lay ahead for her in Bermuda, and part of her wished that she could escape and stay forever on *The White Heather.* Lost in thought, she was absently tracing the grain of the rail with a fingertip when a cry went up from the crow's nest high above the decks.

"Ahoy! Land bird to starboard!"

Bridger was standing at the helm lazily looking out across the water. When he heard the lookout's hail, he called Jamie to take the helm. He jumped down on the deck beside Eugénie and grabbed her hand. Together they scanned the sky for the telltale sign of landfall. His keen eyes sighted it first, and he pointed to a faint speck high on the horizon.

"See it there? Follow the line of my finger. You'll see him when the sun glances off his feathers as he rides the thermals. There, see the white flash?" Eugénie caught his excitement and grabbed his arm as she, too, saw the glint of white against the turquoise sky.

"Bermuda?" she breathed.

"Yes, sweeting," he answered, using the endearment he had adopted for her during their private moments. "I never fail to feel my heart lift at the first sight of land or one of her messengers." Looking up into his face, she watched as the joy suddenly faded from his eyes. The pain she saw in their depths caused her to cry out in alarm.

"What? What is it?"

"It's nothing, Eugénie, nothing but the feel of my heart being wrenched from my chest," he answered hoarsely. "Like a thief in the night, you've slipped in and stolen it for your own, to beat only at the whim of your will. It turns over at the flicker of your eyes and swells with gladness at your touch. Your face is my soul, your laughter my very breath. You are all my tomorrows. Without you the darkness closes in and there is nothing but emptiness. Nothing, no breath, no pulse, no sight. Nothing."

Her eyes glistened with unshed tears, and she felt a leaden hand grip her heart as a strangled sound came from her throat.

"How soon?" she whispered. The joy of the day had vanished.

"We should make land by tomorrow evening," came the terse reply.

"Maybe it's a false sighting, or the bird has strayed farther from land than we know. Or its home is other than the island of Bermuda. Or perhaps it's not a bird at all but some bewitching phenomenon of light cast by the sea's reflection." Babbling like a sentenced man clutching at straws to stay the executioner's hand, Eugénie tried desperately to ward off the inevitable.

"Nay, my heart, it's only the first of many bells tolling this journey's end. But come. There's life in this voyage yet. Let's not mourn the body prematurely. A lifetime can be had between now and Bermuda's shore." And with a quixotic change of mood that Eugénie had come to value in this complex man, Bridger lifted her up lightly above him and twirled her around. "We'll make the most of the time we have, prizing each moment as though it were the most precious of gemstones. And when the end comes, as come it must, you and I will be standing side by side in the crow's nest to greet landfall together as the doughty sailors we are! What do you say?"

Rallying to his call, Eugénie looked down into his laughing face, her heart in her eyes. "Aye, aye, my captain! It's a splendid conspiracy you plot, and I your willing *confrère*."

"*Frère* is far from what I have in mind for you," he murmured, his blue gaze deepening in a fashion and with an intent that had become familiar to her. Nonetheless, it never failed to send heat to her face and tightness to her belly.

"Then, sir," she said archly, "I must go and prepare myself for the occasion." At his raised brow, she said firmly, "Alone."

"See that your preparations don't take too long," he growled, reluctantly letting her go, "or they may be unceremoniously interrupted."

A short time later, a sharp rap on the cabin door interrupted Eugénie as she was completing the final touches to her toilette. The rap was followed by Bridger's voice.

"The beauty of the evening sky has sent me to call you forth from your sanctuary."

Laughing at his flimsy excuse, Eugénie opened the door to behold a vision in full military regalia. Bridger had gone to great lengths to dress for the occasion. He stood before her in a uniform that boasted enough braid and brass to mark an admiral of the first order. He drew his sword from its sheath and executed a series of flourishes. He finished with a final swish through the air, drawing the sword's hilt to the tip of his nose and extending his elbow straight out from his shoulder.

"Sir Captain, how gallant!" Eugénie exclaimed.

Bridger sheathed the sword, swept his tricornered hat from his head, and, placing it over his heart, bowed deeply. "I'm at your service, milady."

Sweeping him an answering curtsy, Eugénie laughed up at him. "Shall we go and see what the beauty of the sky has to say for herself?" she asked.

Befitting the spirit of the occasion, the sky paraded all her best hues and tones before their dazzled eyes. Just when they thought the heavens could perform no further, the various shades of apricot, peach, and gold continued to deepen and glow. Bridger turned to Eugénie. His words died on his lips. The vivid colors gilded her skin and reflected off the tissue-thin fabric of her gown, bathing her with its glow.

"Bridger," she whispered, "may this sky, this sunset, last a lifetime." As if hearing her prayer, the panorama above them gave one last burst of glory that hung suspended for a long moment, etching its magnificence forever in their minds. Then, as they watched, it began its slow farewell into dusk.

Later they sat enjoying yet another of the cook's culinary triumphs in the cozy intimacy of the captain's cabin.

"Tell me about Bermuda," Eugénie said, popping a grape into her mouth.

"It's hard to capture her in simple words," Bridger said, toasting her with his eyes. "There's a magical quality to that isle that captures all who set foot on her shores. In her early recorded history, she was called the Island of the Devil, or some such thing, owing to the strange and eerie sounds heard by seamen sailing by, and the treacherous shoals and reefs that ring the island that have claimed many lives and ships.

"Later, William Shakespeare immortalized her in his last play, *The Tempest,* and called her 'the enchanted isles.' The play was based on the somewhat fulsome reports of one William Stratchey, a historian aboard the *Sea Venture,* the first British ship of record to arrive on Bermuda's shores. Well, 'arrive' is perhaps a generous term for what actually occurred. She was on course for Virginia when she was blown off her path by a hurricane and foundered on the reefs of Bermuda.

"Luckily for her and everyone on board, the *Sea Venture* was saved from sinking because she was wedged so securely between the reefs. Stratchey's elaborate praise and Mr. Shakespeare's romantic tale drew settlers to her shores in droves. It was soon discovered that the piercing screeches and yawlings reported in earlier times were nothing more than a large herd of wild pigs and millions of cahows, a pigeonlike seabird, that mated in burrows on the island. The birds were tame enough to land on your shoulder. Aside from these creatures, the island was uninhabited. The bounty of the pigs and birds, as well as the fish that infested the shallows, fed the early settlers quite handsomely."

"What a romantic beginning!" Eugénie exclaimed. "You say there seems to be something magical about her?"

"Quite so," Bridger answered, tracing the curve of her soft cheek. "Her reefs are still dangerous to the unschooled, giving rise to unscrupulous wreckers at the west end of the island, but, once safely ashore, there are few who can resist the spell she casts."

Warming to his subject, he continued, "She's little more than twenty miles long, running east to west, and probably no more than two and a half to three miles at her widest point, north to south. If you were to draw a straight line from her westernmost point to the mainland, the closest point of land would be the coast of North Carolina. The seat of her government and the British governor's house are in St. George's, on the east end of the island. The family of your friend, St. George Tucker, resides in the westernmost parishes, Somerset and Southampton, at the other end of the island. His father, Colonel Henry Tucker, is a shipper, as are other branches of the Tucker family. Their relatives, the Jenningses, who live in Flatts in the middle of the island, are one of the most successful shippers on the island."

"Wouldn't it be more convenient to be nearer St. George's?" Eugénie asked, sipping the ruby-red claret and feeding Bridger a particularly succulent piece of capon.

"Mmmmm, is it the fingertip or the bird that offers the sweeter morsel? Ah, the fingertip, to be sure," Bridger said drawing her finger into his mouth. He grinned as he watched her silver gaze turn smoky. She snatched her finger back and made a great pretense of concentrating on cutting up her ham.

"You were saying?" she asked, looked up at him innocently.

"Now where was I? Ah, yes, on the contrary, as you probably know, government customs extract their due based on the size of the cargo in the ship's hold. The smaller the cargo, the smaller the customs fees levied. Many shipments pass quietly into private warehouses that dot the wharves and inlets along the coasts of the west and middle parishes, before the ships are presented to the St. George's customs agents. Hardly a safe occupation to carry out right under the government's greedy nose, wouldn't you say? Far better to seek as great a distance as possible from the government and its agents. The Tucker family and the other leading families didn't gain their wealth dotting every 'i' and crossing every 't' of the onerous governmental regulations. Given my own livelihood, I've a natural sympathy for that group," he chuckled. "But, I daresay, my present loose affiliation with the British authorities makes me and my family not particularly welcomed by that Bermudian group. No, the Tuckers and their ilk steer a wide berth around the presiding governor, one George James Bruère, and his people. As if the situation weren't ticklish enough, the colonel's oldest son, Harry Tucker, is married to the governor's daughter, Frances. Harry lives not far from Bruère in St. George's, placed there by the colonel to keep an eye out and to further the family's cause." Eugénie had been listening to Bridger's narrative with rapt attention as she enjoyed the lightness of the superb cheese soufflé.

"You seem well acquainted with what happens on Bermuda," she managed to say between bites.

Bridger gave her a wry smile, "I assure you, it's not due to any great knowledge of the world or any burning curiosity on my part. But I must admit, I'm very single-minded about what's important to me. It's quite a short list. I have an insatiable appetite for anything to do with ships, shipping, trade . . ." he said, his eyes gleaming with mischief, ". . . and you." The words and the intensity of his stare caused Eugénie to choke on the meat that she had been nibbling. Bridger enjoyed her agitation immensely.

"As a sea captain and trader, I recognize Bermuda's unique strategic position, lying as she does at the 32nd parallel. What is the significance of that, you may ask?" Eugénie, her composure restored, nodded, fixing him with her silver gaze.

"Where were we? Oh, yes, the thirty-second parallel," he went on doggedly. "Because of the winds, the currents, and Dame Fortune, the early shipping lanes to the New World lay much farther south. The first ships from Spain and Portugal discovered their gold and treasure to the south along those lanes. To return home, because of the prevailing winds, those ships had to sail due north to the thirty-second parallel, where the winds and tides shift and allow them to turn due east and sail for home."

At this point Bridger would have gladly given up the explanation, but, seeing Eugénie's fascination with the subject, he gamely labored on. "Given Bermuda's geographic position, it behooves those of us in trade to be well acquainted with that island. As I mentioned before, Bermuda's captains and shipmasters enjoy the reputation of being the best in the world today. There are no trading lanes left uncharted by them. They sail at their own peril, those who venture to trade without due respect for and knowledge of Bermuda's shipping oligarchy and the treacherous reefs and shoals of the thirty-second parallel.

"In fact," he continued, "I think it's safe to say that Bermuda was one of the early leaders in the carrying trade that developed between the West Indies, along the ports of the eastern seaboard, all the way up to Nova Scotia and Newfoundland and across the Atlantic to the ports of Europe. Today, their ships range all over the world.

"More than most, I guess, I've made it my concern to stay informed about the inhabitants and happenings on that island, and I've come to have the utmost respect for the Bermudians. Were I not as appealing to them as last week's fish, I would gladly seek a closer relationship."

"They've made much of the island, from what you say," Eugénie said, in an effort to pull him out of his contemplative mood. "It would seem the early Bermudians were of plucky stock."

"Yes, a particularly resilient sort they were, from all reports," Bridger said, looking up and smiling. "A trait, I might add, that has manifested itself in each new generation. After the 'accident' of the *Sea Venture* that brought the island to the attention of the Virginia Company, those seeking Bermuda for her own sake came to the island mostly from England and Scotland, looking for fortune, religious freedom, or simply adventure. Their numbers fell mainly into three groups: supervisors who represented the English shareholders overseeing their land investments, tenant farmers who contracted with the landowner to split the proceeds from the crops they grew, and a smattering of indentured servants. This last group found that the mainland's colonies were a better bet in the long run. Once their service was completed in Bermuda there simply wasn't any land to get on the cheap. Most of this group eventually migrated to the mainland.

"I remember hearing that a captain sailing up from the West Indies brought the first red man and black man to the island. But as early as 1619, Bermuda's government tried to discourage people from bringing any more slaves, who were mostly African blacks, into Bermuda. Large numbers of them weren't necessary, since the economy was based on shipbuilding, shipping, and trade. Today the population is about two-to-one white to black, and of the blacks, the men outnumber the women."

Puzzled, Eugénie asked, "If, as you say, the land is limited and therefore large acreage devoted to crops is nonexistent, then what purpose does the slave population serve?"

"First," Bridger answered patiently, "it isn't just the limited acres that dissuade them from growing crops. They tried tobacco, but found it inferior to the Virginia crop. The soil itself is a porous, stonelike substance overlaid with no more than six inches of topsoil. The land can't match the sea as an easier and more lucrative source of income and adventurous livelihood.

"To get back to your question, even the poorest whites have one or two black slaves. It's the slaves who're the highly skilled pilots, sailors, shipbuilders, fishermen, masons, carpenters, and on and on. A Bermuda crew usually has a white captain, first mate, and possibly bo'sun. The other four or five who make up the crew are blacks. You'll see, when you seek to bring a boat to shore through the rocks, reefs, and shoals, it is a black pilot that'll guide you through.

"The slaves in Bermuda are nothing like their brothers and sisters in the West Indies and on the mainland. There's a far closer bond between the owners and the slaves on Bermuda than elsewhere. That's not to say there aren't exceptions in both camps, but the size of the island and the lack of natural resources exacts a tremendous toll on all who live there. They need close cooperation and a spirit of goodwill. To survive, Bermudians of both colors have finely honed the traits of resiliency, enterprise, courage, a jealously guarded independent spirit, and the ability to take what opportunities fate throws their way and make the best of them. They have the highest regard for Nature's power, and they devoutly believe in God's good grace, should they trip over or have to bend man's shortsighted laws and regulations from time to time. They consider themselves to be upstanding subjects of the British Crown, with a good measure of leeway and autonomy thrown in, since they're so far from England."

"Are you saying that they're unscrupulous?" Eugénie asked.

"Nay, on the contrary," Bridger interrupted her. "By their lights, they have very strong scruples. They care for and protect their own to the best of their ability. They look to no one to shore up or rescue them, nor will they brook any interference from those temporarily on their island or those at a distance."

"I see," Eugénie said softly, and thought to herself how much in common the Bermudians had with this fiercely independent man, who shared the same creed he had just described so eloquently. "You've drawn a thorough picture of the island and her people. I'm now much less apt to put a foot wrong. I'd imagine there are those whose interests may be in sympathy with the patriots, considering how closely they are bound in trade."

"To be sure," Bridger agreed. "Colonel Tucker and others like him zealously guard their trade routes. But do not be misled. There are many on Bermuda who, if not staunchly loyal to the Crown, see their interests best served by being fervently neutral. And then there are those who are blindly loyal to England."

Bridger reached across the table and took her hands in his. "Knowing where your sympathies lie and your purpose here, be warned that it's a prickly path you're walking. Much is at stake on all fronts. You're of no consequence in this game. You'll be dealt with as quickly and with as little thought as a twig in the wind, should you become a nuisance."

He took his hands away and leaned back, giving her a minute to let his words sink in before going on. "Bermuda's strategic importance is now more than ever apparent to the masterminds of the European courts. She attracts agents to her shores like bees to honey, and they are just as well disguised as you. Even the colonials have gotten into the game. One Silas Deane crossed only recently on John Tucker's ship. Need I remind you to tread with care?" His eyes burned into hers, beseeching her even at this late hour to turn from her purpose and allow him to captain her home.

During the voyage, each had worked at coming to terms with the different forces that drove them, and they had succeeded to some extent. Neither would have considered passing judgment on the other's actions or would have attempted to persuade the other to their own point of view. That Bridger would breach this pact and speak so bluntly drove home to her the magnitude of his concern. Eugénie knew that Bridger, through some combination of instinct and information, had full knowledge of her true purpose in the colonies, so she wasted no time in throwing up even a token protest. Looking him square in the eyes, she cut to the heart of the matter.

"Each of us has burdens enough on the paths we've chosen. On no account must we add concern for the other to that burden," she softly chided him. Her eyes glowed silver at him in the candlelight. "To do so would cause our vision to cloud, our step to falter, distracting us when we most need to be clearheaded. Instead, let me borrow from your strength and your courage to affirm my own, and from your brave heart to lift and carry me lightly on my way. In return, I give you the best that's within me, to be with you always." She drew his hand to her lips, kissed it, and pressed it to her breast.

The expression in her eyes shifted and she said huskily, "Can't we find a better pastime to while away the dark hours than this?" In answer, he drew her up against him and initiated the age-old dance, shifting the feast from the table to each other's arms.

In accordance with their compact, the next morning they embraced the day, reveling in each other's company, jealous of anything that separated them even for a moment. He teased her unmercifully when a passionate embrace caused her hand to falter at the helm and the sails to luff, drawing a cry of alarm from the crew.

"If I didn't know your eagerness to reach Bermuda and seek Marie's assistance in repairing your disheveled state, I'd accuse you of practicing your wiles on me to stretch out this journey," Bridger said, laughing into her eyes.

"Hah!" Eugénie replied indignantly. "You're responsible for my deplorable state. You refuse to lend a hand even for the simplest tasks to rectify my *déshabillage!*"

If only I could enjoy your *déshabillage* for every moment of every day for the rest of my life, Bridger thought, admiring her lithe form, unencumbered by stays. Her loose-fitting blouse opened at the neck, offering him a glimpse now and then of her softly swelling breasts. The full skirt belled over only one layer of petticoats, which, when lifted by the wind, exposed dainty ankles and curving calves that made him hot just remembering. He answered her recriminations with a chuckle.

"You, milady, have a natural touch for the helm." And for other things, he added to himself. "You're an adept pupil. Beware, lest the Bermudians discover your skill as a sailor and call on you to do an honest day's work."

"Hah!" she said again, but smiled at his compliment and leaned naturally into the curve of his arm. "This ship is a joy. How I shall miss her!" And you, she said to herself. "Perhaps I can introduce the cedar hull and Bermuda rigging to our captains in France."

"The value of Bermudian-crafted ships has long since been known to your captains," Bridger told her. "It's common knowledge that at the outbreak of a war or even in anticipation of one, your countrymen, no fools they, immediately order several Bermudian ships to be built. Nay, French ports are no strangers to these sweet birds."

———

As the afternoon stretched out, the increasing numbers of land birds claimed their attention. The seabirds as well held them spellbound. They watched enchanted as the shearwaters skimmed the sea, plucking tasty morsels from the waves, and then soared heavenward, cavorting with one another in the sky. They followed the flights of the longtails, climbing and diving in a complex series of acrobatics, their white feathers gleaming in the sun.

Eugénie, accustomed as she had become to the sea air, suddenly caught a shift in the breeze, and some knowledge deep within her identified the change. She smelled land. She turned to Bridger. He, too, had lifted his nose as a hound to a new scent. Nodding to her, he called for Jamie to take the helm. Then, taking her hand, he turned with her toward their cabin to enjoy their last dinner and to prepare for their climb up the mast.

XVIII

꧁꧂

The sky was dark above them as they began to climb the ratlines toward the crow's nest. Bridger went first, his movements swift and sure from a life spent aboard ship. The brightness of the moon illuminated the night sky, casting shadows and patches of light through the shrouds. The lapping of the water against the hull of the ship set a steady rhythm that matched their ascent.

"Watch where I put my hands and feet, and place yours exactly where mine have been," Bridger warned, raising his voice above the howling wind. "Don't look down! Even a seasoned sailor can have vertigo climbing the rigging. Once we're in the crow's nest, you can safely look out or down to your heart's content."

Eugénie's heart was in her throat as she heeded his words and inched up the rigging behind him. What had seemed like a dandy landfall ceremony when she stood on the solid timbers of the deck seemed far less appealing to her now, as the wind buffeted her body and tossed her hair in her eyes. She tried with little success not to dwell on the fact that all that lay between life and death was her tenuous grip on the rigging, slippery with the sea's mist. She was acutely aware of the voices of the ship that clamored around her: the clatter of the shrouds snapping against each other, the creaking of the ship's superstructure, the whining and whistling of the sails, taut and straining against the wind.

Finally, Bridger hoisted himself up onto the partially enclosed platform of the crow's nest. Reaching down with one hand, he grasped Eugénie's wrist and drew her up beside him. In the moonlight, he could measure the extent of her fear by the paleness of her face, the wideness of her eyes, and her unsteady breath that came in short gasps. Gently, he disengaged one of her hands that clutched his shirtfront and placed it beside his own on the railing of the crow's nest.

"The first rule aboard ship: One hand for you and one for the ship," he said. Putting his other arm around her trembling figure, he pulled her close to him. "You've earned your stripes this night. You've passed the final test with flying colors! No true sailor can claim the name till he's climbed the mast and scaled the crow's nest," he murmured close to her ear. His nearness calmed her, and his words sent her blood singing along her veins.

"I did it, didn't I?" She laughed gaily up into his face, remembering to keep a firm grip on the rail. "Oh, what a beautiful night! The stars seem close enough to touch. And look there, at the moon's path on the water!" She infected him with her excitement. As if for the first time, he looked at the canopy of the night sky above them, the stars and the white globe of the moon, seeing them freshly through her eyes, another gift amongst countless others that she had given him.

As they stood side by side staring in awe at the heavens, a light streaked across the sky.

"Bridger, what was that? Did you see it?" Eugénie gasped.

"Aye, sweeting, 'twas a shooting star, considered by the ancient mariners to herald good fortune. Seen on the eve of a voyage or some great endeavor, such a sighting is said to predict a propitious outcome. At planting time, it's believed to predict an abundant harvest. It favors the beginning of any important undertaking. A babe conceived under a shooting star, it's claimed, will have a life marked in some extraordinary fashion. Even lovers are known to make wishes on them," he said, nuzzling her neck with his lips.

"There's no yearning of my heart that you haven't fulfilled and fulfilled again," she said, her breath brushing his ear. "I've ascended with you to paradise and heard the angels' sweet voices sing in the firmament. Those memories lie deep in my soul, and once I'm gone from you, I need only to reach deep down to that place where the remembrances of you nestle within me, to be with you once more."

"Ah, Eugénie," he said, his voice hoarse with emotion. He leaned down to press his cheek against her soft curls, committing their sweetness to memory. "How long I have loved you. My heart knew you long before my eyes beheld you standing amongst the crowd in the stableyard. When first I touched your skin, my fingers sighed in memory of its texture. I had known the music of your voice from my dreams. I've lain with you in times past. How often have I loved you, as often as I've breathed in wakefulness and in sleep." His last words floated out on the winds. In silence they stood, joined by a language of their own, at one with the night. They gazed out into the blackness. Far in the distance appeared the first, faint twinkle of shore lights. In the dark, their hands sought and clasped one another as they stood side by side facing landfall. Bridger held that moment for an instant. Then he called out to the decks below, his voice carrying high and clear above the wind.

"Landfall!" Even at their great elevation above the decks they could feel the excitement of the crew as they responded to Bridger's cry.

"Must we return to deck at once, or may we linger here a bit longer?" she asked, beseeching him with her eyes.

"Dear heart, these will probably be some of our last moments alone together for a very long time. We'll be parted soon enough," Bridger answered. "Jamie has often been master of the ship. I happily leave him to it for the moment. We're of much greater use right where we are, acting as the eyes of *The White Heather* to sight other vessels in the vicinity." Bridger suddenly grasped Eugénie's arm and turned her toward what appeared to be a field of tiny lights dancing on the water just off the starboard bow. "Look there! We have a welcoming committee!"

"Oh, Bridger, what is it?" Eugénie asked, her eyes straining to see where Bridger was pointing.

"It's a school of phosphorescent fish that give off that unholy light."

"They're magical," Eugénie breathed, enchanted by yet another of the night's entertainments. They watched until the school of fish was out of sight and then turned to look again toward the Bermuda shore.

"The beacons are getting close," Bridger said reluctantly. "It's time to drop anchor lest we add our number to the voracious appetite of the reefs." Their descent seemed much quicker to Eugénie. Strong hands grasped her and lowered her gently to the deck. Eugénie looked around, startled, when a cheer went up from the crew.

"Milady, for your pluck, you've won the hearts and admiration of every member of the crew," Jamie said, his respect for her shining in his eyes. "There are those of this hard-bitten crew who quake at the very thought of the crow's nest."

"If the truth be known," Eugénie whispered to him, "my knees are still knocking together. I have a new regard for the way the crew scampers over the rigging at will."

In short order, the anchor chain was rattling through the metal fitting, the sails furled and lashed, and *The White Heather* resting quietly at anchor. Soon, the ship and all aboard were settled down for the night.

As the first streaks of dawn crept across the sky, Eugénie stirred. Anticipation mixed with regret brought her to full wakefulness. She looked with longing around the dimly shadowed cabin that had been her home.

Another parting to endure, she thought, as she rose slowly from the comforting softness of the four-poster. This mission has been a series of partings and losses, but this will be the cruelest yet. Protesting muscles reminded her of the strenuous climb up the mast to the crow's nest. She splashed cold water on her face and turned one last time to her trusty satchel, looking for something that might be remotely appropriate for her arrival in Bermuda.

She emerged from the cabin to see a swirl of activity on deck. Bridger, she learned, had gone below to tend to the roan. Knowing that the horse's trust in Bridger was almost equal to his trust in her, she left the two to enjoy their last minutes together. She took herself to the rail and stared out across the water to look at Bermuda for the first time.

What met her eyes was a low-lying landmass that seemed to balance precariously between a towering sky and a vast sea of the most brilliant turquoise she had ever seen. At such a distance she could only make out what appeared to be an unending stand of evergreens, their feathery silhouettes flung up against the backdrop of the morning sky. Small dots punctuated the water surrounding the larger landmass. They looked as though they had been cast adrift from the main body of the island. She remarked on this to Jamie, who stood nearby directing the unlashing of the whalers.

"Aye," he said. "There are some three hundred islands in all. What you see stretched out before you are but the mountaintops of one large mass that lies beneath the sea. An ancient volcano threw up her offerings on the waves eons ago, but outcroppings have been known to disappear and others to appear suddenly at the whim of the shifting seas."

"Where do we stand off the island?" she asked, wondering at the breadth of his knowledge.

"We stand off Ely's Harbor, in Somerset parish. 'Tis on the western end of the island," he replied.

Eugénie turned her attention back to the deep-green crescent. As the morning light grew brighter, she began to see cottages and other structures painted a variety of pastel shades and sharing one characteristic in common: they all appeared to have similar stark-white roofs. Just as she was about to question Jamie on this point, a cry went up from beyond the ship's rail.

"Ahoy! Ahoy! *The White Heather!* St. George Tucker requests permission to come aboard!"

"St. George!" Eugénie exclaimed, running in the direction of the cry. Leaning over the rail, she waved wildly at the flotilla of small crafts bobbing below her in the lee of the ship. St. George stood in the prow of the lead whaler.

"Eugénie!" He called out waving happily up at her. "We've come to be of assistance." Jamie, who had joined her, tied a rope ladder to the rail and then flung the other end into St. George's outstretched hands. When the whaler was made fast, St. George climbed the ladder, leaping nimbly onto the vessel's deck.

"She's a true beauty, she is," he said, flinging his arms wide to embrace *The White Heather's* length. "For days I've been scanning the sea from my cousin Henry's roof walk, not knowing from which direction you might come. Then last night, word reached me at Father's of an unscheduled vessel's lights. I took the chance and requisitioned these whalers and a barge for the roan to transport all of you ashore. We set off with high hopes, knowing if she were simply a stray ship, the exercise would serve to prepare us for when you finally did arrive. So, here we are, spit-polished and at your service."

"Oh, St. George, you're incorrigible," Eugénie laughed, throwing herself into his arms and hugging him warmly. As she was making introductions, Bridger joined them. He clapped St. George on the back. "The roan thanks you for your forethought," he said. "It would've been a shaky passage for the beast on one of my whalers. It's good to see you, even though it means that I must part company with the newest member of my crew. Your father could look far before he'd find a better helmsman than Mistress Eugénie."

Gracefully bridging what could have been an awkward moment between the two men, Bridger continued, "The arrival of your conveyances has bought us some time. Without your help, we would've needed to disembark immediately for the roan's sake while the tide was out and the ocean's surface smooth. Will you join us for a modest repast that the cook has gone to great lengths to prepare for Mistress Eugénie? He was crestfallen when he thought all his efforts were to be relegated to fishbait. You'll win the cook's undying appreciation if you allow him to present Mistress Eugénie with his final hurrah."

"Who am I to thwart his culinary arts? Truthfully, if I may be so blunt, I'm so famished at this point that I'd fall upon salted jerky if it appeared before me," St. George said, delighted at the prospect of the delicious meal. The three happily took themselves to the main galley and did justice to the lavish feast the cook had so lovingly prepared.

A hubbub ensued when all hands were called to move the roan from the ship's hold to the awaiting barge. More than one of the crew found himself enjoying an unexpected swim in the ocean. Eugénie laughed until tears streamed down her face at the antics of the roan. With the agility of a cat, he evaded their grasping hands, moving this way and that, leaving the astonished crew clutching at thin air. Only her soft whistle finally quelled his loud protests and turned him from a raging Tartar into a placid lamb. Once securely lashed to the sturdy timbers of the barge, he cast his eyes about him with a look of utter disdain, as if to ask what all the commotion was about.

Seizing the last fleeting moments before she, too, had to leave, Eugénie took Bridger's hand and led him to a secluded nook. Now that the moment was upon them, they hesitated to speak. Instead, they reached out to each other with their eyes. Eugénie noticed the early-morning breeze stirring and lifting his hair where it fell across his forehead. She watched the pulse at the base of his neck quicken under her gaze.

"Thank you for leaving the imprint of your eyes in the turquoise of these waters," she whispered, trying to muster a smile.

"The radiance of your face will be with me in every morning's sunrise." He spoke softly, brushing the chestnut curls back from her cheek with gentle fingers. They embraced, straining to hold back the moment of parting.

"If the need arises, somehow get word to me and I'll come," he said, with urgency. "I'll send one of my own men from time to time to see how you are faring. It's beyond my endurance to go long without knowing of your welfare."

"Ah, Bridger," Eugénie sighed with relief. "I didn't know how to ask. Thank you. Will you go ashore with us in one of your whalers?" she asked, knowing the wiser choice lay otherwise.

"Nay, dear heart," he said holding her closer. "It would only prolong this pain. It's far better to share our final parting in private." With one last deep embrace, they went back to join the others.

Bridger helped Eugénie onto the rope ladder and watched as she climbed down and stepped gracefully into the whaler. She called her thanks and farewells to Jamie and the crew who were lined up on deck. Then her eyes sought Bridger's and lingered there as they shared messages without words.

Slowly the flotilla of small boats tacked their way toward shore. Eugénie watched as the sleek lines of *The White Heather* receded toward the horizon. When she could just barely make out Bridger standing alone at the rail, she threw up her hand in one last jaunty salute. She saw his answering wave, then turned her eyes toward Ely's Harbor.

XIX

❧❧❧

It was slow going through the reefs that lay off Ely's Harbor. True to Bridger's prediction, both the whaler carrying Eugénie and St. George and the barge that brought up the rear were piloted by black men. Eugénie was struck by the easy camaraderie between St. George and his pilot, who spoke to St. George with surprising familiarity, at one point saying, "That easy Virginia life sho' makin' Master St. George sof'." Is it common to the island or just St. George's amiable nature? Eugénie wondered.

St. George called Eugénie's attention to the points of interest as they went along. He pointed out a particularly high point of land that jutted out into the water then curved like a bent finger, creating the entrance to Ely's Harbor.

Using that analogy, he said, "Look where the second knuckle extends out into the sea. That promontory is known locally as Wreck Hill. The shoals below it are especially treacherous. False beacons placed by unscrupulous hands have caused many ships to founder in the dark of night and crash on those reefs. The wreckers waste no time going aboard the unfortunate ship, murdering all on board and stripping her of her cargo."

St. George noticed Eugénie shudder involuntarily and he continued, "Aye, it's well to fear their kind. That lot has little respect for life— their own or anyone else's. Wreckers have little to lose. They are the rabble of the West End that secret themselves in the nooks and crannies of the western parishes. Even the stoutest of us knows to be careful when venturing out on the cliffs on a dark, moonless night."

"Is there no law enforcement to deter these fellows?" Eugénie asked.

"Being so far removed from 'the protective arm of government,'" St. George answered, drawing out the last words to emphasize his lack of trust in that august body, "we're left to fend for ourselves, which suits us just fine. Every so often, when their activities have become particularly offensive, we locals get together and scour all their known hideouts, round them up, and serve them their just deserts. It's a little bloody, but it tends to settle 'em down for a while."

The dispatch with which he dismissed this group of mankind showed Eugénie an altogether different side of St. George.

"You flinch at our local approach to law and order?" St. George asked, his genial expression back in place. "'Tis only expedient on an island that can ill afford disruptive elements. There's plenty of work for honest hands. It's best for all concerned that those who'd wish to do otherwise find a more accommodating habitat than Bermuda.

"For a short period in our history," he went on, "this island was a hiding place for bands of cutthroats and other unseemly characters. They learned quickly that their kind was not welcome here. Since then, we've enjoyed only infrequent unpleasant episodes of the homegrown sort, and when such weeds spring up, we pluck 'em out."

Although less grisly than the earlier descriptions, this homey metaphor, presented in such a mild tone, left Eugénie with a sense of unease. She cast about for a less-distasteful aspect of Bermuda's flora and fauna and was relieved when her eyes lighted on an interesting rock formation looming up in front of the whaler.

"Oh, what a sight!" she exclaimed.

"We call them Cathedral Rocks, for their lofty spires. It's a phenomenon of nature that you'll find nowhere else on the island," St. George explained with pride.

"Shortly, we'll pass through Somerset Bridge, which connects two parts of Sandys parish—it's spelled S-a-n-d-y-s, but it's pronounced

'Sands,' without the 'y'. It's known locally as Somerset, probably after Sir Thomas Somerset, the captain of the *Sea Venture,* the first recorded English ship to arrive in Bermuda. The bridge is of special note because it has a trapdoor that allows larger vessels to come and go between the Great Sound and the ocean. Otherwise, they'd have to go all the way around. It isn't necessary for the trapdoor to be raised in our case, but to make a little show for you, I've paid the bridge master for the service." He grinned at Eugénie's obvious pleasure.

Eugénie listened closely to St. George's geography and history lessons. She was struck by the beauty of each scene that passed before her eyes and began to feel the enchantment of the place, just as Bridger had predicted.

As they passed by Cathedral Rocks, the traffic around them picked up considerably. St. George hailed several friends and was hailed in return. It was clear to Eugénie that much of life in Bermuda occurred on the water and, from the boisterous nature of the exchanges, that the Bermudians were naturally friendly and high-spirited. Their barge carrying an exceptionally large horse drew curious stares from every craft in the vicinity.

Noticing the stares, St. George explained, "Horses aren't very common on Bermuda." Eugénie was reminded of an earlier conversation they had had at the Whittingtons'. "Ships and smaller watercraft are a far easier mode of transportation," he had told her then, "given the rocky terrain and the limited number of passable roads on the island. The roan will be the talk of every household by teatime. We may have few roadways, but we have a highly developed gossip mill."

St. George chuckled, turning to wave at yet another skiff's skipper that had hailed him. He was thoroughly enjoying the notoriety of transporting the huge beast on the barge in the company of a young lady of exceptional physical attributes. This was not lost on Eugénie as she smiled at her friend.

Eugénie noticed that every cottage and structure along the shore had a dock of some sort. Wharves were also common, and watercrafts of all shapes and sizes were either moored near to shore or attached in some manner to the ubiquitous docks. She remarked to St. George about the clatter and hammering that she heard coming from several directions.

"Aye, the sound is so familiar to me I don't even notice it," he said. "The shipwrights have benefited from the many years that your French and my Brits have been having at each other. Destruction on the one hand spells fortune on the other," he went on breezily. "Our cedar-hull Bermuda riggers are in high demand when the great European courts seek the weapons of war to settle their differences. Coin is coin. Be it English pound or French franc, it spends the same. You're hearing the din of the shipyards that ring the Great Sound from Mangrove Bay to Salt Kettle and back again. That incessant tinkering is music to our Bermudian ears. 'Tis our prosperity. Ironically, for all this water around us, as well as the shipping and trade that sustains every living soul on this island, there's not a drop of fresh water that comes up from the ground." At Eugénie's look of surprise, he explained, "You may've noticed the sparkling white roofs that grace every structure you see. It's not for beauty, that. It's a design of slope, tier, and gutter drawn to capture the rainfall and carry that precious liquid to cisterns that provide all the fresh water used in Bermuda."

Ah, Eugénie thought, another reason why planting is so scarce on the island. I'd wondered why I'd seen so few flower gardens here, compared to Virginia's abundance, since they both seem to share a similar gentle climate. I'm beginning to see what Bridger meant when he spoke of Bermuda's resourcefulness, making the most of her treasures and finding a solution for her shortcomings.

Eugénie was suddenly distracted by an explosion of activity on the water's edge and the sight of their pilot leaping up to grab a line thrown to him by a burly, red-faced man who was barking orders at an urchin standing by his side.

"We'll use the line as a guide so's ye'll not slide sideways through the bridge," he yelled to St. George's pilot, then he turned and continued to bellow at the young boy. "Hurry, lad! Hurry! 'Twill be nighttime if you don't get a move on! Raise up the trapdoor and be quick about it, so milady can see the invention of the bridge." The lad in his frayed britches and bare feet was already off and gone, scampering with monkeylike movements up the bank and out of sight.

"Look, look!" St. George called to Eugénie, pointing to the bridge structure as he cleated down the line. Above and ahead of her, she saw the young boy appear on the bridge. With lightning speed, his agile fingers unfastened the leather strips that held the trapdoor secure, and, with a flourish, he flopped it over to one side, then executed a jiglike step to show his delight. As the whalers and the barge passed through the bridge, he honored them with a crisp salute.

"*Quel petit charmant!*" Eugénie said, laughing at his antics. "Never have I had such a royal welcome. How can I thank the lad?"

"Your smile is more than enough," St. George answered. "Seldom is the lad even noticed for his pains, and I've well rewarded his master for the 'privilege' of passing through the bridge."

Apparently, she thought, the Bermudians hold their coins close. With good reason, I expect, since they have to fight simply to survive. Eugénie turned to give the little fellow another wave, only to see him already hard at work restoring the trapdoor to its original position.

"Look there, up on the hill to your left!" St. George cried. "That's Henry Tucker's house. He was my cousin and is now my brother-in-law, as well, since he married my sister, Frances. He's the one who lent me the barge." Eugénie turned, shading her eyes to follow where his fingered pointed. She saw a handsome, square-built, pale yellow house, corner trimmed in white block with large, dark-green shuttered windows and the familiar sloping, white-ridged roof. It was an imposing structure compared to the cottages that dotted the banks they had passed. It boasted a roof walk, which was filled to overflowing with people of all ages and sizes. Apparently, they had been waiting for the waterborne entourage, because as Eugénie turned to look at them, a roar went up, accompanied by the waving of arms, handkerchiefs, and brightly colored banners. Somewhat overwhelmed by the reception, Eugénie managed to smile and wave back. A few minutes later several children emerged from the ground floor and tumbled down the bank to subject her and the huge horse to closer inspection.

"I must beg your pardon, Eugénie," St. George said, blushing beneath his deep tan. "I've spoken much of you since my return home, and everyone wishes to see for themselves if what I've said is true."

"Oh, St. George, their bright faces of welcome are as pretty a sight as I've ever beheld. I'm truly grateful to you and your family for extending to me such warm hospitality." As she spoke, she stood carefully in the whaler and made a deep curtsy to the waving crowd.

It was well into the afternoon by the time the little group rounded the last turn and saw ahead a well-appointed wharf. At long last, they were coming to the end of their voyage. Eugénie breathed a sigh of relief, stretched her arms, and flung back her head to allow the afternoon breezes to blow through her hair.

As they drew nearer to shore, they saw a young black boy sitting on the wharf. He looked to be about the same age as the bridge master's helper, but better dressed and better nourished. Clearly, he was the lookout designated to report the arrival of St. George and his illustrious guest. He sat deep in concentration, whiling away the time by using a makeshift net to capture the fish swimming in the shallow waters. As they watched, he suddenly yanked the net out of the water. Even at their distance, they could see a shiny fish flipping and flopping about in the net. With a quick twist of his wrist, the young fisherman neatly pitched it into the pail sitting at his side.

"Ho there, Jeremy!" St. George called out to him.

"Master George! Master George!" Jeremy turned around so quickly that he almost upset his pail. His eyes grew as large as saucers as they came to rest on the great roan. "Holy Jesus and Mother of God!" he shrieked. Then, horrified at his outburst, he clapped his hands over his mouth. "I mean, Master George, I never seen a horse so big as that!" Eugénie noticed that his speech was considerably more educated than that of his Virginian counterparts and that his cadence had a distinctly musical quality.

"Jeremy, where are your manners?" St. George said sternly. Belatedly remembering the appropriate decorum called for in such circumstances, to say nothing of the responsible role that had been entrusted to him, young Jeremy turned reluctantly from gazing at the roan and bobbed his head in Eugénie's direction.

Standing tall and straight, he proceeded to reel off a speech of welcome so well rehearsed that the words, coming in an unbroken string, were virtually unintelligible.

"Welcome mistress welcome from one and all at The Grove ma'am we is pleased pleased pleased!" At this point in the spiel his voice rose with enthusiasm as he began to gain momentum. "To make welcome to you mistress from all of us at The Grove welcome mistress welcome . . ."

"Hold, Jeremy!" Realizing that Jeremy, once started, had lost track of how to finish, St. George had to shout to break through the boy's trancelike concentration. "Excellent, excellent. 'Tis a fine speech of welcome, Jeremy. Now," St. George proceeded in more normal tones, "if you'd be so kind, please take Mistress Eugénie's satchel and go up to the house and tell the others that we have arrived and will need some help with the roan." Interpreting correctly the child's blank stare, he quickly amended his words. "The horse, the horse. We'll need assistance with the horse."

As comprehension swept over his young face, Jeremy broke into a huge grin. "Roman! I know's what's a roman, Master George. I sees romans alla time!" Immensely pleased with himself at having established his knowledge and familiarity with "romans," Jeremy wasted no time snatching the satchel from St. George's hand. Then, grabbing his pail in his other hand, he shot up the path through the tangle of seagrape.

Eugénie had been choking down her merriment from the beginning of Jeremy's welcoming speech. When she could see that the earnest young lad was well beyond earshot, she collapsed against St. George, laughing until her ribs ached.

"Roman," she gasped, struggling for breath. "Roman. Of course, I should have known all along. 'Roman' is just the name I've been searching for!" The roan, who had been waiting patiently for his mistress to get around to releasing him from the restraining ropes he had endured entirely too long, looked wholly unperturbed by his sudden name change.

It was a triumphant, if weary, column that some time later straggled up the path with young Jeremy in the lead, announcing often and in loud tones to one and all, "I knows a roman when I sees a roman. Why I'd knowd a roman any time, any place."

Only when St. George exclaimed fiercely, "That is quite enough, Jeremy!" causing Eugénie to have to suppress another outburst of laughter, did the young fellow finally cease and desist.

The entire household had turned out to welcome Eugénie. As the motley entourage emerged from the seagrape and underbrush that fronted the broad lawn, two figures separated themselves from the group on the veranda and made their way forward with smiles of welcome.

As they walked toward her, Eugénie looked at them closely. She would have recognized Colonel Tucker as St. George's father in any crowd. He carried himself erectly and, except for the look of speculation in his eyes, bore a strong resemblance to his son. Beneath his jovial countenance, she detected a will of iron.

Anne Butterfield Tucker had a gentle, intelligent face that was far less easily read than the colonel's. Eugénie suspected that her pleasant facade enabled her to manage a vast household and raise six boisterous children without ever having to raise her voice to have her wishes carried out to the letter. Eugénie liked them both on sight.

"You are all and more than we expected from St. George's glowing reports," Colonel Tucker said, beaming his welcome. "I'm anxious to hear more about the affairs in the American colonies."

Prepared by St. George for his father's bluntness, Eugénie smiled charmingly.

Before she could respond, Anne Tucker slipped her arm through Eugénie's and said, laughing, "Come, come, Henry. Can't you see Eugénie is fair wilted from her trip? Eugénie, pay him no mind. Your Marie has your room all prepared, and she's been up since dawn awaiting your arrival. We must not have her wait one minute more. The rest of this throng can cool their heels until tea. 'Twill be soon enough, then, for them to meet you. That will give you a little time at least to rest and get settled." With that, Anne Tucker hastened up the veranda steps with Eugénie in tow. Eugénie noticed the unusual cadence and pattern of the Tuckers' speech and wondered if it were typical of all Bermudians.

She didn't have long to pursue that thought, for she was barely past the threshold when Marie came rushing down the stairs. Her usual composed demeanor shattered at the sight of her mistress. The two women flew into each other's arms, tears of joy mingling on closely pressed cheeks.

"Marie, Marie, I've missed you so! Your crossing was without incident? I see you're blooming from the Tuckers' kind hospitality," Eugénie cried, her words coming out in a rush. "Let me look at you." Stepping back, but still holding both Marie's hands in her own, Eugénie looked closely at Marie's face. "I see there must be magic on this island, just as I've been told. You look completely recovered from all the ordeals." Indeed, Marie's lovely face had lost the pale, pinched look that had settled on it at Jacques's death. Her eyes twinkled and only a slight roundness gave any indication of her advancing condition.

"Dear Mistress, it's the sight of your beloved face that returns the bloom to mine. I swear I've not breathed since I left you." Marie's voice trembled as she spoke. "But I've thoughtlessly kept you waiting here. You must be exhausted. Let me show you to your bedchamber."

"Yes, yes, dear girl," Anne Tucker said, touched by the sight of the reunion. "But don't tarry, I won't be able to hold this group back much longer."

Marie's efforts made short work of Eugénie's disheveled appearance. Refreshed by a quick bath, Eugénie slipped into a light, sprigged-cotton frock and sat patiently as Marie's deft hands artfully arranged the shining chestnut curls. Gone was the sea gamine, replaced by a radiant young woman.

It was this vision that greeted the Tucker family a short while later in the sprawling front parlor. Anne Tucker preempted St. George and briskly made the introductions.

" 'Tis seldom that our whole family is assembled these days under the same roof," Anne explained to Eugénie as she moved around the circle of her four sons and two daughters. "Harry, here, and his Fanny live t'other end of the island in St. George's. Our dear Frances and her Henry live at Bridge House in Somerset. I fear we've lost Nathaniel and Thomas Tudor permanently to lands beyond our shores. Thomas's wife is upstairs. She'll be down shortly. They've only just arrived from the colony of South Carolina.

"You'll meet the rest of the clan at the upcoming wedding of one of Henry's cousins, who is, of course, our cousin as well, but further removed," she said, nodding at her son-in-law.

Eugénie's head swam with the complexity of the relationships and the similarity of the names. One need only mention Henry or Harry in this room and several heads would bob up in unison, with Fanny and Frances not far behind. She held her breath as they approached the last person in the circle.

"Eugénie, this is our Elizabeth," Anne said, much to Eugénie's relief. "She's our family scribe. Her prodigious letter-writing keeps account of all of our group wherever they may be." Everyone chuckled good-naturedly as Eugénie smiled at the young woman. A merry countenance and bright eyes overcame what otherwise would have been an extremely plain face. It was soon apparent that Elizabeth's unrestrained vitality and interest in everyone and everything gave her a special position in the family circle.

"Would you like to join us in our version of the celebration of Beltane, tomorrow?" she asked, immediately folding Eugénie into the group. At Eugénie's baffled expression, Elizabeth explained, " 'Tis an old pagan ritual practiced in Scotland on or about the spring equinox. We're running a bit late for those who are sticklers. The traditional English equivalent, the Coming of the May, is celebrated on May first. Tomorrow. It calls for young maids to go up into the hills at sunrise and collect wildflowers to twine into wreaths for their hair and to cavort about in some dance ritual, which is supposed to call forth the spirits from their long winter's nap. The Scottish Beltane was originally somewhat more bloodthirsty, with sacrifices and all. But these days it's been tamed down quite a bit. For our purposes, the Coming of the May will suit us just fine. It's a convenient excuse to have a good frolic and to welcome the sunrise, which is so beautiful this time of year." Her mother spoke up just then, much to Eugénie's relief.

"Lizzie, our guest has barely made it to shore. No doubt she'd appreciate at least one good night's sleep to restore her strength after the rigors of her travels before we throw her into the activities of our mad household. And where are my own manners? Forgive me, Eugénie. I'm as bad as the rest, keeping you standing here when you must be famished. You'd best help yourself to what's left of tea, now that it's been plundered by this brood of pillagers. Really, Nat! Isn't that your fourth, or is it fifth, helping of clotted cream?" Anne Tucker's sharp words were softened by her indulgent smile. Eugénie needed little encouragement to plunge into the heaping plate that St. George had prepared for her.

" 'Tis fortunate we are," Colonel Tucker said, embarking on his favorite subject, "that we don't suffer from the shortages felt by so many in Bermuda. Government policy is strangling the shipping. Trade is tightening up daily. Now there's word of an American embargo. It won't be long before there'll be people starving on this island." These dire remarks were met by nods from his sons, and a heated conversation began, extolling open trade and damning governmental restrictions. The voices receded around her as Eugénie thought of her recent discussion with Bridger on the same subject.

She barely remembered making her goodnights and climbing the stairs to her bedchamber. As she settled beneath the lavender-scented sheets, she thought, The outbreak of war will increase the license already taken on the high seas. I'm glad to be on solid ground once more. Bridger's face was the last image that floated before her eyes just as sleep came to steal her away.

XX

❧❧❧

Eugénie awoke the next morning to the sounds of birds twittering just outside her window. Bright sunlight streamed into the room, setting the dust motes dancing in the light air. She lay quietly, contemplating the room. A floral valence surrounded the four-poster bed. The open top allowed her to see the ceiling molding, which resembled an upside-down tray. This graceful architectural detail also gave the room the impression of greater height. The room was open and airy compared to the spacious but low-ceilinged architecture in Virginia and her recent quarters aboard *The White Heather.*

The furniture was simple but skillfully built. The rich, dark wood was highly polished to an almost mirrorlike finish, as were the doors, woodwork, and floor. Along one side of the room were built-in cabinets with wrought iron hardware. The windows were flanked by yellow curtains of such light material that they swayed easily in the morning breeze. Shutters were affixed to the window moldings as protection, she guessed, from storm and cold.

"Time to get up, sleepyhead," she said out loud. Reluctantly, she climbed down from the bed, which, because of its raised height and proportions, reminded her of her own in France. She gave a start of pleasure as her bare feet came into contact with the smooth, polished floor. It felt almost warm to the touch.

She began to investigate her surroundings. Rummaging in the drawers of a spindle-and-spool highboy, she discovered that Marie had carefully unpacked and put away all of her clothes in anticipation of her arrival. When she opened an oversized armoire, she was struck by a pleasant smell that she had noticed the night before when she entered the Tucker home. Taking out the gown she had chosen for the day, she noticed that the pleasant smell lingered.

Ah, this must be the scent of the Bermuda cedar. It has a slightly different smell from the cedar materials we import to France.

She looked around the room with new eyes, realizing that the wood had been used throughout the room, not only for the beautiful floors and woodwork but for the lovely furniture as well. She couldn't resist running her hand along the smoothly polished surfaces. On closer inspection, she noticed that the furniture blended the familiar elements of famous English cabinetmakers with what must be the interpretations of local artists. Eugénie found the overall effect uniquely attractive.

She dressed quickly and was just tying back her hair when Marie entered carrying a tray laden with delicious-smelling rolls and steaming coffee.

"Mistress Tucker thought you would enjoy breakfast in your room this morning after your long journey."

"How thoughtful she is," Eugénie exclaimed. "But I'm sorry to make extra work for this busy household."

"The family was up early," Marie said, setting the tray down on the lady's desk in front of the window. "Miss Elizabeth convinced all the ladies, even Mistress Tucker, to join her in celebrating the first day of May. The men are down at the warehouse overseeing the unloading of the cargo from the ships that arrived last night. The house is as quiet as a tomb this morning."

Eugénie admired the needlework on the seat of the Queen Anne chair as she sat down and devoted herself to the repast before her. "Mmmmmm," she said. "Is this the loquat jam St. George spoke of? It's delicious!"

"Yes, that it is." Marie smiled at the look of sheer delight that lit her mistress's face. "I see the salt sea air has not diminished your sweet tooth one bit."

"If anything, the rigors of the sea voyage seem to have made it more insatiable," Eugénie laughed, slathering the delectable golden jam on yet another roll. "What talk have you heard here about the battles in Massachusetts?" she asked Marie.

"When the news first came, it caused great excitement. Then people quieted down," Marie said as she shook the bedclothes and started to make up the bed. "They fear a trade embargo by the Americans. The word is that this end of the island is in sympathy with the patriots' cause, even so. As you know, Mr. Silas Deane came to Bermuda when I did on Mr. John Tucker's ship. He's known to be an American agent. He was a guest here when he first arrived. Since then, he's been entertained in several homes that share Colonel Tucker's views." Marie lowered her voice. "These views are not expressed publicly and are only discussed amongst those they trust. On the surface, little is said, but seldom does an evening pass that doesn't see many comings and goings and conversation well into the night. The Tucker sons have all assembled for the wedding, but much is going on that has nothing to do with that event. Mr. St. George's and Mr. Thomas's passion for the Americans' cause is known to the British authorities here. There's concern for their safety, but it's believed that the Colonel's political influence will safeguard them for the time being."

Eugénie digested Marie's words. "Then, there is true division on the island?"

"It would seem so, although the real issue is trade. The livelihood of Colonel Tucker's family and his friends, and this island's survival, both depend on trade and shipping," Marie answered.

"Marie, your words lead my thoughts down a dark and winding path," Eugénie said slowly. "If shipping is the issue, to service these trade routes it'll be necessary for Bermuda to trade with a former friend that is now an avowed foe. Voicing sympathy amongst confidantes is one thing. Trading with the enemy . . . *mon Dieu!* Marie, that's treason!" Eugénie's eyes grew wide at the implications. "Marie, what have we stumbled into?"

Eugénie jumped up from her chair, her breakfast forgotten. She moved distractedly around the room, stopping here and there to finger some object as her mind raced back and forth.

"Marie, this is more than we bargained for." Eugénie stopped in front of her servant and said urgently, "We've leapt from the frying pan into the fire!" She whirled away and began pacing once more. "Local animosities aside, Virginia was far from the center of the storm. Colonel Tucker, as the leader of the American sympathizers, is right in the middle of it! And here we are. We can hardly pretend to stand above the fray when we're accepting the Tuckers' hospitality. We're tarred with the same brush. Being an agent for the cartel was nothing compared to this. Now, I'm collaborating with American sympathizers! The mission is compromised, not to mention the danger I've placed us both in. How in God's name am I going to be able to get the information I need? I can hardly go dancing into the other camp and expect to be welcomed with open arms. *Mon Dieu,* what have I gotten us into?"

"Mistress, Mistress, don't distress yourself so. The Tucker clan and their compatriots have been tweaking the governor's nose since long before the disturbances in the American colonies began. Colonel Tucker's own son, Harry, acts as a go-between. Their ships flagrantly bypass the custom agents, throwing a crumb to them just often enough to keep from being hauled up in front of the magistrates—which would be a sham, in any case, since their relatives and friends fill those offices.

"The governing bodies, the Bermuda-chosen Assembly and the governor's appointed Council, are riddled with these men," Marie went on. "What recourse does Governor Bruère have but to turn a blind eye? Harry reports to his father that the governor is forever hounding Whitehall with *les billets* of complaints describing the disorder on the island and with pleas for warships to assist him and for foodstuffs to alleviate Bermuda's shortages. All to no avail. So far, Whitehall has turned a deaf ear. If the Bermuda ships ceased slipping in with their additional cargo, the plight of this island would be truly desperate. The governor is all too aware of this."

"Marie, Marie," Eugénie insisted. "What you describe is child's play.

In the past, the governor may well have been able to tolerate or even overlook the devious methods practiced by Colonel Tucker and others, since they brought much-needed cargo to the island. But now there is a war going on! Bermuda is British until and unless she comes out and declares otherwise. Governor Bruère cannot permit the Bermudians to correspond, much less trade, with the Americans. They are the enemy. The enemy! These are acts of treason! As governor of this colony, he is accountable for the deeds of Bermuda's citizenry. No doubt, he has had spies who reported on these activities in the past. Now, I shudder to think what network he must have in place and what lengths he will go to preserve his own reputation.

"How far do you suppose these Bermudians are prepared to go to protect and continue their trade with the Americans?" Eugénie continued. "Will their economic need be enough to force them to join the Americans' revolution? Or will they stand aloof from the fight and attempt to continue to trade with the seaboard colonies, thinking they can do so with impunity? They walk a narrow path between two precipices." Eugénie paused, looking down at her hands, and was stunned to see that in her distress she had shredded her monogrammed cambric handkerchief. She opened her hands, letting the pieces drift to the floor, lowered her head, and closed her eyes.

Marie watched her mistress, alarmed at the extent of her distress. Just as she was about to go to her, Eugénie lifted her head and took a deep breath. "It's not for us to judge these people or to fear for them. Our purpose, rather, is to determine whether Bermuda will or will not join the Americans in their fight. Our sympathies must not cloud our judgment or influence our actions. If the Bermudians' operations help the Americans' effort and thwart the British, then all well and good. In the end, should this island throw in its lot with the Americans, its strategic position and its fleet will greatly enhance the cause. If, on the other hand, Bermuda remains a British colony..." The implications of her words hung ominously in the air.

"Marie," she said, her face grave, "you and I walk a path no less dangerous than theirs. For the first time since we began this mission, I truly fear for our safety. I only hope that we can manage to survive and that we haven't irreparably compromised the mission." With a last sip of her coffee, Eugénie mentally shook herself and said, more brightly, "It's foolish to cast a pall on the present worrying about what might or might not happen in the future. Conjuring up a wolf at the door is sheer foolishness. If a wolf comes knocking, then we'll have to figure out how to deal with his fangs. For now, enough said."

Eugénie stretched out her arms and twirled around. "Marie, I've been cramped aboard ship too long. Come, help me dress. I think I'll wander out and enjoy this glorious day." Marie was only too happy to oblige.

Eugénie was relieved to have the grounds and gardens to herself. She walked at will, remarking as she went on the exotic plants that grew side by side with the more familiar European varieties. She remembered St. George telling her that the island had few indigenous plants and that the sea captains had brought plant specimens back to the island from all over the world to flourish in Bermuda's gentle climate. She noticed that stone block was used for walls and pathways, steps and platforms. It was grayish in color, rough to the touch, and appeared to be porous.

This must be the material that lies just beneath the thin layer of soil, she thought. It must be plentiful and available. The main house had several dependencies, all built of the same materials. She came upon the buttery, which stood round and tall with slit windows near the top just below the cone-shaped roof. Walking a little farther, she arrived at the kitchen building and smokehouse. They were surrounded by a walled garden where a young black man was industriously hoeing fresh furrows in the dark earth. She stood and watched him, enjoying his rhythmic motion. He must have felt her presence because he turned, and, seeing her, his face split into a broad grin.

"Dat big hoss is a mighty fine animal, Missus," he said, courteously doffing his hat. "Young Jeremy thinks he come jus' fo' him. He spends every spare second he can squeeze out just to be with dat hoss. I never

seen the likes of how he skedaddled through his chores this mornin'."
Eugénie noticed that the gardener's voice held the same musical quality that she had heard in Jeremy's the day before.

"Is Jeremy your brother?" She asked.

"No, ma'am!" He laughed, finding something in the question amusing. "Our peoples are from the West Indies. After his family died of
the pox, he just moved in with my folks and sort of attached hissef to
me. He was a good little fella and not much trouble. When he learned
Colonel Tucker's people were going to bring me up here, he set up
such a ruckus dat they finally let him come along, too. So, I guess you
could say we are pretty near brothers after all." He smiled at the thought
and returned to his task.

As Eugénie passed along the kitchen wall, she saw two men building an addition on the end of it. She stopped to watch. She was fasci-
nated to see one of them using a simple saw to cut symmetrical blocks
from a large chunk of the porous material. The other was pulverizing
the same material. As she watched, he added the powder to a solution
that he stirred into a paste and then applied it to all the surfaces of the
block. They worked methodically, setting the blocks row by row with
no wasted motion. She was about to question them about their work
when Anne Tucker came around the corner.

"Oh, there you are, Eugénie," she said. "What sort of hostess am I,
leaving you to wander about by yourself?"

"Please don't be concerned on my account," Eugénie said. "I've
been having a perfectly wonderful time enjoying your beautiful gardens. It's been very educational, too. I'm astonished at the wide variety
of your planting."

"Did you see Ethan?" Anne said, smiling, pleased at the compliment. "He's responsible for the gardens. Actually, there's very little
around here that he doesn't have a hand in. He's a master carpenter,
and we often loan him out to the shipwrights. I'm loath to do it,
though. Everything just seems to go to rack and ruin in his absence.
He's teaching Jeremy his skills, and the lad is an apt student. I'm sur-

prised he isn't around here somewhere. He's seldom far from Ethan's side. Oh, of course, I'd forgotten. He's completely entranced by your horse. 'Roman,' isn't it? I must say, quite an unusual name."

Eugénie laughed and explained the origins of the roan's name. Soon both women were laughing heartily at Jeremy's antics.

"Yes, that's Jeremy, all right," Anne said, catching her breath. "I don't know how we got along before he came. I was just on my way to the rose garden. We're having guests tonight, and I noticed this morning that the arrangements in the house were beginning to look a bit tatty. Will you join me?"

"I'd love to," Eugénie answered delightedly. "Roses were always my mother's favorite flowers. I imagine that's where I inherited my love for them." They stopped at a small building constructed in the same manner as the others. Anne Tucker outfitted her guest with thick cloth gloves and offered Eugénie her choice of wide-brimmed palmetto hats similar to the ones St. George had brought to Mary Whittington. Then, equipped with clippers and baskets also made from the palmetto fronds, they set off down the path to the rose garden.

Eugénie was surprised at the assortment of rose plants. Climbers trailed over the post-and-rail fence that enclosed the garden. Bush roses were blooming profusely, as were the rose trees that lined the center walk.

"I've never seen such abundance so early in the season," Eugénie exclaimed.

"We were blessed with a rainy but mild winter this year, and since Ethan has been with us the roses have been exceptional. He uses fish emulsion, which has the most awful odor, but the plants gobble it up and then compete with each other, pushing out buds and blossoms in every direction."

The two women fell fast to work snipping and pruning the vigorous plants. Eugénie had a moment's pang of homesickness, thinking of her own roses whose first blush she had already missed. She wondered if she would have the chance to enjoy any of her beloved "Eugénie" this season.

It's useless to pine, she chided herself and bent her mind, instead, to learning the names of the unfamiliar varieties in Anne's garden.

"We owe a great debt to the Orient for contributing this beauty to the world," Anne said, cradling a large, deep-red blossom in her hand. "Roses have always been such a part of my life that I find it hard to believe there was a time when they didn't exist."

Eugénie nodded, breathing in the rich scent of a multipetaled, ivory-colored bloom. The two women worked in companionable silence for several minutes, then Anne Tucker gasped, looking up at the sun's position.

"My word," she said, "the men should be back with growling bellies by this time. With the news of your arrival, no doubt there'll be some extra company along as well. Let's collect just a few more, then we'd best get back and tend to our hungry sailors."

Indeed, on their return, the house was brimming with people. Children's voices, raised in play, danced above the deeper male voices holding forth on a myriad of subjects. The women were clustered in age groups discussing preparations for the Tucker wedding. Eugénie overheard one woman discoursing on the necessity of including the governor's guard.

"Their bright coats will add just the right touch of color. They're such handsome young men and stand so beautifully." She appeared to be completely oblivious to the cool stares that met her words.

Dressed in a starched white jacket and carefully pressed britches, Ethan served a steady flow of drinks to the convivial crowd. Jeremy was in constant motion carrying out Ethan's orders. Female servants moved between the kitchen and the broad veranda replenishing platters and trays, their brightly colored calicos floating in and out like fluttering butterflies' wings. Satisfied with the smooth functioning of her household, Anne Tucker guided Eugénie through the crowd and made introductions. She described and defined each person by parish and family antecedents.

By the time people began to drift off to their sloops, whalers, dinghies, and other seacraft, Eugénie felt as though her head were swimming with names and intertwined relationships. Butterfield, Jennings, Cox, Trimingham, Darrell, Smith, Dill, Harvey, and on and on and on. Most of the men, it seemed, were engaged in shipping or were investors, to some degree, in trade.

With so many of their men at sea for such long stretches of time, the women appeared to Eugénie to be far more self-sufficient and independent than their European or even their Southern American counterparts. It was not unusual, she learned, for these women to be responsible for running their households, maintaining their properties, and overseeing the family store that sold the cargo from their ships.

The stores, she found out, were open for certain hours each day and certain days a week, depending on how successful the voyages had been. The cargo from the voyages was stored as well as sold from the family warehouse, which was either on the ground floor of the family home or in a separate structure on the waterfront. Sometimes a very valuable cargo was dispersed amongst several warehouses so that, if word came that the "Searchers," as the customs agents were called, were planning a raid, the smaller quantities of goods could be moved easily to a new location, once again thwarting the agents.

St. George was regaling Eugénie with just such a story as they sat finishing their drinks on the veranda. She laughed at his description of furtive creatures sneaking about playing an adult game of hide-and-seek. The Colonel, who was coming up the stairs, came over to join them. He slapped his son on the back. "Filling our guest's ears with the local lore, are you, son? There are endless tales about us upstanding citizens leading the Searchers on a merry chase. Don't always come out on the winning side, though, truth be known, but often enough to keep us interested. One such time, a cousin of ours, in his haste to elude the customs net, underestimated the tides and ran afoul of the shallows, getting himself and his craft well and fully stuck. He had no choice but to ditch the lot. He spent the next week, much to his displeasure and loss of pride, spending considerable coin paying divers to reclaim his losses. He never did come out on the winning side of that one. Soured him a bit. Didn't seem to have the same gusto for the game, after that. 'Tis not an exercise for the faint of heart, this stuff."

Still in a conversational tone, he continued, "This evening, Miss Eugénie, there'll be some menfolk stopping by to share a pipe and a port. We'd greatly appreciate it if you'd join us and give us the benefit of your observations about the American colonies."

Caught off guard by the abrupt change of subject, Eugénie nevertheless replied smoothly, "Colonel Tucker, you overestimate my knowledge, but you're welcome to whatever small contribution I can make."

The Colonel gave her a long look and then said jovially, "Isolated as we are here, young lady, we're starved for news. Anything, however insignificant it may seem to you, could be of great consequence to us." He appeared to be about to say more but was interrupted by a group of Harveys who came over at that moment to bid their adieus.

XXI

❧❧❧

The last of the sun was fading from the deep indigo sky as twilight crept across the horizon. She had always enjoyed this time of day, Eugénie thought. She listened to the night sounds of birds seeking their nests and the rustling of small animals in the underbrush, as nature's creatures settled down for the night. She could faintly hear the low hum of the servants' voices and the rattle and clatter of dishes, pots, and pans coming from the kitchen building.

She knew that Colonel Tucker's guests had begun to arrive. She was thankful for the few quiet minutes she had to collect her thoughts and prepare herself before she went to join them. The light from the house illuminated the yard, and she walked easily amongst the shrubs, drinking in the scents released by the evening air. She plucked a spray of night-scenting jasmine, absently sniffing its heady smell. She smiled as the star-shaped flower tickled her nose.

With a sigh, she turned back toward the house, knowing the time had come to make her appearance. As she walked around the side of the building, she heard the cricket population striking up its nightly chorus. Torches and chairs had been arranged in a circular fashion on the lawn. Colonel Tucker and his friends were already enjoying their port. Young Jeremy was ceremoniously presenting each guest with a packed clay pipe and, with a flourish, lighting each with a flint contraption.

Does that child ever sleep? Eugénie thought as Jeremy completed his rounds and scampered off in the direction of the house to carry out a request from one of the guests. Looking around the group puffing in different rhythms on their glowing pipes, Eugénie thought that the gathering looked innocent enough. Just a group of neighbors who'd come together to share a warm spring evening.

"Miss Eugénie, how kind of you to join us," Colonel Tucker said, as she walked forward. At his words, the men rose to their feet in unison. The Colonel introduced her around the circle. Eugénie was relieved that she could remember some of the names and just about all of the faces. The group was made up of the four Tucker sons, several Tucker relatives, and neighbors related closely through ties of shipping and trade. Having completed the pleasantries and settled Eugénie into the chair next to him with a glass of claret, the Colonel immediately broached the subject uppermost in everyone's mind.

"We've been discussing the serious dilemma facing Bermuda. That is to say, the Americans' quarrel with the Crown and the possibility of an American embargo of our trade. We've been considering all the angles. Mr. Harvey, here, points out that even if we can manage to per-suade the Americans not to embargo us, and we continue to bring in the necessary foodstuffs from the mainland to Bermuda, it'll mean that we'll be sailing against our own. You see, if we're considered to be adversaries, we can be seized as contraband. If they can catch us, that is. We're used to outrunning the French—pardon me, Miss Eugénie—as well as the Spanish, the Dutch, and all the rest of 'em, but it'll take some getting used to, to see the Union Jack and have to make a run for it."

Mon Dieu! Eugénie mentally shook her head. He's more concerned about the inconvenience of outrunning his fellow countrymen than becoming an outlaw. What madness is this?

"Now, John Cox, on the other hand, points out that since we're so close geographically to the American colonies and have members of our families who live on the mainland, not to mention the relation-ships we've developed over the years, it might seem a natural step to join in their fight." At Eugénie's startled expression, he continued, "We've agreed to lay out all our cards on the table for you. Otherwise, you won't be able to evaluate the situation or understand the extreme nature of what we're up against here. John's point of view is not as outlandish as it sounds. It's just plain foolishness to think that we aren't bound to be caught up in the fray, one way or another. Strategically, we're a hazard to the Americans if we remain attached to the British Crown. Under the circumstances, none of us thinks it's far-fetched to imagine that they'll have no choice but to invade us and neutralize us, if not take us over. The danger of invasion is a real one.

"Another choice is to sit back and seek aid from Britain: food supplies, warships to protect our shores, and so forth." He raised his hands in a flapping motion to quell the negative mutterings that met this suggestion. "Past experience suggests that the chances of receiving this aid and sustenance is about as likely as expecting ol' St. Nick to pop out of that bottle of rare port sitting over there on the table."

When the chuckles and laughter subsided, he continued, "As far as we can figure out, that about sums up our choices. Either we sit on our bums—you'll pardon the expression, Miss Eugénie—and hope for a miracle, or we throw in our lot with the Americans and fight for freedom from the Crown. Or, we come up with some plan to encourage the Americans to resist embargoing our trade. I grant you, each of these alternatives has its drawbacks. Are there any other choices I've overlooked?"

The Colonel looked around the circle. Silence stretched out as the men pondered the ends of their clay pipes or stared into their goblets. Finally, a Smith broke the tense stillness. "'Tis been a little over two weeks since the hostilities began. Maybe our best course for the time being is to let it play out a little longer and see how the Americans' fortunes go. In the meantime, young Harry here is in an excellent position to keep us informed of Governor Bruère's plans and any correspondence that arrives from Whitehall."

Well, I surely am amongst my own, Eugénie thought wryly. We're all of us agents and spies here. Somehow the thought did not give her a sense of well-being. Quite the opposite.

"But how long can we hold out, man?" a voice from the other side of the circle called out. "All our stores are depleted already. I lost two ships and valuable cargo over the winter in those infernal storms off Newfoundland. And recently the Goodrich scum waylaid a third, and they claim loyalty to the Crown. Out for themselves, more like it," the man added, grumbling.

At the mention of Goodrich, Eugénie was careful to keep her face expressionless. Other voices joined in, adding the losses and disasters they'd suffered. Their descriptions were so vivid that Eugénie could almost see the broken ships and waterlogged cargo and hear the screams of the drowning victims.

Colonel Tucker broke through the jumble of voices. "We're in accord on that subject, at least. We suffer losses in the best of times. Present circumstances promise more of the same. That is precisely the reason we're all here tonight. Muttering amongst ourselves serves no purpose. We must have a plan, and there's no time to spare. It will call for courage and deadly intent. Now is not the time to be squeamish. To the vote, then." His voice never rose a note, but his tone demanded attention and restored order. Eugénie saw that the men in the circle hung on his every word.

"First, it's hard to argue with Mr. Smith's words. Waiting and seeing is a wise course, so long as we remain active and alert while we wait and see. Are all in agreement on this point?" He was answered by a wave of "Ayes" from the group. "Good, then, we have a beginning. I understand this first vote to mean that, for the time being . . ." He paused over the last words for emphasis and then went on, "we'll neither join the Americans, nor will we sit back on our, uh, heels awaiting providence. Am I accurately stating our wishes?" Again, his words were met with a round of "Ayes."

"Then it's apparent to me that we've arrived at the middle course. That is to say, we'll seek some means to persuade the Americans not to embargo our ships and trade." The chorus of "Ayes" came on cue this time without his encouragement. "We'll have to choose a persuasive tool to accomplish this. As the good book says, 'Seek and ye shall find.' May I hear suggestions?"

At once the men started throwing out ideas that, though plentiful, were quickly scotched as useless, too far-fetched, or in some way inadequate. Then Mr. Trimingham, an exceptionally successful shipper and merchant, spoke up.

"'Pears to me we should narrow our considerations to things that would promote the Americans' success in battle. To begin with, what are their shortages?" A skeptical murmur rose from the group. "Hear me out!" he said sharply. "All night we've been talking about our needs and our fears. To bargain effectively with them, we must put ourselves in their shoes. What are their needs?"

"I believe I see your line of thought, laddie," Colonel Tucker interrupted. From his expression and tone, Eugénie had the strong suspicion that the Colonel did indeed know where Trimingham was headed and that he had spent the whole evening manipulating the discussion to arrive at this very point.

"If I'm following you correctly," Colonel Tucker said, "we must assemble a list of things that our American cousins need to carry out their objective. In other words, the materials of war."

Never let it be said that the Colonel is not the consummate showman, Eugénie thought, and an articulate showman at that.

Now clear on the concept, the men poured forth suggestions like quartermasters outfitting a war machine.

"Ships! Guns! Men! Foodstuffs! Gunpowder! Uniforms! Horses!"

"We can eliminate certain ones of these right off," one voice spoke up. "We're short of foodstuffs ourselves. That's what got us started on this whole thing to begin with—that, and protecting our shipping and trade interests. I see no means of our supplying uniforms. As for horses, I hear tell that Miss Eugénie has sent a whole shipload back to France. Now, just maybe she'd be generous enough to divert them back to the patriots in our name to help our cause."

"'Tis not appropriate or seemly to indulge in quips at this time," Colonel Tucker said sternly. "Most especially at the expense of my guest, who has kindly agreed to give us the benefit of her knowledge and who also resides under my roof. This is a serious business confronting each and every one of us, and should be dealt with in such a fashion. Those who think otherwise are free to leave." No one stirred. Everyone carefully avoided looking at their reprimanded neighbor.

"Then let's get on with this. It's getting late. We've listed accurately all the tools of battle, most of which are beyond our ability to supply to the Americans, as our friend pointed out. It's hardly our intent to ingratiate ourselves to the Americans by bankrupting ourselves in the bargain. We can't afford to bulk up their nonexistent navy by handing over our ships to them, but we can increase the output at our shipyards and offer them for sale. We have no foodstuffs to spare. Horses are a scarce commodity here on Bermuda. I doubt that even Governor Bruère would fail to notice if our good wives and sisters suddenly took to making uniforms, even if we had the materials to do so. If we start supplying men to their battles, that will be an altogether different kettle of fish. As for guns, swords, and the like," he said, waving his hand in a deprecating fashion, "I doubt that we have enough in good working order, as it is, to protect our own.

"We've come up with a good list, but, as you can see, all the items but one either would cost us dear or aren't in sufficient quantity to be of interest to the Americans. There is only one that's available to us, will cost us no coin from our own pockets, and is of desperate need to them. It is, without a doubt, the most dangerous of all the items we've mentioned." He paused for effect. "I speak of gunpowder. The gunpowder that, even as we speak, nestles in the magazine up in St. George's."

The stunned silence that met his words soon exploded into a raging argument between those who denounced the idea, horrified that it was mentioned even in the safety of the group, and those who praised the ingenious nature of such a simple solution.

"Simple it may be," one man said angrily. "And simple you are if you don't see that such a plan places our necks squarely in the hangman's noose!" During the melee, the Colonel motioned to St. George to replenish the empty goblets and tankards.

"I think we could all use a respite to wet our whistles," he said, unruffled by the storm that raged around him. During the lull that followed, Eugénie looked around the circle, assessing which attitude would prevail. She had no doubt that these men, carefully picked by the Colonel, would protect if not go along with whatever plan he conceived, no matter how extreme. Whatever transpired after this evening, they were witnesses to the plot and therefore conspirators in it. These were pragmatic, no-nonsense men who knew that their attendance was tantamount to signing a compact of collusion.

"Now that we've had a moment to refresh and reflect, let us proceed," Colonel Tucker said calmly. "The idea put forward is simply a suggestion. It's now on the table to examine, test, assess, and ultimately decide upon. The stakes are high. None of us here would impetuously risk his life or that of his family or his neighbor. Should we decide to act on this suggestion, it'll be undertaken only with the greatest caution. We must first find out if such an offer is of interest to the Americans. Mr. Silas Deane is here on the island. He's a good place to start that investigation. If that discussion is met with the enthusiasm that I expect, then we must determine how the actual transfer can be carried out, minimizing the risk to us as much as possible.

"You have all met Miss Eugénie Devereux. I imagine each of you wonders why she is with us this evening. There's much you don't know about this unusual young lady," he said, smiling at her. All eyes focused on him as he described Eugénie's pedigree and her journey from France to the American colonies and now to Bermuda.

Eugénie struggled to keep her face impassive. She felt like one of the horses presented on the block at the Whittingtons' auction. She felt exploited, exposed, and angry. All the fears she had expressed to Marie that morning ran through her mind. She understood his purpose, at least in part, and she couldn't help admiring his tactic. By describing her in such a fashion, he was vouching for her and proclaiming to this group that her investment was no less than theirs. She was on an equal footing with them. He was including her in their inner sanctum. Now, she, like they, had a stake in the outcome. After that night, no one could act to protect himself unless it ensured the protection of all, nor could anyone in the group risk the welfare of the others. She had not asked for this, and probably, had he asked, she would have been adamantly opposed. But now it was done, and perhaps it was a protection of sorts, at least for the time being.

The Colonel concluded by saying, "Miss Eugénie, you've been kind to join us this evening. We'd be grateful for any knowledge you have about the situation in the American colonies." Earlier in the evening, Eugénie had been quite aware of the curious looks directed her way. Then she noticed the curiosity change to wariness. At this point the looks were downright suspicious, if not hostile, in spite of the Colonel's introduction.

Eugénie nodded to Colonel Tucker and gazed around the circle of men. She decided what she must do if she were to have a chance of carrying out the objectives of her French constituency. She must throw in her lot with these men and somehow gain their trust. Taking a deep breath, she launched into a summary of the events that had led to the patriots' decision to fight for their independence. She underlined their commitment and baldly stated their own assessment of the pitfalls and shortages that faced them.

As she continued to speak she could feel a change in the group's manner toward her and see a reluctant acceptance, even admiration, on some faces. Perhaps she could salvage the mission after all.

She finished by saying, "I may have begun this journey for reasons of my own that had nothing whatsoever to do with the betterment of mankind or any other such lofty thought. The American patriots may have started down this path with only the intent of resisting a series of taxes, levied at a distance, to pay off a debt not of their making. That has changed dramatically over the last few months. Now, there is a new and fierce dedication that has carried them to another plane. No one can walk amongst them or listen to their words and not know that they and those who aid and succor them are joined together as instruments of destiny, a destiny that transcends the meager needs of survival.

The world is bearing witness to a people who have come together to create a natural order for mankind, be he pauper or king, loftier than any that has been conceived of or attempted by the minds and hands of men. They seek far more than mere independence. They seek freedom to create a system of self-government."

Eugénie's voice did not falter as she described the truths as she saw them. Her words carried such conviction that those listening felt the presence of the colonials standing before them. "These people, these patriots," she continued, "have sought out the very best amongst them to draw up a political philosophy, a social contract, based on the great thinkers in history. They're undertaking what Mr. Thomas Jefferson calls a 'grand experiment.' I often heard him say that he and the other architects of this plan have gleaned political wisdom as far back as Plato and Aristotle and, more recently, John Locke, Edmund Burke, Jean-Jacques Rousseau, and others of the present day. In fact, it was Burke's words he quoted when last I heard him speak, when he said, 'People crushed by law have no hopes but from power. If laws are their enemies, they will be enemies to laws; and those, who have much to hope and nothing to lose, will always be dangerous, more or less.'

"I devoutly believe," Eugénie continued, "that Mr. Jefferson and the other political thinkers and writers wouldn't have chosen to fight had they thought there were any other recourse left to them. But now that they have chosen this course, I see nothing in their nature that suggests that they'll back down until they have spent their last shell and shed their last drop of blood. I believe beyond a shadow of a doubt that their commitment and conviction are absolute."

She smiled, breaking the spell that her words had cast on them. Speaking softly, she finished saying, "You've taken me into your confidence this night. I will respect and protect that trust." No one spoke, and Colonel Tucker let the silence stretch out for a few moments.

"We will do no less," he said. "This night, the warp and weft of a single fabric has been woven amongst us. We're bound together by a shared knowledge and a shared commitment. As we look ahead, it behooves each of us to consider the words of Thomas Paine, another patriot, who said, 'The summer soldier and the sunshine patriot will, in this crisis, shrink from the service of their country; but he that stands it now deserves the love and thanks of men and women.' I thank you, Miss Eugénie. I think we can call it a night."

XXII

❧❧❧

Sleep came slowly to Eugénie that night. Her dreams were peopled with shadowy figures giving her messages she couldn't understand.

She found herself in an unfamiliar landscape that seemed threatening to her. Looking about, she could find no reason for her fears. But the feelings persisted. A faceless form emerged from the gloom and beckoned her to continue along the path in front of her. Eugénie started to obey, when, to her horror, the ground before her fell away, and suddenly she was standing on the edge of a steep precipice. Far below, she could see turbulent waters crashing on jagged rocks and boulders.

She awoke with a start, chilled to the bone.

Slipping out of bed, she went to the highboy in search of something to put around her shoulders. She selected a silk-fringed woolen shawl. Settling it snugly about her, she crept beneath the sheets once more, pulling them tightly up to her chin.

What do you expect, you ninny? she chided herself, trying to take her mind off her chattering teeth. The path you've been on since you left France has been dangerous enough, but your attendance at last night's meeting and your own words have placed you on the brink of an abyss. The dream just laid it out for you. This island's people have not survived this long by taking a passive role in their own welfare. It's a dangerous game they've been playing with the governor, sailing their ships according to English law only as long as it suited their purposes. Now Colonel Tucker and his cohorts have even more at stake and will go to any lengths to protect their own interests. And they've made you a part of it.

As she wrestled with these and other dismal thoughts, she noticed the gray light of early dawn chasing the darkness from the room. Thank God, morning is here, she thought. Somehow things always look better in daylight.

It was a cheerful face that greeted Marie a few minutes later when she came to rouse her mistress. It took little time for Eugénie to inform Marie of all that had happened at the meeting.

"Have you learned anything more about the Bermudians' loyalties?" she asked Marie when she had finished her account.

"No, only what I've already mentioned," Marie answered. "It's clear that The Grove is the center for those who bristle under Governor Bruère's tight rein. There's a strong faction that supports the governor, but they're far less organized and hold few positions of influence. I gather that it's less a matter of loyalty for one side or the other than it's a matter of how the Bermudians feel about their freedom and the degree to which they think it's being affected. If they think their livelihood and welfare are being imposed upon, then they'll take action to prevent it. Bermudians may differ on many things, but they share a fiercely independent nature. To them, a distant Whitehall is far better than the impositions of a people a few hundred miles from their shore."

"Marie, I warrant that the 'independent spirit' you speak of was the reason for my troubled sleep. From the start, I've been concerned for us, but now we're surrounded by those who may become increasingly heedless of our safety should they perceive that we place theirs in peril. Last night I felt like a hare in the midst of the hounds. I don't know whether it was that I was French, that I was a woman, or simply that I was a stranger, but my presence was very unpalatable to them, with the exception of Colonel Tucker, of course."

"It's probably a bit of all three," Marie replied, "although, from what I've seen, our sex doesn't appear to suffer particularly from any form of inequality on this island. Your presence breached their secrecy. It's probably as simple as that. Under the circumstances, it would be cause to worry had they not shown such wariness."

"Well, the precedent for my attendance at their meetings has been set. *De l'eau est sous le pont,*" Eugénie said, taking the pragmatic view. "*Certainement,* after last night there's no mystery about my identity. The harm's been done on both sides. Perhaps there's some protection for us in that."

Eugénie grabbed her head with both hands and exclaimed, "Oh, Marie, I don't know what to make of all of this. My mind just keeps going around in circles. Perhaps I'm being unduly concerned."

"Only time will tell, Mistress. I wouldn't fret too much just yet. But it's been our experience on this mission, as my sainted mother has so often said, that 'chance favors the prepared mind.'"

"Yes, only time will tell," Eugénie agreed. "For now, we've made all the preparations we can. Having said that, my concern about our safety heightens with each passing day. I won't take an easy breath until we're once more on French soil.

"Come. Let's turn our minds to more pleasant things. *S'il vous plaît,* help me into these things. After breaking our fast, St. George has promised to give me my first lesson in those quaint, little boats they call dinghies."

Eugénie didn't appear to have a care in the world when she greeted St. George on the dock. The sun shone warmly and the wind was brisk on the Great Sound as he took her through the steps of mastering the small craft.

"'Pears to me you're a natural at this, Eugénie," St. George said, smiling at her after she again took the little boat through the wind and continued to hold the course he had set for her. She noticed he had fallen back into the Bermudian speech pattern. "I vow, by May twenty-fourth, Bermuda Day, when the waters are declared fit for bathing and we begin our old Bermuda tradition of the fitted-dinghy races, you'll be ready as can be and leading the fleet. From the skills you've shown this morn, you'll soon be ready to take this little craft out through the cut and test your talents on the open sea!"

"Oh, St. George, you flatter me," Eugénie answered. She chuckled, thinking of the many hours she had spent at the helm of *The White Heather* under the instruction of that ship's captain, a fact she chose not to share with her current skipper.

"Surely," she continued, "outside of the protection of the harbor the seas and currents must be considerably more challenging."

"Well, as long as you remain in the lee of the land, the feel is very much the same," St. George said. "Should a sudden squall come up or if you stray too near the reefs, that's an altogether different story. See here, we're already passing Scaur Hill. In no time we'll be at Watford. There's no time like the present to try out your skills on the open waters. We'll sail through to Mangrove Bay. Then, 'tis only a short distance from there to the ocean."

"Oh, St. George, your confidence in me leaves me breathless, but I'm ready if you are." Eugénie's eyes sparkled with the challenge.

In no time they were skimming across Mangrove Bay. For the first time that day, Eugénie wished she could slow the speed of the small boat so that she could watch the bird population noisily foraging in the high-water grasses and inspect the rich overgrowth of mangroves that grew in a wild tangle right to the water's edge. The boat skimmed over the water's surface. The forward motion lifted Eugénie's hair and dried the moisture that had formed at the base of her neck and trickled down between her breasts.

They tacked around the upper finger of Mangrove Bay, the only spit of land that separated the harbor from the ocean beyond. Eugénie's spirits soared as she watched a longtail swooping high above them like a beacon leading them on to infinity. Out of sheer high spirits, she whooped with laughter. Her sudden movement in the stern of the boat sent the craft into such wild gyrations that the little vessel was saved from capsizing only by St. George's quick reactions.

"The first rule aboard ship is to keep your center of gravity low and your movements deliberate." His words sobered Eugénie. "Other than

that near-disaster," St. George continued, "I applaud your performance. I had the same reaction the first time I skippered one of these
tiny boats out onto this vast ocean. The horizon stretches out forever,
and, on a day like this, the sky reaches all the way to heaven." His eyes,
as they turned to gaze on her face, matched the blue of the sky above
them. Their color deepened and an expression appeared in their
depths that caused Eugénie quickly to look for a way to distract him.

"Dear St. George," she said, keeping her tone light, "considering
that I nearly plunged us both into the sea a good three weeks ahead of
Bermuda Day, you're generosity itself." Her words had the desired
effect of breaking the awkward moment. "That's enough excitement
for one day. The last moments have left me with my heart in my
throat. I'd be eternally grateful if you'd take the tiller and guide us to
the nearest bit of shore where we can enjoy this lovely basket of good-
ies while we still have an appetite."

Very deliberately, they exchanged places in the boat and St. George
pointed the craft toward shore. They were soon nearing a wide
expanse of beach. Running the bow of the boat up onto the sand, St.
George rolled his britches well above his knees and hopped over the
side. Once he had steadied himself and the boat, he reached up to Eugénie, who gratefully accepted his gallant offer to carry her to shore.

Eugénie spread out a striped cloth on the startlingly white sand and
soon they were enjoying tangy goat cheese, spread generously on
thick, crusty bread still warm from The Grove's oven.

"Eugénie, did my father's unorthodox manner last evening upset
you?" St. George asked without preamble as he sipped the fine claret
from the Tuckers' cellar. "I worried about it, but you seemed to take it
well in stride."

"I appreciate your concern," Eugénie said, smiling at him. Their
friendship was such that they did not hesitate to speak openly with
each other. "I must admit that I was amazed that your father included
me in such a close-knit group and then proceeded to discuss me at
such length and in such detail. Moreover, I was astonished that he and
the others were so forthcoming in front of a stranger—and a woman

at that," she concluded. She was surprised to see her hands shaking as she added a slice of capon to her bread and cheese. She wasn't sure whether it was anger, fear, or both.

"Father is the recognized leader of the group, as I'm sure you surmised. They've been meeting in such a manner for as long as I can remember to discuss mutual concerns about trade and the shipping business. As for last night, I understand your reactions. I believe Father had a specific purpose for what he did. Unfortunately, there was no way to do it without putting you on the spot. It was his way of vouching for you. Your unique position cancels any worry that the others might have had about your nationality and why you're here. As for your being a woman, my dearest Eugénie, there's not a man alive that doesn't rejoice in the Lord's gift of you to mankind," he said, his eyes speaking eloquently of his own appreciation of that gift.

Clearing his throat and averting his eyes, he continued more evenly, "Were you a West-Ender heading a lucrative shipping business, woman or not, no doubt you would've long since been in their ranks. Father caught everyone off guard with his suggestion about the gunpowder. Believe me, that was much more the cause of their disquiet than having you thrust into their midst." He paused as he caught his lower lip between his teeth and chewed on it thoughtfully. After a moment he continued. "I wager, by the end of this day, Father will have already received word about how Mr. Silas Deane reacted to our overtures on the subject. I don't know whom Father entrusted with that assignment, but I know that it will have been carried out with alacrity."

"Wouldn't such a *liaison* with the patriots compromise the group's independence?" Eugénie asked. "Mightn't it even pull them into the conflict? And what would Governor Bruère and the others on the island close to the British Crown make of even the slightest hint of such an action?"

"Those were my concerns precisely," St. George nodded. "Which is why I took the earliest opportunity to address these questions to my father this morning. He put my concerns to rest by reminding me that the exchange we are considering is simply a matter of expediting a business necessity and holds out not one jot of a promise beyond that. He said that furthermore, when he broaches the subject with their Commander-in-Chief, General Washington, he'll define the limits of the association. We don't appreciate any assumptions or presumptions on our freedoms. 'Tis why we may well be willing to go to such lengths to maintain our trade. As to your last concern, we're past masters at concealing our movements and plans from the government. We have all the more reason, considering the extent of risk involved, to practice utmost discretion." Eugénie could hear the Colonel's reasoning, if not his very words, in St. George's answer. But her skepticism was tempered little by his assurance that the oligarchy could elude the British governor on the one hand while soliciting the patriots' cooperation on the other. Seeing nothing to be gained by pursuing the subject, Eugénie turned their conversation to the upcoming nuptials.

"It'll be a joyful day all around, that one," St. George said, chuckling. "They've been the light of each other's eyes long since, and they have the blessings of both families, since their union binds together two thriving shippers. All in all, a good day's work."

Eugénie, who had been absentmindedly sifting the soft white sand through her fingers, gasped suddenly, "Oh, St. George, it must be getting late! We've not a moment to lose. Your mother kindly delayed making the bride's and groom's cakes until we returned so that I could take part in the tradition. Come, we must hurry back."

"Set your mind at ease," St. George reassured her. "You've only missed the preparations for the preparations, if that. I'll have you at the dock with plenty of time to spare."

His words proved correct. When Eugénie arrived at the kitchen, she found all the servants were just assembling at their stations. No commander in the field has ever held the attention of his troops more closely than Anne does at this moment, Eugénie thought as she watched her guide them through the painstaking steps of the tradition-steeped procedure.

Anne Tucker explained that even the slightest deviation from the strict observance of the custom could put the future happiness of the couple in jeopardy. In between her instructions, she elaborated on the traditions of Bermuda weddings to Eugénie. "Weddings last for three days or longer. There's much music and dancing. The young people will deck their favorites with rosemary, the symbol of love and faithfulness. There's always at least rummy punch and pipes of tobacco, if not a more expanded feast of some sort. Although it's still infrequent, we're beginning to see a wedding ring included as part of the ceremony. Until recently, such a thing was unthinkable since it was considered to be the height of popishness. Anything that smacks of Rome is very much looked down on, you know, by most Protestants.

"We continue the time-out-of-mind custom of separate batters. There are other interpretations, but it's commonly held that the bride's fruitcake will bring her fruitfulness and the groom's pound cake represents the weightiness of his obligation."

As the last stages of the cakes' decorations were carried out, the sprinkling of silver dust for the maid's dowry and gold dust for the young man's future prospects were added to the appropriate cake. The afternoon light glinted off the cakes' surfaces.

"'Tis not only Mother's position as close kin that caused Auntie to choose her to prepare the cakes!" Elizabeth exclaimed, beaming at the two splendid examples of her mother's housewifely skills. "Mother's known for the artistry of her wedding cakes."

Anne Tucker clucked her tongue but looked pleased nonetheless. "Now, for the last," she said, bringing forth a basket of trailing English ivy and a pot that held a small, feathery seedling. Draping the groom's cake with the ivy, Anne explained, "Ivy isn't always used, but I think it adds a lovely touch. If we adhere to the old beliefs, it'll ensure the young man's faithfulness, clinging to the marriage vows as closely as the tendrils of the ivy cling to a solid wall. And now for the *pièce de résistance*," she said, winking at Eugénie. "Lizzie, if you'll carve out the center of the bride's cake, we'll be ready to place this cedar seedling in its proper position.

"You see, Eugénie, when the first people arrived in 1609, these islands were blanketed with Bermuda cedar. It wasn't long before the cedar was being cut down right and left, in part to clear the land to build houses, in part to make just about anything you can imagine— ships, boats, flooring, doors, framing, fence rails, utensils, plates, cups, furniture of all kinds.

"The early houses, or cabbens, were built of cedar, too, until the first hurricane hit and blew them all out to sea. After that it was proclaimed that no more houses were to be built of cedar. That's when those resourceful early settlers discovered how good the limestone that lay just below the soil was as building material. But back to the cedar. By the end of the 1600s, many stands of the cedar had been devastated." Here, she stopped to give Elizabeth instructions and then continued.

"Where was I? Oh, yes. The governor at the time, wise man that he was, saw that the cedar, which had been the salvation of the island and its only valuable resource, would become extinct if things kept going the way they were going. So he put a stop to the rampant destruction of the forests. From then on Bermudians have protected the trees just as the trees had protected the Bermudians in their time of need. Now, there's plenty of cedar, if used judiciously, for furniture, ships, and building materials. In the last century, whole stands were fired to kill the rat population brought ashore by the ships. Can you imagine? That's long since been outlawed.

"From the time of that wise governor—you probably thought I'd never get to the point of all this—a cedar seedling has graced the bride's cake, signifying longevity, strength, and endurance. After the wedding ceremony, the guests accompany the bride and groom to their new home and witness the new married couple planting the little seedling. The idea is that it and they together will grow and flourish, so that one day their children, their grandchildren, and on and on will play beneath its boughs. You may have noticed ours in the back yard. Its greens have decorated many a Christmas table at The Grove.

"Now, my goodness, all my talk and everyone's holding their breath waiting for the final touch." Anne smiled warmly at Eugénie. "If you would be so kind, Eugénie, I would take it as a special favor if you'd place the seedling. I'd consider it particularly propitious for the young people's future joy and happiness."

"Anne, I would be honored," Eugénie answered. Taking the little pot from Anne's outstretched hands, Eugénie carefully placed the seedling in the center of the cake. Everyone clapped delightedly.

"Mother, this time you've even outdone yourself!" Elizabeth announced.

"Thank you, dear child," Anne beamed at her daughter. "I think just a bit more gold and silver, and we'll be done." As the last dusting settled over the cakes, Anne stepped back and clasped her hands together. "They're indeed beautiful, if I say so myself!"

XXIII

❧❧❧

The week leading up to the wedding was a frenzy of activity at The Grove. Guests arrived by boat in droves. The wharf was soon crowded with every variety of small craft.

Eugénie learned firsthand that the Bermudians were a high-spirited group who enjoyed their food, drink, dancing, and music in equal measure. There was rarely a moment of the day that she couldn't hear a fiddle somewhere on the property.

In spite of the merrymaking, preparations for the wedding moved steadily forward under Anne Tucker's resolute direction. It seemed that only the weather was beyond her command. That subject was seldom far from everyone's thoughts. No one passed through the dayroom at The Grove without a quick glance at the weather-forecasting shark oil in the glass beaker.

Midweek, St. George found himself at loose ends and sought out Eugénie's company. He finally discovered her in the flower garden where, on Anne's orders, she was plaiting flower stems together into a garland that would decorate the wedding pair's dinghy on the important day.

"Dear Eugénie, have mercy on me and give me a few minutes of your time," he implored her. "Surely your nimble fingers deserve a few moments' rest from Mother's demands."

"Ah, St. George," Eugénie said, laughing at his baleful expression.

"These nimble fingers, such as they are, have been tangling more than plaiting for the last few minutes." Eugénie stretched and tossed her head back to relieve her tight muscles. Looking up, she saw less-than-friendly clouds hovering to the east.

Following her glance, St. George said, "Had I known better, I'd swear that Mother has even leashed the weather spirits to her will. See the clouds as they hang there? They'll soon be blown down the island away from us. By evening, St. George's will suffer their sprinkles and we'll feel nary a drop. In general, Port Royal and Somerset are sunnier than most other places on the island because here the wind is from the southwest. The island runs south-west, north-east, and so when it heats up and the clouds form out over Gibbs Hill, over the ridge of Bermuda, they head down that way and tend to rain in the middle and eastern parishes a bit more than they do in Somerset, you see." Eugénie wasn't at all sure she did see, but nodded in agreement since she was in no position to question this bit of local knowledge.

With an abrupt change of subject, St. George said, "I heard one of Father's friends speaking again about the possibility of invasion by the Americans." At Eugénie's startled expression, he continued, "It might not be such a far-fetched notion. Bermuda might do well to look to her defenses."

"Surely, the patriots wouldn't divide their attentions, considering the enormity of what they already face," Eugénie said.

"As you know, the significance of Bermuda lies in her strategic geographic position," St. George answered, "standing as she does within a few leagues of the route from the Caribbean and the British southern colonies. She's also a link between the northern colonies and the West Indies. Should the patriots believe that Whitehall might stage an attack on them using Bermuda as the base of operations, they might well choose to have the advantage of holding Bermuda in their own hands rather than leaving her to become a part of Whitehall's battle plans. 'Twould serve my purposes well, should the Americans seek to link with Bermuda. Whatever the outcome of this war, I plan to make my life in Virginia. She's won my heart long since. For others it may be a matter of intellect or purse. For me it's a matter of the heart."

Eugénie turned their conversation to a lighter vein while tucking away these shocking bits of information. At that moment, a calico cat came tearing around the corner of the house with Jeremy in hot pursuit, yelling at the top of his lungs. "Damme! Damme!" He cried, his voice loud with outrage. "Dat pesky cat done knocked over the shark awl, lappin' it up like hit was thick cream and I bein' responsible and all to the Mistress to keep the big eye on the awl day and night, so's we'd know the first inklin' of storm. She gonna skin me alive! Master George, please, oh please, hep me. Where'm I goin' to get some awl, so's I can fix things up befo' Mistress Tucker see's what's happened?"

St. George managed not to laugh. "Come along with me. We'll set things straight in no time." Eugénie smiled as she watched Jeremy trotting off at St. George's side, trying manfully to match his master's long stride. His equanimity restored, Jeremy looked up at his savior with adoration in his eyes.

Eugénie picked up the garland, glad to put her nervous fingers to good use. Invasion! *Mon Dieu!* Her mind shrieked, recoiling at the idea. Surely not! I didn't think it was a serious consideration when it was introduced at the Colonel's gathering. Could this rumor have originated with Mr. Silas Deane? I haven't heard of anyone else who's here from the colonies who's a member of the Americans' inner circle. And what purpose, but mischief, could such a rumor serve? Perhaps whoever is responsible is trying to further alienate the island from the mainland. Or maybe, if they know about Colonel Tucker's plans, to hasten them along. Ah, this wedding brings together all the opposing factions on the island. It looks like it's going to be nothing short of a tinderbox.

The comings and goings before the wedding appeared innocent enough to Eugénie, completely devoid of any unusual political overtones. Whatever storm was brewing seemed temporarily held in abeyance. True to St. George's predictions, the weather, too, remained mild, with brilliant blue skies and gentle winds.

On the eve of the wedding, the celebrations started with an elaborate feast and lively music. Eugénie was taking a well-earned respite after a particularly lively reel with one of the Tucker cousins when Colonel Tucker bore down on her with a distinguished-looking gentleman, dressed in full military regalia, in tow. "Ah, Miss Eugénie, how fortunate to find you," the Colonel said, beaming at her with a curious glint in his eyes. "Governor George James Bruère, may I present the Comtesse de Beaumont, Eugénie Devereux, who is residing with us on her way home to France after a successful sojourn in Virginia, where she purchased impressive bloodstock for the French racing syndicate." The governor bent low over Eugénie's hand. She read warmth and intelligence in the eyes that lifted to meet hers.

Eugénie curtsied gracefully. "Governor Bruère, it's a pleasure to meet you."

"My dear Comtesse, the pleasure is all mine. I heard of your kindness and generosity to my brother-governor in Virginia, who was quite smitten by your charms. Poor man, those were happier days. I received a report only recently that he's been driven from Williamsburg by the revolutionaries and must conduct his governing responsibilities aboard ship offshore." Eugénie struggled to maintain an expressionless demeanor in the face of the governor's almost indifferent delivery of such a report.

"I'm saddened to hear of his hardships," she replied quietly. "He was the soul of kindness to me."

"There are fine men on both sides of this conflict," the governor said, matching her tone. "As history has shown us, in times of war, actions are taken by men of conscience that would be repugnant to them under more normal circumstances."

Was there a veiled warning in those words? Eugénie wondered to herself, and if so, for whom? Out loud, she asked, "If I'm not mistaken, sir, your surname suggests you have ancestors that were countrymen of mine, *n'est-ce-pas?*"

"*Ah, oui,*" the governor answered, "*c'est vrai. Nous avons . . .*" At that moment, he was interrupted by the appearance of two little boys who ran up and wedged themselves between Colonel Tucker and Governor Bruère.

Eugénie saw at once their remarkable resemblance to the two men standing before her. "These must be your grandsons whom I've heard so much about," she said, smiling down at the two bright faces.

It was clear that both grandfathers were quite taken with the two little boys who were scampering in and out between the legs of their doting relatives. "Here, here," Colonel Tucker finally said as the two little ones threw themselves on the grass and began to wrestle with each other like two exuberant pups. "Masters Tucker, on your feet at once and pay your respects to our honored houseguest, Mademoiselle Devereux!"

His indulgent expression belied his stern words. Nevertheless, the two boys hopped quickly to their feet and proceeded to bob their heads and execute the prescribed bows in Eugénie's direction. Then, their obligation fulfilled, they turned, gave both grandfathers quick bear-cub hugs around the knees, and were off like two shots across the lawn.

"Please pardon them, Miss Eugénie," Colonel Tucker said. "We're all so delighted with Harry and Fanny's offspring, I fear we've gravely overlooked the matter of their comportment."

"If anyone is to blame for their unrestrained manner, we alone are the culprits," Governor Bruère agreed, smiling at his in-law. The two men nodded at each other, looking somewhat rueful. "It's beyond our power to do anything but indulge the lads. They're the light of our eyes."

Eugénie laughed. "They're utterly charming. And as my father always said, 'A little spoiling can't hurt if the stuff is there to begin with and if the stuff isn't there, well,' she gave an expressive Gallic shrug, 'then, a little spoiling won't make any difference anyway.'" The two men joined in her laughter.

"A wise man, your father," Governor Bruère said. "My thoughts exactly. Mistress Eugénie, I'd like to extend an invitation to you to visit me in St. George's during your stay."

Eugénie's mind moved quickly. This might be the very opportunity she was looking for to learn about sentiments at the other end of the island.

"Governor Bruère, I'm honored. It would be a pleasure to accept your invitation. As a matter of fact, I'd been thinking of joining Harry and your Fanny on their trip home after the wedding to enjoy the sights at the other end of the island. Would that suit you?"

"I can't think of a more opportune time. You'll all dine with me at Governor's House," the governor said gallantly.

Eugénie nodded and was about to speak when St. George arrived. "Ah, I've found you at last, Miss Eugénie, in the company of the dot-ing grandfathers." Linking his arm through hers, he continued, "No doubt, they've been bending your ear about the one subject they never tire of discussing and upon which they're in complete accord. Let me whisk you away for the next allemande before their praise of the two scamps sets your ears ringing, if they aren't already."

Bowing deeply to Eugénie, the governor said, "It's been a pleasure, milady. I look forward to entertaining you at Governor's House."

"Yes, yes," the Colonel agreed. "You young people run along and enjoy yourselves. We'll make do with a bit of Anne's own rummy-punch concoction. And a right good refreshment it is on this warm day, if I say so myself."

The day of the ceremony dawned clear and bright, promising the cou-ple a warm welcome into holy wedlock. Spirits were high amongst the assembled family, friends, honored guests, and servants. A great cheer went up the moment the clergyman pronounced the bride and groom man and wife. The young couple turned to each other and, lost to all around them, gazed deeply into each other's eyes. Linen handkerchiefs immediately appeared, dabbing at many pairs of eyes.

From where Eugénie stood, the couple was framed by the Great Harbor behind them. She captured in her mind's eye the beauty of the scene—the sky, the water, and the stand of cedar reaching to heaven on the distant shore. Her breath caught in her throat and her vision blurred, softening the edges of the bright day. She clasped her hands to her chest as she closed her eyes and took a deep breath, seeking to regain her composure.

"Mistress Devereux, are you ill?" The voice at her side abruptly brought Eugénie back to herself. She turned to see Silas Deane hovering solicitously. "Silas Deane, at your service."

Mustering a smile, Eugénie replied, "Mr. Deane, I thank you for your concern, but I'm quite all right. I lost myself for the moment in the happiness of the newly wedded couple and the beauty of this place and this day."

" 'Tis no wonder. It's an eloquent moment, to be sure," Silas Deane agreed. "I'm a far from sentimental man, but I found myself moved by the ceremony," he said, smiling briefly. "I understand that I almost had the pleasure of your company on the crossing from Virginia aboard John Tucker's ship. I've heard much about you. I'm delighted that our visit to this fascinating island coincided. I trust there were no ill effects from the unfortunate occurrence that befell that magnificent beast of yours. Have you had a chance to go horseback riding here?"

Eugénie managed to maintain a smooth demeanor as she wondered how he had such intimate knowledge of her and the events at the Whittingtons'. She also quickly squelched her unpleasant memory of him at the auction and replied smoothly, "Mr. Deane, our paths cross with such frequency, it would appear that we have many acquaintances in common. As for the roan, he's little the worse for the experience, but I daresay he'll be even more unruly by the time I have occasion to ride him again.

"He's now thoroughly accustomed to the rank indulgence he's enjoyed since his arrival. I've discovered, much to my surprise, that Bermudians have been transporting Virginian bloodstock to the island for some time. They hold them in such high regard that they treat them in a manner close to reverence. So far, I haven't had the opportunity to ride the roan. I understand that horseback riding is not particularly common here, given the scarcity and condition of the paths and byways. Indeed, I hear it's a prerequisite for safety to have a servant trailing along behind on foot in case an accident should occur on the rough terrain. Riding in Bermuda must be an adventure beyond any in my experience." She laughed at the image she conjured up of the fearless roan reduced to carefully picking his way along a path.

"But what of you?" Eugénie asked, seeking to shift his attention from her activities. "Will you be visiting long in Bermuda?"

"Ah, dear lady, circumstances may intercept the most carefully laid plans," he answered enigmatically. "I fear . . ." He stopped, as something over her shoulder caught his attention. His face suddenly tightened in anger.

Eugénie turned to see what had caused such a reaction. At first, she saw only the governor surrounded by members of the British regiment. As she watched, the group shifted. Suddenly she froze as she saw Darby talking closely with the man next to him. Then she saw the unmistakable profile of Bridger Goodrich bending in conversation to the upturned face of a dark-haired young woman entirely unfamiliar to Eugénie, but who bore a striking resemblance to Eugénie herself.

The shock of Darby's presence, combined with the appearance of Bridger and her look-alike, threw Eugénie completely off balance. By turns, she felt herself grow hot and cold. Her head swam and she staggered. She took a deep breath and let it out slowly. She was relieved to find herself still standing and the earth once more solid beneath her feet. She glanced at Silas Deane to see if he had noticed her dismay. He was too distracted himself to be aware of anything else.

He turned to Eugénie and said in harsh tones, "It's an outrage that Goodrich shows his face at this occasion and amongst the Tuckers!" At Eugénie's look of surprise, he continued, "He's a turncoat and an out-and-out ruffian. He and his kin have made no secret of their sudden antipathy for our cause and, as if that betrayal were not enough, they prey on our shipping, crippling and pillaging at will. There are even rumors that this one has been laying off Bermuda's shores singling out Tucker and other worthies' ships for his rapacious appetites. He's unconscionable! He deserts the land of his birth and has no compunction about turning on his supposed new allies. The sheer arrogance of presenting himself in their midst today! He's a thoroughgoing scoundrel. I've a mind to face him down and send him packing!"

Eugénie knew she must ward off a disastrous scene in which Silas Deane would most certainly come off the worse for wear. If he carried out his threat, the loving efforts of the Tucker clan would be reduced to ashes, the suspended political animosities would erupt from their fragile tinderbox, and the serenity of the day would be shattered beyond repair. "Mr. Deane, I don't doubt that all you say is true. Perhaps his attendance can be explained by his close friendship with St. George Tucker, whom I see standing nearby. The families' generous hospitality has brought together this day many who otherwise would not tolerate or seek out each other's company."

Eugénie paused, giving Silas Deane the time and the excuses the proud man needed to compose himself and pull back from an impetuous action that would have breached the very hospitality he sought to defend. "Miss Eugénie, I'm forever in your debt. I thank you for reminding me of this very special occasion, which even that unwelcome presence can't blemish. Your words have also reminded me of duties that I've been shirking." Bowing to her, he took his leave. The awkward moment had passed, and Eugénie was overcome with relief to be alone and to have the afternoon salvaged.

"He serves the patriots' cause well," she murmured to herself. "Perhaps I should put aside my initial misgivings about the man." She drifted away from the crowd, seeking a private nook in the garden where she could regain her composure. She settled on a stone bench concealed from the lawn by a trellised arbor.

"I thought I'd never find you alone." Bridger was suddenly at her side. Startled out of her reverie, her head snapped up. The intensity of his eyes took her breath away. "I've been prowling the Bermuda waters trying to get a glimpse of you, sweetheart. My spies tell me you've fared well since you arrived on these shores." His quirky smile implied that he saw himself as the butt of the joke.

"Bridger, when I saw you in the crowd surrounding the governor, I thought my heart would stop in my chest. What in the name of God are you doing here?" She rose and clasped his hands in hers. "There are those here who'd like nothing more than to destroy you. If you have no care for yourself, then have a care for me and my heart that you treat with so little concern."

Again, the wry grin spread over his face, but fell short of reaching his eyes. "Ah, Eugénie, to be so near and not see you has tested me to the limits of my endurance, my strength, and my will. Jamie is thoroughly disgusted with me. When Governor Bruère extended a personal invitation to accompany his regiment, I couldn't have kept myself from you even if it had meant that I would've been drawn and quartered on the spot. I would have reached out and embraced that death a happy man."

His declaration carried Eugénie into his arms. Gone caution, gone reason, swept before the passion of reckless abandon. For a moment, they stood motionless in each other's embrace. Then their hands began to move, rediscovering, remembering the feel, the touch of the other. Slowly, as if in a dream-state, their lips met and clung, savoring the sweetness of the reunion. The kiss deepened and took on a violence that lifted and carried them away to a place where there was no fear, only bright promise. No suspicion, only trust. Where the giving and the taking blended together and became one.

Bridger recovered first and pulled back. How could he leave this woman, again? How could he live his life without her in it? He took her head in his hands. His long fingers molded the skull beneath the chestnut silk as he tilted her face up to his. "My heart, my very breath, what spell have you cast on this poor soul who stands before you?" he said harshly, crushing his mouth down on hers.

She tore her lips away. "Oh, Bridger, we've started something that can't be stopped. There's no turning back. Even if I would, I could not." She gently traced the line from his brow, along his cheek, down to his chin, learning again the smooth texture of his skin. "I fear for you here," she whispered, her emotions darkening the silver of her eyes. "Your activities are known and your exploits have lost whatever sympathy there may have been here for you. The governor's protection means nothing to a certain element. In this neighborhood, an accident . . ."

"Shh, shh," Bridger said, placing a forefinger on her lips. "My training with the Iroquois will stand me in good stead. There's no one who can slip up on me unheeded. Nor are there ears that can hear me, or eyes that can see me if I don't choose for them to do so. On the other hand, while I've been sailing these waters, I've seen the activities of Tucker and those who associate with him. It could be very damaging to them, should word of those activities reach the ears of the British authorities. But even amongst thieves there is *honneur*." This time the grin reached the blue eyes. "The information is safe with me. Board their ships, lift their cargo, claim their vessels in Prize Court—yes, I will do all that and more, but not one word will I utter of the deeds of disloyalty they carry out daily beneath the Union Jack. More importantly, Eugénie, I must warn you about your own danger. I overheard a man named Darby here today talking about a Frenchwoman residing with the Tuckers who bodes ill for the loyalist and British cause on the mainland. I've reason to know about him. He's truly dangerous. Do not underestimate him. Promise me!" When she nodded, he pulled her to him. "Give me your sweet lips once more before I go." Eugénie put her fears and protests aside and lifted her lips to his.

"Oh, sweet Jesus," Bridger said huskily, taking a moment to get his breath. "I will see you in the morning sun and the evening sky and every moment in between until I'm with you again. Eugénie, always remember that I'm never so far away that I can't be reached if you need me." As he spoke, he placed something in the palm of her hand and closed her fingers around it.

Eugénie nodded. "I'll see you in my dreams, awake and asleep," she said, smiling into his eyes. *"Adieu, mon amour."*

He was gone so silently and so completely that she wondered for a moment if it had all been a dream. Her eyes drifted down to her clenched fist. She opened her fingers slowly. There in the palm of her hand lay a golden band. Looking more closely, she saw etched on the surface the silhouette of a heather blossom entwined with the letters "E D" and "B G." Holding it against her heart, she bowed her head. Then, rallying herself, she stood, straightened her skirts, and went to join the others. ·

XXIV

❧❧❧

When it was clear that the celebrating would last well into the night, Eugénie and a small contingent from The Grove made their adieus and promised to be at the fish fry at noon the next day.

"I swear, I don't know how you young people keep up such a heady pace," Anne Tucker said, smiling at Eugénie as she settled herself in the small parlor, a short time later. Her fingers were already busy with the needlework that was never far from her hands. "Why, you must have danced every single step over the last three days."

"The music was irresistible," Eugénie said with a laugh. "I've learned a new step or two to introduce into my French circles. They're so lively, they're almost like a romp. I must admit I breathed a sigh of relief when you said you were returning to The Grove. My dancing slippers were well-nigh worn through." She noticed that the longer she was in the British colonies, the more her speech sounded like theirs.

"That reminds me of when Henry and I were married," Anne reminisced, a gentle smile lighting her face. "Now that I think about it, I did wear out three pairs of slippers and had to borrow a pair from my cousin, whose foot was considerably smaller than mine. I never thought my feet would ever be the same. Mercy! I haven't thought about that in years."

Eugénie offered to help with the mending, and soon the two women were working industriously in a companionable silence.

"Anne, perhaps you can solve a mystery for me," Eugénie began. Anne's hands stilled as she looked up from her work.

"And what might that be, child?" she asked.

"There are two things puzzling me, actually. First, there was a young lady at the wedding whom I hadn't seen before today who resembled me to a surprising degree," Eugénie answered. "In fact, I almost felt that I was standing in front of a looking glass. I was wondering who she might be."

"I know exactly who you mean," Anne exclaimed. "She's one of the young Tucker girls, cousins who live at 'Bellevue' in Paget. Her name is Elizabeth Tucker." At Eugénie's look, Anne laughed. "It does become confusing, doesn't it? I hadn't seen her in ever so long. It never ceases to amaze me how you can live on this small island and miss seeing people, even ones in your own family. I'd forgotten just how pretty that young lady is. Not that she can hold a candle to you, my dear, but I certainly did note her resemblance to you. She had her share of admirers, didn't she though? Even the young Goodrich whom St. George is so fond of was attentive at one point. My, what a handsome lad he is. Henry says he's becoming something of a nuisance, sad to say. I was always rather fond of that family. We used to see them when we visited in Virginia. I don't know what's gotten into them. Well, he was a great help to you, and for that I'm grateful."

Eugénie had noticed that once a person came under her roof, Anne Tucker considered that person a member of her family unless there was good reason to feel otherwise. It explains why Anne has such a wide circle of friends and is held in such warm regard by so many, Eugénie mused.

"This wedding couldn't have come at a better time," Anne said thoughtfully. "It's brought everyone together and given everyone something pleasant to think about. It's taken all of our minds off the conflict over in the American colonies and our own troubles right here at home."

A frown creased her usually calm demeanor. "Far be it from me to make judgments about who's right and who's wrong. All I know is that scarcity bears no sympathy for either Whig or Tory. Bermuda is already feeling the pinch. Well, let's leave that subject alone. There's nothing that can be accomplished by fretting about it. It's for smarter minds than mine. After tomorrow, the men will be back at it with a vengeance, I daresay. And what was the other mystery?"

"I noticed a man named Darby at the wedding who was keeping company with the governor's people," Eugénie replied. "Do you know the one I'm talking about? I first saw him at the Whittington auction and then several times after that. I wondered if you knew what business he had here in Bermuda."

"I must admit I didn't pay much attention to the people who were with the governor, dear, so I'm afraid I can't be of much help on that score. Ask Henry. He and the boys keep an eye out for any unfamiliar face at these gatherings. Here I've been prattling on and haven't even asked if you'd care for a little refreshment before we call it a day."

"Thank you, Anne," Eugénie said, "but if you'll excuse me, I think I'll put this early evening to good use and catch up on some much-needed sleep."

Embracing the younger woman warmly, Anne said, "You go right along, dear. I intend to follow your good example very shortly. I'll wait up a bit longer for the stragglers, but not much longer, I vow. You stay abed as long as you like in the morning. The fish fry is the last of the festivities and will not start a jot before one o'clock. I, for one, intend to arrive fashionably late!"

With Marie's help, Eugénie was soon beneath the fresh linen sheets and, without a thought in her head, drifted off to sleep.

The roan whinnied softly and tossed his head, impatient with the rough terrain.

"There, there," Eugénie said, stroking his neck and speaking to him in soothing tones. "You're a Virginian, born and bred, and used to that gentle countryside. But there's beauty here of a different sort." As she spoke, she slipped from the saddle and knelt down by the water's edge, trailing her fingers in the cool wetness. Around her, she could hear the rustling and chirping of the birds that made their home in the dense thicket fringing the magical inlet.

She gazed down at the softly lapping water and saw his face join hers on its smooth surface. His hand reached out and clasped hers, bringing it up to his cheek. He turned his head and drank from her palm, kissing the drops from her fingertips. At his touch, a sensation started to build in the deepest part of her, and she began to tremble. He took her gently into his arms, crooning softly to her. He drew her closer, holding her with one arm as he pulled his jacket off with the other.

The heat from his body radiated through her and fired her own body's response. He turned her in his arms and laid her back across his chest, support- ing her against his body as he slowly untied the ribbons of her bodice. He spread the two halves back and let his eyes sweep down the slender column of her throat to the beauty of her shoulders, then let them come to rest on the gentle swell that lay exposed above her pale, pink chemise. Her eyes never left his face as she took his hand and brought it to her breast.

He read the invitation in her eyes and freed the ends of her bodice from the waistband of her skirt. He carefully slid each arm out of the sleeves. Then, with a touch as light as a butterfly's wing, he slipped the restraining straps of her chemise off her shoulders. With a whisper, the delicate silk settled in folds at her waist.

His breath came in a rush, and she felt the rhythm of his heart quicken against her cheek as he gazed down at her breasts, shaped round and firm as though by an artist's hand, the pink tips already springing to life under his gaze. She moaned as they began to ache, seeking his touch.

"Soon, soon," he said in answer to her need, while his hands began to unclasp the skirt's fastenings. She lay back languorously and closed her eyes, surrendering to his hands that seared a path down her thighs and calves as, with meticulous care, he guided the split skirt and underthings down her body. Lift- ing her gently, he put them aside. Her short boots and stockings soon followed.

Only one barrier remained. He leaned over her and buried his face in the chemise gathered at her waist, breathing in the scent of her. He slipped his hand beneath it and slowly slid it over her hips and down the length of her body, treasuring its delicacy. At his touch, her body responded violently, spasming as if in pain. Her arms reached up reflexively. Her fingers grasped the dense muscles of his back.

"Please, please," she moaned as she arched her body up to his, seeking to pull him down to her.

"Not yet," he said, his words coming harshly. *"We've waited too long for this moment to hasten it now."*

Her head thrashed on the pillow. She clutched at the bed covers and moaned softly in her sleep.

With torturous restraint, he gently disengaged her arms and returned them to her sides. Then, tenderly, he laid her down on his jacket as he removed his own garments, until, clothed only in his britches, he crouched beside her.

He lifted her back into his arms and for a long moment cradled her there, unmoving. His eyes closed as if in prayer, stretching out his anticipation of what was to come. Finally, he opened his eyes. Keeping his body still, he let his eyes roam at will over the beauty of her body. He felt the breeze on his back that flicked across her nipples, increasing their erection as he watched, and stirred the curls of her downy thatch, causing the muscles of her stomach to quiver convulsively.

She lay limply, unable to move, her eyelids too heavy to lift. She was sealed in darkness. She felt the gentle play of the breezes. Behind closed lids, she felt his eyes move over her body as she lay spread before him, exposed and raw. Heat started at her center and swelled through her until even the tips of her fingers tingled with it. She felt an intimate throbbing and reached to soothe it with her hand. She cried out as he took her hand away and drew both of her arms above her head in a gentle grip. With his other hand he softly parted her legs.

"Surrender to the breezes. Let them cool your heat," he told her. *Beyond will, she ceased to struggle. His words released her last anchor. She was intensely aware of eddies of air moving over and around her. She gave herself up to them as they invaded her, reaching into her and sucking her forth. She was completely immersed in the feel of the currents playing across her sensitive skin. Her ears throbbed. Her face grew hot. The fingers of air caressed her neck and her exposed underarms. They slid between and over her breasts, swelling them, drawing forth and deepening their sensitivity, the taut nipples riding high and hard on their crests.*

The air currents trailed down her ribs and belly, lifting and playing with the fine hairs. They lapped at her reddened lips and tweaked her swollen maiden-

head. The cool breezes played over her body, reaching into openings and crevices, leaving a path flaming in their wake, building tension in her thighs and calves, lingering over her curved arches and the tips of her toes.

She was robbed of strength and will, and at the same time she felt strung as tightly as a finely tuned bowstring. Her breath came in short gasps, and white shots of light exploded behind her eyelids as wave upon wave ripped through her. A moan escaped her lips, and her hands clenched and unclenched in his grip. Her feet arched and stretched as her head moved from side to side, her lips open in a silent cry.

The deep blue of his eyes darkened as he watched the dance of the breezes on her body and her body's rich response. Watching her in her most private of woman moments, he watched her body continue to be lashed, riding its internal storm. He watched the fine beads of sweat form on her brow, the flutter of dark lashes against vermilion cheeks. He watched the lips lush and ripening as the rush of blood reached those tender cells, the jumping pulse at the base of the beautiful throat. He watched the rosy blush suffusing the skin from the tips of the delicate toes, up the calves, the thighs, around the glistening triangle where the peak stood proud, engorged and deeply red, across the trembling hips and belly, to the high breasts that were rounding and filling with her body's need, carrying their nipples swollen and straining, rising up and down, taunting him with each ragged breath that escaped her parted lips. He watched.

The teasing fingers became more insistent, demanding more of her. They entered her and dallied, stroking the roof of her cavern, probing deep, then deeper. An animal sound exploded from the depths of her throat as her springs burst forth deep within her, drenching her walls and soaking the outer crevices and the tendrils that guarded the opening of her. Her aching deepened and spread, carrying her beyond thought, out of mind. The torture mounted. Her legs thrashed mindlessly, stretching farther apart, straining to capture the coolness of the air currents, only to be inflamed more by their touch.

She felt her heart bursting in her chest as tears slipped beneath her eyelids and slid down her cheeks, gathered up there by the fingers of air. Thirsty for her moisture, they tracked her tears to her lips and lingered there, tracing the tender curves. Her mouth opened with a sigh, and her tongue reached out, seeking to mate, and touched the fingertip she craved. Her tongue circled it, bathing it, feeling its texture. She tasted the salt of her own tears on its tip. With a whimper, she drew it gently between her lips, into her mouth, and suckled.

The light fingers of the breezes feasted on her body, sipping up the droplets of moisture that sprang from her, cooling her even as they brought her to heat. They held her captive for the human fingers and human lips that joined them in the ravishment of her.

His fingers and lips ran lightly over her forehead and eyebrows, cheeks and lips, before trailing down her neck, pausing to kiss the erratic pulse at its base, flaying her nerve endings. The mouth retraced its path, moving up to an exposed ear, breathing into it as lips and tongue captured the sensitive lobe. The sensation that hit her as the moist invader entered that virgin cave sent shock waves through her. Her body arched blindly and his hands slipped beneath her, serving up her breasts to his hungry mouth. Her hands, now freed from his grasp, clasped his head to her.

First with his finger, and then with his licking tongue, he circled her puckered aureoles, satisfying their need. He fed at each bursting nipple until her first liquids released for him, and he groaned as he tasted the sweet liquor on their tips. He lifted one rounded breast and, with sensitive fingers, gently stretched the nipple out to its full length. He pinched and twisted the erect, swollen stalk, now readied for him, while his teeth nipped and chewed its tip. The openings of the nipple dilated, rewarding him with the full flow of her. His hands pressed in on the sides of the breast as he sucked deeply at her spout. He coated his lips with the rush of her, then licked it up with his tongue.

She whimpered, shifting to bring the other aching breast to his mouth. When he had nursed it in like fashion, he lifted his head to gaze down at their magnificence. He gathered them together in his hands and buried his face in their fullness. He drew his beard stubble across their rigid peaks before taking each one again into his mouth, grinding them gently with his teeth as his hands kneaded and molded the surrounding flesh.

The sweet pain caused her breath to come in short gasps and strange sounds to burst from her throat. His lips closed over hers, drawing her cries into his mouth, as his hands followed the path of the breezes, stroking the softness of her *underarms, traveling down her sides, encircling her tiny waist with his hands, splaying his long fingers out across her abdomen, teasing the springy hairs at the edge of her dark triangle with the tips of his fingers.*

She moaned when he took away the lips she had been hungrily feeding on. He reached behind her. Filling his hands with her buttocks, he lifted her belly up to his mouth and thrust his tongue deep into her navel, licking her, sucking its center. Her hands raked across his back, seeking purchase on his ridged muscles.

A finger crept between the full globes of her buttocks and entered the back of her channel. She froze and fought to pull away.

"Lie back. Open to me," he commanded, while his other hand stroked her inner thighs with feathering caresses. "We have but entered the rear door when it's the pleasure of the front portal that we seek." She sank back and gave herself up to the exquisite agony of his touch. Her breath caught in her throat when his finger found the first opening, circling and playing with it before moving forward along her furrow. He found her next entrance hot and wet, ready for him. He measured it with a long finger. He felt her inner walls spasm, grasping him, pulling him deeper into her. Reluctantly, he withdrew and moved on, drawing his finger forward along her groove as he soothed and inflamed her with the practiced touch of his other hand. His finger paused and then gently brushed across the reddened bud at the mouth of her channel. Her breath came in a rush and she cried out.

"Stay with me, stay with me," he ordered softly. "The next will continue your preparation for the final journey we take together." He opened her thighs wider and held them apart as he bent his head to her, following the path with his tongue that his finger had just traveled. His tongue circled, then plunged into her rear entrance as he gently blew on the hairs of that nether, moist region. She moaned and reddened with shame at the pleasure she felt at his violation. Again, she felt the pressure building within her.

With his fingertips, he combed out the lush tangles of her corolla and with infinite care spread back the outer lips, blowing lightly along each exposed crease. Carefully separating and parting the inner labia, he watched as the tender folds, thus set free, filled and swelled, their color deepening beneath his gaze. Holding the outer lips apart, he stroked their walls with his thumbs and softly blew along the length of her. He lowered his bristled chin and rubbed back and forth along the tender fleshes, leaving them raw and tingling. She moaned deeply, and her whole body quaked in response to this new awakening of her body.

He took each plump fold between his teeth, nipping and sucking each in turn, bringing them to their full engorgement as she writhed beneath the ancient rites he was performing on her. Having paid homage to that ripened flesh, he sought the summit of her and found it standing fully distended, erect and readied for him. He took the throbbing bud-head into his mouth, worshiping it with his teeth and tongue. Finally, he drew it out farther, sucking its hardness as he inserted the full length of a finger into her, moving it slowly in and out to the rhythm of his suckling. Her body exploded into paroxysms as she cried out and thrashed beneath his hands and mouth.

"Ride it, my sweeting. Go with it. Let it take you," he coaxed her softly. "Soon, soon, my heart, I will join you. There's but one last stop I must make if you're to be completely readied for our journey together." He slowly withdrew his finger from her, flicking his tongue once more along the troughs between the engorged folds. Then, intensifying the pressure on her swollen peak with his thumb and forefinger, he drove his tongue into the center of her, entering and withdrawing, coring her inner canal. When his tongue found and pressed against the sensitive spot that pulsed in the roof of her, her body stilled and then tightened convulsively. She shuddered in violent contractions. With a moan, she melted apart and her body rewarded him with the flood of sweetness he sought. He lapped up the juices, dizzied by the abundance and lusciousness of her flow. He buried his face in it, breathing in her rich scent.

In one motion, he dispensed with his britches.

"Look at me, Eugénie," he commanded, his voice harsh in his throat. She obeyed, her eyes traveling the length and breadth of him. Then slowly, she raised her arms up to him, issuing her own command.

He took her then, entering her, feeling the tightness of her walls opening to accommodate him. They hung suspended together for a long moment, gazing into the depths of each other's eyes. Then, slowly, they began their rhythm. He traveled deep into her, found her barrier and thrust through, taking her cry of pain into his mouth.

"Now," he whispered into her ear, "we have nothing between us and paradise. Come with me, my beloved." They moved as one in the dance as ancient

as time, seeking and finding, holding and releasing, carrying each other to the very edge of fulfillment, then withdrawing to build even higher. Her legs encircled him, opening farther to his thrust. He lifted her buttocks to drive deeper into her, reaching the very edge of her womb.

They rode the tide as it carried them upward, winding them tighter and tighter, bringing them to the brink of unbearable pain. Then, just as every nerve and sinew, stretched past enduring, screamed for release, the heavens shattered into a million pieces and an ecstasy beyond knowing swept over them and carried them together over the edge of space and time and on to paradise.

In that instant, Eugénie felt her soul leave her body. She watched with a lightness of being her sleeping body far beneath her as she soared above the earth. She floated weightlessly in this other dimension, filled with a peace beyond any she had ever known. She knew that this dream, this experience, had joined her soul forever with Bridger's and that, if their earthly bodies should never meet so intimately on the earthly plane, their souls had traveled together to paradise and were linked there for all eternity. At the moment that she knew this with certainty, she felt her soul descend back through the ethers, down to earth, to merge once more with her physical body.

She awoke, renewed, just as dawn began to lighten the dark skies. She remembered vividly the night's journey, and she understood the full meaning of that experience. She knew she would carry it with her for the rest of her life.

XXV

❧❧❧

A regatta of small boats was commandeered to transport the guests to the fish fry the next day. Eugénie, Elizabeth, St. George, Fanny, Harry, and their two boisterous sons had been assigned to one of The Grove's fleet. As one by one they clambered aboard, the little boat listed dangerously to one side.

"St. George, I'll happily join the next party," Eugénie said, eyeing the boat with alarm.

"Come, come, Miss Eugénie," St. George said. "We have our orders. I'm not going to be the one to arrive at the fish fry without this boat's full complement of people and have to answer to Mother. Here, give me your hand. I'm steadying the boat. You'll be as safe as safe can be." The two little boys chose that moment to throw themselves against the boat's far side. The side nearest Eugénie tipped up. She missed her footing, and her toe caught the edge of the gunwale.

In an acrobatic effort, Eugénie managed to fall into the boat and sprawled on top of St. George and Elizabeth. Harry, standing on the dock, quickly grabbed the boat and steadied it, just barely avoiding disaster as the three thrashed about trying to disentangle themselves.

"Boys! Boys!" Their mother spoke sharply, grabbing them both by the scruff of their necks. "Sit down this minute and be still, or we'll leave you both right here! There've been enough of your antics for one day." The two pups chose to obey their mother's orders and sat

251

down, peeking at each other beneath lowered lashes. Harry, the last, climbed in without incident and took up the stern oar.

"St. George, shove off and we'll get under way."

In no time, they made their way into the mainstream, joining the floating parade headed for the last event of the wedding festivities. Soon the skippers of the small crafts were barking challenges back and forth to each other across the water.

"What do you say, Brother?" Harry shouted forward to St. George in the bow. "Shall we take them on?"

"Aye, aye, Captain," St. George said, turning to salute his brother. "Hold on, ladies, it's apt to get a bit choppy." Eugénie, Elizabeth, and Fanny heeded his words and immediately grasped the gunwales, leaning forward as if to aid the boat's speed with their posture. The two young boys held fast to their mother's skirts, for once completely subdued.

"Look out on the left!" Eugénie cried as one of the neighbor's boats threatened to steal a march on the Tucker craft. The two boats were neck and neck, leaving the rest of the fleet well behind. The other boat had the advantage, carrying only four people compared to the five adults and two children in The Grove's boat. Less encumbered, their challenger sat higher in the water and fairly flew across the sparkling surface of the harbor. Even so, they were no match for the sheer determination of the Tucker brothers, whose oars plowed through the water at an ever-increasing rate.

With all eyes glued on their competitor, no one in the Tucker boat noticed the fast-approaching wharf. Had it not been for Elizabeth's shriek, they would have smashed head-on into it. At the last minute, Harry angled his oar and managed, in spite of the boat's forward momentum, to steer away from the disastrous course and swerve up alongside the dock only seconds ahead of the other boat.

Harry and St. George collapsed forward, holding themselves up by their oars. Their faces were red with exertion and wreathed in smiles as shouts of congratulations rained down on them from people in the other boats and from the people on shore who had watched the impromptu race.

"Well, Brother," Harry said, clapping St. George on the back, "'tis clear we have some work to do if we're to uphold our honor on Bermuda Day."

How remarkable these Bermudians are, Eugénie thought. They can carry on normally, even acquit themselves with *joie de vivre,* in the face of imminent shortages and a conflict that rages so near their shores. What a resourceful, resilient people they are. She glanced at St. George and noticed a pensive expression on his face. She laid her hand on his arm and drew him aside. Lowering her voice, she said, "What is it, St. George?"

St. George turned to her, making no secret of his feelings.

"I haven't wanted to dampen anyone's fun during the festivities, least of all my own, so I've kept this to myself for the last few days." His face was uncharacteristically serious.

"St. George, what are you talking about? What's the matter?" Eugénie exclaimed, thinking only the most dire circumstances could cause this transformation in her friend.

"Harry's mention of Bermuda Day reminded me that I won't be here to share in that celebration," St. George answered in a quiet voice. "It's common knowledge that my sympathies lie with the patriots. My presence here attracts unwanted attention to this end of the island. It's no longer safe for me to remain here. It's time for me to return to Virginia. On all accounts, my place is there. I can be Father's eyes and ears, as well as his spokesman to the Americans."

"Oh, St. George, so soon?" Eugénie asked. "Only the other day, your mother spoke of how sweet it was having you home again after you'd been away for so long. My heart aches for her."

"Ah, Mother is a plucky soul. I've no doubt that she'll bear up just fine," he said, love and respect clear in his voice. Then his expression shifted subtly. "Will I ever see you again, Miss Eugénie?" He took her hands in his and looked down into her face.

"St. George," she chided, trying to lighten the moment. "Wiser ones than I say that our world is shrinking day by day. Your famed Bermuda rigging has brought France ever closer to the New World. I shall expect to have the opportunity to repay you, your family, and the many good friends I've made here with the same generous hospitality that's been extended to me on this side of the ocean." She patted him gently on the arm. "What are your plans? How soon must you leave?"

"I wait only for a favorable tide. The ship is stocked and ready. It'll be no more than two days at the very most."

"Well, then," Eugénie said brightly, determined to lift the shadow from his face, "we've not a moment to lose. Every instant between now and then must be enjoyed to the fullest. Come, let's join the others and celebrate the fortunate couple with dancing, dining, and drink. I'm fast learning the style of your Bermuda merrymaking!" Swept up in her enthusiasm, St. George grabbed her hand and set off to do just that.

At dusk the following day, Eugénie wandered down to The Grove's dock and stood looking out across the water, enjoying the play of the long shadows on its smooth surface. After the crush of people and events over the last few days, the sounds of lapping water and the other voices of nature were soothing to her. A movement behind her jarred her out of her reverie, and she whirled around to see St. George making his way through the tangle of mangroves.

"St. George," she exclaimed. "You gave me such a start."

"Eugénie, I've been looking all over for you!" His concern for her caused him to speak sharply. "What are you doing down here alone? It's not safe on this island to wander about unaccompanied once night begins to fall. Even at The Grove. You must listen to me. For all your ferocious independence, you are a woman, and easy prey."

"St. George," Eugénie said, laying her hand on his sleeve, "I appreciate your concern for me. It's protected me through everything. I'll miss you terribly when you leave, when I can no longer rely on you to guard my safety. St. George, what will I do without your sweet companionship?" Eugénie was surprised to feel tears spring to her eyes.

She realized suddenly how much she would miss this steadfast friend who asked so little of her and gave so much.

St. George gathered her into his arms, murmuring endearments. Eugénie gently pulled back, knowing how easy it would be for her to take advantage of his feelings. "Forgive me," she said quietly. "I presume too much on your kind nature."

"Dear Eugénie, you must know the extent of my feelings for you. You could never presume too much," he spoke hoarsely. "I only wish you could regard me as more than a friend." He shook his head and then said in a firm tone, "I didn't seek you out to talk of such things, but rather to discuss the matter of your safety. I spoke with Bridger during the wedding festivities." Looking at her hands, which rested in his, he failed to see the look of surprise on her face. "His concern for you is as great as my own. We've worked out a plan, should the need arise."

He paused for a moment and laughed. "The one man who sends my father into the final stages of apoplexy at the very mention of his name, whose interests run counter to ours at every turn, who—and you needn't deny it to me, who knows you so well—has conquered the tender heart that I wish so much for my own, is the one man I would trust above all others to guard your welfare in my absence. I've taken Marie into my confidence as well. If, for any reason, she has cause to be alarmed for your safety or hers, she'll know what steps to take and who to contact."

"Surely, St. George, your fears are unfounded," Eugénie protested. "Marie and I are not without . . ."

"Eugénie," he said sternly, "these are good measures put into place to safeguard your welfare, should, God forbid, circumstances call for them. I will not have them brushed aside by your proclamations of self-reliance. Now, if I may continue. Bridger told me that, even when his own ship isn't plying the Bermuda waters, he always leaves behind a smaller sister ship, captained by Jamie, the big Scotsman. I chose not to burden our friendship by asking too closely about the purpose of his constant vigilance," he said wryly before continuing.

"He's placed one of his crew ashore, a man named Roland, who's now employed by the owner of Pelican's Reef. Roland has struck up a romance with one of the tavern wenches there who's a great source of information. Apparently, in short order he's made himself indispensable to the establishment, and no one seems suspicious of him. Roland is our link. We've set it up so that one of Bridger's ships will pass daily by this end of the island. Should the need arise, signals can pass between ship and land and bring aid to you immediately.

"The waterways are already busy," he went on. "Now we're nearing the end of May, with only the summer to build the stores the island needs for the long winter. The trafficking in these waters will increase even more. Such activity attracts those who'd prey on fat cargoes. I overheard Governor Bruère complaining that all his letters to Whitehall seeking supplies to sustain the populace and warships to patrol these waters have come to nothing once again, which means he'll mandate the customs agents to increase their vigilance. We all know that the Searchers will stop at nothing. All this suggests that there will be bloody scenes on this end of the island before the Americans' fight is over."

St. George paused, looked at Eugénie intently, and then continued, "The increased incidence of arson and the loss of ships on the reefs speak to the evil that creeps abroad in the darkness. Activities on all fronts are stepping up apace, as will Father's efforts to carry out his plans with the Americans. I warn you, Eugénie. Take heed for your own safety. These are uncertain times. When the bush is shaken, more than berries may fall to the ground. Whatever falls to earth won't lie there long before its scent draws the rats. Speaking of rats, that Darby fellow has made his appearance and is nosing about where he's not welcomed. Keep your eye out for him, and trust no one unless they make themselves known to you by a sign that you recognize. Promise me!" he said urgently, grabbing her hands.

"I promise, dear St. George, but when will I meet this Roland?"

"Yes, yes, I was coming to that." He picked up the lantern that he had placed at his feet. Lifting it high above his head, he lowered and raised the cover, paused, then repeated the same sequence twice more. Almost immediately, a dark form separated itself from the shadows along the bank. First they heard the muffled sound of oars pulling through the water and then a soft thud as a boat nudged the wharf. Eugénie, her nerves strung tight by St. George's warnings, felt the hair rise on the back of her neck. A figure alighted from the boat and walked toward them.

St. George moved quickly forward, thrusting the lantern in the face of the newcomer. "Roland," he said with relief, "I didn't expect you so soon, but I'm glad you were laying by so near. Good, we can make quick work of this, and you can be off. I'm afraid that if other evening strollers stumble upon this *rendez-vous,* it'll be hard to explain. More importantly, your face will become known, which will make you of no use for our purposes."

Nodding to St. George, Roland turned to Eugénie and said, "Mistress, I've met your maidservant, Marie, and now the circle is complete. My first charge is your safekeeping. I'm wholly at your service, should you ever need my assistance. I hope with all my heart that the need will never arise."

Eugénie looked closely at the man standing before her who might one day hold her life in his hands. She had noticed the refinement of his speech and wondered how he had come to be a lowly crew member so far from his native England. Even in the dim light, she could see the intelligence in his face and the sharp eyes that missed little. His average height and leanness disguised the strength she sensed was there. Bridger had chosen well.

"Roland, your presence is a great comfort to me," she said with feeling. "I, like you, hope never to put these preparations to the test, but Marie and I will sleep more soundly, knowing you're near. Now, you must go before you endanger yourself."

"Milady, it's an honor to serve you," Roland said, bowing. "Do not be surprised if you see me at The Grove or in this vicinity. One of my duties is to bring stuffs from the tavern and the master's market to houses hereabouts. Should I receive messages for you, or should you have ones to send, it's the perfect ruse. If there's nothing further, I'll take my leave." In a quick motion, he was in the boat and melting once more into the darkness.

Eugénie and St. George were approaching the house when they heard the Colonel's and Harry Tucker's voices raised in anger. They could see the two men sitting on the back veranda, pulling on their clay pipes. The smell of rich tobacco lay heavy on the air.

"I tell you, Father, you ask too much!" Harry's voice was harsh with ill-concealed rage.

"Harry Tucker, you're my firstborn—my firstborn son and name-sake. Your duty, you may feel, is an onerous one, but the marriage that I sanctioned positioned you to have intimate knowledge of the com-ings and goings of the governor's household. You were eager enough to assume the office of the secretary of the Council, as one of the gov-ernor's own men. Authority and influence have been yours. Now, when your position can, as it was intended to, serve and inform your family and our associates, you begin to whimper and shrink! I've no patience for such! You'll carry out your responsibilities and obliga-tions."

"Father, I've never shirked my duty to you and my family," Harry said hotly, then stopped and took a breath before continuing in a calm tone. "Nor do I intend to do so now. I said only that my position is dif-ficult, standing as I do between two camps. It becomes more so daily, as the Americans' war accelerates. You'll hear everything I'm privy to, but I'll act with discretion. I wouldn't for all the world act in any man-ner that would wound my dear Fanny. It's hard enough, knowing that my family loyalties betray the governor. He's placed his trust in me and, as you pointed out, I have much for which to be grateful to him. Ah, St. George and Mistress Eugénie, come join us. You've arrived just in the nick of time. I saw the glint in Father's eye. One more word out of my mouth and I daresay, old as I am, it would've been the strap and the woodshed for me."

St. George marveled at his brother. Harry had always been the boldest and staunchest of the lot, except when it concerned their father. Then Harry would always take it on the chin and never attempt to defend himself. He would even take punishment silently to shield his younger brothers and sisters. Were it not for his feelings for his wife, Fanny, and the governor, no doubt, he would not have spoken up on this occasion.

"Harry, I'd just begun to get used to having you heft the load for me again," St. George said, quickly picking up his brother's call for help. "Just the way you always used to. Now I'm off once more to brave it alone. It's been a pleasant respite. Your Fanny is glowing, and the boys are living up to their early promise. When next I see them, they'll be replacing me in the bow of your dinghy!" The last remark caused everyone to laugh, since Harry and St. George had long been the terror of the dinghy races.

"Should that day ever come, they'll follow in a long and fine tradition," Harry said, smiling fondly at his brother.

"Well, well," Colonel Tucker said, "I've a mind for a second pipe and a nip of refreshment." As if on cue, Jeremy pushed through the swinging door, bearing a loaded tray before him.

"Stand aside, Jeremy," Anne Tucker said, coming through the door with the rest of the family. "Wait until everyone is seated, then you may serve the dessert. Maisie, place the candelabra there, and there. Good. That's better. At least now we can see our hands in front of our faces." The remainder of the family arranged themselves in available seats, and soon all were enjoying the sweets and beverages.

When Jeremy began making the rounds for the second time, Colonel Tucker cleared his throat to draw everyone's attention. "We've been celebrating aplenty these past few days, but I'd be remiss were I not to call upon us to take special note of this moment when we're gathered here together. We're thankful that the wedding of our cousins brought our flock together to The Grove for a precious few days. We've long been scattered hither and yon: Nathaniel to Edinburgh, St. George and Thomas Tudor to the colonies, and Harry to the far end of the island in St. George's, where he sometimes seems as far away as

Halifax. Thank God for our Fanny, whose Henry takes her no farther away than Bridge House." The Colonel and Anne Tucker exchanged a smile. "We're soon to be scattered once more. The days and months ahead will be trying ones for us all. As it is, due to information that we've just received, St. George, you must leave on the morning tide, rather than tomorrow evening as we had planned originally. And so I'd like us all to raise a glass to this moment when we are together in the bosom of our family. Let us go forth to follow our duties and obligations, strong in the knowledge that we carry with us the love and loyalty of each and every one of us."

At the conclusion of his words there was a moment's silence. The Colonel looked around the ring of faces as though to mark each person indelibly on his memory. Then, with a solemn expression, he raised his glass and was immediately joined by the rest. Together, they quaffed the contents of their goblets amidst a chorus of "Hear, hear!" "Cheers!" *"Salut!"* and "Bottoms up!"

Spontaneously, everyone rose to their feet and embraced one another. The unspoken question in each mind was how long would it be before they would relive this happy scene and what would occur in their lives in the meantime.

"The morrow will break soon enough," Anne Tucker said, linking her arms through St. George's and Harry's. "I, for one, am off to bed." With one last kiss all around, she sailed through the door, followed closely by the Colonel. The others dispersed quickly with wishes of pleasant dreams and promises to meet at the wharf at dawn.

XXVI

❖❖❖

All was in readiness for St. George's departure when Eugénie arrived at the wharf the next morning. Servants were milling around, busying themselves at this and that so that they could be part of their young master's send-off. Family members were tucking last-minute items into St. George's satchel or repeating once again some essential bit of information or piece of wisdom.

Jeremy had been chosen as one of the crew of the longboat that would carry St. George out to where the *Fanny* lay at anchor outside Ely's Harbor. In his excitement, he was jumping up and down and making a general nuisance of himself.

St. George turned as Eugénie approached him, watching her graceful figure as she drew near. Even in the dim light, he noticed the glossy shine of her chestnut curls, the faint blush across her high cheekbones, and the silver luster of her eyes. Her beauty never failed to affect him deeply, but this time, looking at her for perhaps the last time, he felt a constriction in his chest. With an effort, he took a deep breath and forced a smile on his face.

"Miss Eugénie, how refreshed you look for this early hour," he said.

"Dear St. George, I was hoping somehow that this moment would never come. Listen to me! What sort of send-off is this? I come to speed you on your way, and instead I add stones to your knapsack, as my mother used to say. You must promise to write to us faithfully and tell us all the news of Virginia and the Whittingtons. Here are two letters for them if you have room to take them."

St. George took the letters and carefully wedged them into his already bursting satchel. "Even if I didn't have room," he said, laughing, "I'd carry them in my hand all the way to Oak Knoll, knowing that I'd be turned away at the door by John and Mary were I to arrive without bringing written word from you." Then he continued more seriously, "I shall write to you and the family without fail."

"Ha!" exclaimed Elizabeth, who arrived at his side in time to hear his last words. "Perhaps we'll hear from you more frequently now that you have some hope of receiving word of, or from, Eugénie." She smiled broadly at her brother, taking some of the sting from her words.

St. George's face turned a bright crimson and he sputtered, "Confound it, Elizabeth, you know that I correspond more regularly than the rest of our brothers! It's not the writer who's at fault, but the mode of delivery that needs attention."

"And I say 'Ha!' again," Elizabeth snorted, enjoying the rare opportunity to goad her brother. "The best of a bad lot, I'd say. And, as for the countless letters lost on ghostly galleons that disappear mysteriously into the mists, I have my doubts about that!"

"Come, come, Elizabeth," Anne Tucker joined them, laughing. "That's no way to send off your beloved brother, all red in the face and angry at you."

"Well, at least he's stopped moping around, looking like he's going to the gallows," Elizabeth retorted with a toss of her head. "Brother mine, I'd rather my parting glimpse be of you standing tall on the decks with the glint of adventure in your eye." Her gentle ribbing had accomplished just that.

Fully recovered from his momentary gloomy spirits, St. George grabbed his sister around the waist and gave her a resounding kiss on the cheek. "And you've done that, Sissy. My blood's up and fairly boiling to feel the roll of the sea beneath my feet and the salt spray upon my face. Thank you for the timely boost. Now," twirling her around, he continued, "I don't want to hear that you've gone off and gotten yourself engaged to some stoop-shouldered, lame lad while I'm not here to fend the swain off. You hear me?"

This time it was Elizabeth's turn to color brightly. "And how am I to find the time for such goings-on when my every free moment is taken up with my correspondence to my dear brothers who've chosen to travel to the far corners of the earth? Answer me that!" she squawked to cover her confusion.

Before the two could launch into another exchange, Colonel Tucker clapped his son on the back. "'Tis time, Son." No Pied Piper had a more devoted throng following in his wake than St. George did as he turned and made his way to the dock at his father's side.

After one more round of embraces, St. George hopped nimbly into the longboat. Once he had settled his satchel, he turned and waved to the bright faces lining the dock and shore. "I'll send word with the returning tide!" he shouted.

The pilot in the stern barked out the order "Stroke!" and the longboat shot off across the water.

A pang went through Eugénie as she watched the boat disappear out of sight. It seems that this journey is a constant series of partings and comings and goings, she thought, like a tapestry whose threads weave in for a short time and then out again. Will I ever see these people again?

She had little time to dwell on her thoughts before the Tucker family caught her up in their ranks and swept her off toward the house.

St. George's boat was hardly out of sight when a small craft appeared around the bend of mangrove from the other direction. It swooped up to the wharf, and two men alighted on the dock, barely taking the time to tie up before hastening up the bank toward Colonel Tucker.

"Henry! Henry!" they shouted, catching up with the entourage.

The Colonel, who had been in close conversation with Eugénie, stopped to greet his two friends. "Jack and Andrew, have you forgotten your manners? Miss Eugénie, I believe you've made the acquaintance of Jack Darrell and Andrew Harvey?"

Eugénie was nodding her response when, with uncharacteristic shortness, Jack Darrell stepped abruptly around her and grabbed the Colonel's arm, causing his brow to rise and a tightness to appear around his mouth.

"I say, Jack . . ."

"My pardon to you, Mistress, and to you, Henry, for my breach of manners," Jack said quickly. "But we have news of the greatest importance that we must convey to you at once!" Infected by Jack Darrell's urgent tone, Colonel Tucker took Eugénie's elbow and hastened up the sloping lawn to the house.

He ushered the two men to matching wing chairs by the fireplace in the dayroom, settled Eugénie on the settee opposite, and dispatched a servant for light refreshments. "Now, what's the urgent business you speak of?"

"My head pilot, Lawrence, roused me out of bed before dawn to attend to my warehouse, which was on fire down at Salt Kettle," Darrell began. "It was burned past saving by the time I arrived, in spite of my men's best efforts. It bears the same markings as the other fires we've seen over the last couple of months. This time, the scoundrels weren't as fortunate evading capture. We caught one of them, who lingered too long enjoying his handiwork. We're questioning him now. We all lost a tidy piece in that night's business."

"Were that not enough," Andrew Harvey continued, "I learned this morning that only one of the five ships we sent on the southern route last March made it back through the blockade set up by the Goodrich gang. In addition, the captain of the ship that did evade the blockade heard during his travels that Bermuda ships are being turned back from the American ports."

Colonel Tucker slammed his fist down on the cedar mantle, causing a pair of heirloom candlesticks to rattle. Eugénie's expression went from curiosity to alarm to shock as the Colonel shouted, "This has gone far enough! We cannot and will not tolerate these actions to continue against us!" Clasping his hands behind his back, he lowered his head in thought and paced back and forth in front of the hearth.

Slowly, his color returned to normal. Thrusting his hands into the pockets of his britches, he spoke more calmly. "We don't have a minute to spare. Every warehouse will have a double contingent of armed guards. This will be done, immediately! It's only a lucky accident that none of our people's lives have been lost so far. Anything or anyone that appears in the least bit suspicious must be investigated at once."

"There doesn't appear to be a connection, as yet, between the governor's people and these fires," Jack broke in. "But we can't rule out such a thing. The one we caught was common riffraff. It won't be difficult to learn what he knows and whom he works for."

In the silence that followed, Eugénie spoke. "Colonel, the earlier fires may have no connection with the loyalist faction on the island, but this most recent one comes so closely on the heels of Darby's appearance at the wedding that I can't help but wonder if he or his connections might not have instigated it. I've experienced firsthand the effect he can have on common riffraff. This morning's fire smacks of his imprint."

"Eugénie, I know you have every reason to be wary of this Darby…" Colonel Tucker began.

"Henry, to support what Miss Eugénie says," Andrew cut in, "we have reports that the Searchers have been sniffing around the wharves and taverns recently, letting it be known that there's coin to be had for certain services rendered. Who's to say that the lowlifes frequenting those areas aren't in league with this Darby, as well as acting for the customs agents. That way, the riffraff cuts a deal both ways."

"Ah," Colonel Tucker interrupted, "I see your direction. By carrying out this mischief sanctioned by the government men as well as by this infernal Darby, the ruffians can line their pockets in two ways at our expense. We'll know for sure once we get the scum's confession. Either way, we'll lodge a formal protest with Bruère, signed by us all, apprising him of these lawless acts. If there's no action forthcoming, we'll take matters into our own hands.

"As for the Goodrich clan's piracy," he went on, "our position with the governor is somewhat tenuous. I think we have no choice but to continue to bypass customs at St. George's, just as we have in the past. Even if we do lose a ship or two here or there, we still come out ahead in the long run. Henceforth, all our merchant ships will be armed. We must be prepared to give as well as we get.

"It's clear we've been moving too slowly with the Americans. We must increase our correspondence and lay out our plan more explicitly to them. Silas Deane is our man. He leaves shortly to return to Philadelphia."

"This is a change in Mr. Deane's plans," Eugénie remarked. "At the wedding, he appeared ready to leave for the Continent. What happened to alter his plans?"

"Events are moving at such a pace," the Colonel answered, "that he felt compelled to delay his trip to the Continent. When he arrives in the colonies, he'll be armed with our assurances that we'll assist the Americans in procuring the gunpowder."

The Colonel's words were interrupted by Maisie's appearance in the doorway. "Yes, yes, Maisie," Colonel Tucker said impatiently, "what is it?"

"Pardon me, Colonel Tucker, sir. The new man from the tavern is here with the stuffs Mistress Tucker ordered. I cain't find her or Miss Elizabeth, nowhere. What am I s'pose to do with him?" Colonel Tucker was at a loss for words.

Eugénie rose from the settee where she'd been frozen throughout the remarkable conversation. "Colonel Tucker, Anne and Elizabeth went off to Bridge House. I'll be happy to attend to this."

"Miss Eugénie, I'd be mighty obliged."

The Colonel had already resumed his conversation with the others by the time Eugénie had reached the hallway. "Maisie, where is the young man?"

"He's awaitin' down at the dock."

"Well, ask him to bring his wares up to the kitchen, and I'll meet him there," Eugénie told her. Lifting her skirts, she fairly flew up the stairs to her bedchamber. She burst through the door to find Marie lacing her linens with sprigs of fragrant lavender and carefully folding them into the dark cedar armoire.

"Marie, much has happened, but I'll have to tell you about it later. Quickly, bring me my quill and paper. I must pen a note to Bridger. I fear his recent actions against Colonel Tucker and his associates will bring their ire down on his head. I must get word to him and warn him of the danger."

"Mistress, take heed for your own safety. He's their enemy. Were they to learn that you . . ."

"Marie, should something happen to him because I haven't done my utmost on his behalf, it would hurt me far more than any treatment I could receive at their hands. Fear not. I'll be careful." Her note completed, she blotted the ink with sand from the tray on her lapdesk, folded it, and secreted it in her skirt pocket. With a quick smile at Marie, she was gone, leaving her servant looking after her with concern.

Eugénie hurried along the graveled path to find Roland bringing the last of his load through the kitchen garden. Once he had deposited it, she gestured for him to follow her back down toward the dock where his small boat lay waiting. In the light of day, she saw that he was an exceptionally handsome young man, which explained to her how he had so quickly made his way amongst the ladies of the island.

He broke into a grin at her report of his captain's exploits, but even he uttered a low whistle when Eugénie told him the number of ships Bridger had managed to capture. "With the patriots and the Bermuda trade looking for his scalp, he'd better keep an eye peeled," Roland said. Eugénie slipped her note into his hand, urging him to deliver it to Bridger as quickly as possible. "It'll be in Jamie's hands by nightfall and soon afterward in the captain's," he assured her. "Remember, you have only to send Marie or come yourself to Pelican's Reef and leave word for me at the tavern. I'll find a way to help you."

She grabbed his shirtsleeve as he turned to go. "Roland, there's one thing more. Are you familiar with a man called Darby and where I might find him? Captain Goodrich seemed well acquainted with him."

"Yes, I know of him, but his movements are well concealed. I don't know his present location," was the guarded reply. "He's a dangerous one. Why do you ask?"

"Don't question me. You must find him at once and come tell me his whereabouts."

"Miss Eugénie, you put me between a rock and a hard place. When the captain left me with explicit orders to carry out your wishes, I'm sure he didn't have anything of this sort in mind." With a deep sigh, he continued. "I'll do as you ask, but only if I go with you." Eugénie opened her mouth to protest. "No! Those are the conditions, and that's final. Farewell, milady." With a wink and a wave, he continued on to the dock, leaving Eugénie to mull over the plan forming in her mind.

Finding her thoughts poor company, she took herself to the stables in search of some solace there, only to discover that the head stableman had chosen that day to put all the horses out to pasture while the stableyard and stalls were being mucked out from stem to stern. As she wandered back in the direction of the house, she heard the sound of hoofbeats coming at a fast clip. The lane that led to The Grove was so infrequently used for horseback riding that it could only mean that something of great importance had happened.

For the second time that day, Eugénie grabbed her skirts in both hands and raced toward the house. She arrived just as the horse and rider pulled up to the rail. Flinging himself out of the saddle, the rider doffed his hat and said, his breath coming in short bursts, "Mistress, my name is Rorick Hamilton. I've been sent with information of the utmost importance for the Colonel."

Mon Dieu! What more could happen this day? Eugénie said to herself. Aloud, she said calmly, "Come, I'll take you to him." She led the way through the front door and down the dim hall. She could hear male voices coming from the dayroom. The three men looked up as Eugénie entered the room.

Jumping to his feet, Darrell said, "Rorick, what news do you have of our captive? Has the interrogation been successful?"

Rorick nodded. "Very successful, sir. He and his accomplices are responsible for all the firings of the warehouses that we've been suffering over the past several months. The man knows only that 'a man of influence,' as he calls him, has been ordering the fires. He has no information about the man beyond that. Whoever it is knows exactly when the shipments are coming in and where they are going to be stored. This person then contacts the leader of these ruffians, who recruits whoever happens to be around. The scum admitted that he and his brethren have lured several ships onto the rocks on the west end. Wreckers they are, and proud of it. We may have bagged more than one rabbit this day."

"The hell you say!" Darrell exploded. "My pardon, Miss Eugénie. Wreckers, are they? We must set a trap to snare their hides and put an end to the damage they do once and for all!'"

"My sentiments exactly," Colonel Tucker agreed. "It's clear that these scoundrels have grown bold these past months—urged on by coin from the coffers of one of our own. If the informant is to be believed, only one of our own circle would be privy to our ships' schedules and our storage locations. We must unmask this 'man of influence' right away, before our plans for the gunpowder can go a step further. First of all, how do you plan to dispose of our helpful friend? His compatriots must not learn what he's told us."

"He's safely stowed in irons in the hold of an outgoing ship on its way to a distant port," Rorick replied. "If he survives the conditions of that fine vessel, which I doubt, never fear: the crew will make short work of him, a confessed wrecker."

"Well done!" Harvey said. "Now we can move ahead with a scheme to trap the others and expose the traitor in our midst. We dare not go forward with the Colonel's gunpowder plan until we've dispensed with that one. It's a sad day when we're betrayed by one of our own. For the life of me, I can't fathom who he might be or what could have driven one of us to such lengths."

"I don't give a damn about the motives of one who is lower than the lowest scum!" Colonel Tucker said angrily. "Begging your pardon, Miss Eugénie. I only know that he endangers the welfare of each and every one of us, and our families, and I won't rest until he stands before us unmasked. If you're all in agreement, I'd like to send Rorick immediately to tell Henry Tucker of the Bridge and my two Jennings cousins about this matter. But only them. If the circle becomes too large, we may include the very one we seek to trap." The two men nodded. "We've much to discuss before Rorick and the others join us this evening. These developments could not come at a worse time, but when has ill-fortune ever been known to come conveniently? Eugénie, will you please see to some refreshments for Rorick, and whatever else he may need for his journey? Young man, until this evening."

With the Colonel's words of dismissal, Rorick quickly followed Eugénie from the room. "Mistress, please pardon my lapse in manners. I'm truly grateful for your willingness on my behalf, but it's not necessary. I'll see to my horse and be off."

"I wouldn't hear of it, Mr. Hamilton," Eugénie said. "Far be it from me to break the long-standing reputation of Tucker hospitality. Besides, it's my pleasure," she added with a smile.

Eugénie moved briskly about the pantry, unaware of the burning gaze that followed her every move. She ushered him to a chair and put before him food and drink sufficient to last him, if not a good fortnight's time, well past when he would return to The Grove that evening.

"I'll see that your horse is fed and readied for your departure," she said, leaving Rorick Hamilton to his own company, much to his disappointment. Without her companionship, he made short work of the refreshments and was just walking through the front door when he saw Eugénie approaching the house. She was conversing with a stable-hand, who was leading his mount.

Eugénie turned to Rorick. "Mr. Hamilton, I hope my efforts with you have been as successful as Leonard's have been with your horse."

"Please," Rorick stammered, "I'd be honored if you'd call me by my Christian name, Rorick."

"I would be pleased to, Rorick, and by all means call me Eugénie."

"Dear lady," he said sweeping his hat to his chest, "I am forever in your debt for the care you've rendered me and my horse. I look forward to returning at day's end with the hope of conversing with you further. Until then." He was in the saddle and cantering down the lane before Eugénie could catch her breath.

XXVII

❧❧❧

Anne and Elizabeth returned from Bridge House, accompanied by their cousin Henry Tucker. It was clear that Rorick Hamilton's curt message had left them completely in the dark.

Since the Colonel was still closeted in the morning room with Jack Darrell and Andrew Harvey, it fell to Eugénie to explain. Eugénie finished by saying, "Mr. Hamilton said that he expected he'd be back before nightfall with the Jenningses."

"My, my, what an unfortunate turn of events," Anne said, looking at Cousin Henry, who stood by the window mulling over the startling information. "I'd say it's an ambitious plan to cover such distances on these roadways by nightfall."

"Indeed," Henry agreed. "And it looks like it'll be a long evening for all of us once they arrive."

"Well, I'd better get busy if I'm going to be ready for them. The simple fare I'd planned will be no match for those hearty appetites. I must talk to Cook at once." Anne turned toward the door. "Oh, dear me, I do hope that young man from the tavern arrives in time to . . ."

"Anne," Eugénie interrupted her, "in all the excitement, I failed to mention that he came this morning. Everything you ordered is at the kitchen. I asked him to put your stores there, not knowing what your plans were."

"Oh, thank the good Lord! Isn't he a nice young man? I don't know what any of us would do without him. We've become so accustomed to his help. My goodness, Eugénie, you've had your hands full while we were away. Thank you, dear, for all your help."

"It was certainly little enough," Eugénie demurred. "But what can I do to help you now?"

"An extra pair of hands would come in mighty handy," Anne agreed. "Let's see. We'll put the Jenningses in the south bedroom. Cousin Henry, will you stay the night? No, no, never mind. Of course you will. That means the east bedroom must be readied as well, and we must prepare the sleeping porch for young Mr. Hamilton. Elizabeth, dear, will you make sure Sally has aired the linens and freshened those rooms? Eugénie, will you see that they have fresh flowers in them? You might as well repair the arrangements in the rest of the house as well. I noticed when I came in that they were all looking quite bedraggled. Good, now that I know all those chores are being looked after, I'll turn my attention to the dinner." The women went off to attend to their tasks, and Henry of the Bridge went to join the men in the morning room.

As good as his word, Rorick Hamilton delivered John and Richard Jennings to The Grove just as evening began to fall. Because of the lateness of the hour, the host and hostess dispensed with the usual amenities and sent the new arrivals off to refresh themselves while the rest of the household gathered for the evening meal.

"Rumors are flying up and down the island about the blockade that cost us the four ships," Richard Jennings said as he, his brother, and Rorick Hamilton took their seats at the table. "It isn't known who's responsible for setting it up, but we do know that the early reports accusing the Goodriches have proved false."

"It was certainly an understandable mistake," Andrew said. "Those rascals have a well-earned reputation for pirating and all manner of mischief. It's no surprise that this most recent thievery was laid at their feet."

"And Bridger Goodrich is the most audacious one of the lot," the

Colonel said, speaking up for the first time. "He'd better not show his face in these parts if he knows what's good for him. There are those who would shoot him just on general principles." Eugénie shuddered inwardly. These men could carry out even the most extreme threat if it were their wish to do so.

"If not the Goodriches, then who?" Harry asked, returning to the subject of the blockade.

"Some say the Morgan brothers, some say Edward Teach," John Jennings answered.

"Aha!" Colonel Tucker exclaimed. "The infamous Blackbeard! We're to assume it was the work of pirates?"

"That's what we're hearing down in Flatts. Out-and-out piracy," John agreed. "Whoever the rascal or rascals are, they must command a sizable fleet to inflict the damage we've seen. We must take whatever precautions are necessary and find some means to strike fear in their numbers."

"Yes," Colonel Tucker nodded. "We've been working on a plan all afternoon to do just that."

Throughout the conversation, Anne Tucker had been growing increasingly agitated. "Oh, dear God!" she burst out. "Pirates! You young people don't remember, but during my childhood we lived in mortal terror of pirates. And now they're coming out of their dark holes again?"

"Put your mind at rest, my dear. They were driven from our waters back to the Bahamas and the West Indies then, and we shall drive them away this time as well," the Colonel said with conviction. "It's weakness that attracts their villainy. A show of strength will send them scurrying back where they came from. We've devised just such a plan."

Seeing her mother's distress, Elizabeth searched for some way to distract her. "Have you chosen your dinghy teams for Bermuda Day?" she asked brightly, looking at the non-Tuckers seated at the table. "This year, The Grove has a new entrant." Once she had everyone's attention, she turned to Eugénie. With a dramatic gesture, she declared,

"May I introduce to you Skipper Eugénie Devereux!" Varying degrees of surprise registered on the faces around the table as she went on. "St. George discovered that Eugénie is a natural-born sailor. Over the last couple of weeks he's been honing her nautical skills, and I'm proud to say he selected me as her crew."

"My word!" said her father, at a loss for words.

"Yes," Elizabeth continued, "we've been out just about every morning practicing under his sharp eye."

"Well, I declare!" her mother said. "Who would have thought?"

"Actually, I had my doubts, too, when St. George first proposed it," Elizabeth said with a smile. "We thought it best to keep it a secret until we were sure we could perform. Our last run before St. George left was the clincher. We took him on and just squeaked by. I don't know who was more surprised, him or us. I doubt if he'll ever live it down." She laughed, clapping her hands. "So what do you think? An all-female boat."

"Why, Eugénie," Anne Tucker said, "isn't this simply wonderful! I had no idea you girls were up to this."

"Well, I'll be, Henry," Andrew chuckled. "Will wonders never cease! I expect I'd better put my team on notice that they'll have a run for their money." His smug expression belied his words. The rest of the men except for Rorick looked clearly skeptical about the unorthodox Grove team but politely refrained from expressing their doubts.

"Miss Eugénie!" Rorick exclaimed. "What a capital idea! I'm not entered this year. I'd gladly find a crew and pace you and Elizabeth, now that St. George is no longer here to help you."

"Elizabeth and I would greatly appreciate your help," Eugénie said, quickly accepting his offer. "We need all the practice we can get, and now that our secret's out we won't have to do it at the crack of dawn."

"Good! It's settled, then. Let me know when you'd like to start," Rorick said, clearly delighted to have an excuse to spend time in Eugénie's company.

"I'm sorry to put a damper on this happy diversion," Colonel Tucker said, "but we have much to discuss on a more serious note, and the evening is not getting any younger." With that, he rose from his chair and ushered the men down the hall. Rorick lingered with Eugénie and Elizabeth to set up a practice schedule, and then he, too, hastened down the hall.

"Well, this has surely been a full day," Anne said. "St. George sails on the morning tide. Elizabeth and I go to Bridge House to deliver this year's loquat jam and return to find all these goings on, and now we learn that we're to have a unique dinghy team on Bermuda Day. My, my, my! Lord have mercy, what a day!"

"After all that's happened," Eugénie said, laughing, "I guess it's past time for me to retire. It appears to be official that I'll captain The Grove team. If I'm to conduct myself *avec honneur,* I'd best not, as you say in English, burn the midnight oil."

"I'm close on your heels," Elizabeth agreed, yawning. "I'm worn out."

"You girls get along to bed." Anne said, giving each a hug. "I won't be long myself."

Eugénie slept later than usual the following morning. She awoke slowly to the pleasant smell of baking bread wafting through the open windows, signaling that The Grove ovens were well into their weekly baking schedule.

"*Mon Dieu!* It must be late," she exclaimed as her eyes flew open to see Marie sitting quietly by the hearth, her hands busy with needlework. "Marie, how could you let me sleep away the morning?" she scolded, throwing the covers back and leaping out of bed.

"You were long overdue after all those early-morning practices. Anyway, there was no reason to disturb your rest. This day's practice has been postponed," Marie answered. At Eugénie's questioning stare, she explained. "Mistress Elizabeth has been called away to a neighbor's to help at a birthing, and Mr. Hamilton was dispatched to Warwick by the Colonel. I think it had something to do with the warehouse fires."

"Ah, they're wasting no time putting their plan into action," Eugénie mused aloud. "Well, I see no reason not to practice on my own, then. No telling when Elizabeth will be home, and Rorick will surely be gone most of the day. The better I know the tides, the currents, and the wind, the happier I'll be. For that, I need only a boat and a beautiful day. Let's see, where are my britches and vest?"

"Mistress, shall I come with you? I don't think it's wise for you to go sailing by yourself."

"No, no, Marie. Truth be known, I feel very much at home in the little craft. She handles like a dream and, look, there isn't a cloud in the sky."

"It isn't fitting," Marie grumbled. "What must the Bermudians think of French ladies when you behave as you do?"

"That has never been my concern, as you well know," Eugénie said. "I'll leave that for you to fret over, dear Marie, while I go off and have a perfectly delightful sail on this glorious day. No, not the bonnet. Where's my cap? It'll hold my hair out of the way and not blow off in the wind."

Disgruntled, Marie put down the bonnet and dug in the drawer of the cedar bureau. After much searching, she found the cap.

"Mistress, if you must, you must, but it would be far more seemly and safe if I were with you."

"Marie, it's not like you to grumble so. It must be the babe that's causing you to be so fussy. Besides, you know since you've been *enceinte* that water travel has not agreed with you. If you were in the boat, I'd spend all my time worrying about you. I do that enough as it is, even though I have to admit you are the picture of health. Why, if I didn't know better, I'd never guess you're with child and by our calculations at least three months along. That is, I'd never guess as long as you stay on solid ground," she said, trying to tease a smile from her friend. Then she changed the subject. "Now is as good a time as any to tell you all that happened yesterday." Wasting no time, she brought Marie up to date.

"And you're going out alone in that boat with . . ."

"Really, Marie, I am not going out on the high seas. Nor am I sailing some merchant ship. I'll be perfectly safe."

"Mr. St. George would not like this one bit," Marie protested.

"Marie, I'm not going to discuss this any further. I'm wasting good time that could be better spent out on the water. Now give me a smile, and if Elizabeth comes back in time, tell her to hail me from the dock and perhaps we'll be able to salvage a practice after all."

Before Eugénie could speak further, there was a knock on the door. "Come in," Eugénie said brightly.

"Oh, Eugénie, I'm sorry to disturb you, dear," Anne Tucker began breathlessly. "Are you still planning on going to St. George's with Harry and Fanny? If so, I realize this is awfully short notice, but with everything that's happened, Harry thinks he should get up there without delay. They're planning on leaving within the hour. Oh, dear, oh, dear! How complicated and confusing everything's become."

Eugénie rushed to her side and put her arm around the older woman. "Please, Anne, don't be concerned on my account. Yes, I would love to join them, and it won't be any trouble at all for me to be ready in time."

"Oh, I'm so relieved, dear. I know how much you were looking forward to going. This is perfect then, because Harry mentioned that a gathering was planned at Governor's House this evening, which means that you'll be able to see the governor as well. How wonderful! I'll send Jeremy with you to pilot you back. Good, good, good, everything is working out just perfectly." As she opened the door to leave, she added, "The Colonel said he had a few things he'd like to discuss with you before you go. He's at his desk working on the accounts, when you're ready."

"Please tell him I'll be right along," Eugénie said, then turned to Marie as Anne closed the door softly behind her. "Well, so much for dinghy practice. Now, finally, I'll have a chance to see the governor in his own setting and hear the other point of view on the island. Marie, while I'm gone, if something should happen that needs taking care of, don't wait for my return. Get a message to Roland, immediately."

"Shouldn't I be with you to attend to your needs?" Marie asked.

"I don't think so. It'll be such a short time. I expect to be back by tomorrow evening, if not before. I'm sure there's someone at Fanny's house who can help me." As Marie looked meaningfully at Eugénie's tousled curls, Eugénie laughed, saying, "Yes, yes, I know. My hair is always a challenge. Well, do what you can with it now, and I'll do my best to act like a lady and not disturb it. I'll manage somehow this evening. Oh, stop looking so skeptical and help me get ready." True to her word, Eugénie was dressed, packed, and knocking on Colonel Tucker's door in no time.

"Eugénie? Yes, yes. Come in, come in," he called out. "Well, well, well. Things are popping, that they are. Now, let me see. I was wondering if you'd be willing to do me a great favor." When Eugénie nodded, he went on. "Good. While you're dining at the governor's, I would appreciate it greatly if you'd find a moment to slip out and take a good look at the magazine where the gunpowder is stored. I trust you'll return with the information we'll need to carry out our plan if it comes to that. It's right there near Governor's House, so it'll be simple for you to find it. Should someone come upon you, with your quick wits, you'll easily allay their suspicions. On the other hand, if a gentleman were found wandering around there in the dark of night, he'd have a far harder time of it. Keep your ears pricked for anything you hear of note while you're mingling with the governor's guests. Who'd have thought this would work out so well for our purposes?" the Colonel asked, beaming. "Now go along and have a good trip. You certainly have a beautiful day for it. I'll be eager to hear what you have to report when you return." With a smile and a pat on her hand, the Colonel swung his chair around and returned to the mound of papers on his desk.

D'accord! I think I've been dismissed! Eugénie laughed to herself. No questions, no chance to answer. Just do it, Miss Eugénie! Well, it's nothing that I wasn't planning to do anyway. She hurried down to the dock to join Harry and Fanny.

The trip by boat to St. George's went without incident. The two little boys were a constant source of amusement to Eugénie, if not their parents. When they finally collapsed on each other to take a catnap, Eugénie leaned back against her seat and enjoyed the scenery as it slipped by. Jeremy managed to resist his usual antics, except for occasionally bursting into song in a language completely foreign to Eugénie. The tunes were so infectious that he soon had the other two members of the crew harmonizing with him. After a while, even Eugénie and the Tuckers found themselves humming along. Eugénie found the whole experience thoroughly delightful. When the boat pulled up at the dock in St. George's, she realized that she hadn't spent one second thinking about what she had to face later that evening.

Eugénie noticed, as she was standing in Governor Bruère's informal receiving line with Harry and Fanny, that she felt surprisingly refreshed and ready for anything. Almost anything, she mentally corrected herself. *Harry's directions to the magazine seem clear enough. He certainly hadn't appeared startled when she asked him about it. I just hope there's enough moonlight to see where I'm going. Wandering about in the total darkness . . .*

The governor's words broke through her thoughts. "Ah, Mistress Eugénie, what a pleasure it is to see you again! How kind of you to come."

"Governor Bruère, I'm delighted to be here. Thank you for your kind invitation," Eugénie replied smoothly, with a deep curtsy.

"I trust my grandsons haven't made a complete nuisance of themselves, and your accommodations are adequate?"

"Absolutely not, sir, to the first question—and a resounding Yes! to the second." Eugénie moved on as the next guest claimed the governor's attention.

The evening was successful from Eugénie's point of view. There was no end of conversation about the strong support that England could expect from the eastern end of the island. She even heard two men discussing, with the full agreement of those around them, that England should use Bermuda in any way that was necessary. Eugénie had no question about this gathering's loyalty to the Crown and the lengths to which these people were willing to go.

There was one ticklish moment when a well-meaning guest asked her, "Comtesse, I must have been misinformed. I was told that you've been staying at the home of Colonel Henry Tucker. My source must have been mistaken. Certainly, no clear-thinking person would associate with such as he?"

"Au contraire, c'est vrai." Eugénie answered, smiling sweetly. *"Oui, um, um . . . comment dîtes-vous, um . . . ? Excusez-moi, monsieur, parlez-vous français?"* With a Gallic shrug, she looked around wide-eyed at the circle of guests who now hung on her every word, whether they understood one single syllable of what she said or not.

Eugénie had barely caught her breath when a florid-faced man stepped forward, his thumbs stuffed in the pockets of his brocade waistcoat, and said, "Mademoiselle Eugénie, please accept our apology. I'm sure my good neighbor here didn't intend to catechize you about your purely innocent sojourn here in Bermuda. It's no crime to accept the hospitality of Anne and Henry Tucker, even if they do hold peculiar political views." He paused as those around him laughed good-naturedly. "We're in a complete state of disarray on the island, not knowing from one day to the next what to expect. We are upside-down and suspicious of our own shadows. I understand that you're a skilled equestrian and that you bought a stable of racing bloodstock of outstanding quality while in Virginia, which is now on its way to France. Come, tell me about it as I escort you in to dinner."

Eugénie was grateful for his generous gesture, but his neighbor's accurate assessment of her put her on guard. She had been lucky this time to be able to use feminine giddiness and the excuse of ignorance to slip out of a sticky situation. But what about next time? Her earlier euphoria evaporated. She was on her toes and alert for the rest of the evening. To her relief, the subject of the Tuckers did not come up again. If anything, she became a sympathetic character who had been harshly put upon by the poor, hapless soul who had had the temerity to bring it up.

At the first opportunity, Eugénie signaled to Harry that she was going on her errand. He knew to stand by.

The night was dark, but the moon gave off enough light to guide her across the garden and through the woods to the edge of the clearing where the magazine stood. Its very solitude gave off an eerie feeling. Eugénie shivered as she gazed at its impressive height. Not a sound, not a breath of air disturbed its tranquillity. Eager to complete her mission and be gone, she quickly estimated its height and width and made note of the native block used to build it. Because of where it was situated, she saw that anyone who approached it would be out in the open and exposed.

Eugénie slipped across the clearing to assess lookout positions and to see what access there was to the water. Finding answers to both questions, she stopped to think whether she had overlooked anything. Satisfied, she was just turning to retrace her steps when she heard a sound. She kept to the trees that fringed the clearing as she made her way soundlessly around the periphery. Straining her eyes and ears, she watched for someone to show himself. She hoped to reach the side of the magazine nearest Governor's House, before she was forced to make her move. Just as she was within a few steps of her objective, a distinguished-looking man whom she recognized as a guest of the governor's stepped into the clearing, puffing on an elaborate pipe and gazing out to the water away from where she stood.

Eugénie thought quickly. Now she had a choice. She could either make her way as silently as possible back to Governor's House along the moonlit paths and take the chance of being sighted, or she could brazen it out, rely on her quick wits, and take her chances. Of the two, she preferred the latter.

Making no effort to cover her approach—in fact, purposely stepping on dry leaves—she walked nonchalantly into the clearing, staring around her as if lost. Only at the last minute and with apparent shock did she turn and exclaim to the man standing there, "O, *mon Dieu! Pardon!* I didn't expect . . . I hope I'm not disturbing you."

The man looked at her closely for a moment and then said quickly, "Ah, Mistress, don't distress yourself. If I'm not mistaken, you and I are both attending the governor's gathering tonight. Allow me to introduce myself. I'm George Westbrook. Please call me George. I must confess, dear lady, you've found me out. I had hoped to slip away and have a quiet smoke. I'm in something of a personal dilemma: an affair of the heart."

Eugénie breathed a sigh of relief. Here was a man so distracted with his own concerns that he was hardly coherent enough to question what she might be doing in the vicinity of the British magazine. "Then I did intrude. Oh, dear, forgive me. It's my first visit to Governor's House, and I'd heard such glowing reports of the gardens. I'd so looked forward to seeing them. Since I must leave early in the morning, I thought I'd just slip out and see them by moonlight. I was having the loveliest time. They are simply beautiful, aren't they? Somewhere, though, I must have taken the wrong turn, for I seem to have lost my way and ended up here." Eugénie stopped abruptly and stared in the direction of the magazine. "What in heaven's name is that?"

Her companion laughed heartily. "It's called a magazine. It houses the government's munitions."

"O, mon Dieu!" Eugénie exclaimed, her hand at her throat. "How terribly dangerous! We must leave at once! Where are the guards to warn people to stay away from here?"

"You needn't be afraid, my dear. To my knowledge, there have never been any guards, which probably means they don't think there's any danger. Otherwise, it would stand to reason that they'd post them. So you see, you're perfectly safe." When he saw Eugénie shudder, he offered gallantly, "Come, I'll escort you back. You know, you really shouldn't be out here wandering around in the dark, alone." She took his arm and allowed him to lead her out of the clearing and away from the magazine.

They arrived back at Governor's House to find that the evening was drawing to a close. Seeing Fanny and Harry nearby, Eugénie thanked her escort, bid him goodnight, and quickly went to join them.

As she was thanking the governor for his hospitality, she slipped in a few remarks about the splendor of the gardens in the moonlight. He said graciously that he hoped she would have the chance to come again before leaving Bermuda so that he could show them to her in the daylight. On that pleasant note, the three made their farewells and hastened home to the Tucker house, all too happy to call it a day since Eugénie and Jeremy had to make an early start the next morning.

XXVIII

⚜⚜⚜

"Marie, we simply are not going to discuss this any more!" Eugénie said firmly. "I'll be perfectly safe. Roland will be with me." When her remark was met with silence, she looked up from her breakfast to see Marie looking at her with concern. "All right, all right, what is it? When I see that look, I know there's something I need to know for my own good," Eugénie said.

"Your last instructions before leaving France were to avoid any unnecessary risks. Simply to observe, listen, and learn the nature and extent of the colonials' quarrel with the British Crown as a witness only," Marie said, her face set. "You escaped danger in Virginia by the skin of your teeth, only to be drawn into a conspiracy here. You return yesterday after carrying out the orders of the leader of that conspiracy, and now this! What if it had been a British soldier who stumbled on you there at the magazine? What if the governor himself had . . . ? Oh, I don't even want to think about what might have happened!"

"Shhh, Marie! Nothing did happen, so stop fretting. The Colonel didn't ask me to do anything that I wasn't planning to do anyway. Had I not gone to St. George's, I wouldn't have learned the views and opinions of the other faction on the island. Also, now I know the full extent of Bermuda's armaments and how loosely they are guarded. So by appearing to go under the Colonel's orders, I've not only gained his trust, but I also have gathered essential information for our mission.

"Believe me, I much prefer the role of witness," she went on, "but if it's participant I must be to serve our purposes, then so be it. Today I have no choice. Roland has located Darby, and I must find out what he's doing here in Bermuda. I have every reason to believe that it has something to do with me. You know I'm not safe as long as he's at large. I promise not to take any unnecessary chances," she concluded airily. For fear of upsetting Marie further, she chose not to admit that she shared Marie's concerns.

"That hardly makes me feel any better," Marie grumbled.

"Come, Marie, help me with this disguise. I can't leave Roland hanging around the kitchen much longer without arousing suspicions," Eugénie said, putting an end to the discussion.

It was midmorning when Eugénie and Roland found themselves in Salt Kettle, entering a seedy tavern near the docks. Despite the dimness of the room, they had no difficulty singling out their quarry at a table near the wide, rough-hewn bar. Darby's clothing set him apart from the establishment's clientele, in general, and from his cronies, in particular. While Roland nonchalantly laid claim to a table between the bar and the door, Eugénie wandered up to the bar, staggering slightly, and ordered two tankards of ale.

"Sir, 'tis tailor-made for our purposes, sounds like," she heard one of his companions saying. "You have a grudge against them swells up west. Well, like I see it, you've come to the right place, long as you make it worth our while."

"You've heard about all the warehouse firings and the shipwrecks over the last few months," Darby said, his voice low. His next words froze Eugénie in her tracks. "You make this one at the Tuckers' look like the others, and I'll more than make it worth your while." At that moment, the barmaid shoved two brimming tankards toward Eugénie, who threw some coins down on the greasy surface. With an unsteady gait, she carried them over to Roland.

"Don't you think you're overdoing the staggering a little bit?" Roland asked quietly as he quaffed his ale.

"Never mind that!" Eugénie hissed. "He's plotting mischief against the Tuckers. We must do something!" Giving Roland an owlish stare, Eugénie tilted the tankard and downed a hefty portion, then smacked her lips and wiped the foam off her mouth with the back of her hand. According to plan, she was soon back at the bar ordering two more of the same.

"When next we meet, I'll tell you the time and place," Darby was saying, "but stay clear of the others who are operating up on the west end. It won't do to have them find out we're moving in on their territory."

Just then Eugénie stumbled and bumped into one of the ruffians' chairs, pouring cold liquid down his back. "What the . . . !" was all he managed to roar before Eugénie gagged and spewed vomit down his shirtfront, splattering his face in the process.

The outraged man sprang to his feet, but before he could lunge at Eugénie, Roland appeared out of nowhere and thrust her behind him. "No offense meant, mate. He's young and hasn't had much practice with the brew," he said mildly.

"Not bloody likely!" was the reply as the man made a grab for Eugénie. With a quick movement, Roland drew his knife and barred the man's way. Eugénie, who had been crouching, suddenly stood up, a dagger gleaming in her hand. For a moment no one moved. Then the others at the table were on their feet, knives drawn. "Lads!" rang a shout from the doorway. "Looks like an uneven match. Let's have at it." A short-lived brawl ensued, and the four conspirators were soon subdued.

"Thank you, mates, for coming to our aid," Roland said.

"Speak nothing of it," came the reply. "There are too many of their kind showing up around here lately. We're grateful for the excuse to lay these four out. We'll see that they're on the next ship leaving Bermuda. Good riddance."

"Damn!" Eugénie said as she and Roland watched the local men haul the four away. "Damn! Damn! Darby got away!"

Roland gave her a long look. "My, my, my. Miss Eugénie, you've more courage than brains. I hate to think what would have happened in there if the locals hadn't shown up when they did, and you're undone that Darby escaped? We know the man now. We know some-thing of his plans. All isn't lost. You alert the Colonel, set up a guard at The Grove, and I and mine will see that Darby doesn't take a step that we don't know about. Now, more importantly, what in God's name caused you to start that fracas? And when did you learn to vomit at will and to handle a blade so deftly?"

"We had to do something, didn't we?" Her eyes twinkled. "It was all I could come up with on the spur of the moment. As to that disgust-ing behavior, when I was a young child, I found it was a very convinc-ing method to avoid doing something I didn't want to do. The dagger is just one of the weapons my father taught me to handle from the time I could hold them in my hand."

"You've an unusual arsenal of talents, to be sure," Roland remarked dryly.

When Eugénie arrived back at The Grove, Colonel Tucker was nowhere to be found. She left a note on his desk, told Marie she was going for a short sail, changed into fresh britches and blouse, and in short order was off to the dock by way of the kitchen.

She gladly accepted Cook's offer of some freshly baked bread and a wedge of cheese from the buttery wrapped up in a gingham cloth. As she approached the dock, she smiled at the dinghy bouncing merrily on the water, tugging at its line as though impatient to be off.

"Not one whit more impatient than I," she remarked out loud. Wasting no time, she untied the painter from the iron cleat, flipped it into the boat, and quickly hopped into the bow. Her fingers, clumsy with the unfamiliar lines only a few weeks ago, easily unfurled and raised the single sail. It luffed in the breeze as she used one of the oars to push off from the dock.

The little craft turned and headed up into the wind. Pushing the tiller to port, she trimmed the sail in close. Immediately the wind swelled the canvas and the boat glided out into the Great Sound.

Time passed quickly as Eugénie took the dinghy through its paces. She practiced several maneuvers until she was satisfied. Although the surface of the water remained smooth and the breeze true, she noticed that the current seemed to be getting swifter. Pleased with her progress, she decided it was much too beautiful a day to go back to shore. On a whim, she pointed the boat to the mouth of the sound and was soon sailing toward the beach where she and St. George had enjoyed their picnic.

It's just as beautiful as I remembered, she thought as she rode the dinghy up onto the sand. Removing her boots and rolling up her britches, she hopped into the water carrying the gingham sack. Once ashore, she grasped the painter and dragged the bow up on the beach, leaving the stern bobbing on the gently lapping waves.

Kneeling down, Eugénie opened the cloth and spread it out on the warm sand. She was delighted to find that Cook had also added fruit and a chilled bottle of wine to her feast. Looking at the food reminded her that she had rushed off with Roland without finishing breakfast. She poured a glass of wine, as she chewed a bite of the crusty bread and dark cheese. The sugared orange rinds melted in her mouth, and the plump peach was the sweetest she had ever tasted.

All too soon, she was sipping the last drop of wine from her glass. She plucked the bread and cheese crumbs from her shirtfront and licked them off her fingertips, sticky with peach juice. Then, stretching her arms high over her head, she indulged in a huge yawn. Why, I'm just like my dear old tabby after she's filled her belly with rich cream, Eugénie thought. I can see her now, stretching out each long leg and then flopping down in a patch of sunlight for her afternoon nap. Hmmm, not a bad idea after such an adventurous morning.

She picked up the half-finished bottle of wine and the wrappers and set them aside. Just a short nap, was her last thought as she stretched out on the cloth, cradled her head on her arms, and fell fast asleep.

She slept as the afternoon melted away. She slept as clouds formed on the horizon and moved up across the sky, darkening as they came. She slept as the breeze stiffened. She slept as the seas churned and grew angry before the wind. She slept as the seabirds cried their alarm and raced for shelter. She awoke as a clap of thunder rolled across the sky and the first drops of rain pelted down on the hot sand.

In one motion, Eugénie spun over and came up to a sitting position, catching the gingham cloth as it threatened to fly away. Her first effort to stand failed as a sheet of rain driven by the wind caught her square and knocked her to her knees. Leaning into it, she struggled to her feet and stared in the direction of the storm.

Oh my God! she thought. With the wind from the south, this is no short squall. Thank God, St. George took such pains to explain the weather patterns to me. I'd better find shelter—and quickly, by the looks of it!

At that moment, she noticed the dinghy. While she slept, the tide had begun to come in, weakening the boat's purchase on the sand. Now the waves and wind were angrily rocking it back and forth. As she watched, the little craft came loose and started to float out to sea.

With a cry, she quickly knotted the gingham cloth around her waist and ran into the surf after the boat. Flailing forward, she was soon in water up to her chest. She flung herself toward the boat, and just managed to grasp the gunwale. The next wave caught the dinghy and lifted it, tearing it out of her grip and hurling it away from her.

The wall of water crashed over her, knocking her down and sucking her under. When she finally struggled to her feet, she looked wildly around for the dinghy and saw it floating away from her. As she moved toward it, the wave rolled away from the shore, carrying the dinghy with it.

Eugénie felt the undertow dragging at her body. Fighting to keep her footing, she exerted every ounce of her strength to get to shore and finally fell forward onto the sand. Not pausing to catch her breath, she hauled herself up on her hands and knees and crawled farther up on the beach. Battered by the wind and rain, she dragged herself forward until she reached a tangle of seagrape and crawled under it for shelter. Clasping her arms around her knees, she sat with her head bowed, taking in great gulps of air.

As her breath returned to normal, she raised her eyes and stared out to sea. To her amazement, she saw the dinghy high on the crest of a wave riding into shore. Like a giant hand, the water lifted the boat on its curl and tossed it up on the sand. Before the sea could reclaim its gift, Eugénie raced back down the bank, grabbed the side of the boat with both hands, and wrestled it out of the reach of the next wave.

Miraculously, the sail and rudder were still intact. Fighting the wind and rain, she furled and lashed the sail before dragging the dinghy farther up the beach. Her first thought was to turn it over and use it for shelter. She quickly discarded that idea, imagining the cold wet sand, the rain pounding on the wood, and the wind howling around her.

The storm had darkened the sky, but by her reckoning it was still only late afternoon or early evening. Prodding herself to find a more suitable haven from the storm's fury before the light was entirely gone, she staggered up the beach, straining her eyes to see through the gloom.

How could this ominous stretch of deserted shore have looked so inviting only a few hours ago? Where are those cozy little caves St. George pointed out when we were here last?

She tripped and almost fell before she caught herself and stumbled up the bank. She leaned into the wind, her bare feet stinging where she had scraped them on the rocks, but she hardly noticed. Just when she was about to believe her search was in vain, she saw a break in the undergrowth. She stepped carefully over a rock formation and found herself standing in front of an opening to a small cave.

Stretching her hands out, she felt her way into the darkness. The wall of the cave was slimy to her touch, and the wet sand on the floor oozed between her toes, but no tapestried wall or carpeted floor had ever felt so palatial or enticing to her. She peered into the recesses of the cave, trying to judge how deep it was, but saw only a solid wall of blackness. No telling what creatures lurk in that darkness, she thought.

She shuddered, thinking of hairy things with bright eyes and sharp teeth and claws. "No need to go any deeper. I'll just settle right down here," she muttered out loud. "Have no fear," she spoke louder, "I won't disturb your habitat. There's plenty of room for all of us. I'll not bother you, if you don't bother me."

She thought she heard a distant rustle and flutter but decided not to dwell on the possibilities. Instead, she chose a position far enough into the cave to protect herself from the weather but near enough to the entrance not to threaten her erstwhile companions. She sat down gingerly and leaned back against the wall, wrapping her arms around her legs and resting her head on her knees.

She tried not to notice the chill of her sodden clothes seeping into her bones or the possibility that the storm could last for days instead of hours. In spite of the ferocity raging around her, she soon fell into an exhausted sleep.

XXIX

⚜ ⚜ ⚜

Eugénie stirred in her sleep, causing her cramped muscles to protest. Now fully awake, she looked around her. She was surrounded by thick blackness. She had only the damp floor beneath her and the cold wall at her back to remind her of where she was.

"*O, mon Dieu!*" she exclaimed, as it all came back to her in a rush. The storm had not diminished while she slept. A bolt of lightning cut across the sky, followed by a crashing roll of thunder. The wind roared and the rain slashed at the world just beyond the cave's entrance. She huddled closer to the wall, her teeth chattering.

At first she thought it was her imagination. Then she heard it again, far off: a voice calling. She inched from her hiding place. Braving the storm's fury, she stared out into the darkness. Yes, there it was again. She was sure of it. Human voices. With the next slash of lightning, she could faintly make out dark figures far off down the beach. Rain and darkness distorted her vision. It was impossible for her to estimate their distance or imagine their purpose.

She shrank back farther into the cave. She remembered St. George's description of wreckers and shipwrecks.

A series of lightning flashes illuminated the scene before her. Not far from shore, a ship had foundered on the reefs. Roughly dressed men surrounded several small boats gathered on the beach with their bows pointing out to sea.

At that moment, she saw a flickering lantern high up on the bluffs. Wreckers! The word ripped through her mind.

Above the scream of the storm, she heard a strangely familiar voice shouting out commands. She saw lanterns come to life and men scrambling into the boats and heading out to the crippled ship. She recognized the leader by his fine clothes and arrogant stance before he doused the flame of his lantern.

Once more, everything was thrown into darkness except for the bobbing lights on the boats making their way out to sea toward their prey.

These must be the very ones who've been burning the warehouses and causing the shipwrecks, Eugénie thought, a chill slithering through her. Why does their leader seem so familiar to me? Something teased at the edge of her mind, but try as she might, it continued to elude her. They must have great confidence in their prowess to venture out on a night like this. *Mon Dieu,* I've got to get away from here. But how?

She could only stare out through the storm, hoping that somehow she would go undetected.

Some time later, she noticed that the small dots of light appeared to be moving back toward the shore. In horror, she saw that the swift current was depositing the boats on the beach right in front of her cave.

"Well done, mates," came the voice of the leader, who had moved down the beach to meet them. "A good night's work, all around. Straight up the bank there are good-sized caves where you can store the booty."

In her terror, Eugénie almost missed the next words. "Mr. Trowbridge, sir, when will we divide up the spoils?"

"As soon as the storm plays out, the wrecked ship is discovered, and curiosity has died down, Mr. Painter. It'll be safe enough till then, as long as you and Limey are here to safeguard it. Move along. After all our hard work this night, 'twould be a shame for the rain and wind to bring our efforts to harm. I'm off now. See that you secure the boats in the caves when you're done, lads."

"Mr. Trowbridge," Eugénie gasped. "A confidant of the Colonel's!"

Before Trowbridge had finished his commands she crept out of the cave and slipped behind a wall of seagrape that grew near the opening of the cave.

No sooner had she secreted herself behind the protective curtain than she heard the men thrashing up the bank, groaning under the weight of the booty. "'Tis sheer madness, I say, out on a night such as this," one said.

"He's the Devil's own," grumbled another, as their footsteps passed right in front of where she was hiding.

"Aye, ye speak true, but the element of surprise, my lads, the element of surprise," another spoke up. "The high and mighty around these parts ain't going to mount sentries in this weather to watch for our kindly lanterns beckoning their fat vessels into our welcoming hands, now are they?"

"Shut your mouths!" rang out a voice with authority. Eugénie recognized the voice of the one whom Trowbridge had called Painter. "Save your breath for the carrying and dragging. Any of you lowlifes who don't like the work and pay can answer to me. There's plenty others to take your place. Now, step it off!" After that the men quieted down to only an occasional mutter.

If I ever escape from here, I'll have much to report to the Colonel, Eugénie thought. To her horror, just at that moment, she exploded with a sneeze.

"What was that?" one of the men shouted.

"There's someone spying on us!"

"I think it came from over there!"

"Spread out! Find him!"

Eugénie turned and tried to bury herself deeper into the seagrape, only to find her way barred by the dense branches.

Suddenly, rough hands grabbed her from behind and dragged her kicking and clawing out onto the beach. "And what have we here?" Eugénie heard the rough edge of Painter's voice. "'Pears to be a young lad, from the size of him. Still wet behind the ears."

Eugénie turned her head suddenly and sank her teeth into the hand that gripped her arm. Painter let out a howl and backhanded Eugénie across the face, sending her sprawling onto the sand. She rolled away from him and leapt to her feet just as he lunged at her and threw her back on the ground. He fell heavily on top of her, knocking the wind from her lungs. She lay still.

"A spirited one, ain't ye?" he growled, climbing off her. He gave her a kick as he brushed the wet sand off his clothes. "And look what ye've done to me hand. I've a mind to . . ."

His words caught in his throat as Eugénie in one motion rolled up on her feet and drew the dagger strapped to the inside of her leg. Fueled by fear and anger, she thrust the blade up into his midsection with all strength she possessed. The shock of the blow sent a sharp pain up her arm. Somehow she held on, driving the blade in with both hands. He cried out and staggered to one side, pulling her with him.

"What are ye waiting for?" Painter bellowed above the roar of the storm. "Grab him and get him off me!" Eugénie released the dagger. She twisted away from the hands that reached for her and tore off down the beach.

Blinded by the rain and whipped by the wind, she knew only that she had to escape. Her breath came in short bursts, and her bare feet stumbled over rocks and pebbles. She could hear footsteps pounding behind her. It's a nightmare! her mind screamed. It's all part of a nightmare. I'll awake soon!

But she did not awake, and the footsteps were real. A white light exploded behind her eyes and, abruptly, the wind's howl ceased and the rains died. She didn't feel the hands that hauled her up and flung her over a hard shoulder.

She woke up with a jolt to hands slapping her face. With each slap, hot pain seared through her head. "That's more like it," a harsh voice said. "Can't have ye sleeping when there's answers to be had. Who sent ye here? Who're ye spying for?"

In answer, Eugénie turned her head and with a moan retched into the sand. Another slap cracked across her cheek. With her hands and legs bound, she could do nothing but lie there in the vomit.

Before the rough could strike her again, Painter shoved away the hands that had been tying a rag around his wound and shouted, "Enough! He'll be no good to us dead, ye fool! There'll be time enough for that when we've learned what he knows. Then ye can do what you want with him, but only after I've settled my score. I'll persuade him to give us some answers while the rest of ye finish up storing the booty in the cave. Ye heard me! Get on with ye!"

Eugénie turned her face up into the rain and let it rinse the filth from her face. "There's life in ye yet, is there, lad?" Painter said as he grabbed the gingham cloth at her waist and wrenched her up on her feet.

The pain in her head was blinding, and Eugénie bit her lip to keep from crying out. One thought repeated over and over in her mind. Thank God for the cap! Thank God for the cap!

Painter picked up a torch and peered into her face. "Let's get a better look at ye, laddie. Oh ho! What a pretty lad you are! There are those here who might have special plans for ye, but if ye help Painter, he'll protect ye from those lecherous hands. Best ye look to ol' Painter for your salvation."

Eugénie felt her heart stop in her chest. Fear slammed into her like a living thing. She clamped her teeth together to stop their chattering, but she couldn't stop the tremor that coursed through her body.

"I see ye understand your situation some better now. Just tell me who sent ye and how ye knew of our plans this night?"

"No one sent me, sir. I came here by chance and got caught in the storm," Eugénie mumbled, trying to lower her voice and disguise her accent. Painter scowled into her face, not pleased with the response.

Before he could speak again, one of the men standing nearby said, "Alone or sent by others don't matter none. He's seen us. That decides it. We've wasted enough time already. I say we get rid of him and be done with it."

As he spoke, he glanced down at Eugénie, whose face was still lit by the torch in Painter's hand. "Christ's blood, man! Where are your eyes? This ain't no lad. It's a woman!" He hauled Eugénie over to him by her shirtfront. "I wager there's more than a lad's shag cut hidden 'neath that cap!"

Not waiting for Painter, he snatched the woolen cap off her head and watched as her hair, tangled and wet from the rain, tumbled down her back. Before their eyes, she was transformed from a pretty young boy into a beautiful woman.

"Jesus Christ and the Heavenly Hosts!" Painter whispered. The other wreckers crowded around them, gawking.

Confronted by the worst of her nightmare, a strange calm settled over Eugénie. Her trembling stopped. She drew herself up and stared, unseeing, over the heads of the men who circled around her. Had she looked, she would have seen eyes gleaming and tongues licking dry lips.

Painter saw all this and more. "Back! Back!" he hollered. "She's mine till I'm done with her." He gripped her roughly by the arm and turned her to face him. Stepping in close to her, he grabbed the front of her shirt and with one swift motion ripped it from top to bottom. His violence destroyed her calm, and with a gasp her eyes flew to his face. "Sweet, sweet," he growled. His eyes held hers as the fingers of one large hand closed over her breast and squeezed it, sending a sharp stab of pain through her. He laughed deep in his throat. Tearing off the rest of the shirt, he ran his hands over her, devouring her with his eyes.

Painter's pleasure was interrupted as a burly man separated himself from the circle and stepped forward. "Who says she's yours, Painter? I'll fight ye for her!" He shoved Eugénie aside. Grappling Painter around the waist, the challenger threw him to the ground and fell on him, pummeling him with his fists.

Painter, agile despite his size, shoved his assailant off and sprang to his feet. The other man recovered quickly and leapt up. The two men faced off. Hands clenched into fists, they crouched in wide stances. The rain and wind went unnoticed as they slowly circled each other. Their comrades formed a large ring around them, yelling out encouragement.

Eugénie took advantage of the mob's fascination with the fight. She sank to the ground and, using elbows and heels, slithered away from the brawl. With each movement, the ropes cut into her wrists and ankles. Hot pain shot through her head, almost taking her breath away. Pebbles and grit tore at her bare flesh. She finally managed to creep under the protection of a large bush. Curling into a tight ball, she stopped to catch her breath. She moved her wrists to test the bonds and found some play in them. While she struggled to work one hand loose, she listened to the progress of the fight.

With a violent wrench, one hand came free. Quickly, Eugénie untied the other and reached down to release her bound ankles. Once she was free, she searched around under the sheltering bush for a weapon and found a sharply pointed rock.

The sound of the fight ended. She held her breath and waited.

"Where's she got to?" Painter's voice came from close by. "She couldn't have got far." She heard him thrashing through the underbrush right beside her and tensed for the inevitable. Heavy arms grabbed her around the waist and pulled her up against a heavily muscled chest. She smelled sweat, blood, and rank maleness. Sour bile rose in her throat and she fought the impulse to gag.

"I've won you fair and square, Miss. There's none going to challenge Painter now. We can relax and take our sweet time. You be nice to me and I'll be nice to you. If'n you please Painter, well, maybe he'll let you stay . . ."

Suddenly, gunfire exploded in every direction, followed by the ring of metal on metal. Painter's shout of anger caught in his throat, and Eugénie was hurled to the ground. She looked up to see a giant throttling Painter. She scrambled to her feet and took off down the beach, holding tightly to the sharp rock. Almost immediately, strong hands lifted her from behind.

Her fury overcame her fear. *"Non! Non!"* Flailing and kicking, she lashed out with the pointed stone.

"Don't be afraid, Mistress. I won't harm you. I only wish to rescue you from the bandits and return you safely to your home and family."

Eugénie's eyes flew to the face hovering above her. The size! The voice! Could it be . . . ? "Jamie! Oh Jamie! Please God tell me it's you!"

"Mistress Eugénie! By all that's holy! We've been searching everywhere for you. How in God's name did you come to be here?" Setting her carefully on her feet, he yanked the sailor's smock from his back and gently covered her nakedness.

Pulling the sodden garment around her, Eugénie collapsed against her friend and wept. "Jamie, Jamie." She gasped for breath, burrowing into his warmth. "I thought you were another one of them. I couldn't fight any more. It was over. I would have welcomed death."

Patting her on the back, Jamie chuckled, "Sure as God, ye could've fooled me, milady. You were fightin' right well, I'd say. Come, we must see how my men are farin' and attend to the harm those scoundrels did to you."

With the wind tossing her hair in a wide circle around her and the rain streaming down her face, Eugénie looked up at him.

"You saved my life, Jamie. Thank you," she said simply, and fainted at his feet.

XXX

✢✢✢

As Eugénie floated up through the layers of darkness, her first sensation was a slow, even, rocking motion. She lay quietly. A throbbing pain held her head in a vise. Gingerly, she reached up to touch it and was startled to discover that her head was completely swaddled in cloth. When she opened her eyes, the light streaming through the portholes sent a searing pain through her.

A ship? How did I come to be here? What happened to me? A violent wave of nausea swept over her. Without thought, she hauled herself to the edge of the bed and vomited wretchedly over the side. Purged, she fell back against the pillows, spent. She lay panting, eyes closed. The fine sheen of sweat that had covered her body began to evaporate, leaving her chilled and shaking. She huddled beneath the covers, teeth chattering.

She heard footsteps entering the room and felt a warm hand on her forehead, smoothing her hair back with a gentle motion. She whimpered. Even that light touch caused her pain. She struggled to open her eyes, but the eyelids were leaden, unresponsive to her command. She forced a hoarse whisper through her dry lips, *"De l'eau, s'il vous plaît, de l'eau."* Immediately a strong arm slipped beneath her pillow, lifting her, and the rim of a cup touched her mouth. She sipped the cool water and felt it slide down her parched throat. As a finger tenderly applied a fragrant ointment to her cracked lips, she slipped back into a deep sleep.

The next time she awoke, the throbbing in her head had almost completely disappeared. She opened her eyes slowly, remembering the previous blinding flash of pain, and found herself looking into blue eyes that gazed at her with such tenderness that her heart caught in her chest.

"Bridger!" she breathed.

"My dear heart." His voice was deep and ragged with emotion. "I feared, oh how I feared, that you were gone, that you were lost to me. Thank God, you've come back."

"How did I arrive here? Where am I? What happened?"

He took her hands in his and raised them to his lips. "Don't talk, dearest. Save your strength. There'll be time enough later to answer all your questions. For now, let sleep heal your wounds and refresh your spirit. I promise I won't leave you. I'll be here when you awake. Sleep." He leaned over and brushed her lips with his own as her eyes closed and slumber carried her away.

Three days later Eugénie was sitting up without pain and nausea. She reveled in the simple pleasure of it. Bridger had joined her in the captain's cabin to share a light noonday meal.

"How did you know where I'd gone? How did you find me? How did Jamie know that I was missing? And how, in the name of all that's holy, was he able to maneuver in that storm and come ashore?" The words tumbled out of her mouth. Jamie's rescue had been nothing short of a miracle.

Bridger feasted on the sparkle that once more shone in her eyes and the rosy glow that had returned to her cheeks. Gone were the lost, bewildered expression and the terrifying vacant stare.

Exasperated at his silence, Eugénie's eyes shot silver. "Bridger, are you listening to me? I am not a ghost. I am fully recovered. Please answer my questions. I feel as though I've returned from a long way off. I need to feel my feet once more solidly beneath me, which won't happen unless I get some answers."

"You remember, then?" Bridger asked softly. "For the past three long days and nights you suffered with delirium. I despaired for your sanity. You spoke only of your mother and father and your beloved France, except for one time when you appeared to awake and recognize me. You spoke my name."

Eugénie looked thoughtful and then said, "From the time I thanked Jamie for saving my life until I awoke this morning, I recall nothing except vague, frightening images and a moment when your dear face came to me and then disappeared. Please don't keep me in suspense any longer. Answer my questions. I must know how this miracle occurred."

"Indeed, it was a miracle," Bridger agreed, "or a series of the most fortuitous events that I've ever heard of that saved you from a fate that I shudder to think about. Marie became concerned when you hadn't returned by the middle of the afternoon, for you'd said you were only going for a short sail. When it was clear that a storm was brewing and you still weren't back, her concern grew into fear and she took action. She managed to get a message to Roland, who sent Jamie out to search for you.

"His patrolling took him farther and farther along the beaches. As fate would have it, he'd drawn closer to shore because of the weather. By then the storm had come up full force and was venting its fury up and down the coast.

"With the help of lightning, he saw a ship grounded on the reefs. He went to investigate, thinking to aid the survivors. As he drew near, it was clear to him that the vessel had not foundered there by accident. It was the work of wreckers."

Bridger stopped abruptly when he saw her face turn pale. He went to her then and knelt before her, taking her into his arms. "Eugénie, there's no need for you to hear this and relive that awful night. If only I could've borne your humiliation and pain, I wouldn't for all the world cause you anguish anew by bringing back these memories. You're safe with me now. I'm taking you back to The Grove with all the speed of wind and ship that's within my power to provide. That nightmare is over and gone. Let's leave it there where it belongs." He rocked her gently, crooning quietly against her soft curls.

"Bridger, I must know," she said, her voice muffled against his chest. "How I wish I could stay here safely in your arms forever, never speaking of that ordeal again. But I cannot. We must discuss it. That's the only way I can set that night and its horrors aside and heal the wounds of my mind and heart, just as the wounds of my body are healing."

"Very well," Bridger sighed. He hesitated, then rose and walked over to the sideboard. He poured two stiff measures of brandy and returned to her. "I think we're both in need of some bracing." He tossed his back, and Eugénie followed suit. She gagged as the potent liquid burned down her throat and brought tears to her eyes. Impatiently she brushed them away. Once more composed, she pinned him with her silver gaze. Bridger resumed his seat across the table from her and reluctantly continued.

"Aided by the darkness, the storm, and the wreckers' spread-out operation, Jamie and his men were able to slip ashore and position themselves without the wreckers' knowledge.

"From their vantage point, they were able to watch what the scoundrels were doing. They settled in and waited for the opportune moment to strike. They didn't have long to wait. The last of the stolen cargo was being stored in the caves along the cliffs, when all of a sudden a skirmish broke out between the man who appeared to be the leader and a young lad who Jamie had no way of knowing was you in disguise." Bridger chuckled. "Little did you realize that the diversion you caused was expeditious for Jamie and his men. Staying close to cover, they closed in around the scoundrels. Once the brawl broke out between the leader and his challenger, all eyes were fastened on the fight.

"After the leader dispensed with his adversary and turned his attentions once more to you, Jamie and his men moved in quickly. Jamie went after you once he'd immobilized the leader, a man named Painter who, you'll be interested to know, is trussed up, as we speak, below decks." Seeing the frightened look that swept across her face, he added quickly, "Fear not, my love, his days of attacking innocents and luring men and ships to their ruin are over. The punishment administered to wreckers is sharp and swift.

"When Jamie caught up with you, you still had some fight left, as the gashes and bruises on poor Jamie's hide can attest." Bridger laughed, recollecting the battered appearance of his comrade. "There aren't many who can lay a hand on that giant, much less leave a calling card." Bridger's mirth was infectious, and soon they were both laughing, tears rolling down their cheeks.

When Eugénie finally caught her breath, she cried, "Oh, poor Jamie! How will I ever make it up to him?"

"Ah, dear lady, you have already. You see, never before have Jamie's attentions caused a lady to swoon at his feet. Jamie considers having such an effect on the gentler sex a great feather in his cap. He takes full credit for it. He hasn't paused to consider that your swoon could have been caused by blood loss, exposure, exhaustion, fear, or a myriad of other things that would've taxed the strongest constitution.

"No, in his eyes he's fully redeemed. I daresay, right at this moment, he's strutting about, a somewhat scarred, but otherwise proud, peacock. I've no doubt he'll point to whatever battle wounds he may still be carrying as badges of honor." Their eyes caught and held, their faces wreathed in smiles. Slowly the smiles slipped away, and Bridger said softly, "Dear heart, my mind, heart, and soul recoil when I think that you would've been lost to me forever had it not been for a few lucky happenstances. Never to see your beautiful eyes gazing upon me, never to feel the warmth of your smile, to hear the music of your laughter, never to touch you again is beyond my poor faculties to imagine. If you weren't somewhere in this world that I live in, if you were gone from here to another place, then I'd have no use for the heart and the breath that bind me to this earthly place. I would leave and follow you."

He held up his hand as Eugénie started to interrupt him. "No, let me finish. When we last parted, I felt a love for you that filled my whole being, a love that deepened the brilliance of the oceans, that freshened the scents of the earth and magnified the radiance of the skies at day's end. I had only to think of you to see, taste, smell, and feel you. Then a short time ago, you came to me as I slept, not as you've come to me every night since I first laid eyes on you, but you, the essence of you, came into my dream. I held you and felt the texture of your skin. I smelled your scent. I tasted you. I heard your breath in my ear, and when I lay with you, when we were joined together, the pulse deep within you surrounded me and beat in rhythm with my own. When I awoke in the morn your taste was still on my lips."

"I know," Eugénie breathed, "for I experienced the same thing. Somehow, somewhere we crossed a dimension and came together in one dream. In that dream, we joined forever beyond this earthly plane."

"I felt your danger," Bridger said, his level gaze communicating to her in ways his words could not. "I moved heaven and earth to reach you. I arrived early the next morning and met Jamie's ship laden with the stolen cargo, the wreckers that had survived . . . and you. Together, we transferred the human cargo to my hold, along with an exact listing of the contents of the lost ship. The wreckers had disposed of all life on that unfortunate vessel. The circumstances of that night made that cargo repugnant to us, even though naval law would bequeath us the booty. The full contents will be returned to the rightful owners once that can be determined," Bridger finished grimly.

He rose and came to her, taking her face in his hands. "When I think . . ." he whispered, "when I think of what might . . ." and clasped her to him.

"No, no, don't torture yourself, *mon chéri,*" she said, holding him in the circle of her arms. "It's over. It's past. The wounds of my body are all but healed, and now my mind and heart are whole as well. And all to the good. After all, it brought you to me," she said, her eyes twinkling. "I'll have to think of less extreme measures next time."

"There will be no next time," Bridger said sternly. "You are incorrigible! If they weren't such a reprehensible lot, I might almost feel pity for those hapless wreckers at your mercy." Eugénie smiled at him, happy to hear the playful tone return to his voice.

"Now, my love," he said, his expression signaling an end to their lighthearted banter, "to bed with you, and to sleep. I've kept you up long enough. I know from experience that head wounds can be deceiving.

Only sleep can bring you back to full health. And I'll settle for nothing less." He lifted her up and tenderly placed her in bed. Drawing the covers up to her chin, he thoroughly kissed her parted lips before turning to go.

"But, Bridger," Eugénie began.

"Not another word!" he barked. Then he looked at her with a rakish grin. "See you in my dreams."

Colonel Tucker looked out at the harbor as he often did upon arising. Turning back toward the raised canopied bed, he said, "Anne, there's a strange ship at anchor out in the harbor across from our wharf."

"There's so much traffic coming and going these days with all the messages that have been flying back and forth, I'm hard pressed to know even a small fraction of the vessels," Anne answered, carefully stepping down the bed steps as she slipped into a duster.

The Colonel smiled, watching his wife, who looked as fresh to his eyes as she had the first morning of their married lives so many years ago. The early morning was their favorite time of day. Before the bustle of the household infringed on them, they would share a cup of tea in bed or sit together on the window seat looking out over the harbor, discussing this and that.

Joining her husband and linking her arm through his, she followed his gaze. "I wish one would arrive bringing news of dear Eugénie," Anne said sadly. "We have scoured every nook and cranny searching for any sign of her. She has vanished without a trace."

"I feared foul play, my dear girl, once her dinghy was recovered with no sign of her." The Colonel patted her hand. Turning his eyes back toward the ship, he said, "'Pears to be activity aboard that vessel. They're lowering a longboat."

"Why, Henry, it's pointing toward our dock!" Anne exclaimed. Already in his britches and waistcoat, Colonel Tucker grabbed his black broadcloth jacket and started toward the door in his stocking feet.

"Your shoes, Henry, your shoes!"

"Ah, thank you, my dear," he smiled at her tenderly. "Perhaps it's the word I've been waiting for from the Americans," he called back to her as he hurried down the hall.

"Never has the sun shone so brightly or the air smelled so sweet." Eyes closed, her face tilted back, Eugénie took a deep breath. Only minutes before, Bridger had handed her down into the longboat that was now skimming across the water toward The Grove dock.

"Aye, Mistress," Jamie agreed as he pulled hard on his oar. "Looks like there's a little fella mighty glad to see you." Eugénie's eyes flew open, and she saw Jeremy on the bank, leaping up and down, dancing about and waving his arms wildly to get their attention.

"It's Missy Eugénie! Missy Eugénie is comin'. Missy Eugénie is comin' home!" His words, screeched in a high register, carried easily to them across the water. They saw Colonel Tucker dashing across the yard with Anne, her duster flying, not far behind.

By the time the longboat had pulled up to the wharf, the dock and the bank were filled to overflowing with The Grove people.

"Dear, dear child," Anne Tucker cried as tears of joy streamed down her face. "I'd despaired of ever seeing your beautiful face again!" Eugénie was standing just on the edge of the dock. Barraged by questions and expressions of welcome, she staggered and would have fallen had not Jamie's strong arm been there to steady her.

Seeing her precarious position, Colonel Tucker stepped forward. Raising his arms for silence, he said, "Come, come. Everyone step back and give Miss Eugénie some room. We don't want to lose her into the harbor just when we've gotten her back."

As he took Eugénie's arm to lead her off the dock, Jamie elbowed his way to the Colonel's side. "If I may, sir."

Colonel Tucker turned to see a giant stranger blocking his path.

The Colonel looked quizzically at Eugénie. "Colonel Tucker, forgive me," Eugénie said, answering his look. "In my joy at being reunited with your family, I quite forgot my manners and some very important news. May I introduce Mr. James Mackenzie, my dear friend and first mate to Captain Bridger Goodrich."

The smile on the Colonel's face vanished and his eyes turned cold at the mention of Bridger's name. "Sir," the Colonel bowed his head slightly. Then he turned and directed his words to Eugénie. "Neither The Grove, nor I, nor any member of my family welcomes anyone or anything that's in any way connected to that man. I will not countenance that name in my hearing. I would appreciate it if you'd kindly escort Mr. MacKenzie off this property and into that longboat. I'm overjoyed at your safe return, Eugénie, and will await you at the house to hear of your adventure."

He turned to go but looked back with surprise when Eugénie laid a restraining hand on his sleeve. "Colonel Tucker," she began in a soft voice. "We all have much to be thankful for due to Bridger's and Jamie's efforts these past few days. I, for my very life. I implore you to suspend your feelings of animosity long enough to hear Jamie out. I believe that once you've heard what he has to say, you'll agree that he and Captain Goodrich deserve our gratitude, not our condemnation."

"You pique my interest, child," the Colonel responded, his expression softening. "For your sweet sake I'll suffer this man's presence long enough to hear what he has to say." Turning to Jamie, his face hardened once again. "But I make no promises."

When Eugénie, Jamie, and the family were settled in the parlor, the Colonel dispensed with any pretense of hospitality and came right to the point. "What do you have to say for yourself, young man?"

Jamie's face flushed with anger at Colonel Tucker's tone, but he managed to answer mildly enough. "At this moment, sir, we have in the hold of our ship yonder what we believe are the remains of the ring of wreckers, who've been terrorizing the west end of this island for some months now, luring ships onto the reefs and firing and burning the warehouses of the local gentry."

At his words, Colonel Tucker's closed demeanor broke wide open.

"What's that you say? Come, come, man, explain yourself!"

"During the recent storm, I brought my ship into shore seeking shelter," Jamie continued. "We came upon the men now in our hold preying upon the remains of a ship that they, no doubt, had lured onto the rocks."

Jamie's words came out harshly. While he paused to collect himself, the Colonel spoke. "Don't be ashamed of the depth of your feelings. All we seafaring men share a common rage and disgust at the slime you describe. Your feelings are commendable. Please continue."

"Thank you, sir," Jamie replied. "I have personal reasons for wishing to wipe their kind off the face of the earth. I hastened ashore with my crew to capture the vermin and bring them to justice. Our task was made easy because their attention was riveted on a brawl that had broken out between the professed leader of the gang, one Painter by name, and another one of the rascals. It was only later that I learned that they were fighting over Miss Eugénie.

"One thing led to another, and in the melee some of their number lost their lives. A quick death is too good for the likes of them. Unfortunately, some of my men were overzealous. Afterward, my first concern was to carry Miss Eugénie to safety, for she had suffered a serious head injury and other wounds at their hands. In the meantime, my crew rounded up the survivors and the stolen cargo and stored them in the hold of my ship.

"We awoke the next morning," Jamie went on, "to see that the storm had passed and that Captain Goodrich and his ship were riding at anchor alongside of us. On the captain's orders, we transferred onto his ship the remainder of the wreckers and Miss Eugénie, who was still unconscious. It was he who considered it your due to dispose of the wreckers as you saw fit. Despite your feelings toward him, he also felt it was his duty to transport them here to you. He entrusted me with the task of inventorying the recaptured cargo in the hopes that such a list would help to identify the rightful owner. Because of the damage done to the ship by the storm and the wreckers, all identification was lost. Captain Goodrich thought you might know the ship's owner from the list of the contents that are now in the hold of my ship, lying at anchor outside Ely's Harbor. The list is now completed. My orders are to carry out your wishes on both these matters—the wreckers and the cargo. In conclusion, it greatly saddens me to report that no life was spared aboard that ill-fated ship."

A stunned silence hung over the room. Colonel Tucker was the first to recover. "What an extraordinary story! Is your captain aboard the vessel we see anchored in the harbor?" he asked.

"Yes," Jamie answered.

"Jeremy, Jeremy!" The Colonel shouted, knowing that the young lad was never out of earshot when there was something afoot. Immediately, the bright face popped around the doorway.

"Yessah, you call me?" Jeremy asked, his eyes as big as saucers.

"Quick, Jeremy, go to the longboat tied up at the dock and tell those aboard to bring their captain here as quickly as possible."

"Yessah, yessah," Jeremy called over his shoulder, already off to discharge the Colonel's bidding.

"Young man, you and your captain are to be praised and applauded for your actions, which you carried out at no small risk to yourselves and your crew," Colonel Tucker said to Jamie. "There's a price on the heads of that gang of thieves and miscreants, and a substantial reward offered for any information about them. Both will be immediately forthcoming to you, your captain, and the crew. To this I add my apologies for my rudeness, Mr. Mackenzie." Jamie graciously nodded his acceptance.

"That's not to say that the ex-Virginian is absolved of all past deeds against the properties of my associates and myself," Colonel Tucker was quick to add. Eugénie noticed that the Colonel had managed to adhere to his cardinal rule of not uttering the name Bridger Goodrich.

"It appears," he went on, "that you and your captain have rid us of the scourge that has harried the west end of this island for many months—except for one detail: the identity and capture of one of our own, who led and masterminded these villainous exploits. Were he also in our grasp, we might all rest easy in our beds once more," the Colonel said regretfully.

"Colonel Tucker, I think I can shed some light on that subject," Eugénie spoke up, causing all the heads in the room to turn in her direction. "Before I was discovered by the wreckers, I overheard their conversation. I recognized the voice of the man who was their leader, but I couldn't put a name to the voice. Then the man Painter called him by name. He's Stephen Trowbridge, who, if I'm not mistaken, is a member of your inner circle."

"Trowbridge!" Colonel Tucker exclaimed, aghast. "He's my old and trusted friend! Why, as boys, we dreamed of our futures together. I was the best man in his wedding and am the godfather of his oldest son. My God, what brought him to this? What manner of man could turn on his own in such a fashion? He's worse than the slime he led to attack us."

"Henry, Henry, he's sacrificed everything with his despicable deeds," Anne Tucker spoke to him soothingly. "Don't waste one moment's thought on him."

"Thank you, my dear. I'm grateful to you for bringing me back to my senses. Instead, we must plan a way to capture him," he said grimly.

Again Eugénie spoke up. "I heard him say that he would return for the booty after all interest in the wrecked vessel had passed. Within my hearing, he spoke only to Painter and left him to safeguard the treasure. He didn't speak to anyone else and would have no reason or means to contact any of the others. In fact, it would be highly suspicious if he were seen in the company of such men."

"I see your head injury has not clouded your wits, Miss Eugénie," the Colonel said, beaming at her. "We must send a welcoming committee at once to greet Mr. Trowbridge. Meanwhile, we'll keep his erstwhile comrades under wraps until he's safely in our grasp."

"Sir, perhaps I can be of service in this matter." All eyes turned to see Bridger Goodrich standing in the doorway. "I'll gladly dispatch members of my crew on that mission. If Trowbridge is returned to you somewhat the worse for wear, I'll consider the debt he owes to all seamen of conscience partially paid," he said quietly, but with authority. Across the room, the Colonel's eyes locked with those of the younger man. Neither gaze wavered.

Finally Colonel Tucker spoke. "Come in, young man." Everyone in the room breathed a collective sigh of relief. "I salute you for the courage and honor that you've exhibited in the events I learned about today, not the least being your bravery in setting foot on my property." At his wife's show of alarm, Colonel Tucker spoke quickly to reassure her. "I've heard it said that politics make strange bedfellows and stranger enemies of those who might otherwise be friends. In this matter, you and I are in total accord, and the people of Bermuda are in your debt, Captain Goodrich. My head's still spinning from this incredible turn of events. Now, please, have a seat and let's get down to cases. First of all, I accept the offer of your men and ask only that it be done with all speed."

Bridger nodded. Appreciating the need for haste, he turned to Jamie. "Jamie, go at once to my ship and pick three stout men to accompany you. We impatiently await your return. Good hunting and Godspeed."

Bowing briefly to the Colonel, Jamie kissed Eugénie's hand and was gone. "In the meantime," Colonel Tucker said to Bridger. "We must attend to the men you carry in your hold, and I must read the list of the cargo and see if it sheds any light on the ownership of that luckless vessel."

"I should think the less stir we make until we have our hands on Trowbridge, the better," Bridger said, drawing the list from his waistcoat and handing it to the Colonel. "It would be a shame for any word of this to reach his ears and give him an opportunity to escape his just rewards. It would seem to me that the simplest course would be to keep the rascals where they are till Jamie delivers Trowbridge into your hands. Gagged and bound as they are, they cause me little trouble, and a few days more without food may increase their amenability." The two men shared a smile, discovering that at least in this instance their minds ran along parallel lines.

"Dear child," Anne Tucker said, bustling over to where Eugénie sat. "It looks as if these men have the situation well in hand. After all you've endured, you must be close to collapsing. Why, your devoted Marie doesn't even know that you've returned to us. Come along with me. I'll help you up to your bedchamber. You must have a cool bath and go straight to bed and rest, so that you can get your strength back."

Realizing suddenly that she was barely able to keep her eyes open,

Eugénie smiled gratefully at the older woman and said, "Anne, I don't need any persuasion on that score."

"Eugénie, your information has been invaluable to us," Colonel Tucker said, walking over and taking both of her hands in his. "I only regret that it came at such a high cost to you, my dear."

"*Merci,*" she replied. "Were it not for Bridger's and Jamie's timely arrival, I would've paid a far higher price. Those criminals would have succeeded once again, and would have continued to subject the good people of this island to more of their atrocities." Before the Colonel could answer, Marie appeared in the doorway. With a cry, she ran to Eugénie and threw her arms around her mistress.

"Dear God, I'd given you up for lost," she sobbed, tears streaming down her face. "I just heard you were back safely. I was down at the stables with the roan. We've been a great comfort to each other. Oh, Mistress, I can't imagine what I would've done if I'd lost you."

At her words, Bridger quietly bowed his head. "Amen," he said under his breath.

Marie's voice broke. "Thank you, dear Lord, for bringing her safely back to me."

Those in the room had only known Marie as a quiet, dutiful servant. Witnessing her reunion with her mistress, they realized the extent of the suffering she must have endured, stoically and alone.

"There, there," Eugénie murmured to her distraught friend. "It's due to your quick wits that I'm back safe and sound. Come, dry your eyes. I've so much to tell you, but at the moment I must admit that my adventures have left me a bit weary. Help me upstairs before I fall sound asleep on my feet."

Arm in arm, the two women guided each other from the room. For those who watched, it was impossible to tell who was leaning on whom.

XXXI

※ ※ ※

He found her the next morning sitting in the rose garden, staring with such concentration at the rose in her hand that he hesitated to intrude. Undecided whether to stay or go, Bridger stood taking in the beauty of the tableau before him. Dewdrops still sparkled on the blades of grass and glistened on the petals of the roses. Their colors ranged from whites to creams, from blush pinks to rich yellows, from vivid reds to deep cerises. The blossom that held Eugénie's intense gaze matched the bright shade that tinted her cheeks. Her hair was swept back from her face in a simple bow made from the same material as her white gown. A light breeze played with the hem of her skirt, which fell in loose folds at her feet.

She turned as though sensing his presence. Seeing him, her face lit in a bright smile. She beckoned him to join her.

As he sat down beside her on the stone bench, she offered him the blossom for his inspection. "The rains have washed the earth clean and set free all of her delicious scents. Have you ever smelled air so fragrant as it is this morning?"

Her joy infected him, and he laughed out loud at the sheer pleasure of her. "Ah, Eugénie." Taking her hand, he turned it over and kissed the soft palm. "You shame me. I woke this morning dwelling on weighty thoughts and concerns. But you, who've just escaped death, are radiant with the day, speaking about the beauty of the earth and her treasures."

"Bridger, when I awoke on your ship and found myself whole again

317

and in your safekeeping . . . there are no words that can describe the feeling that swept over me. I'd returned from a place between life and death. The only thing I remember from that time was the brief moment when I opened my eyes and saw your face before me. Then I was pulled back into the blackness again. I've been sitting here reliving that first moment when my life was restored to me. How I rejoiced with each breath, each heartbeat. Each second that passed was a confirmation of my life. That I lived. But even while we were talking that day, I feared that any minute the blackness would come back to reclaim me. Last night, as I lay down to sleep, I didn't know if I would see this morning. When I did awake . . ." Her voice caught in her throat. Bridger put his arm around her and drew her against his side. She rested her head on his shoulder, breathing deeply.

After a moment, she continued. "When I did awake this morning, I felt such joy, such fullness. I felt so thankful for this gift of life that's been returned to me. I shall treasure it for however long it's entrusted to me. I'm humbled by the magnitude of it, this precious, precious gift. To be alive after where I'd been, to have come so close, so close to never seeing the faces of those I love, to never walk at will on this beautiful earth, to miss her sights and sounds and smells, the taste and feel of her. Every blade of grass, every petal of this rose, the strength of your arm holding me, tells me that I am alive. Alive. There's nothing that doesn't pale in comparison. I'm actually thankful for that experience and those lost days." She laughed at his startled expression. "For without them I could never fully appreciate the value of simply being alive. Does any of this make sense?"

"I haven't been where you were," he answered gravely, "or experienced the terror you felt, or passed through the place between life and death as you did, but there have been times when I've had to lay my life on the line. Each time I prevailed and survived, I felt something akin to what you describe. I do know, when you awoke whole from that long sleep, I felt a gladness beyond measure." His arm tightened around her. For a moment he rested his cheek against her hair. Then he sat up straighter and turned her to face him.

"Which is why I sought you out this morning. Your mission placed you in danger in Virginia and again puts you in peril on this island. Your association with the Tucker family adds immeasurably to it." He put up his hand when she started to interrupt.

"Hear me out," he said sharply. "We've spoken of this before. Their activities are well known to the government in St. George's. Simply by accepting their hospitality, you're tarred by the same brush. We know that Darby tracks you and will not rest until . . ." He dipped his head, unable to say the words they both knew. "Eugénie, we were lucky that our method to protect you worked this time. We may not be so fortunate in the future.

"I have eyes and ears on this island that report to me," he continued. "I've been informed of what's being planned on this end of the island. Anything that occurs in this neighborhood is under the scrutiny of Colonel Tucker, if not instigated by him. If you can't dissuade him from this foolhardy venture, promise me, Eugénie, that you'll distance yourself from it and from him before it's too late. My spies tell me that Governor Bruère has ended all communication with the Colonel since the wedding. In spite of the governor's fondness for his son-in-law, Harry, Tucker and his cohorts' lawless deeds make it impossible for Bruère to continue even an arm's-length relationship with the Colonel. Given any provocation—any at all—he'll prosecute these men to the full extent of the law."

He grabbed her by the shoulders and said urgently, "Eugénie, once your strength is restored, you must make plans to leave this place. No mission is worth your life. You must return to France."

Eugénie covered the hands that gripped her shoulders with her own, and her eyes locked with his. For a moment she hesitated, seeing the tenderness and love there.

"Oh, dear heart, were it only that simple," she said softly. "You know something of my mission, but not all. I came across the Atlantic to measure the extent of the American colonists' disaffection with their mother country. Would they or would they not expand their dispute into an all-out war for independence? I found the answers to those questions in Virginia, but I also learned while I was there about the strategic importance of Bermuda. Once I realized just how important, geographically and militarily, this small island might be to the eventual outcome of the war, I knew that my mission would not be over until I found out which side held the Bermudians' loyalty. I have yet to learn that answer. I will remain here until I do."

"Eugénie, this is madness! This is not your war! I cannot and will not stand by and watch you do this!" Bridger shouted at her, his eyes hard and flat with anger. He stood up abruptly and strode away from her, then swung around. His body bristled with such emotion that she shrank back from him. "You speak of the gift of life, and yet you dally with it as if it were of no value at all to you, placing it daily in danger for some misguided reason. I imagine it's something to do with heroism or some such lofty, utterly useless emotion," he growled at her.

His eyes caught and held hers for a long moment in an unblinking stare. Then he spoke, his voice all the more dangerous for its softness.

"Those who sent you over sit safely across the ocean in France. No doubt, if they knew your circumstances, you would be recalled at once." He said no more, his intent clear. Eugénie sprang to her feet.

"Bridger, if you so much as breathe a word . . ." She stopped, knowing that such an approach would only drive him to do the very thing he threatened. She returned to the bench and sat very still, plucking absentmindedly at her gown, thinking. "Why is it I speak so freely to you, telling you my innermost thoughts?" she asked him. "I don't hesitate to say anything to you, even when it would endanger my life! I speak to you as I speak to myself, as though you were a part of me. Ah, I've answered my own question. I speak to you so easily because you are a part of me."

She gathered her thoughts and then looked up into his face. "Bridger, how do I make you understand? I made my choice long ago, and I've never wavered for one minute from my commitment. Even were I recalled, I wouldn't go until I've learned the answers to my questions.

"The Americans have ventured forth to meet their destiny," she continued. "Armed with new truths and a new social order, they'll change the political face of their nation if they succeed in their bid for independence. As a witness, I've played a small part in their effort. I've watched a political philosophy become a call to arms that men are willing to fight and die for. I must do what little I can to help in this effort. I must stay until I know whether or not the Bermudians will embrace the Americans' cause and, if so, what role they'll play. Then and only then will I return to France and, together with others, plead the Americans' case to our Ministry. I can and will do no less. I wish you could understand the importance of my undertaking and not fight me on this. I know you have a different allegiance: the allegiance to your family. With your pragmatic mind, you place no importance on what I do. You simply see me as a French spy, and that galls you." Her voice was barely above a whisper.

"Eugénie, you understand me so well, but know me so little! I couldn't give less of a damn if you're a French spy. Why can't you see what I'm trying to tell you? Your association with these traitors—and, make no mistake, they *are* traitors—and your participation in their acts of treason place you at risk from their enemies. You have enough enemies of your own." The silence stretched out between them.

Finally, Bridger sat down beside her. "There are many in the fight, I daresay, whose motives bear little resemblance to the lofty principles of which you speak so eloquently, motives that strike closer to home, that have more to do with mundane matters than with noble ideals. I grant you, many of the leaders appear to be inspired by a revolutionary political order that may well overturn more than just a burdensome Stamp Act. You're right. I don't aspire to their vision, nor am I stirred by either set of emotions, the noble nor the mundane. I don't care on which side of the boat the oar is pulled so long as the craft stays afloat. In all of this, you, and you alone, Eugénie, are my concern. I wish only for your well-being and safety. That's all I wish, all I've ever wished."

He sighed deeply, his face suddenly tired, his eyes bleak. "You thwart my love for you at every turn! If only I could pluck you from my heart and be free of you!" he said vehemently. Sighing again, he took her hand and held it to his cheek. Then, turning it over, he traced the long lifeline on her palm.

"Would you really want me to be different from what I am?" she asked him quietly. Instead of answering, he turned away from her and stared off across the garden. She watched him in silence, memorizing the strength of his profile, the lofty forehead, the straight aquiline nose, the full lips, set now in a grim line, the chiseled chin and the eyes, the beautiful blue eyes, ringed with dark lashes that contradicted the sandy hair streaked with sunlight.

His gaze moved back to her. "Forgive me, dear heart, for distressing you and for burdening you with my fears. I wouldn't want you to be anything other than who you are. Were you otherwise, I couldn't love you as I do, with all my soul."

Then, with a lightning change of mood, he gently gathered her into his arms. "I'm torn between two desires. On the one hand, when you go, as one day you will, I'll be relieved to know that you are going to your homeland and to safety. On the other hand, my heart will grieve the loss of you for every minute of every day for the rest of my life."

"My love," Eugénie began, but her words were interrupted by the sound of hoofbeats coming down the lane toward the house. Startled, they rose and hurried out of the garden and across the lawn. They came around the side of the house just as Colonel Tucker strode through the front door.

The expression on the Colonel's face would have daunted even the bravest spirit, but the disheveled man held in the tight grip of Rorick Hamilton seemed not to notice. He jerked himself free and demanded, "Henry, what in the Devil's name is the meaning of this? As I was attempting to salvage the remains of one of my ships that smashed on the reefs in the last storm, I was apprehended by a trio of strangers who, from all appearances, were nothing better than cutthroats. Then, with no explanation, they coerced me into their vessel. The next thing I knew we were at Salt Kettle, where men joined us whom I've known all my life, but who acted like strangers. They forced me on a horse to go who-knows-where. Finally we arrive here, much to my relief, at the home of one of my oldest and dearest friends. Henry, such methods are hardly necessary. You know all you'd have to do is send a message and I'd come at once."

"Yes, Stephen, explanations are in order," Colonel Tucker said with deadly calm. "Miss Eugénie, if you would, please." He gestured to her to precede him through the door. "I think with this number of people we'd better gather in the large parlor."

As Eugénie walked down the hallway, she heard the heavy tread of the men behind her. She felt fear sweep over her at the sound of Stephen Trowbridge's voice. Then a cleansing anger surged through her as she thought of how lightly this man and his cohorts had held her life and the lives of the people on the crippled ship he claimed as his own.

When she took her seat, Jamie came and stood beside her. She noticed that Bridger had hung back in the doorway until everyone was seated. Then he moved quietly into the room and lounged against the wall within easy reach of Trowbridge, who was so focused on Colonel Tucker that he was unaware of the other man's nearness.

"This is a tribunal, of sorts," Colonel Tucker began. "I see that we have a quorum of merchant seamen from the west end, so we can proceed. When last we met, we were tackling the pernicious problem of the increased frequency of warehouse burnings and shipwrecks. We have always ensured the safety of our waters and the protection of our families and properties by policing our own and meting out swift justice. This time we've had outside assistance, for which each of us should be eternally grateful. We are also fortunate to have a witness to the most recent act of the willful wrecking of one of our ships. Miss Eugénie, are you willing to bear witness?"

Even though Eugénie had known that this moment was coming and what her decision would be, she hesitated, knowing that her words would cost men's lives. She felt Jamie's hand on her shoulder, and she glanced up at him briefly, silently thanking him.

Looking directly into the Colonel's eyes, Eugénie answered, "Yes, I am."

"You understand the gravity of your words and their consequences?" he asked her quietly.

"Yes, I do."

"Then, tell us your experience, if you will," he said.

Eugénie described being marooned by the storm and seeking shelter in a cave to wait it out, how she had fallen asleep and wakened to the sounds of voices.

"At first I thought it was my imagination. No one would choose to be out in that weather. But then I saw a lantern shining high up on the cliffs. I saw men looting a ship that had crashed on the reefs. I heard a voice directing the others that sounded familiar, but I couldn't place it. He was clearly the leader. As the men came closer, I could hear their conversation. At one point, I heard one of them address the leader as 'Mr. Trowbridge.'"

She felt, rather than saw, Stephen Trowbridge's sudden intake of breath. "How dare . . ." he began.

Colonel Tucker interrupted him. "Miss Eugénie, you're quite sure you heard the name 'Trowbridge'?"

"Yes, I'm quite sure, Colonel Tucker," Eugénie replied calmly. "The man whose name I learned later was Painter said something like, 'Mr. Trowbridge, how soon can we split up the booty?' Mr. Trowbridge, as nearly as I can remember, answered, 'Once the storm is over and curiosity about the wreck has died down,' or words to that effect."

"This is an outrage!" Trowbridge's sudden outburst caused Eugénie to start in her chair. "You can't believe the word of a perfect stranger. She's lying! It's her word against mine. We've known each other all of our lives. Who're you going to believe? She has no proof. How do we know this isn't a figment of her imagination? She's implicating me to cover up her own responsibility for the deed. For all we know, she's the leader that she accuses me of being. What other purpose would she have for insinuating herself into your household and into your confidence?"

He looked into the faces of those assembled in the room and received only cold stares in return, except from the giant standing beside the chit who accused him. The pity that he saw in the depths of those eyes struck fear in him. None of this showed on his face as he held on tightly to his anger and outrage and continued to take the offensive.

"We have only the unsupported word of this young woman," he said with a sneer.

"I know what I saw and what I heard," Eugénie responded, unruffled, "but . . ."

Her words were lost as Trowbridge's thin control snapped. With a roar, he lurched up from his chair and lunged at her. So blinded was he by his fury that he hardly felt the strong hands that clamped around his throat, then dragged him away from his target and flung him to the floor, or the fists that smashed into his face and body.

The red haze before Bridger's eyes began to recede as restraining hands tore him off the nearly unconscious man and hauled him to his feet. "There's not a man in this room who doesn't wish to tear that bastard limb from limb," the man said to Bridger. "But we're not done with him, yet. He has much to answer for before he goes to his great reward."

Bridger's breath began to return to normal. He brushed the hair back from his forehead and ran his sore knuckles across his lips. His only regret was the expression of horror frozen on Eugénie's face at the sight of his unleashed fury. "My pardon," he said dryly to the man who had reprimanded him. "I wouldn't for the life of me deprive such a deserving soul of all that's rightfully coming to him. I meant only to encourage him to speak with more respect to the young lady."

The man chuckled and moved away. Bridger bent down to Eugénie and whispered, "Dearest, forgive me. I didn't mean to frighten you so. If you wish to withdraw, do so, for there's no further need for you here."

"I'm fully recovered," Eugénie said quietly, her eyes expressing her gratitude for his concern. "Fully recovered from the effects that I'd most certainly have suffered at his hands had you not so gallantly intervened on my behalf." Her playful expression convinced him far more than her words that she had regained her composure. Bridger straightened and took a position on the other side of her chair. Above her head, his eyes met Jamie's in a silent message. Across the room, Trowbridge sat slumped in the chair where he had been unceremoniously dumped by two of his former friends, who then stationed themselves on either side of him.

"Let me make myself perfectly clear," Colonel Tucker said to him harshly. "You deserve no explanations, but your accusations give me the opportunity to say some words on Mistress Eugénie Devereux's behalf. First, Mistress Devereux is above reproach. Her word alone is sufficient to hang you. It was the strength and courage that she exhibited that brought your sorry skin to justice. I'm pleased to inform you that even were we not fortunate enough to have Miss Eugénie's account of your perfidy, we have an array of scoundrels and cutthroats, formerly your associates, who are at this very minute enjoying the hospitality of Captain Goodrich's hold. They're only too eager to confirm your guilt." This announcement was met with silence from Trowbridge, who sat staring blankly at his hands.

"I see no reason to detain Captain Goodrich and his crew or to prevail upon his good graces a moment longer," Colonel Tucker said solemnly. "In accordance with traditional precedents, I propose that, without further ado, we put to vote to convict or acquit this person and his associates for the aforementioned acts of piracy, murder, and destruction of property attested to by Miss Eugénie Devereux. Do I hear a second?"

A chorus of "Second!" rang out.

"All in favor to acquit, say 'Aye.'" An ominous silence followed his words.

"All in favor to convict, say 'Aye.'" Loud shouts of "Aye!" pronounced the verdict.

"It's done then," Colonel Tucker said in a voice filled with emotion. "By the power vested in me as magistrate of the Court, I hereby sentence those held in custody aboard Captain Goodrich's ship to be hanged until dead and that Mr. Stephen Trowbridge bear witness to their deaths. After which time, he shall be strung up and hanged likewise, then buried in an unmarked grave as befits the common criminal that he is."

"Henry, have mercy!" Trowbridge gasped. "I beg you, for the sake

of our long, close friendship and association. For the sake of my innocent family, I beseech you!"

"And what mercy have you shown to the strangers whose lives
you've willfully taken? And what concern did you show for the property and well-being of your close and longtime friends and associates?"
The Colonel spoke chillingly, looking straight ahead, not deigning to
grant Trowbridge the respect of looking at him. "Your pathetic whee-
dling disgusts me. Have you no dignity? Ben, Jack, take him away! He
fouls the air with his presence. I hope to God never to lay eyes on him
or his like again!" the Colonel thundered, his voice filled with contempt.

Eugénie felt Bridger's hand on her arm and looked up at him,
thankful once again for his presence throughout the ordeal. "Come,
my love," he said softly. "There's nothing else that you can do here." He
turned to Jamie and directed him to assist the Colonel in any way he
could to remove the prisoners from the ship and take them to the
appropriate location on shore.

I, like the Colonel, am glad to see the last of them, Bridger thought,
as he extended his arm to Eugénie and escorted her from the room.

Left to their own devices, Eugénie and Bridger wandered about the
gardens, enjoying the long shadows of the late afternoon, pausing here
and there to sniff a fragrant blossom or pluck an errant weed. They
watched the flight of a pair of longtails as they swooped and soared in
tandem, carving a design against the sky, their snow-white feathers
catching and reflecting the last of the sun's rays.

Savoring each other's company, they spoke rarely and felt much. In
accord, they drifted back to the rose garden where the day had begun.
The earlier angry words forgotten, they stood with their hands clasped
loosely around each other's waist, bent toward each other, their fore-
heads touching.

Slowly their heads shifted and their lips met. The gentle kiss held
and deepened. Their hands turned harsh and demanding. Their bodies strained, seeking to melt into each other. She felt his heart beat
against her own, matching. She heard her blood roaring in her ears.

She could not get her breath. She was awed by the power they held between them. They pulled apart. Searching the depths of the other's eyes, each found the benediction they sought.

"I'll be gone with the evening tide," he spoke, his voice barely audible. Clearing his throat, he said, "After all, I wouldn't want to overstay my welcome with the Colonel." His irrepressible humor lightened the moment of departure.

"Ah, but wouldn't it better serve his ends to have you where he could keep a sharp eye on you?" Eugénie asked, her eyes twinkling through unshed tears. Chuckling in answer, he gently kissed the corner of each eye and tasted the salt that lingered there. His lips brushed the curve of her throat. Not trusting himself, he paid only brief homage to her parted lips.

Taking her hand, he led her out of the garden. "Aye, but without the distraction of shipwrecks and warehouse fires, I doubt that he would fail to notice my ship preying upon another vessel that abides beneath his very roof, adding one more offense to his long list of grievances against me." She rewarded him with a burst of laughter. He was so pleased with himself that he couldn't resist swinging her up in his arms and giving her one last, long kiss in the shadow of the veranda.

XXXII

❧❧❧

The days flowed one into another, but the thought of Darby and his whereabouts was never far from Eugénie's mind. Bermuda Day dawned with brilliant blue skies and the promise of heat. True to his word, Rorick had schooled Eugénie and Elizabeth in all the subtleties of dinghy racing so that The Grove craft had acquitted itself well. When the little boat finished in the fleet's top ten, the raucous reception by The Grove at the finish made it look as though it had carried away all the ribbons and prizes.

There had been one awkward moment that day when the two grandfathers came face to face for the first time since the Tucker wedding. The air fairly crackled around them, and everyone nearby held their breath, anticipating verbal sparring or actual coming-to-blows. Elizabeth had danced in place, looking from her father to the governor and back again.

The moment had been saved when Harry's two sons came running up, exclaiming that, since their family included both the St. George's and the Port Royal picnics, hosted by the two grandfathers, they didn't know which one they were supposed to go to and what they were supposed to do.

The question of British authority versus private enterprise had been immediately supplanted by the need to resolve the dilemma of two small boys. The governor and the Colonel had looked in consternation at each other, clearly out of their element when it came to handling such knotty questions.

Anne Tucker had stepped forward, her diplomatic skills finely honed in this area. "Boys, boys, boys," she had said firmly, her voice ringing with the authority that all little boys recognize. "This is a simple matter. You'll draw straws. The short straw will go to Grandfather Bruère's picnic first, and the long straw will go to Grandfather Tucker's. Midway through the afternoon, you'll switch places. That way, both grandfathers will have the pleasure of your company and you, theirs. Now, how's that?" she had asked brightly.

"Grandma, where shall we find some straws?" the elder brother had asked, clearly accepting his grandmother's solution.

"Come with me," she had answered. "I know exactly where we can find just the perfect straws for such a special occasion." Taking a small hand in each of hers, she had hastened off in search of the appropriate tools for the high-level decision.

Those who witnessed the scene had drawn a collective sigh of relief. The two grandfathers had proceeded to make small talk with each other. Appreciating how closely they had come to an explosive situation, they soon wisely chose to wander off in the company of their own constituencies.

Eugénie observed the confrontation between the two men and saw that the chasm between them was wider than she had realized. Bridger had been right. It would take little to bring the British authorities down on the west end of the island, specifically on Colonel Henry Tucker. She had shuddered, thinking about the Colonel's ambitious plan, which was already well under way.

The days were stretching out, and soon they were approaching the summer solstice. Eugénie remembered her father, an avid astronomer, explaining to her that twice a year the sun appeared to have no northward or southward motion. The times occurred around the twenty-first of June, at the northern-most point of the sun's path, and around the twenty-first of December, at the southern-most point.

Her parents had always held a special celebration during the day and evening of the summer solstice, using the longest day of the year as an excuse to showcase their renowned gardens. They invited their friends and neighbors from far and near, including a healthy sprinkling of children for Eugénie's benefit. The château's staff had a celebration the following day with a presentation of gifts and awards from the Comte and the Comtesse in gratitude for everyone's efforts over the past year.

Since her parents' death, the day of the summer solstice had held a particular poignancy for her. She found that this year was no exception. Even at such a great distance from the château, she still felt the powerful ties to the home she loved and the strong pull of memories.

Anticipating Eugénie's mood, Marie sought her out on the morning of the twenty-first and found her at the roan's stall, nuzzling the great animal's muzzle. The horse whinnied a gentle welcome to Marie as she approached.

"Mistress," she said softly, stroking the glossy coat, "I guessed you might be here. I, too, have felt the twinges of the *mal du pays.*"

"Marie, *ma chère amie,*" Eugénie said, smiling, "how is it that you know what's in my heart almost before I do?" The two women stood silently side by side, each lost in thought.

"I'd appreciate your company while I groom the roan," Eugénie said quietly as she offered a carrot from the kitchen garden to the horse. The roan lipped the offering from his mistress's fingers with a delicacy surprising for one of such size and strength, causing both women to giggle. As though sharing in the joke, the huge animal snorted and rolled his eyes, which made them laugh even harder.

"Better than that, I'd enjoy helping you curry and rub him down," Marie replied.

"In that case, I'll take him out of the stall for, although it has been mucked out recently, it's no place for your dainty footwear," Eugénie said, opening the stall gate and leading the roan out into the paddock. Soon the two women were busy brushing away. It was obvious that the horse was basking in this special attention, as he stood stock-still, his eyes closed, his long tail swishing his contentment.

"How are you feeling, Marie?" Eugénie asked, broaching the subject she rarely discussed, not wanting to remind Marie of Jacques's loss.

"I feel extraordinarily well," Marie replied. "I calculate that I'm past my fourth month, for the babe quickened in my womb a few weeks ago. Each time he moves, I feel such joy. I rejoice daily that I have the gift of Jacques's life within me." She spoke softly, her face radiant.

"Oh, Marie," Eugénie exclaimed, "then you've recovered from his loss?"

"Dear mistress, I realize you've avoided this matter in deference to my feelings. Thank you for your thoughtfulness. I'll always carry his loss with me, but it's no longer so painful that I can't talk about him. Each day, I'm one day closer to holding a part of him in my arms. The happiness of that has softened the grief of the other."

"I'm so glad that we can talk about it freely," Eugénie said, hugging her. "I'm looking forward to the arrival of the babe almost as much as you are. You've not forgotten your promise that I'll be the godmother?" Eugénie asked with mock sternness.

"Certainly not," Marie laughed, "if I have any hope of continuing my position in your household."

"I'm amazed at your trim figure. Thank goodness the Tuckers believed our small falsehood that you were wed in France before sailing with me to Virginia. I hope that we'll be safely back at the château when the babe is born."

"Don't fret," Marie assured her. "I come from good, strong birthing stock. When the moment comes, be it here, in France, or on the high seas, the babe and I will perform beautifully. After all, Jacques would have it no other way!" The two women smiled at each other, remembering his Gallic tenacity.

"Well, you handsome devil," Eugénie said, addressing the roan. "Aren't you the fortunate one, privy to all this fascinating female gossip while being rubbed and stroked at the same time?" In answer, he pawed impatiently at the dirt and threw back his head, trumpeting a protest.

"I know, I know. My sentiments exactly," Eugénie laughed, reaching up to yank playfully on his forelock. "It's time for us to finish our business here so that we can set sail for home and introduce you to your new country. There's a herd of eager fillies awaiting you there to vie for your attentions. Patience, you beautiful beast. It won't be much longer. The Colonel is as impatient as you to see the conclusion of the game he plays, as long as he's the winner. Once his plan is carried out, we'll lose no time boarding the first ship leaving for France."

Eugénie led the roan back into his stall. With a loving slap to his flanks to move him out of the way, she replaced the grooming gear in its proper place and the harness on its hook.

As she closed the latch of the roan's stall, she said to Marie, "Even he reads the tension that's mounting in the household. Young Jeremy is off his feed, too. Why, I can't think of one bit of mischief that he's gotten into this week."

"It's true," Marie agreed. "The steady stream of messengers coming and going has everyone on the edge of their seats. At first, I thought Mr. Hamilton's daily visits were contrived to pay suit to you, but even his demeanor has taken on a somber cast these past few days."

Leaving the stableyard, the two women made their way through the grove of trees that gave the house its name. "Oh, for heaven's sake, Marie. Mr. Hamilton is simply attracted to the aura of mystery that he attributes to me. He's a kind young man whose humor and talents are a pleasant diversion for the family as well as for me."

Marie looked askance at her mistress. "It isn't Elizabeth that he composes sonnets to or follows around like a lost puppy. Keep a sharp eye out for those talents you speak of. You have enough on your hands without contending with an entanglement with that young man."

"Marie," Eugénie said with exasperation in her voice, "you've always worried too much about me, but if it makes you feel better, I promise I'll watch my step with Mr. Hamilton."

"Speaking of whom," Marie murmured under her breath as the object of their discussion came into view, hurrying in their direction.

Rorick Hamilton's face lit up when he caught sight of Eugénie. Seeing it, Eugénie thought, Oh dear, perhaps I should take Marie's words a little more seriously.

"Miss Eugénie, how are you on this beautiful day?" Rorick asked when he reached her side, red-faced and breathing heavily.

In contrast to the obvious effort he had made to catch up with them, his commonplace greeting caused Eugénie to bite her lip to keep from laughing. "It is a beautiful day, and I'm very well, thank you." She smiled prettily up at him while resisting a look at Marie, who suddenly seemed to have caught something in her throat. "We've been down at the stables all morning and were just returning to the house. Won't you join us?"

"I stopped off at the house first to deliver some urgent messages to the Colonel, before coming to look for you. But I'd be pleased to accompany you, thank you. Allow me," he said, offering his arm to Eugénie in such a formal fashion that Marie once again began making odd choking noises. Rorick turned to look at her quizzically. Rather than embarrass the young man, Eugénie placed her hand lightly on his arm, with a mental sigh of resignation.

As they approached the house, the veranda door flew open and Jeremy scampered out and down the steps, pulling up short when he saw them. "Miss Eugénie, I's been lookin' all over for you!"

What now? Eugénie exclaimed to herself. "Yes, Jeremy?" she asked out loud.

"Mistress Tucker says I'm to ask you if'n there's anything I can do for Roman 'cuz I'm gettin' too much underfoot in the house," he said, shamefaced.

"Why, Jeremy, you've come just in the nick of time."

Jeremy's face brightened considerably. "I have?"

"Yes, indeed. I was just saying to myself that the roan sure could use some exercising. If you'd be so kind as to harness him and walk him around the ring for a good period of time, I'd be ever so grateful. Then, if you still have time on your hands after that, I heard Ethan was shorthanded today, and I imagine he could really use your help." She hoped Ethan wouldn't expose her little ploy.

His dignity restored, Jeremy executed a jaunty bow.

"Yes'm, yes'm. You can count on me, Miss Eugénie. I'll be exercisin' Roman, if'n anybody asks for me. If'n nobody be needin' me after that, I'll give Ethan a hand like you says. I knows he can always use my hep." Off he went in the direction of the stables, whistling merrily. Eugénie smiled to herself. The whole household at one time or another conspired to find ways to exhaust Jeremy's boundless store of energy. Today it was "Roman" and Ethan's turn.

"Plucky lad," Rorick remarked as they crossed the veranda.

Eugénie laughed. "He's that and more. He's the most willing little fellow. There's nothing he won't try his hand at. Elizabeth has been working with him on his letters and numbers. She's quite amazed at his quick grasp." They were still chuckling when they arrived in the hallway.

"Eugénie," Anne Tucker said, coming out of the dining room. "Have you seen Jeremy? I sent him off to find you. I was hoping that you'd come up with some task to keep him busy and out from under foot. With all the comings and goings around here these days, I've enough to say grace over without worrying with him."

"He is well and truly occupied, attending to 'Roman,'" Eugénie reassured her.

"Thank the Lord," Anne exclaimed. "How one little person can keep a whole household in an uproar is beyond me! We're just gathering for dinner, Rorick, if you'd like to join us."

"Thank you, ma'am," he replied, cutting his eyes briefly in Eugénie's direction. "I'd like that very much. It seems, with everything that's happening, I can't remember when I last had a good home-cooked meal." Marie rolled her eyes and escaped down the hall.

"It's my pleasure," Anne Tucker said graciously. Everyone had noticed that the young Hamilton had become something of a fixture at The Grove, first as a courier for the Colonel, then as an instructor for the dinghy race, and now for just about anything that needed doing. It wasn't lost on anybody that the honey for this particular bee was Eugénie, who seemed to handle his attentions with enormous grace.

When Eugénie entered the dining room, she noticed that there were several faces at the long cedar table that she didn't recognize. It had been that way for the past several weeks. The Tucker home had become the central meeting place for the west end of the island. With the increased traffic of messages and visitors, it was clear that there was much afoot.

"The food shortages are already bad, and it's not the end of June yet," one neighbor was saying as Eugénie took her seat and helped her-self to hominy and succulent slices of freshly smoked ham. Although the Tucker stores were abundant, Eugénie knew that many families on the island were suffering from loss of trade with the American col-onies. Anne Tucker's efficient management of The Grove accounted for the plentiful meats, fresh vegetables, and fruits on The Grove table. Eugénie also knew that St. George's close relationship with the Amer-icans was the key to the many Tucker ships that slipped in late at night laden with cargo.

"What do you hear from Harry up at St. George's?" the man seated next to Eugénie asked. "He has the ear of the governor, even if the rest of us are persona non grata."

"We receive documents from him daily," the Colonel said, "thanks to the relay that we put in place, which will also serve us well in the not-too-distant future when it'll be of the utmost importance to send and receive messages with all speed. To answer your question, I'm afraid the news is not good from St. George's. Harry reports that Governor Bruère writes to Whitehall continuously, pleading Bermuda's plight. The response is exceedingly discouraging. They claim that they can't divert goods to Bermuda, that all shipping and supplies are needed for the American conflict. They've even implied that the shortages are a false claim. Governor Bruère continues to plead for warships—in his words, to protect Bermuda from invasion. This is most alarming and could cause untold mischief should Whitehall comply. Not only would the presence of such ships seriously hamper the running of our day-to-day affairs, but it would most probably preclude our carrying out our plan. We can't allow that to happen. The gunpowder is our only bargaining tool with the Americans."

Silence met his words. For a few minutes the only sound was the clicking of silverware against fine imported porcelain as each person mulled over the gravity of Colonel Tucker's words.

"Has there been any progress on that front?" asked one of the men unfamiliar to Eugénie.

"St. George is acting as our go-between. So far we've received no direct response to our initial approach to Mr. Washington, but we're in contact with an intermediary who is a well-connected member of the influence peddlers. We have substantiated his credentials. He has the authority to carry out the steps that are needed from their end.

"We're now negotiating the fine points," the Colonel went on. "One stickler is the extent of our involvement in the actual transfer of the gunpowder from the magazine. Our position is that we'll make the gunpowder available, and they'll be responsible for handling it while we oversee the transfer. That way we cannot be held accountable for the amount or condition of the barrels. We know that their appetite is whetted and their supplies of powder are sorely limited. I have every confidence that we'll resolve these issues very shortly."

Those around the table nodded and murmured in agreement.

"What can we do here to help alleviate the food shortages that so many are already suffering?" a neighbor asked.

"Thomas Tudor and St. George have been working on that as well. They've found a good supply of rice available that should be shipped this week or next," the Colonel replied. "Till it arrives, we'll gather the stores of last year's corn and sell them at our warehouse stores at a reduced price. It's all we can do for now." This plan also met with approval around the table. "But," he added, "we must pray that the Americans agree to lift the embargo, in return for the gunpowder, before it is too late."

"It's a dangerous game we're playing," the man to the Colonel's right said, "but we have no choice."

"Aye, and even if there were one, we're too far down the path to turn back now," another said. "Let's pray that Whitehall continues to ignore the governor's pleas for warships."

"Aye, I'm thinking those pesky Searchers are nuisance enough, without royal warships to back them up," said one of the Harveys. "Maybe while we're praying, what say we put in a word for the colonials' navy keeping the British navy occupied until we can carry out our plan?"

The levity of this last remark brought forth a laugh, and the meal ended on a light note.

XXXIII

❧ ❧ ❧

The next morning Colonel Tucker and the other men wasted no time using the relay system to spread the word amongst the merchants about the sale of corn at the warehouse stores. Each household was responsible for bringing their sacks out of storage, inspecting them, and attesting to the weight and condition of the contents. Depending on the number of sacks that had been laid away and how and where they were stored, it could be a large undertaking.

Anne Tucker, Elizabeth, and Eugénie were up early. Anne sent Maisie off to assemble the women in the ground-floor storage rooms. Meanwhile the three women ate an abbreviated breakfast of fresh fruit, beaten biscuits spread with The Grove loquat jam, tea for the Tuckers, and *café au lait* for Eugénie.

The Grove, like many Bermuda houses, was built into a hill. This gave it strength to weather heavy storms. The land on the other side of the house sloped away, creating an additional lower level, which was not visible from the two-storied side. This space served many purposes, but it was most often used for storage and to house the servants.

Houses built in this fashion had no access from the ground floor to the first floor. An outdoor staircase gave access to the first floor. Usually it was a walled double staircase. The stairs were wider at the bottom than at the top. This created an open, graceful impression, which gave rise to the name "welcoming arms." It seemed only right that Bermudians, known for their hospitality, would incorporate a feature in their homes that expressed their friendly nature.

The ground floor was often recessed, fronted with arches that acted as supporting structures. At The Grove, the welcoming arms led to a veranda that ran the length of the house. This was not a common feature because of Bermuda's raw, rainy winters and hot, still summers. At The Grove, even on the hottest days, there was a steady breeze that blew fresh off the water. The family seldom missed an opportunity to gather on the veranda from the first of April to the end of October, especially after the evening meal.

While Eugénie and Elizabeth chatted over their breakfast, Anne pored over her inventory of household goods. She had an elaborate system, which she had taught Elizabeth. Not a grain of salt arrived, was consumed, or left The Grove that was not recorded. She could pinpoint anything on the property by quantity and location. One year, the winter rains washed away several garden plots. Anne discovered to her dismay that no one, including herself, could remember the number and placement of the plants. After that, there was a layout of each garden for her records.

Her recording system was well known to her friends and even those who were just passing acquaintances. When asked, she generously shared it, but few had the patience to carry out their own system as extensively and as thoroughly as she did.

Glancing over at her mother, Elizabeth exclaimed, "Mama, you are fairly beaming! What in heaven's name for? It can't be the prospect of spending this beautiful day in those dusty storage rooms."

Anne looked up briefly from her ledgers. "It just gives me such pleasure to see everything laid out so nicely. It'll make our task in 'those dusty storage rooms' so much easier."

A few minutes later, Anne slapped her books closed, took a last sip of tea, and said, "I imagine Maisie and the girls are ready for us. We'd better be up and going. Sooner started, sooner done."

The inventory and inspection of the sacks of corn went faster than Anne had expected. Even Elizabeth had to admit that her mother's system was foolproof. By late morning, all the sacks were accounted for and assembled. All that was left to do was to transfer them to the makeshift store that Ethan and the men had built down by the dock.

Wiping her hands on her apron, Anne said, "Good, that part's fin-ished. After lunch, Ethan and the men can move the first of the sacks out and set them up in the store. This afternoon, I'll teach you how to use the weights and measures." She ignored Elizabeth's loud groan. "Then, over the next few days, one of us will have to be on hand at the store to help the girls."

"Mama," Elizabeth asked, "do you really think we'll be able to sell all this corn?"

"What do you mean, child?"

"Well, you know a lot of the people in Bermuda turn up their noses at corn. They much prefer wheat flour or rice."

"In the old days," Anne said, "there was no such thing as corn. The early settlers learned about corn and how to grow it from the Indians over in the American colonies. Once they saw all the uses for it, just about every garden plot had a few rows. I hear, today, it's right popular even in England. There'll always be those who look down their nose at it, as you say, but when people are starving, it's just amazing how tastes can change.

"I know for a fact," she continued, "that our servants and most of those on Bermuda prefer corn. It's infinitely cheaper than rice. Besides, for all rice's popularity in certain quarters, corn is much easier to store. In our climate, as you know, rice spoils easily in storage unless it's kept under very special conditions. Now, come along, we'd better put some food on the table before your father comes down here to fetch us. As a matter of fact, we're having loblolly for dinner, unless I miss my guess."

As they started up the stairs, Elizabeth explained to Eugénie, "The local loblolly is sort of a mush made of Indian corn. It's real popular on the island. We usually sweeten it. It's not unlike spoonbread that you may have had in Virginia. That's made of cornmeal too, but it's dry, not mushy." Eugénie had never been very fond of grain- or meal-based foods, but she had grown quite fond of the beaten biscuits that she had enjoyed in both Virginia and Bermuda.

"I've never been a very adventurous eater," she said to Elizabeth. "Who'd have guessed I would ever eat shark? Maybe I'll become a devotee of your loblolly too."

As usual, several guests were assembled at the table, including the ubiquitous Mr. Hamilton. Anne Tucker took her seat, saying to the Colonel, "Henry, will you say the blessing, please?"

The chatting stopped as all of them bowed their heads and Colonel Tucker spoke into the silence. "Bless, O Lord, this food to our use and ourselves to Thy service. Make us ever mindful of the needs of others and may we rely on Thy bounteous goodness to aid those on this island suffering from the food shortages. These things we ask of Thee in the name of Thy Son, our Lord Jesus Christ, Amen."

"Amen," added the rest of the people at the table. Anne Tucker helped herself to the platter in front of her, and the noontime meal began.

Eugénie was delighted to see that the main course was shark. She caught Elizabeth's eye, and they shared a smile. "Anne," Eugénie said, turning to her hostess, "would you please tell me your receipt again. This time, I promise to write it down."

"Why I'd be happy to, dear. First, let me give you a little background. Shark, along with mullet roe, are old Bermuda traditions and are both considered delicacies. They're fished off St. David's, which is quite a small island off the east end of Bermuda. The roe is found in the mullet only in autumn. It's heavily salted overnight, then cut into small pieces and served with bread and butter. I hope you'll still be with us when it's in season so that you can at least have a small taste. It's harder and harder to wrestle even a family's portion from those St. Davidians. They guard it so jealously.

"Now, about the shark receipt," Anne Tucker continued. "Shark is plentiful all around the Bermuda islands, but we must give St. David's the credit for the best way to prepare it. First, you take the liver out and fry it to extract the oil. Then, using a combination of things, left up to each cook's discretion, you make up a hash, which in turn goes into the frying pan. Next, you squeeze all the juice out of the shark, skin it, and bone it. Then you add a lot of seasoning, like pot herbs, pumpkin buds, and lots of bird peppers and pepper leaves. Everything ends up in the frying pan, where it's stirred until it has absorbed all the liver oil.

Et voilà!" Anne said with a flourish, winking at Eugénie. "The shark is ready to serve."

"*C'est magnifique!*" Eugénie said, swallowing a mouthful of the shark. "I've truly been spoiled by the variety of fish you have in Bermuda. They have much more texture and flavor than I'm used to at home. Our most common fish are *loup de mer* and the *rougets* that are fished in the Mediterranean. By the time they get inland to us, they're heavily salted and bear little resemblance to the original fish. But here, so many of your varieties are fished and immediately popped into the pan. *C'est délicieux!* Mmmmm." To emphasize her point, she popped another piece of shark into her mouth.

"Anne, my dear, I think the Adam's ale is particularly tasty with the shark," Colonel Tucker said. "But then, in this heat, Adam's ale tastes particularly fine with anything!" Everyone laughed good-naturedly.

"Eugénie," Anne said, "the chief staples of Bermudians are fish, potatoes, and Indian corn. We're just very fortunate, here at The Grove, to have ships that bring us a wide variety of foods that aren't usually available. We're also lucky to have land to support some livestock and crops." Anne beamed at her husband.

"Ah, but it's your deft hand upon the helm of this household that's beyond compare, my dear," he said.

Conversation continued to flow around the table, for once devoid of politics. The topics meandered from the new rector who had recently arrived from London, which led to the question of how well he and his family would blend into the community, to upcoming social events, to the burning of stands of cedar to help control the rat population.

"It's a shame that there's no way to keep those varmints from coming here, in the first place," said one of the guests.

"But after all, we're the ones responsible for bringing them to the island," Rorick retorted. Responding to Eugénie's quizzical look, he explained, "There wasn't a single rat or mouse on Bermuda when the first Englishman came here. The nasty creatures fled England aboard ship, much like the rest of us. When the ships arrived here, they hopped ashore and settled in. They've thrived because they have no natural predators."

"But there's such a healthy population of cats. Don't they thin them out?" Eugénie asked.

"It's usually the rat that chases the cat, rather than the other way around," he replied, chuckling. "You'll notice that the cats are seldom fed by the households in the hopes that, out of sheer desperation, they will brave a confrontation with the rats."

"It seems an extreme measure to burn the beautiful cedars that have so many uses on the island," Eugénie said.

"Aye, it is indeed, and it's rarely done anymore. So far the rats haven't carried any of the pestilences that have plagued the Continent and England, but you can well understand that fear of the plague periodically drives us to extreme measures."

One of the Whitcombs sitting to Eugénie's left overheard the conversation and spoke up. "It's not only pestilence that warrants their destruction, but also the damage they do when they invade our stores of grain, meal, rice, and the like. The stone structures of our buildings deter them, to some extent, but many of the more ambitious ones burrow beneath the walls and gnaw through the wooden floor planking to gain entry. Only last week, over at Flatts, a wee babe was nipped as it slept in its cradle. I'd rather face five men with muskets than one of those hungry, sharp-fanged critters."

Eugénie shivered, imagining one of the bloated long hairless-tailed creatures slithering across the floor with glittering eyes and sharp, jagged teeth.

Further discussion of the unpleasant topic was cut short as Anne rose from her chair and beckoned Elizabeth and Eugénie to do the same.

"You rescued me just in the nick of time!" Eugénie said gratefully, with an elaborate sigh, as they left the room. "One more description of those ravenous beasts and I wouldn't be able to sleep for a week! I had no idea that rats were such a problem on Bermuda."

"My mother handed down to me the receipt for an herbal concoction that's always been very effective in driving rats and other pests away," Anne Tucker said as she and the two young women made their way across the lawn to the store. "That's why they're not as bothersome to us here at The Grove as elsewhere. Which reminds me, we'd better make up some of the mixture, or the corn sacks will be riddled with mice by morning."

They arrived at the store and were surprised to see several small boats tied up at the dock. Word had already spread that there was corn for sale. Anne quickly taught Eugénie and Elizabeth how to use the weights and measures. Soon they were fast at work dealing with the crush of buyers who crowded the dock.

It was late afternoon before the business began to slacken. "Elizabeth, quick, come with me," Anne said urgently. "We must mix the rat concoction. Lord, I'd forgotten all about it. Eugénie, will you please stay with the girls? If we don't go now, it won't be ready by nightfall. Where did the day go?"

"Anne, you go right ahead. I've got the knack of it now, and it looks like the crowd's beginning to thin. The girls and I will do just fine. If we have any questions, I'll dispatch Jeremy up to the house to find you."

The young lad seemed to have eyes and ears around his whole head when it came to anything that involved him. He materialized at Anne's elbow, his head bobbing and his eyes alight.

"Yes'm, yes'm. You can count on me. I be right here, jes' in case. Yes, ma'am!" he said, raising his voice at the last for emphasis. "I will not budge from Miss Eugénie's side, neither, in case she be needin' some hep." With that, he planted himself next to Eugénie. The two women glanced at each other, unable to suppress a smile at the young boy's determined sense of duty.

"Well, that's mighty fine, Jeremy," Anne said, which caused the little fellow to beam proudly. "Come, Elizabeth, we'd better be off."

The selling continued at a hectic pace, and Eugénie moved back and forth amongst the girls, weighing here, and measuring there, with Jeremy glued to her side. Before long, he was making suggestions that simplified the measuring and bagging. He managed to maintain his vigil at Eugénie's elbow and to involve himself in every transaction that took place.

At one point, after one of his clever suggestions, she turned to him and said, "Jeremy, you are truly a marvel!" The young lad grinned from ear to ear.

A short time later, Eugénie looked up after weighing a particularly large portion of corn to see Roland leaning comfortably against one of the poles that anchored the store's roof. He stood with his arms folded across his chest and an amused expression on his face. He appeared content to remain as he was, even after he caught Eugénie's eye. She couldn't help but wonder how long he had been there and what his purpose was.

When the sales dwindled to a trickle and no new boats appeared at the dock, Eugénie turned to Jeremy. "Well, young man, it looks like we're about finished for the day." She pushed back stray tendrils of hair from her forehead and wondered how to distract Jeremy so that she could speak to Roland.

"Miss Eugénie, they's not much doin' here now. The girls can be finishing up while I go up and see if Mistress Tucker's rat concoction is ready," Jeremy said, solving her dilemma. "If it is, I'll bring it back down here and hep the girls put everything away for the night."

"Why, Jeremy, that's a splendid plan. If I'm not here when you get back, don't worry, I'll be at the kitchen putting the weights and measures away. When you and the girls have finished, go up to the house and tell Mistress Tucker that I'll be along shortly."

"Yes, ma'am, Miss Eugénie. I'll do that right away. You can count on me!" In a flash, he was tearing up to the house. Eugénie watched while the girls finished the last few sales. Then she told them to tidy up and wait for Jeremy to return to close down the store for the night.

Eugénie glanced over at Roland, who nodded slightly to show that he understood what she intended to do. After she had collected the pouch of coins and notes of trade, she looked around to make sure she hadn't forgotten anything. Then she picked up the weights and measures and started toward the kitchen.

Roland hoisted the sack of grain he had purchased and joined her. "Miss Eugénie, it appears you've got a handful there. May I be of some help?"

"I'd appreciate that very much," she smiled, their eyes almost level. "We haven't seen much of you, lately. How are you on this fine day?"

"Very well, thank you, ma'am," he replied. "Colonel Tucker's store sure came in mighty handy. Pelican's Reef was down to one day's reserve of meal. I imagine I'll be a frequent customer till our own ship gets to port." They continued this innocuous conversation until they were out of earshot of the others.

Then, drawing Eugénie behind a convenient hedge, Roland lowered his voice. "Miss Eugénie, we've been keeping a close eye on the man Darby. He's making a nuisance of himself, but that's about all. If he should make a move of any sort, we'll be ready for him. I'll keep you apprised. I have a letter for you from Captain Goodrich. I was told it was urgent and to bring it to you with all speed. I'll return in two days' time to purchase more corn, so if you have any reply for him, I can pick it up then."

He handed her the letter, which she quickly secreted in the sash of her gown. "Roland, I haven't had a chance to thank you for your part in my rescue. I'm forever in your debt. And knowing that you are dogging Darby's footsteps gives me much-needed peace of mind."

"Dear lady, your smile is thanks enough," he said gallantly. "Now, I'd better be going. I'll see you in two days' time." He slipped around the hedge and was gone.

XXXIV

⚜ ⚜ ⚜

The household gathered around the table that evening without the usual coterie of guests.

Even Rorick Hamilton was absent, causing Elizabeth to remark, "Why, my goodness me, Mister and Mistress Hamilton must have reclaimed their errant son! Mama, is it too soon to restore the sleeping porch, now known as the 'Rorick Hamilton Room,' to its former guestroom status?"

"Now, now, Elizabeth," her mother chided her. "That young man is very good company and a pleasure to have around, not to mention all the help he's been to your father carrying messages back and forth with nary a complaint, no matter what time of the day or night." Elizabeth, her eyes twinkling, looked over at her mother, but held her tongue.

"Indeed, he has been a great help," the Colonel agreed. "At this moment, he's probably down at Salt Kettle. We've been awaiting word from the colonials, as you know. Several ships were due in today, and I'm hopeful that one of them carries the news that we sorely need. Once the postal pouches have been off-loaded, I'm sure Rorick will waste no time coming here. So we'd best not be too hasty in returning his bedchamber to its former status," he said, chuckling at Elizabeth. "I don't doubt we'll be seeing a lot of that young man for some time to come."

"The embargo, Father. Doesn't the whole matter rest on the Americans' agreement to lift their embargo on our shipping, in exchange for our help?" Elizabeth asked.

"Of course it does, my dear," he replied. "But we must receive a clear indication that they'll fulfill our request. This is the confirmation that I'm talking about. Once we've received it, then both sides will have to settle down and work out the last details, which might get a little ticklish. I imagine they'll expect to receive the goods before they lift the embargo. We can only hope that they won't see fit to burden us with a protracted period of time before carrying out their end of the bargain. The survival of our shipping, and perhaps even our way of life, depends on their cooperation. For this cooperation, we are participating in an event that places all of us at great risk."

Eugénie was amazed that the Colonel spoke so openly about his overtures to the Americans and his plan to offer up to them the government of Bermuda's sole supply of gunpowder. There's no court in the land, she reflected, that wouldn't convict him of treason on both counts. Should word filter through to the British authorities that Colonel Tucker and his cohorts were in league with the enemy, the men might be hanged or shot on the spot. The magnitude of the risk they take is beyond measure.

Eugénie was so absorbed in her own thoughts that she lost track of the conversation around her and was jolted back to her surroundings only when everyone began to rise from the table.

"…and so, desperate times dictate desperate deeds," the Colonel was saying as he slipped his arm around his wife's tidy waist. "It's important work that we do for the good of the whole. We won't shirk our duty for fear of a bit of risk to our persons. Our protection lies in the loyalty that binds us together."

Anne drew strength from her husband's words and looked up lovingly at him as he held the door to the veranda open for her. Elizabeth and Eugénie bade them goodnight and left them discussing the events of the day, the Colonel with his pipe and port, Anne with a glass of claret.

Eugénie closed the door of her bedchamber with a sigh of relief and leaned her head against it. She massaged her temples with cold fingers.

"What is it, Mistress?" Marie asked, looking alarmed. "You look so pale. Are you unwell?"

"Oh, Marie, events are moving so swiftly, and I'm afraid of what the outcome will be. My head is pounding with it all."

"Come, I'll help you into your night rail and fix an herbal compress to help you sleep," Marie said, quickly taking charge.

"I'll gladly turn myself over to your ministrations, dear Marie, but first I must read Captain Goodrich's correspondence, which Roland brought this afternoon."

"No," Marie said firmly, causing Eugénie to look at her sharply. "Mistress, this once, I'll have my say. You've made no allowance for the ordeal you endured so recently. It taxed you far more than you're willing to admit. Whatever news is contained in the letter will keep for the night. In the morning, after a refreshing sleep, you'll be able to read it with a calm mind. Right now, you're too overwrought. I'm my mother's child and have her gift for gauging the signs of health and disease. You're on the brink of total exhaustion, and I won't be responsible for the damage you'll cause to your health if you continue to push yourself in this fashion."

"My dear Marie, far be it from me to expose you to your mother's wrath, should anything happen to me while I'm in your care. It's only for your sweet sake that I'm willing to set aside my own desires. But, just this once." Marie smiled at her mistress, glad to see that at least a shadow of her usual humor was still intact.

"Thank you, Mistress, for your generous forbearance," Marie replied, continuing the banter. "I'll endeavor not to exploit your good nature in the future." With a laugh, Eugénie turned herself over to Marie's capable hands and was soon tucked into the four-poster with a soothing compress on her forehead. Almost purring with contentment, she fell fast asleep. Had she opened her eyes at that moment, she would have seen Marie's forehead furrowed with concern as she looked once more at Eugénie before blowing out the candle and slipping into her trundle bed.

Marie's prediction proved true. Eugénie awoke feeling better than she had in a long time. Her sense of foreboding had passed with the night. Sitting up, she stretched her arms high over her head and took a deep breath just as Marie came through the door carrying a tray.

"Oh, Marie, you've worked a miracle. I can't remember when I've felt so well! Mmmmmm, are those wheat cakes I smell? Oh, and honey, my favorite." She shoved the bedclothes aside to make room for the breakfast tray. "Bless my soul! It's a feast you've brought me! I'm not the one who eats for two." Eugénie patted the plump goose-down mattress beside her. "Come, you must help me with this. I shall never finish such generous portions by myself, and you know how it upsets Cook if every last crumb isn't gone."

Marie joined her on the bed and chose a ripe peach from the tray. "You've no need to hurry this morning. Mistress Tucker told me that she was very concerned about your pallor last night. She went to great lengths to describe how a niece of hers died of exposure far less severe than yours. She asked me to tell you that she'll manage the store with the girls. Elizabeth is perfectly capable of assisting her if necessary. She specifically asked that you use this day for, as she put it, 'nothing more strenuous than attending to her toilette, if that.' So you see, you have the whole day to devote to Captain Goodrich's letter, if you wish, without interruption."

"Marie, to be left entirely to myself—how wonderful! Even if you did put Mistress Tucker up to this!" She brushed aside Marie's protests. "Now that I feel so much better, I'll admit to you that I haven't felt like myself recently. However, last night's pallor was due to my state of mind, not the fitness of my body. I'm concerned about Colonel Tucker and his cohorts, not to mention the members of their families.

"What drives them to take such risks? Surely, they court disaster. There must be some other way to reopen trade with the Americans . . . What am I saying? I've become as mad as they! Simply communicating with the Americans is treason! Marie, Marie, they've got a wolf by the ear!"

"Mistress, we've spoken of this time and time again. You speak of your concern for them, but you're no stranger to danger either. You knowingly embraced it the minute you set out on this mission. And now there's Darby to contend with. Please, I implore you, don't become any more involved than you already are."

"Marie, my purpose in coming here hasn't changed. I only want to find out which side the Bermudians will take in the conflict. Under no circumstances will I join in their scheme."

"How can you say that? You carried out the Colonel's orders in St. George's! You stood and bore witness against one of their own, not to mention your ongoing participation in their nightly meetings!"

"Marie, Marie. Don't you see? Everything I've done is for our mission. Although I do believe in the Americans' cause, and I wish them success in this endeavor, I'm not taking up the Americans' banner. I am no Lafayette. I'll also remain as removed as possible from the Colonel's scheme. You have my word, as soon as there's a clear indication of Bermuda's loyalties, we'll be on the first ship out of here heading for France."

"Well, I'm thankful that at least you've conceded that much," Marie said reluctantly. "Now that we've practically licked the plates clean, I'll remove this tray and leave you to Captain Goodrich."

Eugénie gave her a quick hug and, with mixed feelings, picked up Bridger's letter. It must contain information of the gravest sort or he wouldn't have risked sending it. It began:

My dearest Eugénie, I won't take the time or space to tell you that you're with me in my thoughts and in my heart every minute of my days and nights.

She closed her eyes and pressed the letter to her breast. Taking a deep breath, she continued reading.

Eugénie, I have come upon information of the utmost seriousness. There are those in my acquaintance who're entrusted with carrying the correspondence back and forth between Bermuda's Governor Bruère and the policy-makers at Whitehall—most importantly George Germain, who is acting as the British Minister of War as well as carrying out his other duties. It's clear from the correspondence that Bruère is under considerable strain. He's caught between Tucker and his people on the one hand, who systematically undermine Bruère's authority at every turn, and the Ministers of Whitehall on the other, who do nothing to strengthen the governor's position on the island. Add to that the loss of one of his sons fighting on the British side at Bunker Hill, and the wounding of another son in the same battle, and one wonders how the poor man has survived. I fear for his health.

But that's beside the point. Recently I've come to know that Bruère has intercepted letters traveling from Bermuda to Virginia between Colonel Tucker and his son St. George. The governor has informed Whitehall of this and describes the correspondence in minute detail. Although the language is carefully drawn in Tucker's letters, the governor is thoroughly convinced that there's something under way of the most serious nature. In every corre-spondence, he pleads with Whitehall to authorize him to put Colonel Tucker under house arrest on the grounds that, at the very least, he's communicating with the enemy, which is an act of treason. The Ministers, for the time being, have withheld such authorization, saying that the governor can learn more about the Colonel's schemes if he's not alerted by such action. They wrote, and I quote, "Play out the rope sufficiently, and it will suffice as a hangman's noose." They went on to direct him to keep Colonel Tucker and "all those in his company" under close scrutiny and to report all suspicious activities.

Eugénie paused to consider this new development, then read on.

What I've feared all along is now happening. No one near the Colonel is above suspicion. You, dear heart, are considered one of them. Be warned. The governor has already planted eyes and ears in the Colonel's neighborhood. I've no doubt that the Colonel, that wily old fox, has the cunning to carry out his scheme, whatever it may be. But I fear for you, my dearest. The circle is tightening. His destiny is not yours. Eugénie, I beg you, sail for France while you still can! I must close now. Know that you have an avenue of escape as long as I have even one ship under my command.

I commend you into God's hands, B.

Eugénie's hands shook as she folded and refolded the pages, staring unseeing out of the window. *Mon Dieu! Mon Dieu!* What am I to do? I've no choice. I must stay until I have completed my mission. But I cannot and will not continue to place Marie in this danger. I must devise some ploy that will convince her to return to France and take the roan with her. Once I know they're safely on their way, I'll breathe more easily. Then, when I'm finished here, I'll be able to leave at a moment's notice.

Buttressed by her plan, she leapt from the bed with renewed purpose. She hastened to the fireplace and struck a piece of tinder. With great care, she set fire to each page. She watched the corners darken and curl toward the center as, one by one, they turned to ashes.

The bright face that she presented to Marie a short while later gave no indication of the heavy weight that lay on her heart.

"Marie," Eugénie said gaily, "I plan to take full advantage of this beautiful day. Come with me. The breeze is up and blowing. It will do us both good to be out on the water. That is, if the babe won't cause too much trouble with your digestion," she added, throwing down the challenge.

Marie looked askance at her mistress, sensing something. She bit back the words that sprang to her lips, knowing that they would do little good when Eugénie was in such a mood. At least if I'm with her, Marie thought, I can keep an eye on her. She fell in beside her mistress, saying primly, "My digestion is quite fine, thank you very much. The babe and I accept with pleasure."

———

Later, dressed in her britches and a light linen blouse, Eugénie moved agilely about the skiff, raising the sail and cleating down the lines. "Now, you just sit right there," she directed Marie. "I don't want you to do a thing but enjoy this fine day."

At that moment, a puff of wind came up, forcing Eugénie to jibe the sail. Had Marie not ducked in the nick of time, she would have toppled into the water. "Enjoy it sopping wet, you mean." Marie's retort was met by Eugénie's burst of laughter.

"The look on your face, Marie, when you almost pitched overboard was priceless. Now, how am I going to keep my mind on my business if you persist in distracting me?"

"Very funny," Marie muttered, but she couldn't resist smiling herself.

As they zigged and zagged back and forth across the harbor, Eugénie summarized Bridger's letter to her friend. When she had finished the account, both women fell silent. "I'm afraid we must make plans to leave, Marie, even though I haven't completed what I set out to do here. We can't afford to wait. At any moment, the British authorities could change their minds and choose to put everyone at The Grove under house arrest, or worse. I'd never forgive myself if any harm came to you."

"What of the roan?" Marie asked.

"He's just one more reason for us to make our preparations before anything else can happen. We certainly can't slip the huge stallion through a British net, if they should instigate such a thing. You and I could easily pass through in a disguise, but the roan is well known all over the island. We can't just fold him up and tuck him into one of our trunks. I'll waste no time booking passage on the first ship sailing for France."

"*Alors!* What's the matter with me?" Eugénie said suddenly as if an idea had just come to her. "We'll go over to Pelican's Reef this minute and tell Roland of our plans. He can contact Jamie, and we'll sail on one of Bridger's ships."

Marie looked less sure of this inspiration than her mistress did. "Do you think it's wise to sail to France under the British flag? And what will Colonel Tucker have to say about such an arrangement?"

"Dear Marie," Eugénie answered patiently, "Captain Goodrich sails with letters of marque. As a privateer, he has all manner of flags in his hold. The minute we enter French waters, down comes the Union Jack and up goes the Fleur-de-Lis, *et voilà!*" She snapped her fingers. "As for the Colonel, according to his code, he couldn't allow anything untoward to happen to two women in his care. For the moment, a fragile truce exists between him and Captain Goodrich. Nothing would tickle his fancy more than to have us sail away on a British ship right under the nose of Governor Bruère. He would never let us sail on one of his own ships, knowing that they've recently been the targets of the British, the French, and even other Bermuda ships. I'm convinced we have the perfect plan."

As they talked, Eugénie had deftly tacked her way across the harbor.

"Ah, on vient d'arriver!" Eugénie said, smoothly docking the little boat at the tavern's wharf. She hopped onto the wharf and quickly tied down the bow and stern lines, securing the skiff.

Marie began to climb out of the boat. "Mistress, it's unfitting for you to go into the tavern. I'll go in search of Roland."

Eugénie laid a restraining hand on Marie's arm. *"Non, non,* Marie, your dress will attract unwelcome attention. Mine, on the other hand, will blend in perfectly once I've stuffed my hair into this cap." She quickly donned the cap and hastened off toward the tavern before Marie could say another word.

Adapting her posture and demeanor to the occasion, Eugénie pushed open the door and was assailed by the rank odor of stale spirits and unwashed bodies. It took a moment for her eyes to become accustomed to the dim light. It was only late morning, but the tavern was in full swing, attesting to the recent arrival of several ships. The din was deafening. Eugénie could feel the bond of brotherhood amongst the revelers. She knew if she loitered, it would soon be apparent that she was an outsider.

She looked around and saw Roland standing with deceptive nonchalance by the bar, quaffing a tankard of ale. Without appearing to do so, he was keeping a watchful eye on the whole room. Almost immediately, he saw Eugénie standing just inside the doorway. Moving slowly through the crowd, he made his way toward her. He joked with a patron at one table, slapped another on the back, and threw back his head to laugh at a man's jest as he worked his way to her side. He leaned his shoulder against the doorjamb and hooked his thumbs in his waistband.

"Miss Eugénie, what in God's name are you doing here?" he whispered. His harsh tone contrasted sharply with the bland expression he turned toward the room.

"Roland, I must talk to you. Is there a place where we can speak in private?" Eugénie asked urgently.

"High time you showed up," Roland said, raising his voice. "I've better things to do than look after a young pup like you! But I made a promise to your father, so stop gawking and come along. I guess I can find something for you to do that'll keep you out of trouble."

Unceremoniously, he grabbed Eugénie by the arm and fairly dragged her through the crowded room, amidst guffaws from those who had observed the scene.

Glancing over his shoulder to assure himself that no one was interested in their progress, he opened a narrow door and ushered Eugénie into a cramped storeroom. "We won't be disturbed here," he said. "There had better be a very important reason for this visit, Miss Eugénie. Captain Goodrich would not like . . ."

Eugénie cut off his words. "Roland, I haven't much time. Marie is waiting for me in a boat outside. I mustn't leave her there for very long."

Eugénie then launched into her plan. "It's of the utmost importance that Marie not know about this, for she'll never agree to leave Bermuda without me. I'd been having a premonition that something was going to happen. The message in Captain Goodrich's letter is all the warning I need. We haven't a minute to lose. That's why I came this morning instead of waiting for you to return to The Grove tomorrow,

as we'd planned. We must get Marie and the roan off this island without delay!"

"But what about you, milady?" Roland interrupted.

"I'll remain here until I've gotten the information that I came for,"
she replied. "When that's done, I'll be able to leave quickly, since I
won't be encumbered with Marie, the roan, and all our belongings.
Captain Goodrich knows my commitment."

"As you wish," Roland replied with resignation. "I'm not in agreement, but I'll carry out your wishes. Jamie will come to The Grove
when everything is ready. But how will you explain this sudden departure to the Tuckers?"

"Leave that to me," Eugénie said, her eyes twinkling. "I have a plan
that's foolproof."

"I've no doubt you do," Roland said, shaking his head. "I wonder
why I asked. Come now, we'd better not linger. Go out the back way
and around. I'll create a diversion so that no one will notice you getting into your boat and leaving."

"Oh, dear Roland, what would I do without you?" Eugénie asked.
She reached up and kissed him lightly on the cheek. Opening the
door, she smiled back at him and then slipped noiselessly away.

"God go with you, little one," he whispered, but she was already
gone.

XXXV

❧ ❧ ❧

When Eugénie and Marie arrived back at The Grove, they had to wedge their boat between several unfamiliar vessels. Eugénie looked up at the veranda and saw Rorick Hamilton and two men she did not recognize, arguing vehemently. Colonel Tucker stood nearby, his face creased with concern. The words didn't carry as far as the dock, but it was clear that something of great importance had happened while they had been away. Just at that moment, Elizabeth pushed through the veranda door. She was dressed for travel, her bonnet in place and her shawl casually thrown around her shoulders. She was carrying an oversized basket covered with a calico cloth, which seemed to be very heavy from the way she grasped it with both hands.

The men broke off their conversation, and Rorick moved forward to take the basket. Elizabeth smiled at him gratefully and looked back over her shoulder as Anne Tucker came through the doorway, dressed in a similar fashion.

As Eugénie and Marie reached the welcoming arms, Jeremy appeared around the side of the house dressed in his Sunday best and not sporting his usual bounce.

"Anne, Anne, what is it? What's happened?" Eugénie asked.

"My dear girl, we just learned that there's a case of the pox down in Flatts. Elizabeth and I are on our way there with remedies and provisions," Anne answered.

"Give me a minute to change and I'll come with you," Eugénie said, starting for the door.

"No, child," Anne said firmly. "You have a kind and willing heart, but I can't allow you to accompany us. You mustn't expose yourself. Elizabeth and I have both had mild bouts of the disease, so we are quite immune. Even so, I imagine we won't be allowed in the sickroom—although, one way or the other, I'm sure we'll find a way to be useful. Around that sickness, extra hands are always welcome."

"What of the store?" Eugénie asked, "I can certainly manage that while you're away."

"We've closed the store for the time being," the Colonel said ominously. Seeing Eugénie's questioning stare, he explained, "Events have occurred this morning that make it necessary to avoid having outsiders at The Grove for the time being."

From the sharp look that Anne Tucker gave her husband, it was clear that closing the store had caused a quarrel between them.

"It can't be helped, my dear," the Colonel said gently to her.

"There are souls starving on this island," Anne began, and then snapped her mouth shut. Taking a deep breath, she turned to Eugénie. "I've instructed Maisie to prepare the midday meal, dear. You might make sure that all is to your liking. Henry, we should return no later than midday tomorrow. We'll discuss the store further."

"Yes, my dear," the Colonel replied mildly.

"Now, we must be off. Come, Jeremy."

"Yes, ma'am," Jeremy answered, grasping the basket in both hands. Despite his somber demeanor, Jeremy couldn't resist a little skip as he followed the two women across the lawn.

"I couldn't spare any of the men to ferry Anne and Elizabeth to Flatts, but truthfully, we have no better pilot than Jeremy—with the exception of Ethan, who taught him. I daresay, it won't be long before that little fella is running the whole place," Colonel Tucker said with a chuckle.

Eugénie looked fondly after Jeremy's retreating figure.

"He looks considerably taller than he did when I arrived at The

Grove just a couple of months ago," Eugénie said. "It won't be long before we won't be able to call him 'little fella' any more, Colonel. Now, if you'll excuse me, I'll go and make sure the girls are following Anne's instructions. I'll join you shortly in the dining room."

"Thank you, Miss Eugénie," the Colonel said. "All the excitement this morning has given me quite an appetite."

After assuring herself that the preparations for the meal were going according to plan, Eugénie hurried upstairs and changed into a pale-green sprigged cotton. She paused for a moment, fingering the silver handle of her brush. Then with a shake of her head, she quickly ran the brush through her hair, sweeping the shining mass up into a tidy chignon, which she held in place with tortoiseshell combs. She hastened down the wide stairs, her fingers lightly skimming the dark-toned, cedar banister.

The men rose to their feet as Eugénie entered the dining room, and Rorick quickly moved to pull out Anne Tucker's customary chair for her.

When everyone was seated, Colonel Tucker said, "Miss Eugénie, this morning Rorick brought the news that we've all been waiting for. The Americans are eager to have as much gunpowder as we can provide. In return, they've promised to lift their embargo against our shipping at a specific time in the future. I propose a toast to the success of our joint undertaking."

Around the table, five glasses were raised to a chorus of "Hear, hear!"

The man to the Colonel's right rose to his feet. "And I propose a toast to you, Henry, for your audacious plan." Again, the glasses rose in unison. "At last, our feet are firmly placed on the path of action. The days of conjecture and words are past. I'm glad this day has finally arrived."

"Well said, Christopher," the Colonel said, beaming. "You speak for all of us committed to the welfare of Bermuda shipping. Your return from the islands is timely. I will look to you to promote our plan amongst those of like minds in the middle parishes. You know best the men of discretion in Warwick, Paget, and Pembroke." He turned to the other man who had accompanied Rorick and said, "Arthur, I leave Smith and Devonshire in your capable hands." At that moment, the servants arrived to remove the first course of chilled potato soup, replacing it with the main course of turtle meat dripping with sweet oil, baked rockfish, and stewed palmetto heads.

"Maisie, please tell Cook that she has outdone herself!" Colonel Tucker said. "For all the delicacies that we import, the local Bermuda fare will always be my favorite."

Once the wineglasses had been replenished and the servants had departed, he continued, "We mustn't speak of this to anyone outside of our circle. I'm sure that Bruère has his ears to the ground, and there are those who would go to any lengths to creep into his good graces. So beware."

"Have you set a day for the transfer?" Christopher asked.

The Colonel nodded. "Our date with destiny looks to be mid-August. That timing suits the Americans, and I can find no fault with it. The winds are favorable then, and it will give us enough time to set up our part."

Six weeks! Eugénie exclaimed to herself as she scooped another helping of rockfish onto her plate. I haven't a moment to spare. She was only half-listening to the conversation around her as she went through the motions of acting as hostess in Anne Tucker's stead.

The dinner meal concluded with a refreshing junket flavored with vanilla, a spice not often seen on Bermuda tables. Just as Eugénie was about to rise, signaling the end of the meal, sounds of raised voices and hasty footsteps caused everyone at the table to turn toward the doorway. Moments later a young man burst through the door.

"What is it, Tom?" the Colonel asked, recognizing a member of Harry's household.

Twisting a letter in his hands, Tom looked around the table uncertainly. "Master Harry told me to bring this to you as fast as I could, sir. He said it was of the utmost importance, sir." At a loss to know what to do next, the young man shifted back and forth on his feet, his face turning beet-red.

"Tom, you've done real well. Here, give me the letter, and I'm sure you can find some refreshment in the kitchen. When you're finished, come back here in case I have a message for you to take back to Master Harry. Don't dawdle, for you'll want to reach St. George's before nightfall." Tom delivered the letter into the Colonel's hand and, bobbing his head slightly, turned and scurried from the room.

"Now what can this be, that Harry would go outside of our usual channels?" he asked, tearing open the seal and quickly scanning the contents. With no hesitation, he then read the message out loud.

Father, last night I dined with the governor. We were joined by the first lieutenant from a British frigate that arrived in port yesterday morn. The captain of the ship had been taken ill. Seeing no need to be discreet, the lieutenant spoke openly. He said that his ship had sailed here straight from Boston. Apparently, on their way, they ran into a royal naval vessel from England that had news of what was going on there. The news is: the British are hiring Hessians as reinforcements to join their army in the American colonies, and in numbers to outstrip the advantage the Americans have had so far. The lieutenant said they're wasting no time shipping these seasoned mercenaries over.

There was little else of note that he said. By return messenger, Father, tell me if there's anything further you wish for me to do on this score. I trust that you and Mother are well.

I remain, your obedient son, Harry.

"This is alarming news," the Colonel said, folding the letter and slipping it into the pocket of his waistcoat. "It appears that the English are beginning to take the 'upstarts' seriously. We must communicate this news to the Virginians with all speed. But how, and with whom?"

At that moment, Maisie appeared in the doorway. "Maisie, go fetch Harry's messenger," the Colonel barked.

During the stir caused by Harry's letter, Eugénie slipped out of the room. I must set my plan into motion immediately, she thought, as she went in search of Marie.

"Mistress, I'm sure that the Colonel still plans to carry out his scheme," Marie said, after Eugénie told her about Harry's letter. "The Americans' need for Bermuda's powder is all the more critical, now that the British have accelerated the war. If it were dangerous before for us to try to leave, it's now well-nigh madness even to consider such a foolhardy plan. All shipping will be scrutinized by both sides, and I doubt that the Colonel will allow us to go our merry way, knowing all that we know about his plans."

"Marie, dear," Eugénie began softly, trying to allay her servant's mounting fears, "all the more reason for us to act quickly, before events overtake us and hold us captive here for the duration. We were fortunate to get our message to Roland this morning. Even now, I expect Bridger is making arrangements. He won't waste a minute, eager as he is to have us gone from here and out of harm's way. I've further refined the drama we shall perform in which, dear Marie, you shall play the central role."

At Marie's look of alarm, Eugénie continued, "Don't worry, you shall have the central role, but it will call for little or no effort on your part. I, on the other hand, will have to behave quite out of character. You must promise not to laugh or do anything to give me away."

"Mistress," Marie said with resignation, "it won't be the first time, nor, I fear, the last that I play your foil. Tell me what I must do, and I'll do my best to play my part."

"Marie, you're always so wonderful," she said, squeezing her servant's hands affectionately and quickly describing her plan.

"You'll thank me from the bottom of your heart when we're all safe and sound once more on French soil. Go now, and keep watch for Roland or whomever Bridger or Jamie sends to signal us that all is ready. Keep an eye out that no one sees the *rendez-vous*. We must now be wary of the members of the Tucker camp, as well as the governor's men. I shall create a diversion to cover your movements." Eugénie gave Marie a quick embrace and hurried from the room.

As Eugénie made her way down the stairs, she assumed a distracted air that was well in place when she ran into Maisie in the hallway.

"Maisie, the very person I was looking for!" Maisie turned from lighting the tapers in the gleaming brass wall sconces and stood waiting for Eugénie's direction.

"It's Marie. I'm becoming quite alarmed about her," Eugénie said, wringing her hands, knowing that Maisie would soon spread the news of Marie's "malaise" through the servants' quarters. "At first, I thought it was simply the heat, but her indisposition lingers and becomes worse. I fear it's the babe that's causing this malady. I sent her down by the water in hopes that the breeze off the sound would give her some relief. I wonder if I could trouble you to help me prepare a light supper for her?" .

"Oh, ma'am, I had no idea. Oh, dear! I'll see to her tray myself, this very minute."

"Maisie, that's very kind of you. Marie does so hate for anyone to make a fuss over her. I just hope I haven't waited too long." Eugénie ducked her head and dabbed at her eyes with her lace handkerchief. "If you would just let me know as soon as the tray is prepared, I'd be ever so grateful."

Maisie bobbed a quick curtsy and hurried off as the Colonel came out of the morning room. "Eugénie, what's this? Did I hear you say that your Marie isn't well?"

"I'm afraid so," she answered, her voice trembling. "It's so unlike her to be sickly. I've never known her to have an illness. If something should happen to her or the babe while they're in my care, I'll never forgive myself." As she spoke, she became more and more agitated, and tears began to slip down her cheeks.

"There, there, child," the Colonel said, trying to console her. "Anne will be home tomorrow, and she'll know what to do."

"Sir," Eugénie said, collecting herself with an effort, "if you'll excuse me, I'd feel better if I took supper in my bedchamber with Marie tonight."

"Don't say another word, my child. This heat would weaken the stoutest constitution. The shark oil barometer calls for change. Maybe when the weather breaks, it'll bring a much-needed respite from this infernal heat. That would be a relief for all of us."

"I pray that it's the answer to Marie's malaise, sir. I sent her out to enjoy the evening air, but now I think I'd better go and bring her in for supper."

"I wish you a pleasant evening and a sound sleep, my dear," the Colonel said, before returning to the morning room.

"And to you, too, sir," Eugénie said, as she walked as decorously as possible down the hallway and out of the door. As soon as she reached the deep shadows that spread across the back lawn, she grabbed fistfuls of her skirt in both hands and fairly flew over the grass down to the dock, willing Marie to have received word about their departure. As she approached the dock and saw Marie's form outlined against the evening sky, she had a moment's doubt about the ruse she was putting over on her dear friend. Then, knowing that what she planned was in her best interest, she straightened her dress, lifted her chin, and walked resolutely to where Marie was standing.

"Marie, is it the evening air that's brought a blush to your pale cheeks? I've been so concerned."

Marie turned an arched brow toward her mistress, wondering about her stilted speech. Trusting that it would eventually lead to something, she played along. "It's been so pleasant here by the water's edge after the heat of the day. I've been watching the early appearance of the nightbirds. Our old friend, the silver heron, left just moments before you came."

"I'm sorry I missed him," Eugénie replied blandly, gleaning the underlying message, but wondering which of their allies Marie had designated the silver heron. "He's always so amusing," Eugénie blurted out, thinking that she sounded as odd as Marie had and that maybe there was something catching in the night air. Shivering suddenly, she continued, "Come, my dear Marie, I'll look out for you even if you won't." Again, Marie was perplexed by Eugénie's behavior. She turned to gape at her friend.

Oblivious to Marie's stare, Eugénie went on, "I've arranged for us to sup in our room. Here, let me give you a hand." With that, Eugénie put her arm around Marie's waist and practically dragged her up the slope toward the house.

"And what was all that about?" Marie said sharply once they were settled in the bedchamber, a sumptuous meal lovingly laid out for them on the drop-leaf table by the window.

Eugénie put her finger to her lips and shushed Marie with a look, cocking her head toward the closed door. "Mmmmm, the perfect supper in this beastly heat," she said loud enough to carry, "and light enough not to test your tender condition, dear Marie."

Seeing that "dear Marie's" patience was stretched to the breaking point and that enough time had elapsed for the curious Maisie to be well gone, Eugénie quickly described to Marie the scene that she had played out earlier for both the household's and the Colonel's benefit.

"Whether it rains or not tonight, tomorrow it must appear that your condition has worsened during the night. I'll play the distraught mistress to my servant's worsening vapors. In addition, I'll be so alarmed about the outbreak of the pox that I'll demand that we take our leave at the earliest possible moment."

"We know from the message that we received this evening from Jamie that he'll just happen to arrive tomorrow with the very means we need for our immediate departure," Marie said.

The two women grasped each other's hands, looking triumphantly into each other's eyes, the one seeing the green pastures of home, the other seeing her servant and beloved friend on her way to safety.

XXXVI

❧❧❧

Eugénie awoke with a start. Something had intruded on her sleep. She lay very still in the dark, straining to hear. Nothing. The only sound was Marie's gentle breathing nearby on the trundle bed.

Marie is such a light sleeper, she thought. If there were anything moving about, surely she would have heard it. Maybe it's just nerves. I'd better settle down, or I'll never be able to carry out this plan. Marie knows me so well, she'll begin to suspect something, if she doesn't already.

Taking a calming breath, she nestled deeper into the cool linens and was soon fast asleep.

When Eugénie awoke in the morning, bright sunshine streamed through the windows and there was a fresh lift in the air. She sat up in bed, twisting and stretching, enjoying the feeling of her muscles coming to life. She felt surprisingly well rested in spite of her broken sleep the night before.

"You're awake," Marie said, coming through the door just at that moment. "The household is in an uproar with the arrival during the night of Mr. Thomas Tudor from the colony of South Carolina with *ses jeunes filles.*"

"So that's what woke me up," Eugénie exclaimed. "His arrival wasn't expected. I wonder what could've happened to bring him this long way in the middle of the night. And what are you doing wandering about? You're supposed to be sick," Eugénie scolded.

"Don't worry. I'm playing my role to perfection," Marie answered tartly. "I've brought both of us chamomile tea, because Maisie swears ''Twill fix anything that ails ye.' Now, enjoy it and these freshly baked muffins. They're light as air, or at least the air we're blessed with this morning. A summer storm must have passed through while we slept. I've laid out your clothes, and one of the girls will be along shortly with a basin of fresh water."

"Thank you, Marie. You've thought of everything. Mmmmm, this muffin's delicious, but I can't say much for the chamomile tea." Eugénie said, wrinkling her nose.

Marie giggled, "I was of a mind to slip mine over the window sill once your back was turned."

Eugénie's eyes gleamed. "Let's pour it all back into the pot and get rid of the whole thing." Laughing like children, they made short work of returning both cupfuls back into the teapot. Then Eugénie held the pot at arm's length over the sill and dumped its contents. They grinned at each other as they heard the liquid hit the ground.

A light knock on the door caused them to whirl around guiltily.

"One moment," Eugénie said, gesturing to Marie to get into bed. She replaced the teapot on the tray and sat down and resumed munching on a muffin. *"Oui, entrez, s'il vous plaît."*

One of the serving girls came briskly through the door carrying a washing basin, her eyes alight with excitement. "My, my! The household is just a-bustlin' this morn. What with Mr. Thomas and those two beautiful little girls and everything all upside down with Mistress Tucker away. Is there anything else you'll be needin'? No? Then I'd best git myself back downstairs." Her words came out in a rush, tumbling over one another. As she started to leave, she saw the teapot and empty cups. "Oh, you finished all yo' tea. I'll go right this minute and git you a fresh pot."

In unison, Marie and Eugénie shouted, "No!" At the servant's startled expression, Eugénie spoke quickly to soften their odd reaction. "It's very important that Marie rest. I don't want her disturbed, and you must return to your duties. Thank you very kindly, but I'll see to

Marie's needs myself. Now if you will, you may remove the breakfast service, and please let Colonel Tucker know that I'll be down shortly. Thank you."

The young girl looked thoroughly baffled but managed to pick up the breakfast tray. With a brief curtsy, she clattered out of the room.

When Eugénie arrived downstairs a short time later, she saw that Marie's description of the household had been no exaggeration.

She finally found the Colonel and Thomas Tudor in the morning room with the two little girls vying with each other for their grandfather's lap. "Girls, girls!" he was saying, "there's room enough for both of you. There's no cause for squabbling." Eugénie was shocked at Thomas Tudor's appearance. His clothes were disheveled, if not soiled. When he turned at the sound of her footsteps, she saw that his eyes were bloodshot and sunken in their sockets. He wore a good week's worth of beard on his cheeks and chin. His face was drawn and deathly pale. In spite of his evident exhaustion and distress, he rose gallantly to his feet, a ghost of his usual jaunty grin touching his lips.

"Oh, dear Tom," she cried, running to him and throwing her arms around his stooped shoulders. "What has happened to you?"

For a moment he rested his head against her soft curls and then, drawing himself up, he looked deep into her eyes. Her breath caught in her throat at the depth of sorrow and grief that she saw there.

"Ah, Miss Eugénie." Momentarily, his voice cracked. Then he cleared his throat and went on, "My beloved wife. I've lost her. The pox took her from me. And I, a doctor, could do nothing. She fought valiantly to the last. But, when she came to the end of her strength, her spirit simply slipped away, snuffed out like a candle flame in the wind. She died a fortnight ago. Her last words were of her love for me and our dear little girls." While their father had been speaking, the two girls sat motionless in their grandfather's lap. He gently rocked them, comforting them in the age-old manner.

"Oh, Thomas," Eugénie said softly. Holding him closely in her arms, she felt his body shudder and the wetness of his tears on her cheek.

The moment passed quickly. "Thank you," he whispered. Taking a deep breath, he pulled slowly out of her embrace and turned back to his father and daughters. "Young ladies, I imagine Bobbins has had a new litter of kits that need your attention. If I remember correctly from years past, I've no doubt they're, this very minute, nestled in some hiding place down at the stables. Here, come with me. Together, I imagine, we'll find those young kits."

"Yes, yes," the two little girls cried, jumping down from their grandfather's lap, all sadness erased from their young faces.

"Well, let's be off, then," their father said. Taking a small hand in each of his large ones, he led the little ones off on their mission. He looked back over his shoulder at his father and smiled gravely.

"Thank the good Lord for the resiliency of children," Colonel Tucker said, shaking his head sadly.

"That poor, poor man," Eugénie said. "He did love her so. The little time I saw them together here, for the wedding, they were so devoted to each other. And those precious children, so young to lose their mother. Your dear Anne will know how to comfort them."

"Yes, that she will," the Colonel said. "It was dangerous for Thomas to come to Bermuda at this time. His loyalties are well known to the governor. But he did right bringing the girls to us. South Carolina is no place for them, now with their mother gone and a war going on. They'll be safe here."

Considering what the Colonel was planning, his words struck Eugénie with particular force. "Will he be staying long?"

"Only long enough to see his mother and stock his ship. I imagine he'll be off again well before dark."

"*Mon Dieu!* Can't he allow himself at least a few days rest? He looks completely exhausted. He'll sicken, himself, if he doesn't look after his health."

"He's not safe here under the governor's nose," the Colonel said, disagreeing. "His activities in the colonies will be just the restorative distraction he needs. Even if it were safe for him to remain with us, he would only fret and pine away for her. It would do neither him nor the girls any good. No, it's best that he be off, and the sooner the better, before it's known that he's even been here. He can take word of the Hessians' coming, to the Americans. Now, how is your Marie doing this morning?" His abrupt change of subject indicated that the discussion of Thomas Tudor's departure was over.

"Not well, I'm afraid, not well at all, sir," Eugénie replied, but before she could say more, they heard a commotion in the backyard. Eugénie and Colonel Tucker sprang up from their chairs and hurried outside to see what this new development could be.

What met their eyes as they burst out on the veranda was a procession of sorts, with Jeremy in the lead carrying a very ruffled Bobbins, who was struggling for all she was worth to escape her captor. Following Jeremy were the kits, tumbling and falling over one another, as they tried to keep up with the young boy's stride. Thomas' two daughters were dancing and skipping in and out of the scrambling kittens, grabbing first one and then another. Thomas Tudor brought up the rear, manfully enduring the tears and embraces of his mother and sister.

All of this activity was taking place amidst a deafening roar of hissing, spitting, meowing, shrieking, and wailing. Above it all, Jeremy's voice carried easily, as he upbraided poor Bobbins.

"Stop that wrigglin' and hissin'! Stop it, I says. You is not, not gettin' down till we gits to the house. Not one minute before! Now stop that, you hear?" Witnessing Jeremy's performance, Eugénie and the Colonel tried their best to maintain straight faces. In spite of their best efforts, they broke into broad grins.

Clearing his throat, the Colonel waded into the throng of people and animals. "My dear," he said, embracing his wife, "I'm so glad you're home. I see you and our Thomas found each other." A glimpse at her face told him that she had already learned of her son's loss and was trying to decide the best way to put things right.

When they reached the welcoming arms of the house, Bobbins, with a mighty effort, exploded out of Jeremy's arms and at once began to round up her kits.

Eugénie started to console Jeremy. "Dat's all right, Miss Eugénie. I was jes' about to set her down, anyway. I was carryin' her 'cuz I know'd that her little kits would follow right along. That way, Mr. Thomas's little gals could choose which ones they likes best. See there? They's all playin' 'round together. Bobbins never liked me much, no how, but she likes those little gals. She knows that they'll be sweet to her little kits." His assessment of the situation proved correct. With supreme cat dignity, Bobbins pranced up the stairs to the veranda, carrying one of her offspring by the nape of its neck. She was closely followed by the little girls, who, between them, somehow managed to carry the remainder of the litter.

The only hitch occurred when the girls were told that they would have to relinquish their charges to go in for dinner. Peace was restored, however, once they had prepared a nest for the mother and her babies in an oversized wash basket made of palmetto fronds and an old, tattered, down-filled pillow. Pleased with their accomplishment, they allowed themselves to be led off to the dining room. They were assured that it would not be long before they could return and continue their guardianship of the new family.

During the meal, Anne prevailed upon her husband to let Thomas Tudor remain until the next day so that the family could hold a sunrise memorial service for his wife.

"It's only fitting, Henry, that the family here at The Grove and our close friends have the chance to express our grief. I'm adamant about this. It's the only way that the healing can truly begin, for all of us," she said.

"You know best in these matters, my dear," the Colonel said, acquiescing. "But I'm afraid for his safety if he tarries too long. All must be ready for his departure immediately following the ceremony. I've sent word to young Harry about his brother's arrival, so that he can tell Tudor, word for word, what the first lieutenant said. I trust Harry will arrive before long and with discretion." As the Colonel began to bring his wife up-to-date on all that had happened while she was away, Eugénie excused herself and went to prepare a tray for Marie.

———

Eugénie spent the rest of the afternoon deciding which of her possessions to return with Marie and which few things she would keep for the remainder of her stay. She worked quickly so that nothing would appear changed to Marie's eyes when she returned from the gardens where she had been banished to sit quietly and rest.

Eugénie was just closing the lid of the last box when Anne burst through the door. "What's this I hear about your Marie? She's unwell? Oh, dear, I do hope nothing is amiss with the babe."

"Oh, Anne," Eugénie said, assuming an expression of grave concern. "I do worry about her. She kept her condition from me for a whole week, but yesterday the pains and nausea were too great for her to hide them any longer. We must send her on the first ship that sails for France."

"Send her? You're not going with her? Surely, she won't consent to leave without you."

"I've no doubt that she'd refuse if she thinks we aren't going together, but my place is here for the time being—if I haven't overstayed my welcome. I'll need your help to carry out this deception. She may never forgive me for this, but I won't rest until she and her babe are in her mother's safekeeping. Can I prevail on you to help me in this?"

Anne patted her on the arm. "But of course, my dear. You've become very dear to us. We'd love for you to stay as long as you possibly can. Now, the first order of business is a ship," she said briskly, her practical nature coming to the fore. "I'll speak to Henry immediately on that score. He'll know the schedule of every ship that's suitable for her passage."

"Anne, for Marie not to become suspicious, we must count on booking passage for the roan and sending most of my belongings as well."

"Yes, to be sure," Anne agreed. "I'll be sad to see your Marie leave, but with the outbreak of the pox, it's not wise for her to remain on the island and take the chance of being exposed to that awful disease, even if she were feeling fit as a fiddle. Bermudians have always demonstrated a rare resistance to it—a resistance much higher than that of the Europeans. I'm alarmed and mystified to see a case of it in Flatts. I only pray that it's an isolated one. Now I must be off to see to the planning of tomorrow's service."

"Anne, I thank you for all your many kindnesses," Eugénie said softly, surprised to feel tears welling up in her eyes.

"There, there," Anne Tucker said hugging her. "'Tis nothing, nothing at all. You carry much on your young shoulders. We're many and you're but one. If in a small way we can be of help to you, we're only too glad to do so."

At that moment, Marie came through the door. Her pallor was pronounced, aided by Eugénie's rice powder, which she had so carefully applied earlier that day. Marie looked startled to see Anne Tucker but quickly masked her surprise.

"Good day, Mistress Tucker." Marie dipped a curtsy and then turned to Eugénie. "Mistress, Mr. Mackenzie is in the parlor and wishes to speak to you," she said.

"Jamie?" Eugénie exclaimed, appearing surprised at his arrival. "What on earth could bring him here? I do hope there's nothing wrong."

"He said only that he'd come to report to Colonel Tucker that the matter of the recovered cargo had been concluded," Marie replied blandly. "And that he wished to see how you were recovering from the ordeal."

"Well, I must hasten to put his mind to rest," Eugénie said. "Now, Marie, you lie down and rest. Promise me that you'll stay off your feet until it's time for supper." Not waiting to hear the protest that hovered on Marie's lips, Eugénie hurried out of the room with Anne and closed the door firmly behind her.

They found Jamie and the Colonel talking amiably in the parlor, enjoying tall tankards of ale.

"Jamie," Eugénie cried warmly, "it's so good to see you!"

"And you, ma'am," Jamie replied, his face brightening at the sight of her. "'Tis glad I am to see you so improved. Marie is not faring as well,

I hear." Eugénie breathed a silent sigh of relief that Jamie had managed to smoothly introduce the real purpose of his visit.

Jamie followed Eugénie's lead. The expression of concern on his face deepened as she told him about Marie's ailments.

"So you see," Eugénie concluded, wringing her hands, "I must find a way to transport her and the roan to France with all speed. Each day that passes, I worry that she's not in her mother's special care."

"I see that my arrival was fortuitous, indeed," Jamie said. "As it happens, my ship and I are at your disposal, Miss Eugénie. As I was telling Colonel Tucker, Captain Goodrich bade me two days ago to make ready to sail for North Africa to trade our West Indies cargo on that coast. 'Twill be of no consequence to include the French coast as part of our route. I'll see to it myself that Marie and all that you prize arrive home safely."

"Oh, Jamie, once again you've come to my rescue." Eugénie clasped his large hands in her small ones. "You'll join me *dans ma petite mirage?*"

Jamie chuckled. "I'll carry out your subterfuge. Fear not, dear lady."

"How soon can you depart?" Eugénie asked, knowing that his appearance at The Grove meant that he was prepared to leave immediately.

"Since receiving my orders from the Captain, I've been provisioning the ship. I stopped here at The Grove to give the Colonel an accounting of the recovered cargo before going on my way," he answered. "Except for bringing stores aboard to accommodate the mighty roan's stomach, the ship and I are ready and at your service, milady."

"There are ample supplies for the horse in the storeroom," said the Colonel. "Take all you need for the journey. Miss Eugénie, I won't countenance any discussion of payment. Instead, send me a small token from his first winnings. That will suffice. Consider his provisions an investment from The Grove in his successful racing career."

"I find I'm more and more in debt to the Tucker family, sir. I fear I'll never repay the debt I owe you," Eugénie said, deeply touched by yet another example of the Tuckers' generosity.

"It's nothing that your friendship hasn't paid in full already, young lady," he answered gently. "You'd best be about your business, for it appears to me that young Jamie, here, is eager to catch the evening tide."

"Come, Eugénie," Anne said, "while you inform Marie of this evening's departure, I'll round up the boys to bring down your trunks and boxes. Jamie, I'm sure Jeremy is somewhere near by. He can help you with the roan's supplies."

Eugénie needed little encouragement. Her plan was going more smoothly than she could have hoped. Now, all she had to do was see Marie onto the ship and on her way without incident.

XXXVII

⚜ ⚜ ⚜

"What? We sail this evening?" Marie exclaimed, aghast. "But I haven't seen to our things, nor . . ."

"Don't fret, dear Marie," Eugénie replied. "I've been a bundle of nerves since Colonel Tucker received the correspondence from the Americans. I haven't been able to sit still or get a moment's rest. While you were out in the gardens, I organized the trunks and boxes. Jamie's ship is not as large as I would have liked, but we're fortunate that he was able to act on such short notice. If we must leave one or two boxes behind, we must. I'm sure that Anne will see that they're sent along to us on the next available ship. Come now, we must not interfere with Jamie's schedule. Go down to the dock and see to the loading of our things. I'll stay here and direct the men when they come for our belongings."

"Oh, Mistress," Marie said softly, her eyes shining. "I hadn't allowed myself to think about going home. And now the moment is here. Won't it be wonderful to be on our own soil, once more? I've missed it so."

"*Oui, chère Marie,*" Eugénie agreed. "It'll be wonderful to see the shores of France again and to be home at the château amongst our own people. We've been away a long time." Eugénie's voice caught, and she gave Marie a quick hug, knowing that the small gesture would have to last her until they were together again. *"Vite! Vite maintenant!"* she said, gently pushing Marie toward the door. "I'll join you as soon as the last box is carried from this chamber."

Eugénie stood at the window and watched Marie hastening across the lawn toward the dock. Tears sprang to her eyes and slipped down her cheeks.

"*Adieu, ma chère,*" she whispered. A sharp rap on the door brought her around sharply. Straightening her shoulders, she opened it.

"Mistress Tucker sent us up to fetch your boxes and trunks," Ethan said. Pulling his cap from his head, he bowed slightly. "Miss Eugénie, it sho' has been a pleasure knowing you and Miss Marie. I knows young Jeremy is goin' to be heart-broke when the roan leaves."

"Thank you, Ethan," Eugénie answered, touched by his words. "It's been a very special time for us, made so by the many kindnesses of everyone at The Grove."

"We'd best git started, boys," Ethan said, his manner all business once more. "Miss Eugénie, if you'll tell us what you want carried out, we'll have yo' things down to the dock in no time flat."

Three men hoisted the largest trunk up on their broad shoulders.

"Easy; easy, there," Ethan commanded as he and another man lifted the two smaller ones and followed the others down the hall. Eugénie smiled as she heard Ethan continuing to exhort his men all the way down the stairs. They were back shortly, and in no time the room was emptied of all but three boxes stacked in the corner.

Eugénie stood looking around the room that had been their home. Stripped of their familiar things, it now looked bare and lonely. "This may be harder than I thought," she murmured to herself. She turned to look back at the room once more before closing the door softly behind her and walking briskly down the hall.

Outside, it seemed to Eugénie that there were more people than usual milling around, even for The Grove. She saw two stablehands leading the roan along the far edge of the lawn in the direction of the dock, and she made her way toward them. As she approached, the roan whinnied his usual greeting.

"Ah, you beauty," she said softly to him, taking his rein in one hand and stroking his massive shoulder with the other. "I'll miss you with all my heart until we're together again." As if he understood, he rolled his eyes and tossed his head from side to side.

"Now, none of that," she scolded him. "You're the leader. You must set the example for the other Virginians. I don't want to hear when I arrive home that you've been up to any of your pranks. Only glowing reports. Do you understand?" In answer, he pawed at the grass and dipped his head to nuzzle her. Eugénie threw her arms around his neck. Laying her check against his, she laughed. "Well, just see that you do! Oh, I shall miss you so."

When they arrived at the dock, they found a horse barge and a long-boat secured side by side. All the baggage had been loaded onto the longboat, and Marie was standing in the middle of the mountain, checking each piece off on her list. Seeing Eugénie and the roan, she gingerly picked her way through the stacks of boxes, satchels, and trunks and stepped without her usual agility onto the dock. Eugénie, seeing her awkward movements, was glad that she had not wavered in carrying through with her plan.

The Grove people, who had gathered to see them off, quickly surrounded the two women. Most had a thoughtful, handcrafted, parting gift to give them. Others held out bouquets. No one came empty-handed. In return, Eugénie gave each a few coins and French bonbons. Anne, the Colonel, and the rest of the family stood to the side, smiling at the scene.

Out of the corner of her eye, Eugénie saw Jamie gesturing to her. She nodded, whispered briefly to Marie, and walked over to him. "Yes, Jamie, what is it?" Eugénie spoke quietly.

"Milady, see the man yonder? There's something in his manner that draws my attention to him. Maybe it's because he's working so hard not to be noticed."

Eugénie looked around, her eyes following Jamie's gaze. The object of Jamie's concern was of medium height, with nondescript features, dressed in a manner that marked him as neither a servant nor a master. He would have been totally without distinction and would have blended easily into his surroundings, had it not been for his exceptionally erect posture, which, to Eugénie's eye, stamped him as a soldier. She gasped and quickly averted her eyes, lest he feel himself watched and be on guard.

"You recognize him?" Jamie asked.

"Yes, yes, indeed. He's one of the governor's men. At first I didn't recognize him in that garb, but his soldier's carriage caused me to look more closely. I remember him clearly. He was at the Tuckers' wedding, which tells me that he's one of Governor Bruère's inner circle and trusted with the most sensitive duties. I've no doubt that he's here to spy on the Colonel's activities and to inform the governor. I daresay he's already made note of your ship and your presence here."

"From what I've heard," Jamie said, "the Colonel's activities would not bear close inspection. Considering that, I'm surprised that Colonel Tucker is so lax about those who come and go here. Although his son isn't openly strolling around the place, he's the topic of conversation on everyone's tongue. I haven't been listening closely, but even I heard of his unexpected visit. The Colonel may take his own safety lightly, but surely he's more careful where his family is concerned. And others in his household, such as you, particularly considering the threat Darby poses for you and the Tuckers."

"I agree," Eugénie said. "It's highly unusual for Colonel Tucker's vigilance to be so slack. Oh, I just remembered, Harry is expected any time, now! This man mustn't see him. Oh, Jamie, what shall we do?" Eugénie whispered, grabbing his arm.

"Have no fear, little one." Jamie's eyes twinkled dangerously. "I shall see to him. The young man's about to discover an entirely new calling, one that he'll find impossible to resist. At the moment, he's probably unaware that he bears an uncanny resemblance to a member of my crew who jumped ship recently. He'll soon be apprised of that fact. We've been looking high and low for the deserter. How fortunate that our search has finally been rewarded. He'll have plenty of time to repent his sins while cooling his heels in my hold. When the mistake's discovered, he'll be well out to sea, in more ways than one."

"Oh Jamie, you're a rascal—and thank the good Lord that you are!" Eugénie chuckled. "Now, I'd better get back to Marie."

A short time later, while Eugénie was standing at the dock watching the stablehands lead the roan onto the horse barge, she saw Jamie and one of his crew in deep conversation with the governor's man, who was looking at both of them with a mixture of bewilderment and horror. A skirmish began. In short order the man was led off, his head lolling on his chest, his hands bound firmly behind his back, and his feet barely skimming the ground, held fast in the grip of Jamie and his crew. All this took place in the blink of an eye. No one at the dock or on the lawn seemed to notice. Eugénie watched them as they made their way down to a skiff tied to a mangrove some distance from the dock.

I hadn't noticed that boat, Eugénie thought with surprise. I'd better be more alert, or I may find myself caught unawares.

Minutes later, Jamie materialized at her side. "You needn't concern yourself any longer about our unexpected guest. But for future safety, I urge you to put a word in the Colonel's ear. If one man could breach his security that easily, it'll be just as simple for another one to do so. You can be sure the governor will send someone else to replace this one. Be vigilant, Eugénie. It goes without saying that the governor can't confront the Colonel with this man's disappearance, but he'll investigate it nonetheless. The next one he places here will be more difficult to recognize and apprehend. If anything at all appears out of the ordinary, don't waste a minute signaling Roland. Promise me!"

"I do promise you, dear Jamie," she said, softly. "I have every intention of joining Marie in France, not just in spirit but in the flesh. This has been a good warning. I'll be careful."

Then she raised her voice, making sure that those around her could hear. "Jamie, you say the loading is finished? I see Marie is on the longboat. It's time for you to set off for the ship. Once I've seen that the roan is settled on the barge, I'll send it along after you."

"Aye, milady. I'll get under way at once."

"Farewell, Jamie," she said gravely. "You've taken a great burden off my shoulders."

"God go with you and keep you safe, dear lady."

"And you, *mon ami,*" she answered before turning and hastening along the dock to the roan's barge.

Before she reached her destination, she heard a loud cry and turned to see Jeremy thrashing about in Ethan's firm grip. His voice rose in a shriek. Everyone on the dock and those gathered on the lawn turned to see what was causing such a ruckus. Eugénie understood the situation immediately and hurried over to see what she could do to remedy it. Even with his great strength, Ethan was hard-pressed to hold on to the flailing boy. With every ounce of strength in his young body, Jeremy was twisting and turning in the older man's grasp. Young arms and legs were shooting out in every direction. Vainly, Jeremy tried to kick Ethan in the shins while his small bunched fists flew out, aiming at Ethan's head. All the while, he kept up a steady stream of yelling and screaming at the top of his lungs.

"Jeremy, Jeremy!" Eugénie called, trying to pierce the caterwauling.

Jeremy's wild movements intensified. Seeing her as a means of rescue, he cried out. "Tell 'em! Tell 'em, Miss Eugénie! They cain't take my hoss away. They cain't take Roman. Tell 'em! Didn't you put him in my care since first he came here? He's my friend. Who's goin' to look afta him? Who's goin' to know when he's hungry and what his favorite treats are, but Jeremy? Who's goin' to take him out de stall and walk him when he's feelin' all cramped up and lonely? Who's goin' to talk to him and listen to what's on his mind? He'll be all sad without Jeremy. He know'd Jeremy allus be there, night and day, rain or shine. He cain't go, Miss Eugénie. He cain't go away without me. He just cain't!" Suddenly, Jeremy slumped in Ethan's arms and began to weep. Fat tears streamed down his face. "Oh, Miss Eugénie, cain't you do somethin'?" he beseeched her piteously, looking up at her with his tear-stained face.

"Oh, Jeremy," Eugénie sighed, gathering him into her arms. The roan, who up until that point had suffered silently and with dignity his transfer from solid ground to the precarious barge, began to stamp his hooves on the solid cedar beams, making a sound like thunder. Then, throwing back his magnificent head, he trumpeted his protest.

"O, mon Dieu!" Eugénie exclaimed. "Now I've got two of them to contend with." She turned toward the roan and whistled. He calmed immediately. A silent message passed between horse and mistress. The great horse tossed his head as if in agreement and then placidly gazed off across the water.

Gently disengaging herself from the clinging child, Eugénie placed her hands on Jeremy's shoulders and looked down into his face. "Here, come with me. Let's you and I go for a walk." Before he could mount a protest, she took him firmly by the hand and marched him away from the crowd.

No one could hear the conversation that took place between the desolate boy and the determined woman, but when they returned, Jeremy's face was wreathed in smiles and his spirits were completely restored. He looked up at Eugénie with an expression of pure devotion. Her face appeared resigned, if not pleased.

"Alors, ça suffit," she said with a sigh, leading him to the barge. "Come Jeremy, you may say good-bye to the roan, but you must be quick."

Standing there watching the horse and boy say their farewells, she was relieved to see that Jamie and the longboat were well over halfway to the ship. She waved to Marie, who gaily waved back.

"Come, Jeremy, it's time for the barge to leave," she said firmly, taking his hand to avoid any last-minute breach of their agreement.

"Yes, ma'am, Miss Eugénie," he said docilely. "I be seein' you shortly, Roman. In France, Roman! Now don't you go forgettin' your Jeremy, you hear?" Confident in the lasting bond between him and the horse, he said the last words with a light heart. "'Cuz I'm not goin' to be forgettin' you!" He called over his shoulder, skipping off the barge with Eugénie in tow.

"Now, what was that all about?" the Colonel asked Eugénie, hearing Jeremy's words.

"If you don't mind, sir, I think it's best if we discuss it later, in private," Eugénie replied wearily.

"I believe I know already, my dear, and you have my blessing." He smiled at her. Eugénie returned his smile and then looked out across the water at the barge and the longboat.

Even at that distance, she could see Marie's reaction when she realized that the barge was making its way toward her with the roan but without Eugénie. She leapt to her feet, a look of shock flashing across her face.

Marie's cry carried easily across the water. "*Non! Non!* Mistress, don't send me away without you!" She made a sudden movement as if to jump overboard, but Jamie read her intent and grabbed her, holding her tightly against his chest. For a long moment, Marie looked across the water at Eugénie and then slowly turned her face away.

"*Adieu, adieu, ma chère amie.* Please, forgive me," Eugénie whispered and turned back toward the house.

XXXVIII

⚜ ⚜ ⚜

That evening at supper, Jeremy and his future were the topics of conversation. The lighthearted discussion came as a relief to everyone after the emotional scenes of the last two days. The memorial service scheduled for the next morning hung in the back of everyone's mind. Eugénie wasted no time describing her conversation with Jeremy.

"I should have discussed the matter with you first, I realize, but I felt it was expedient to seize the moment before Jeremy disrupted everything and everyone."

"You did exactly right, my dear," Anne said, smiling at her. "The Grove will not be the same without that young man, bouncing about everywhere and into everything, but I know—and I'm certain Henry would agree—that before long, Bermuda would prove too small for the little fella'. It's much better that he goes off to see the world under your good graces than for him to wander off alone at some later date."

"Indeed, I agree wholeheartedly," the Colonel joined in. "I have no doubt that he would have been unfit to live with once the roan departed, unless he had this to look forward to. He was attached to that horse the minute he laid eyes on him. He has the makings of a first-rate trainer, too, unless I miss my guess. How he came by that, only the Lord above knows, but it's in his blood. It's a gift that all the teaching and training in the world can't develop in someone unless it's there to begin with. It's a born talent. Young lady, you'll get your money's worth in that one, no doubt about it. I expect we'll all be hearing about young Jeremy and his exploits in the not-too-distant future. I'd be willing to wager good money on that."

"You have my promise to look after him and see to his schooling," Eugénie said. "Elizabeth has gotten him off to a good start. I agree. He does appear to have a rare gift with horses. I'm truly sorry that I'm benefiting at such a cost to you."

"Don't give it a thought," Anne protested. "You've reimbursed us handsomely, but it's Jeremy who's the true beneficiary. Under Ethan's care, he's learned much since he came to The Grove. But you'll be able to give him opportunities beyond anything we could possibly offer him. With you, he'll have every chance in the world, and he'll be a free man, too. This is a very lucky day for that young man."

"I say amen to that," the Colonel agreed heartily. "Now, if my two sons will join me on the veranda for a pipe, I'd like to go over our strategies and decide the wording of the messages that Thomas will carry back to the Americans." Everyone rose from the table. Harry courteously went around to pull back his mother's chair and then followed his younger brother and father out onto the veranda.

"Well, ladies," Anne said, including Thomas's two little girls in her beaming gaze, "what card game will it be this evening?"

"If you don't mind, Anne," Eugénie said, "I think I'll fetch my shawl and go outside for a walk before retiring. It's been a very full day."

"I, too, must beg off, Mother," Elizabeth added, "if I'm going to finish the correspondence that Tom promised to take back with him."

Anne smiled at the two young women and turned to the little girls, saying, "Well, my pets, it looks like it's just the three of us. Now, if you can find where that deck of cards disappeared to, we'll get right down to business. What do you say?" The little ones each took one of their grandmother's hands and led her off in search of the deck of cards.

Eugénie followed Elizabeth up the stairs, trailing her hand along the curved banister. When they reached the head of the stairs, they bid each other a good night. Eugénie turned and walked down the long hallway and entered her bedchamber. She picked up the shawl of blue Flemish wool that lay where she had flung it earlier that day.

"Marie," she murmured out loud, "how I miss you already! I wish you Godspeed. I pray that you arrive home safely, but not before your temper has had a chance to cool from my little deception. For Jamie's sake, I hope it doesn't take too long." The corners of her mouth turned up at her last words, knowing that, for all Marie's sweet nature, her temper could burn white-hot. She didn't envy Jamie's predicament, being in close quarters with Marie. "I have no fear that I shall receive your forgiveness, for no one appreciates a good ruse more than you, Marie, even when it is played at your expense."

The three men were sitting on the veranda, deep in conversation, when Eugénie passed them. She stepped out onto the lawn. The fresh dew had made the grass slippery under foot. Each step was punctuated with squishing sounds. She was drawn to the rose garden as thoughts of Bridger flooded her mind. She sat down on the bench they had shared and breathed in the fragrance of the roses that mingled with the heady smell of night-scenting jasmine and spicy rosemary. She heard the night creatures' chorus starting up, the high singing of the whistling frogs, punctuated with the mellower peepers' voices. She imagined them in the underbrush and perched in the trees, calling out to their mates. Here and there, she heard a nightbird's call.

As she listened, one caller seemed to be more insistent and appeared to be drawing closer. It suddenly came to her that it was no lone bird seeking another, but a signal meant for her! It was Jacques's signal! A tremor skittered down her spine, and she pulled her shawl closer around her shoulders. Then she remembered telling Bridger that she and Jacques had used birdcalls to contact each other in the dark.

What on earth would Bridger or one of his men be doing here at this time of night? she thought, as concern for their safety replaced her earlier fright. I'd better go find them and warn them off.

She slipped silently out of the rose garden and made her way quickly in the direction of the birdcall. As she approached a thicket of mangrove and seagrape, she heard the call again, near at hand, behind a curtain of growth. Parting the dense foliage, she peered into the dimness. A scream froze in her throat.

Darby! She turned to flee, but he was too quick for her. With the advantage of surprise and his superior size and strength, Darby overwhelmed her easily.

"Ha, so I've flushed the quail! That vermin, Sam Brown, was not good for much, but he did tell me about the birdcall you and your foolishly brave countryman used to signal each other. Well, Mademoiselle Devereux, you've led me a merry chase, but now the chase is over." Hearing these words, Eugénie renewed her struggles. Darby tightened his grip on her mouth. The arm that threatened to crush her ribs moved up her body, and she felt cold steel at her throat.

"I'd be still if I were you, miss," he growled, "I'm not known for my patience. There, that's better. With your countryman gone, you're the only one left with the information to bring the French in against us. Yes, we know all about you and your consortium's plans. You laid it out so eloquently in the letter the Frenchman carried. There are those of us with too much at stake on this side of the ocean to allow you, the Tuckers, or anyone else to get in our way. I'm afraid I have no choice, Comtesse de Beaumont . . ."

"Let her go, Darby!" a voice rang out. Darby swung in the direction of the sound, wrenching Eugénie with him.

"Who's there?" Darby shouted. "Come out where I can see you."

"Give it up, Darby. You're surrounded!" the voice came again. Darby whirled his head around, trying to pierce the darkness.

"One move against me and I slice her," he warned. Eugénie, who had slumped against Darby at the sound of Roland's first words, came suddenly erect, slashing her elbow into his ribs and coming down hard with the heel of her shoe on his instep. Caught off guard, he slackened his grip, giving Eugénie the opening she needed. She whirled, ready to drive her knee into his groin just as Roland hurtled through the air and landed with full force on Darby, sending them to the ground. Eugénie heard Darby's knife strike the earth as he fell. She wriggled out from under the flailing bodies, her fingers searching for the blade. When her hand closed around its hilt, she sprang to her feet. But

Roland's speed and agility had made short work of Darby's height and bulk. The big man lay prostrate at Eugénie's feet.

"Roland, thank God you came, but what in heaven's name brought you here at this hour?"

"I had messages for you from Jamie and Captain Goodrich, but it must have been providence as well, for there's no telling what mischief this rascal would have committed had I not come when I did."

"You're alone, then?" Eugénie asked.

"Yes. We'd been tracking him since he left Salt Kettle. When he led us here, since I had messages to deliver to you, I took over from the others."

"*Mon Dieu!* First the governor's man, now Darby. What's next?" Eugénie exclaimed.

"You must inform Colonel Tucker about Darby's appearance at once," Roland said sternly. "He must be made aware that his security has been breached for the second time in one day."

"But how am I to do that without disclosing your presence here?" she asked.

"Very simply, milady," Roland answered. "Say only that I was on my way to the house with a message for you that Jamie had sent to the tavern regarding Marie's well-being, which happens to be true. I was told to deliver the message as quickly as possible because of your concern for her, which will explain the late hour. When I arrived ashore, I came upon Darby, overpowered him, bound him up, and carried him away. That's close enough to the truth. You can say that while you were out for your evening walk, you happened upon me as I was tying him up. I delivered Jamie's message to you and then went on my way. The Colonel should be only too pleased that I've taken the scoundrel off his hands. Simple enough?"

"Well, it will have to do," Eugénie answered. A moan from Darby interrupted their conversation. Roland stooped to bind and gag him, then continued, "Before he recovers completely, let me say that your Marie was thoroughly piqued when she realized you'd planned to stay behind all along. Jamie had to use all his Scottish wiles, which are considerable, but in the end, he managed to console her. She is none the worse for wear. Truth be known, it's for the best that she's safely gone from here.

"Captain Goodrich already knows about the spy Jamie apprehended at The Grove this afternoon and bade me to set up a watch over you, which is the real reason I'm here this night. He also said that you're always in his thoughts, to guard yourself well, and that he'd have transport ready for you when the time comes to leave the island. You need only to get a message to me, and I'll see that it reaches his hands. But who will carry your messages, now that Marie is gone?" Eugénie quickly told him about the arrangement she had made with Colonel Tucker concerning Jeremy.

"Ah, he's a fine lad," Roland nodded, "with pluck and brains enough for three men, though he's still a mere stripling. I've no doubt he'll serve you well. I'll take Darby with me, and one way or another I'll learn whom he's in league with on the island. Captain Goodrich will know what to do with that information and this troublemaker. If there's anything of importance, I'll see that word reaches you. Now, I'm off. Heed the Captain's words." Without waiting for her reply, he melted into the bushes, and soon she heard him moving through the undergrowth, his footsteps heavy with the burden he carried.

Eugénie wasted no time hurrying across the lawn. She was relieved to see the light of the three pipes still glowing in the darkness of the veranda. After hearing about Darby's appearance and Roland's opportune arrival, Colonel Tucker puffed silently on his pipe for a few minutes.

"This night it was Darby. No doubt, next it will be another of the governor's men," he said philosophically. "Let them do their worst. I have no intention of modifying our plans or activities one whit."

"Father, would it not be prudent to post a patrol?" Thomas asked. Eugénie had noticed the look of alarm that had passed between the two brothers as they listened to her account.

"I already had that in mind, son. I'll see that it's put in place, beginning tomorrow. Don't breathe a word of any of this to your mother or Elizabeth. There's no point in getting them all stirred up. Now, we'd better seek our beds. Too soon, the morning will be here."

Eugénie awoke the next morning still troubled by the Colonel's apparent lack of concern in the face of the danger that had arrived at his doorstep. When she joined the family, she saw that everything was ready for the service. As with everything that Anne Tucker put her hand to, the preparations for the memorial service had been carried out to a fare-thee-well.

Even with such short notice, the minutest detail had been anticipated and arranged. The traditional black-edged notes announcing the service had been delivered. The bed curtains and window curtains throughout the house had been taken down and replaced with white muslin, signifying a house in mourning. Anne had seen that corn and tassels had been looped on the bed curtains as well. The funeral scarves had been quickly sown, crimped, and placed in a large basket by the front door. Food had been prepared for those who would return to the house after the service.

People began to arrive early, to assemble in the carefully prescribed manner for the procession. First came Ethan. As was customary, a family servant was delegated to be the sexton. Anne explained to Eugénie that the closeness between Bermudian blacks and whites had set these customs in place long ago. When one of their people died, black or white, the blacks joined in the preparations and played an important role in the service. Next, the eight men and eight women wearing the scarves and gloves given to them by the family took their places, followed by the leaders, beginning with the nearest male relative to the deceased, who led the nearest female relative, and so on down the line.

The scents of rosemary and nutmeg mingled in the air. As the procession got under way and moved slowly down the path toward the family graveyard, those without a specific duty or relationship fell in behind, with the blacks in this group bringing up the rear. The procession swelled as latecomers hastened across the grass and decorously fell in step with the rest. The usual tradition of getting off to a late start to avoid the appearance of hurrying the departure of the deceased's spirit was suspended so that Thomas Tudor's ship would not miss the morning tide.

Eugénie moved along near the rear of the throng, happy to witness the event from a distance. Her thoughts dwelled on her parents' ceremony. Since their bodies had been lost at sea, theirs had also been a memorial service instead of an interment. She felt that her grief had weighed more heavily on her because she had not had a last glimpse of their beloved faces. Her recent experience at Jacques's funeral was particularly horrific because of the brutal manner in which he had died, his handsome face horribly distorted and his body hideously mutilated. She shivered, recalling the sight of him at the last.

Perhaps it was best, after all, that I couldn't view the remains of Mother and Father, she thought. I'll see them always in my mind's eye as I saw them last, with the light of their love shining on their beautiful faces.

She was pulled back by the voice of the clergyman directing the flow of people as they neared the graveyard. Once everyone was assembled, he spoke from memory the words of consolation written in the Scriptures. Then, one by one, members of the family and close friends spoke, recollecting the one whose life had been cut short so tragically. Soon a picture emerged of a lovely young woman who had given selflessly to all those who had had the privilege to know her. Her two daughters stood on either side of their father, holding his hands, their rosy cheeks wet with tears. As Eugénie watched, Thomas Tudor pulled each child closer against his side, enfolding them in the protection of his arms. He bowed his head to each one, laying his cheek against one soft mop of golden curls and then the other before he straightened up to stand stiffly erect once more.

The tenderness of his gestures brought tears to Eugénie's eyes and she turned away. Looking east, she watched the first streaks of color staining the horizon. The sunrise came slowly and magnificently until it spread across the entire eastern sky, as if, in its uncommon beauty, it were giving heaven's benediction to the flown spirit of the young woman, wife, mother, sister, daughter, and friend.

When the last of the eulogies had been given, the clergyman intoned, "Jesus said, 'Let not your heart be troubled: ye believe in God, believe also in me. In my Father's house are many mansions: if it were not so, I would have told you. I go to prepare a place for you. And if I go and prepare a place for you, I will come again, and receive you unto myself; that where I am, there ye may be also. And whither I go ye know, and the way ye know.'" The clergyman paused to let the words float out over the water and then said, "Let us pray. Unto God's gracious mercy and protection we commit you. The Lord bless you and keep you. The Lord make His face to shine upon you, and be gracious unto you. The Lord lift up His countenance upon you, and give you peace, both now and evermore. Amen."

A collective "Amen" whispered through the gathering. The strict rituals that governed the procession and the service did not carry over after the ceremony was completed. The conclusion of the service released the congregation. Everyone returned to the house in a haphazard fashion.

Eugénie noticed that many of the guests quietly melted away after paying their respects to the bereaved family, respecting the family's need to spend time alone together before bracing for Thomas Tudor's departure. Others joined the family for a short while before making their farewells. Finally, only the closest friends of the family remained until they, too, took their leave and slipped away.

Once the family and Eugénie had finished breaking their fast, Thomas smiled at his mother and said, "As always, Mother, you have accomplished the near impossible. You arrived home after an all-night vigil at a sickbed and prepared for a memorial service within hours without taking a breath. I know what this effort must have cost you, but I thank you from the bottom of my heart. The service, just past, has lifted a great burden from my heart that neither the kindnesses of the Carolinians with all their best intentions nor the ritual of the funeral service so far from the family that I love were able to ease."

Anne Tucker moved swiftly to the tall man who was her son and folded him into her arms as though he were still a little boy, saying, "My dear, dear son, with those beautiful words you have gladdened my heart. Now I can see you off with a light spirit." Seeing that Thomas was about to speak again, she held up her hand. "Say no more, or you'll bring your old mother to tears," she said softly. With a quick kiss on his lean cheek, she continued briskly, "You'd better go now and change into your travel clothes, for the tide does not respect your bereavement and will not wait for you."

XXXIX

⚜⚜⚜

A short time later, everyone arrived at the dock with brave faces in place. Eugénie marveled at the resilience and fortitude of the Bermudians, and in particular the Tucker clan. They were bidding farewell to their beloved son, having just mourned the death of his wife. They were seeing him off to a land swept up in war, not knowing when they would see him again, or if he would be one of the casualties of that conflict. For all they knew, this would be the last time they held him in their arms, brushed the hair back from his smooth brow, and laughed at his quips. She watched as the small group clustered together, trying their best not to look at Thomas's ship anchored out in the harbor.

Eugénie saw Thomas Tudor turn back toward the house, his gaze wandering over its dignified facade, which was braced at either end by stands of evergreens. She watched his eyes roam over the clumps of guava, their blossoms long since gone, and pass on to the myrtle just beginning to bloom red. She saw his gaze linger over the flowerbeds in their riotous summer splendor, bordered by yellowish-flowered woodbine and the showy orange-blossomed nasturtium trailing its vines untidily on the lawn. When he looked at the lavender-and-white lilac bushes, she saw his nostrils flair as if catching a whiff of their heady scent.

As his eyes turned to the silver-leafed olive trees, he said to his mother over his shoulder, "Looks like your faith has been rewarded, Mother. The olive trees have progressed nicely, giving us their deep shade in the summer's heat and their fruit crop come autumn. From the look of their heavy boughs, I'm willing to bet you'll have a fine crop this year. I'll be back for the harvest, you have my word on it."

"That will be the day, Thomas, when you rush home to do an honest day's labor," his mother said, smiling lovingly at him. Her words brought a laugh and broke the tension that had been mounting steadily since the family and The Grove people had begun to gather at the dock.

At that moment, Thomas's two daughters stepped forward, holding a basket between them that looked as though an invisible hand had roved over The Grove property, plucking bits and pieces of flowers, herbs, leaves, and twigs, and then massed them together in a haphazard fashion. The result could only be described as a mishmash.

"Papa, look what we made for you! We've put all your favorites into this basket to remind you of Grandpapa's and Grandmama's house," one said brightly.

The other quickly chimed in, "Jeremy helped us to plant the jasmine around the edges in real soil, so it will live forever! Doesn't it smell good?" Her father lowered his head to sniff the tiny white stars.

"When the other flowers die," she went on blithely, "you can just put in some new ones, any ones you like, and then your garden will always be fresh, as good as new."

"Isn't it beautiful?" the first one piped in, "And we did it all, just us . . . Well, Jeremy helped a little with the jasmine."

"It's the most beautiful garden I've ever seen," their father answered, taking the basket and inspecting its contents gravely. "How did you manage to find every single one of my favorites? Why there's even a bird feather or two. I'll care for this garden faithfully and put it right beside my bed so that each morning when I wake up and look at it, I will see your sweet faces and think of you here with Grandpapa and Grandmama." The poignancy of the moment tested even the Tucker mettle. With remarkable composure, Thomas Tudor swept both girls up in his arms and into the air. Soon their shrieks of delight restored everyone's equanimity.

"Papa! Papa!" the two little girls squealed. "We have another gift for you."

"More? I haven't recovered from the first one! My cup runneth over," their father said, looking askance at his mother, who tried to suppress a chuckle at his expression.

"What could it be?" he asked, not yet completely recovered from their first presentation. Wriggling out of his arms, the two scampered over to the nearby bushes and drew out another palmetto woven basket. Skipping back to their father, they held it carefully between them, looking as if they were about to burst with excitement. They stood ramrod straight in front of him and thrust the basket into his hands.

"What have we here?" he asked, looking down at a mound of blanket in the basket. As if on cue, the mound came to life. First, a small nose and whiskers emerged, followed by a pair of sleepy eyes, then two pointed ears. Finally, the furry, rounded head of a small kitten popped out. Blinking its eyes, it looked around with an almost human expression of bewilderment on its face. With an elaborate yawn, it dismissed the company around it, burrowed back under the blanket, and was soon heard purring contentedly.

"My dear girls, what a thoughtful gift," Thomas Tudor began diplomatically, once he had managed to stop laughing, "but I think the kit is too young to be parted from its mother, and what would it do aboard ship? My dears, keep it safe here with you, and I will reclaim it when I return."

"No, no, Papa!" the girls cried in unison.

"Grandma Tucker said that Bobbins has already begun to wean the kittens, and Paws—that's her name—was the first," one child explained patiently to her father.

"She's also the biggest of the litter and caught her first mouse just last night," the other one added. "I know, because she brought it right into our bedchamber."

"She's a natural hunter, Grandma Tucker says. She'll rid the ship of all the rats and mice, and she will keep you company, too," the first continued in irrefutable child's logic. "She'll be a great help to you on your voyage and when you get back to South Carolina, too."

No match for his daughters' logic and the love that prompted the gift, Thomas Tudor relented gracefully.

"In that case, I can't imagine a finer companion for the journey and for me. How very thoughtful of you," he said, pulling them both to him and hugging them tightly. His daughters clapped their hands, dancing in circles around their father.

The younger of the two stopped in front of her father and shook a small finger at him, saying sternly, "She's my very favorite, so be sure that you take very good care of her. She particularly likes cream, and she'll probably be lonely at first, away from her mother and the rest of the kits, so you must let her sleep with you, so she won't be afraid and have nightmares." At the look of horror on her father's face, she added diplomatically, "Well, maybe, just at first."

Leaning down to kiss the tip of her small imperious nose, Thomas said, "Miss Paws will lack for nothing, I promise. Now, young ladies, it's time for your father and Miss Paws to set off before we miss the tide altogether. Give me one last hug and kiss . . ." His words were cut short by the impact of the two small bodies that hurtled into his arms, smothering him with kisses and hugging him as hard as they could with their strong young arms. As quickly as it began, it ended. The two little girls sprang back, beaming up at their father with such love shining in their eyes that Eugénie felt her heart catch in her throat.

With a basket swinging from the crook of each arm and a small hand in each of his large ones, Thomas Tudor led his little family down to the dock. Outstretched hands took each basket and placed them carefully on the floorboards of the whaler. After final kisses all around, Thomas leapt agilely into the boat, untied the painter, and shoved the little craft out into the water. Standing in the center of the boat, he held Miss Paws in one arm and waved at those crowded on the bank with the other as the boat pulled out into the stream.

"Bye, Papa, bye, bye!" the little girls called across the water, blowing kisses to their father until he, Miss Paws, and the boat were out of sight.

The family members and Eugénie made their way slowly across the grass and up toward the house. Colonel Tucker was in close conversation with Harry. Elizabeth, who was particularly affected by her brother's leaving, walked along beside her mother. When her steps faltered and she brought her hands up to cover her face, Anne slipped a strong arm around her waist to support her.

The two little girls were in high spirits, pleased with the success of their gifts. Each held one of Eugénie's hands as they skipped along, chattering about this and that. Eugénie, deeply touched by the events of the morning, drew comfort from their mindless prattle and their brave spirits.

What remarkable children they are, she thought. So like every member of the Tucker family! Their faith in their father's love and their joy in everything around them leave no room for fear and sadness. They were devoted to the mother who's now lost to them. Their father has just left for who knows how long, after depositing them here in an unfamiliar place amongst people who, for all that they are family, are still strangers to them. They welcome it all with loving hearts and open minds. They never question why or how things came to be this way. They just accept them as they are. My, my, I can learn much from these little ones.

Just at that moment, one of her charges yanked on her hand and tugged at her skirt to get her attention. "Auntie, look!" she cried, causing Eugénie to smile at the upturned face, "A bird's feather just floated into my hand. I put my most treasured feather in Father's basket garden, and now I've received one in return. It must be very special. Good luck, don't you think?"

"Without a doubt. Very good luck, indeed," Eugénie agreed, her grave tone adding to the weight of her words.

Rorick Hamilton and other men were waiting in the front room when Eugénie and the family reached the house. They all began speaking at once. Colonel Tucker plowed into the confusion, holding his hands up for silence.

"Here, here," he said, raising his voice to restore some semblance of order. Just then, Harry recognized one of the governor's secretaries in the crowd and moved quickly to his side. During a whispered conversation with him, Harry deftly worked the man to the door and down the hall. A heavy silence hung over the room.

"Was anything untoward discussed in the presence of that young man?" the Colonel asked in a voice just above a whisper.

"No, sir," Rorick answered quickly. "He arrived just before you came in. None of us recognized him, so we chitchatted about mundane things, like the worsening food shortages on the island and such things as that, so that he'd think we'd gathered here to consult with you about them. Nothing was said that would give him reason to think otherwise."

"Good," Colonel Tucker said brusquely as Harry came through the doorway, looking composed as always.

Still holding Elizabeth's arm, Anne said to the Colonel, "Henry, if you'll excuse me, the little girls ate barely anything for breakfast. I must give them a little something to tide them over until dinner." At the Colonel's nod, she swept Elizabeth and her granddaughters before her and left the room. Just as Eugénie was about to follow, the Colonel stopped her.

"If you don't mind, my dear, I'd appreciate it if you would remain. There's much to discuss here, and I speak for all of us when I say we'd be grateful for your counsel."

"Colonel Tucker, you flatter me, but I doubt that I'd be much help," Eugénie demurred.

"Miss Eugénie, with your knowledge of European politics and your recent stay in the American colonies, you are far better informed than we are on this island, with our paltry resources. I repeat, we would greatly benefit from any assistance you can give us."

"Then, sir, I will give you whatever help I can," she replied, acquiescing. He held a chair out for her and gestured for the others to be seated. Then he turned to his son.

"Harry, would you please tell us what news you bring from St. George's?"

"Yes, Father, but first I'll convey the message the governor's secretary delivered. The governor has seen fit to prorogue the Assembly."

His words caused an outcry from the group.

"Damnation!"

"Not again!"

"How shall we carry out our petition?"

As the voices died down, the Colonel spoke with feeling. "He'll not thwart us this time, my friends. We'll simply call a meeting outside the Assembly, get the signatures necessary, and proceed. Once again he cuts his nose off to spite his face. No Assembly, no salary, for only the Assembly in session is empowered to authorize the governor's salary. So there you have it. The old fox is himself outfoxed!" His words brought forth a resounding cheer.

"Now, Harry, if you'll proceed."

"There are several matters of note. The governor has been receiving, for some time past, a deluge of letters from all over the island pleading for him and Whitehall to solve the food shortage." He paused and looked around, but only received impatient nods in return. This was old news to everyone in the room.

"He has beseeched Whitehall to come to our aid in the past. More recently, he has communicated with Lord Dunmore, the British governor of the Virginia colony. By return post, he received a promise from that beleaguered gentleman that he would send wheat, rice, Indian corn, flour, and any available bread he could lay his hands on. As you probably know, it's a generous but empty offer since he's been driven from the Governor's Palace in Williamsburg by the Virginians and now conducts his business, to the degree that he can, from aboard a ship that lies off the Virginia coast. His only recourse to such supplies is to commandeer and divert such stuffs from stores intended for the British troops. A long shot at best.

"Next, Governor Bruère over the past week has had notices posted at all taverns, churches, public offices, and public meeting places imploring those who are selling wheat on the island to lower the unit price. As you know, certain populations on the island prefer corn and cornmeal and have little interest in wheat at any price. In addition, it's important to note that there is an increased supply of rice in Bermuda, more than there was before." Eugénie marveled that Harry could carry off this statement without a twitch, considering that there was more rice on the island simply because the sloop *Dispatch* was smuggling in large quantities of it from the American colonies. The *Dispatch* was owned by St. George Tucker, Colonel Tucker, Harry Tucker, Henry Tucker of the Bridge, and their kin, Richard and John Jennings. Most of these men were standing in the room, listening blandly to the announcement. Moreover, the price of this rice had been set by the cartel to compete favorably with the price of wheat on the island.

"Even considering all this, the shortages still exist," Harry continued.

"Even if the cost of wheat were lowered, it would not offset the shortages," one man in the group called out, "since there's not enough wheat to meet the demand. Once again, the governor is approaching the problem with flawed logic." These words were met with vigorous nods.

"To continue," Harry went on. "As we know, Governor Bruère's petitions to Whitehall beseeching the Ministers to aid the island with foodstuffs has come to nought. Nor have they come forth with the company of soldiers that he requested—in his words, 'to maintain order on the island and defend the island from invasion by the Americans,' which, by the way, he believes is a strong possibility." Harry was again interrupted.

"'Tis a far greater possibility that it'll be the British who'll invade us under the pretense of requisitioning soldiers here, or some such thing. Damned Redcoats!" Eugénie was aware of the Bermudians' fiercely independent spirit, but until that moment she had not heard this particular sentiment expressed so openly.

"Better the Americans than the Brits," another muttered, startling her even more.

"There's more news," the Colonel said, bringing everyone's attention back to Harry.

"Which brings me to the last," Harry said. "Whitehall has finally responded in the affirmative to the governor's long-standing request for a frigate or a sloop to patrol the Bermuda waters and to support the custom men's efforts. A man-of-war has been commissioned to Bermuda. The warship *Nautilus* has been assigned and is on her way." This announcement was met with shocked silence. Eugénie turned startled eyes toward the Colonel, who stood with his hands clasped behind his back, gazing out of the window.

The silence stretched on. The men avoided one another's eyes, looking down at the floor or at their hands clasped in their laps, hardly daring to breathe. Their worst fears had been realized.

Colonel Tucker turned back to face the room. His eyes scanned one stunned expression after another.

"Come, lads!" he said, at once getting everyone's attention. "Why the long faces? 'Twas bound to happen sooner or later, with or without Bruère's urging. Bermuda is a fair isle, made more so by the conflict in the American colonies. Her strategic position makes her a plump plum ripe for the plucking by either side. Neither the Americans nor the British can countenance the other's use of her as a base from which to launch an offensive, to station troops, or to stockpile weaponry and powder. Not to mention, to exploit her ideal latitude in the trade route.

"If we escape with only a warship," he continued, "so much the better. We should count ourselves lucky and be eternally grateful. We've had experience eluding outside interference in our affairs. I'm not particularly concerned about this new turn of events. We shall play each side against the other, as we've always done. This news simply means we must step up our schedule for the gunpowder transfer. Are there new reports on that score?" he asked. When several heads nodded in reply, he suggested, "What do you say we postpone these reports until after we've satisfied our thirst and our bellies? I, for one, have had enough surprises on an empty stomach for one day. Shall we adjourn until after dinner?"

Relief washed over every face at the prospect of the famous Tucker hospitality. The group needed no urging to follow the Colonel and Harry down the hall to the dining room.

The effect on Eugénie's appetite was quite the opposite. Thank God, Marie is safely on her way, she thought as she hastened up the stairs to collect a shawl for the chill that had settled over her.

XL

❧❧❧

Eugénie entered the dining room just as Rorick was saying, "To that purpose, we had the aid of Captain Samuel Styles."

"Ah, yes," the Colonel nodded, "he's the Georgian who came to Bermuda ostensibly to obtain a cargo of salt. Nice man, that one."

At Harry's puzzled look, Rorick explained, "You remember him, Harry. It was about the time of the wedding. He was sent over here to begin negotiations with us regarding the gunpowder transfer. That seems so long ago now."

Before he could go on, Anne Tucker spoke up.

"Gentlemen, there are tender ears present," she said, looking pointedly at her two granddaughters. "Perhaps another topic would be more suitable."

The focus of her remarks suddenly spied Eugénie and exclaimed in unison, "Auntie Eugénie! Auntie Eugénie!" Again, Eugénie was touched by their innocent inclusion of her in the family circle. "We saved a place for you, right here." Small, eager hands patted the chair between them.

"Girls, girls," Anne admonished gently, "please lower your voices." Eugénie slipped into her place between the two girls and was soon laughing out loud as they competed with each other to see who could choose the most succulent morsels of food for Eugénie. Their gaiety was infectious.

When the Colonel felt enough time had elapsed to pay appropriate

homage to his wife's culinary efforts, he rose from his chair and beckoned the others to follow him. Taking her cue, Anne stood up and said
to her granddaughters, "Come, my dears, it's time for a short nap."
When they started to protest, she said, "Now, now, you don't want to
fall asleep over the candle tallow that we've planned for this afternoon,
do you? Your candles would bend every which way, just like the curl of
Bobbins's tail." Distracted by the picture of candles shaped like cats'
tails, the little ones followed their grandmother out of the room without a peep.

Once everyone was settled in the front parlor with a cool drink,
Colonel Tucker began, "A final word on the subject of our shipping
interests. We must increase our lines of communication. I've received
more reports this week of our merchant ships being preyed upon by
American cruisers, ships of the British fleet, and even our own Bermudian privateers. We must endeavor to alert one another of any un-
friendly vessel lurking along our trade routes. It's well known that we
shippers, at this end of the island, make a practice of approaching the
west end through Ely's Harbor, which sets us up like sitting ducks. I
bring this up not because it is new to us, but because it's getting worse.
Let us beware and remain ever-mindful that our strength and safety
depend on our combined efforts, not on each of us alone. Furthermore, we have reason to believe that there is an offshore ring of loyalists who've come to Bermuda with the sole purpose of thwarting the
patriots and anyone who attempts to aid them. One of them was apprehended here at The Grove last night. I will keep you informed. In the
meantime, keep your eyes peeled, take whatever steps necessary should
you happen on any of them, and report to the rest of us.

"Enough of that subject. Let me bring you up to date on our discussions with the Americans. We've communicated our plight to the
Continental Congress. We've informed them that our soil cannot support the crops necessary to feed our population, which we've told them
is fifteen thousand. We purposely overstated our more accurate number of ten thousand because it's human nature to provide less than is
asked for. Should the Americans see fit to help meet the needs of a

populace of fifteen thousand, all the better. We can solve that pleasant problem by trading the surplus to the West Indies."

"We should wish to have such a problem!" one of the group exclaimed.

"Hear, hear," agreed another.

The Colonel continued as though there had been no interruption. "The renowned Mr. Benjamin Franklin, on his return from his fruitless negotiations in England, has been made president or chairman, or some such thing, of the Committee of Safety in Philadelphia. He has taken over all correspondence with us. He's a sagacious and practical old rascal, and not easily duped. I sent him a letter some two to three weeks past summarizing the situation here, offering our neutrality, our sympathy for their cause, and cargoes of salt. As you know, salt is particularly necessary in wartime to preserve food supplies. In return, I stated that we require foodstuffs from them and open trade between us. I concluded by saying that we hope that this most recent offer will eliminate the need to make the contents of the magazine available to them. I await his reply, which should arrive any day now."

Mr. Hampton, one of the older members of the group, who had appeared to be napping, spoke up abruptly, saying, " 'Twould be a fine thing to hope for, Henry, but shouldn't we lay out our plan, regardless, in order to be prepared if they demand the transfer?"

"Yes, Charles," Colonel Tucker answered, "that we must. To that end, I call on young Jennings here, who's devised a general strategy. James?"

"Yes, sir," Jennings replied, bowing slightly to the Colonel. "I've sketched out a rough plan, but we'll need our best minds working together to polish and finalize it. We have two ways of entering the magazine. One is to cut a hole through the stone roof large enough to lower a man through. He would then unbolt the door from the inside. The other is to secure the keys to the building and unlock it from the outside. We have it on good authority that the governor keeps the keys in his possession at all times."

"That's true," Harry agreed. "Furthermore, he's told me on numerous occasions that they're never off his person and that he sleeps with them under his pillow at night." A discussion followed, arguing the pros and cons of breaching the magazine's roof or somehow getting hold of the governor's keys.

"On the night of the transfer," Harry suggested, "I'll invite the governor and some of the other Council men for dinner and to stay the night. I'll make sure he eats and drinks his fill. As I'm assisting him to bed, I'll slip the keys from under his pillow and return them once they've served our purpose."

"Harry, not only must you be innocent of any involvement in that night's activities, but such a scheme offers too many chances for discovery and failure," said Charles Hampton.

"I quite agree," Colonel Tucker said, nodding, "but an evening of distraction for the governor might prove very helpful, particularly if it could be made to appear that it's the governor's own idea."

"Then we are all in agreement," young Jennings summarized. "We'll gain entry into the magazine by cutting a hole in the roof."

"Wouldn't the noise of such work raise an alarm?" Rorick asked.

"Not likely," Harry answered. "The magazine is a good distance from the nearest house, standing as it does above Tobacco Bay. Also, the governor is so short-handed, he has posted no guard or watchman of any sort to patrol the building."

"Carry on, James," the Colonel said, nodding.

"Yes, sir," the young Jennings replied. "It stands to reason that we must choose someone of small stature, with sufficient skill to cut the stone and the agility to scale the structure. That person must also be light enough to be lowered into the building."

Mon Dieu, Eugénie thought. They're describing Jeremy to the letter.

As though he had read her thoughts, the Colonel said, "Our Jeremy is the perfect choice, for both his physical size and his mental abilities. And since he's planning to go with Miss Eugénie when she returns to France, we could set their departure for the evening of the powder removal, which would ensure that he's out of harm's way once he's completed this task. That is, if you have no aversion to such a plan, Miss Eugénie."

"Jeremy is certainly the right choice," Eugénie agreed. "And were we to leave that night, it would ensure his safety. I have my reservations about delaying my departure until then. But if we receive word from the Americans that the powder is the price for lifting their embargo, then once we have fixed a date for the transfer, we can put out the word that I have chosen that day to schedule my sailing. That way, it won't appear suspicious when I do leave. No one will connect the two events ahead of time and afterward, well . . ." She gave a Gallic shrug. "We can further divert their attention ahead of time. My birthday is August the twelfth. If you choose to carry out the transfer a couple of days afterward . . ."

"Excellent, excellent," the Colonel said, immediately following the direction of her thoughts. "We'll plan a little gathering on your birthday, which will easily cover any unusual comings and goings at The Grove. We'll set the evening of August fourteenth for the transfer and for your departure. James, do you have a plan for the number of men needed to carry away the gunpowder and how it will be transported from our shores?"

"According to my sources, the most recent count was something in excess of a hundred barrels of powder," Jennings answered. "Until that night, when we can view the barrels with our own eyes, we won't know the exact number, nor the condition of the barrels and the powder. I've set a rough estimate of eighteen hundred pounds of powder. The barrels are sufficiently small that they can be carried on the shoulder or rolled easily down the path from the magazine to Tobacco Bay. I'm in the process of handpicking the lads. Once I have compiled a list, I'll bring it to you for your review.

"As for the transport of the barrels off the island," he went on, "it strikes me that it would be by far the safest to load the barrels onto our own small crafts at Tobacco Bay, which will carry them out to the awaiting American ships anchored beyond the reefs. The American vessels are ignorant of the patterns of the reefs and shoals around Tobacco Bay. As it is, they'll look suspicious enough trolling the east end of the island right under the nose of the British seat of government, without hovering too near to shore. If you're in agreement with this plan so far, then the only piece left is for me to tally up the number of small vessels needed to carry the powder to the ships."

No one suggested an alternate plan, so James continued. "I reviewed the plan, such as it was, with Mr. Styles, when he was here. He strongly supported the use of Bermudian craft for ferrying the powder away from Tobacco Bay, pointing out that the 'darkness and the treacherous shoals would place anyone unfamiliar with the terrain at a distinct disadvantage.' So we and the Americans are in accord on that point, at least . . ."

"Unless there's an opinion to the contrary," the Colonel broke in, adding, "I recommend that we place Captain Morgan in command of this stage of the transfer. No one in all of Bermuda has more cunning at evasion than he, or has better knowledge of how to negotiate the reefs." When it was clear that all agreed with the Colonel, James Jennings moved on to the next topic.

"I think we've all been aware of the two American ships that have been visiting our waters these past months. One is *Lady Catherine,* with Captain George Orde, Master. She's Virginia registered."

Harry spoke up, "Governor Bruère is all too aware of her presence. He wrote to Lord Dartmouth, mentioning, amongst other things, that '*Lady Catherine* has been in Bermuda for four months. She is berthed at the Great Sound shipyard for repairs. At least, that's the stated reason.' Until now, he's had no excuse for demanding that she quit the island. We'd better alert her captain to take every precaution to avoid anything that would give Governor Bruère the reason he needs." The group murmured in agreement.

"The second ship is the *Charleston and Savannah Pacquet,* with John Turner, Master, which is registered in South Carolina," Jennings continued. "She's scheduled to depart Bermuda on August eleventh, carrying Bermuda stone for Barbados." Jennings could not suppress a slow grin, as he added, "Both captains were seen in close and frequent company with Captain Styles, and word was passed on to me that the ships were prepared to aid us, if need be."

I've no doubt, Eugénie thought, shuddering, that it hasn't been lost on anyone in this room that the two colonies from which the ships come are the very same ones in which the two Tucker sons, St. George and Thomas Tudor, reside. James's next words brought her back abruptly.

"Lastly, before Captain Styles's departure, I discussed with him the strong position taken by this group to enlist Americans, instead of Bermudians, to carry the powder from the magazine to the small boats once we'd opened the building for them. The Bermudians would be there to oversee the procedure and stand watch. Styles appeared amenable to that and, I believe, spoke to both ships' captains to that effect. I've heard nothing to the contrary, but I'll find a way to confirm that information. This would give us the two alternatives. We can choose whether we want to carry the powder from the magazine to the small crafts ourselves or have the Americans do it once we get closer to the date. I know the Colonel prefers that the Americans carry the barrels out of the magazine and down to the boats in Tobacco Bay, so that they'll be responsible for their condition and number. I'll go ahead and make a list of men, so we'll be ready in either case."

"What of the American brigantine *Retaliation,* which is anchored near Mangrove Bay?" one of the men asked.

"My sources have learned little about the ship," Jennings replied. "One, at the most two, ships are needed to transport the powder back to the American colonies. Perhaps they intend for *Retaliation* to act as a decoy, and perhaps one of the other two ships as well if they only need one ship for transport. I don't know."

"We'd better not invite suspicion by appearing too curious about the *Retaliation,*" Colonel Tucker warned, "since she was not mentioned specifically by Captain Styles. We must guard our tongues, lest the wrong ears hear. It concerned me greatly when Thomas Tudor spoke to me of a certain Harris, who is going up and down the American colonies' eastern seaboard talking indiscriminately of a rumor about an exchange of gunpowder for provisions and a lifting of the American trade embargo. Thomas seemed to think that his babblings would be discredited, based on the man's prior reputation for useless and unfounded information. Whether or not he's believed, it remains that rumors abound and that this closely held secret has sprung some leaks. So guard your tongues, lads. James, have you anything further?"

"Only that the consensus of opinion supports that the American ships should arrive at the appointed time just beyond North Rock," James Jennings replied. "No matter what the level of the tides, that's the closest they can venture to shore without risking the rocks and reefs. Once loaded, they'll make all haste back up here to Ely's Harbor, and from here away to the American colonies."

"The plan appears sound and clear and, I must say, brilliant in its simplicity," the Colonel said. "I commend you, James. Over the next few days, we'll contact Captain Morgan. With his agreement, we'll entrust him with the command of the intermediary transport. We'll enlist those we need to oversee the powder removal and a sufficient number of small craft to carry it from the shore at Tobacco Bay out to the American ships. When we get closer to the date, we'll set the exact time. Now, all that's left is to await the final word from the Americans, as to whether we must make Bermuda's store of gunpowder available to them, or if they will accept my alternative offer in return for supplying us with foodstuffs and the lifting of their trade embargo."

Colonel Tucker had just finished speaking when Jeremy appeared at the door with an air of importance.

"Yes, Jeremy, what is it?" he asked, waving him into the room.

Jeremy looked back over his shoulder and then obeyed the Colonel, saying, "They's a young man jus' arrived here with an important letter, a very important letter, he say, fo' Colonel Henry Tucker. He wouldn't say another word. He jus' keep sayin' he gotta speak to Colonel Henry Tucker and Colonel Henry Tucker, only."

"Yes, all right, Jeremy," the Colonel said patiently, "and where is the young man?"

"Oh, he's standin' right out in the hall there, where I tol' him."

"Fine, then, ask him to come in here, if you please," the Colonel said, trying to control his impatience. Jeremy darted out of the room only to reappear in a matter of seconds, followed by a young man whose self-possession completely deserted him when he saw the stern expressions confronting him. He slunk forward in Jeremy's wake, his eyes darting back and forth. When Jeremy reached the Colonel, he stepped aside, gesturing the young man forward. The young man stood rooted to the spot, unmoving.

"G'won," Jeremy ordered him. "You says you has to speak to the Colonel. Well, here's the Colonel. What's the matter wich you? Cat got your tongue?"

"Jeremy, that's no way to speak to our guest," Colonel Tucker admonished him. With a look of disgust, Jeremy rolled his eyes and moved to the side of the Colonel's chair.

"Come forward, young man. You have a letter for me?" the Colonel asked gently. As if shocked out of a trance, the messenger jumped to attention, saluted, clicked his heels together, and, shoving his hand inside of his coat pocket, withdrew an impressive-looking missive.

He handed it to the Colonel, saying, "Colonel Tucker, sir, I was ordered to place this letter in yo' hands and in yo' hands only."

"Well done, lad," Colonel Tucker said. "You've successfully carried out your mission. Now, Jeremy, see that the young man is well rewarded for his efforts with suitable refreshment."

The look on Jeremy's face eloquently expressed what he would rather do with the young man, but he answered blandly, "Yessuh!" and turned on his heel and led the young man from the room.

Colonel Tucker broke the seal and quickly scanned the contents. He paused for a moment, then said, "Gentlemen and Miss Eugénie, on this day of August sixth, the moment of our destiny has arrived. Mr. Benjamin Franklin, by the powers vested in him by the Philadelphia Committee of Safety, declares that our cooperation in carrying out the transfer of the Bermudian government's store of gunpowder into American hands is a prerequisite to the lifting of the American trade embargo against us. There you have it. There is no retreat for us. We're no longer at a standstill. Our only option is to move forward as planned. The decision is out of our hands, as of this minute."

He paused to let the gravity of the moment register on the others. "From the first, this has been a grave undertaking to contemplate. Anyone, who wishes to withdraw, I offer you this last opportunity to do so. Consider my words carefully. For, once we leave this room today, united in our commitment, there will be no turning back for anyone." Eugénie watched as he lowered his eyes to the letter in his lap and saw a shudder pass through his body. Then, squaring his shoulders, he looked up again at the resolute faces around him. "We're of one mind, then. We're all in agreement that we'll go forward with our plan." Every head in the room nodded.

"Good!" he declared, an air of purposefulness settling once more over his face. "Miss Eugénie, if you will. Please go and inform Mistress Tucker of Mr. Franklin's letter and stress the need to get plans under way at once for your birthday celebration and departure. The rest of us will finish up here with the details of who will do what and when."

By late afternoon, Harry had departed for St. George's, and the rest of the men had returned to their homes, carrying with them the knowledge that there remained only eight short days to prepare for the evening of August fourteenth.

XLI

❧❧❧

The next morning, Eugénie accompanied Anne to the buttery.

"With everything you have to do, I'd be happy to take this task off your shoulders," Eugénie offered.

"Dear child, I have some of my best thinking time when I churn that beautiful cream into butter. I watch it go round and round, and I just drift off. I find it ever so relaxing. I've even been known to doze off now and again, and wake up with some of my best ideas! I'd very much appreciate your company while I'm at it, though." The two women were soon settled in the coolness of the buttery. After the vivid brightness of the sun outside, they particularly enjoyed the dim light cast by the window slits high in the thick stone walls.

"In some ways, it seems as though it's only been a few days since you arrived, Eugénie," Anne mused, "and yet, in other ways, you've fit so well into our household that I can't imagine it without you," she added, wistfully. "All of us will sorely miss you. You've been such good company for Elizabeth. Don't misunderstand me. She's devoted to her brothers, but I know she's always pined for someone to share things with, since Fanny married her cousin Henry and went off to live at Bridge House."

"You and your family have shown me such kindness," Eugénie said, smiling warmly at the older woman, "and I've learned so many new methods of housewifery. I intend to put them into practice at the château as soon as I arrive home."

"Will you ever forget the look on the men's faces when you announced for the dinghy race?" Anne asked, laughing at the memory. "And young Jeremy and the roan, or 'Roman,' as he calls him? And those dastardly wreckers? Child, you gave me the fright of my life, I swear!"

"Anne, had it not been for your fortitude and your knowledge of herbal poultices that even Marie had no knowledge of, I've no doubt that I still wouldn't be right today. How can I ever atone for putting you and your household through that ordeal?"

"My dear," Anne said, patting Eugénie's hand affectionately, "had it not been for that horrible experience of yours, we wouldn't have rid ourselves of that bad lot and their evil activities. I won't hear anything more about atoning on that score or any other. You've been an absolute treasure. With all that's going to happen in the next few days, I'm so glad we're having this chance to capture a few quiet moments together. Ah, look how nicely the cream is thickening."

Just at that moment, Maisie appeared at the door. "Miss Eugénie, Miss Eugénie," she cried breathlessly. "Oh, thank goodness, you're here! I been looking all over. They's a man up at the house to see you! You must come right away." Eugénie and Anne gave each other a look as if to say, What on earth could this be?

"Well," Anne said with a resigned air, "I do declare. I spoke too soon. It appears our quiet interlude has come to an end. Go along, dear. I'm almost finished here. I'll be along shortly myself."

After the dimness of the buttery, the sunlight was blinding. Shading her eyes, Eugénie looked up toward the house.

"Am I so easily overlooked, mademoiselle?" Eugénie froze at the sound of the voice that had haunted her dreams every night. His voice. The memory of it drove her to fill her waking hours with mindless activities, any activity, to keep at bay her need, her desire, her hunger for the sound of it and the sight of him. To hear that familiar voice at such close range . . . Was this some cruel trick of her imagination? He was here? How? She turned slowly.

"Bridger, Bridger," she breathed, whispering his name. He drew her gently into the shadows of the olive trees and took her into his arms, holding her carefully, as if she might break. Eugénie was so startled by his unexpected appearance that all she could do was lean against him, melting into the safe refuge of his arms. Suddenly, her languor evaporated. She clung to him, pulling him to her, pressing his hardness against her body. She took his mouth with her own, drinking deeply, seeking to slake her thirst for him He responded immediately and with ferocity.

They tore apart later, breathing raggedly. With a tentative finger, he followed the trail of tears that traced the curve of her cheek. She took the finger into her mouth, tasting her salt on the tip of it. She kissed it and, drawing it from her mouth, she sketched her parted lips with its tip. Then she took his hand and pressed it to her breast. He felt the rapid beat of her heart and bent down to kiss the pulse at the base of her throat. An ache deep in the center of her exploded, shattering her. She moaned and leaned against him.

"Ah, my little one, my dearest heart, it was no longer within my power to stay away from you. Thank God that Darby gave me an excuse to come to speak to Colonel Tucker." At his words, she pulled away from him, a look of alarm on her face. "You've nothing to fear from that quarter," Bridger reassured her. "He came alone to the island. Once my people put out the word in the taverns, which was his source of manpower, that those in his employ had a strange way of disappearing without a trace, his goose was cooked. Some of his cronies jumped him one night, beat him within an inch of his life, and dumped what was left of him on a ship headed for Madagascar. He'll be a long time getting out of that God-forsaken place, if he ever does. We've seen the last of him," he chuckled.

"Oh, Bridger, I can't tell you what that news means to me," Eugénie said, moving back into his arms.

Rubbing his cheek against the softness of her curls and pulling her hard against him, he murmured, "Eugénie, Eugénie, how have I lived these long days without you, without the sight of your sweet face, the feel, taste, and scent of you?"

Taking a deep breath to gather herself, Eugénie looked up into the dark blue of his eyes. "Bridger, I wish I had the beauty of your speech to describe how I've missed you."

"Eugénie, your body speaks to me with an eloquence far beyond mere words." He was startled to see her eyes shimmering with tears. "What? What is it?" he asked, alarm sharpening his voice. "Come, sit down," he said, leading her over to a nearby bench in the grove. "Tell me. What's the matter?"

"It's just that my heart is bursting. Nothing more," she said softly, resting against him, feeling his strength. Mentally giving herself a shake, she sat up straighter and turned to him. "Let's not waste one precious moment of our time together. Tell me about your adventures," she said brightly.

"Oh, there's not much to tell," he said, a dangerous twinkle kindling in his eyes. "Let's see. I sailed to the stars and back, again, encountered some pirates along the way, captured prizes beyond imagining, and rescued untold numbers of damsels in distress." She rewarded his tall tales with laughter until the last, when she jabbed her elbow into his ribs with such force that he doubled over in mock pain.

"There had better not be a single damsel in distress rescued by you, let alone 'untold numbers,'" was her tart reply.

"As I said," his eyes now twinkling in full flood, "your body's eloquent response is more than a match for my pretty speeches. Now, what is this I hear about your imminent departure?"

"How did you hear about that?" Eugénie asked, alarmed that the Colonel's ring of secrecy had been so easily and so quickly breached.

"I have my sources," he replied mildly. "But don't be concerned, they're for my ears only. Believe me, Eugénie, as long as you're in Colonel Tucker's care, he won't suffer at my hands. For, were I to do so, I'd endanger what I treasure most in this world. I've also heard that he's still planning to go forward with his ill-advised plot. What is your role in all of this? Eugénie, we've been over this and over this! I've begged, I've pleaded with you to keep well clear of this foolhardy scheme!" Eugénie took his hands in both of hers.

"Bridger, Bridger, listen, my mission here is completed! I have all the information I need. I know the condition of Bermuda, its provisions, the number of its inhabitants, its armaments, and the extent of England's involvement on the island, in terms of militia and warships. Based on what I learned at one of the Colonel's meetings recently, I'm confident now that Bermuda won't join the Americans outright in their fight. Her loyalty will remain with the Crown. Don't you see, if that weren't so, Colonel Tucker and his followers wouldn't have to resort to such extreme measures to maintain and protect their trade with the Americans."

She went on to describe Jeremy's pivotal role in the gunpowder scheme and to explain that he would be leaving with her from Tobacco Bay once the magazine had been emptied and the gunpowder carried away. A look of horror came over Bridger's face as she continued calmly, "Colonel Tucker has directed one of his ships to lay off the bay, just outside the inlet, to act as a diversion. Jeremy and I will be on that ship, sailing east as the whalers deposit the powder on the American ships, which will then beat it back to the west end and turn west for the American colonies from there."

"What!" Bridger exclaimed, "This is the very thing I've been afraid of all along! You're going to be at Tobacco Bay in the midst of all this madness? It's bad enough that you're associated with this household, but now you're planning to participate, actually take part in this act of treason? Oh, my God!" He leaned forward, elbows on his knees, his head in his hands. He took several deep breaths, trying to calm himself and to resist the urge to grab her by the shoulders and shake her until every bone in her body rattled. Finally, he straightened up and turned his ravaged face toward her. "You said some of the whalers will be coming back to the west end," he said quietly. "Then there's no need for you to be down there. Jeremy can return in one of them and join you here."

"Bridger, don't you see? He'll be in grave danger. That would place him at even greater risk. If we were to do as you suggest, there would be too many chances for something to go wrong. He might miss getting back here entirely. And I won't leave for France without him," Eugénie said stubbornly, as she saw the beginning of the suggestion in his face.

"And I won't entrust you to a Tucker ship, under any circumstances," Bridger answered, his anger rising to meet hers. "Every vessel, every plank of timber associated with the Tucker name is highly suspect as it is. When the theft of the gunpowder is discovered, Colonel Henry Tucker will be at the top of Governor Bruère's list of suspects. The hue and cry will be heard all the way to Whitehall." When he saw her eyes blaze and her jaw set, he fought to check his own anger and to reason with her.

"Eugénie, hear me out. You know what I say is true. I see the merit of not risking Jeremy on one of the whalers returning to this end of the island under the questionable protection of Tucker's men and American sailors. On the other hand, one of my ships is the perfect solution. The animosity between my family and the Americans is well documented, and it's known that Colonel Tucker merely tolerates me for your sake and the sake of his son St. George. So, no one would expect for me to be a party to any of his foolish schemes to help the Americans or that he would invite me to be. In addition, my ships fly the Union Jack, which places them above suspicion. Also, considering the fact that I'm always coming and going from that end of the island, it would be the most natural thing in the world were my ship sighted sailing away from St. George's. Then, as a loyal subject of the Crown . . ."

"Enough! Enough!" Eugénie burst out laughing, her anger gone. "I concede! I concede! Yours is a far better plan. I'm sure, if the truth be known, Colonel Tucker would be relieved not to be responsible for my safety that night. His hands will be full enough without me adding to his burden." Nuzzling against him and kissing him lightly on the lips, she whispered, "And, if the truth be known, I find this new arrangement far more to my liking. Though in terms of the safety of my person . . ." She allowed her words to drift off as his mouth came down on hers.

———

A little while later, he said, "My dear, I find that you are exceptionally effective with your words when you choose to be. As for my willingness to help the Colonel with his burdens, I can't imagine a more delightful prospect than assuming this delectable burden." With a grin, he lifted her up and plunked her squarely down on his lap.

Leaping to her feet, she grabbed his hand and said, "Come, I feel thoroughly invigorated. It must be the effect of the olive trees, or this shady glen, or perhaps it's the phase of the moon, or . . ." As he made a grab for her, she skipped out of his reach, laughing over her shoulder. "Let's go give the Colonel the good news. You've rescued him once again."

"Yes, but I won't take any wagers that the gentleman will appreciate being in my debt," Bridger Goodrich said wryly.

Colonel Tucker appeared not the least bit surprised when Bridger strolled through the door of the morning room a few minutes later. This gave Eugénie pause for thought. The Colonel was quick to see the virtue of the new plan for Eugénie's departure.

"Young man, your news about that scoundrel Darby comes as a great relief to me, and now you lighten my mind on another score," he said. "Not only will Miss Eugénie be safer on a ship flying the Union Jack, but I'm willing to admit that I've been more than a little concerned about the chances of a Tucker vessel slipping safely past St. George's under normal circumstances. And in this instance, it would've been particularly ticklish." Eugénie looked at him sharply. It was clear to her not only that the Colonel knew that Bridger was privy to his plans, but that he was unruffled by that knowledge.

What a wily old fox he is, she thought, always one jump ahead. Reading her thoughts, the Colonel said, "Young lady, Captain Goodrich and I have our differences, but there's one subject on which we're in total accord. His fondness for you is all too apparent. He's made it his business to keep a close eye on anything and anyone that could affect your welfare. It's not been lost on me that certain ships belonging to a certain fleet have been happening by at predictably frequent intervals since you arrived here. I don't know what ploy you've used with the governor to explain this presence, Captain Goodrich. But for my part, I'm suitably impressed with your surveillance and appreciate fully that, in guarding Miss Eugénie so closely, you must also guard my interests as well, for to do otherwise would endanger this fair young lady. Do we understand each other?"

"Indeed, we do, sir," Bridger answered, unable to suppress a grin at how cleverly the older man had checkmated him. Eugénie was not at all sure that she was delighted to be the pawn in this match.

"Well then, unless it would compromise your arrangement with the governor, I'd like to extend The Grove's hospitality to you for the remainder of Eugénie's stay with us," Colonel Tucker offered expansively, heartily pleased with himself.

Now, what is the old rascal up to? Eugénie wondered. Is this simply an innocent gesture, or is the Colonel choosing to keep Bridger close at hand and out of mischief? In either case, does it really matter, since I'll have the joy of his company for these last days? At that thought, her face grew warm.

"Sir, I accept with pleasure your kind invitation," Bridger answered, smiling even more.

The next few days flowed one into another for Eugénie and Bridger. By dinghy and on foot, they explored the inlets and private nooks along Port Royal's picturesque shoreline, discovering secret caves and secluded beaches, racing dinghies nose to nose between the tiny islands that dotted the Great Sound. They were never out of each other's sight and rarely allowed more than a few minutes to go by before they found an excuse to reach out and touch.

There was a childlike innocence in the pure joy that they took in each other's company. The radiance that surrounded them softened the faces of those in their charmed circle. People found themselves smiling more often or suddenly humming or whistling a tune. It was an enchanted time.

Ever the romantic, Anne proclaimed that Eugénie's birthday celebration would be a picnic by moonlight. The heavenly body cooperated and rose in full, ethereal splendor on the eastern horizon right on schedule. Anne had decreed that everyone would dress in white for the occasion. The effect in the moonlight was nothing short of magical.

It was a happy gathering. Nearby neighbors and family members came who had come to know and grow fond of Eugénie during her stay. Toasts abounded and spirits were high. All too soon, the evening drew to a close. When the last guests climbed into their boats to follow the moon path home, Eugénie and Bridger slipped away to enjoy the beauty of the night alone together.

The next day, a quietness hung over the household, reflecting the change in the weather that had crept in during the predawn hours. Gone were the light air and bright sunshine of the days before. Low clouds loomed on the horizon and blanketed the sun. In Anne Tucker's words, the weight of the air was "thick enough to cut with a knife."

Only Eugénie and Bridger were oblivious to the brooding sky and the oppressive air as they reveled in each other's company. The morning hours stretched into afternoon, and finally the insect chorus heralded the approaching dusk. That night, supper was a simple affair and soon over. Even Colonel Tucker was willing to forgo his pipe and port on the veranda to hasten the end of that long day. Bridger departed to make his way to St. George's, to wait there through the long hours ahead until Eugénie was once more in his safekeeping.

"Keep safe, my love," he whispered into the darkness.

The moon was hidden that night, and there was no star to make a wish on.

XLII

❊❊❊

It had been a hectic morning: up at dawn, a last-minute check of the baggage, and then an early breakfast. During the meal, word had come to Colonel Tucker that James Tucker had made the trek from his home, Bellevue, in Paget, across to Joseph Jennings's house in Flatts to arrange for the promised whalers and men. When he arrived there, his grandfather had told him that he had had a change of heart and had refused to lend the men and the boats. Characteristically, the Colonel had been unruffled by the news.

"We have more than a sufficiency already," he said, scooping another spoonful of porridge into his mouth. The parting with the family had been painful, but finally Eugénie and Jeremy had gotten under way after many tearful promises on both sides to stay in touch and to plan a reunion in the near future.

It had been midmorning by the time they left the dock behind, making their way from The Grove's protected inlet into the Great Sound, around Spanish Point, along the north side of the island, passing by Flatt's Inlet, and on to Bailey's Bay, where they dropped anchor. There, Jeremy had jumped over the side of the whaler and splashed about in the water, seeking relief from the relentless heat. Eugénie had rearranged her few satchels and, sprawling back against them, had pulled the wide-brimmed straw hat over her face and fallen fast asleep. Later, after a quick picnic prepared by Cook's loving hands, they had set off again.

Eugénie and Jeremy arrived in Tobacco Bay just as twilight was fading into night. The heat hung thick in the night air. Jeremy lowered the sail and paddled the little boat into shore. Eugénie was thankful that the waning moon, shrouded by cloud cover, lent little light to the bay and its surroundings. In the darkness, she could not distinguish any openings in the solid wall of vegetation along the shore.

"How can you see where you're going, Jeremy?" she whispered.

"I can see well enough, Miss Eugénie. And I knows this bay like the back of my hand, 'cuz Ethan brought me here to practice my piloting and sailing when I was first learning how. He say this bay has reefs enough to learn on, but not so much as to git me in trouble right off. Don't you mind none, Miss Eugénie, I'll git us into shore, safe and sound." True to his word, he soon had the little boat through the shoals and up on the sand.

"Now, Miss Eugénie, you stay right with me. I knows exactly where I am and where I'm goin.' Captain Bridger say he skin me alive if I let anything happen to you." With that, he stowed the oars and began rummaging around in the hull of the little craft. The next thing Eugénie heard was the scrape of flint against flint. In the sudden brightness, she could see Jeremy lighting the wick of the lantern that he held in his other hand.

"Jeremy, what on earth are you doing? Put that out at once!" she exclaimed.

"I'se signaling Captain Bridger's ship, jes' like he told me," Jeremy answered, unperturbed, as he moved the shutter up and down over the face of the lantern.

"Captain Bridger's ship? How do you know where his ship is? Never mind. Do as I tell you! Put that lantern out this minute!" Cool as custard, Jeremy went on with his signaling.

Just as Eugénie was about to snatch the lantern out of his hand, Jeremy cried, "Look! Look, Miss Eugénie! See out there? Captain Bridger's answering back. He's sending us the signal, jes' like he said he would! Look!" Eugénie whirled around to see a rhythmic blinking coming to them out of the darkness. "We did it! We did it!" He burst out. "He's here, jes' the way we planned, and now he knows we's here, too!"

"Lower your voice," Eugénie scolded him. Then she added more gently, "You've done a grand job, Jeremy. Now, we'd better keep a look out for the other whalers." The words were no sooner out of her mouth than she heard the sound of oars pulling through the water nearby. She felt the hair on the back of her neck rise but managed to get out the birdcall that was the prearranged signal. When she heard the answering call, she let out a long sigh of relief. Soon afterward, several whalers slipped up alongside of them.

The last one to arrive was Rorick Hamilton, who had come the greatest distance. A quick tally was taken to make sure that everyone was there. Then they moved as quickly and as silently as possible up the path that led from the bay to the magazine. Eugénie kept to the fringes of the path, glad to be disguised by her boyish clothing and the deep shadows.

Before they reached the top of the steep incline, Eugénie grabbed Jeremy's arm and quickly went over the plan they had devised on their way to Tobacco Bay that afternoon. Then she took up her post as a lookout, melting into the thick growth of mangrove that circled the clearing where the magazine stood in silent isolation.

It began in the pit of her stomach and spread, like a dark, living thing, into her chest as she watched Jeremy's shadowy form move to the magazine, get a purchase on the rough surface, and begin to climb. She had no defense against it. She squeezed her eyes shut and bent forward, hugging herself. Her breath came in short gasps. She wished for something, anything, that would rivet her attention, demand her concentration, and take her mind off of what was happening before her eyes.

"If he falls, if he gets hurt. If something happens to him . . ." she whispered out loud. Why wasn't she the one inching her way up the wall instead of Jeremy? Inch by painful inch. Instead, she could only stand by, watch, and wait. Her muscles flexed and strained as she watched his slow, torturous ascent. She felt, before she saw, his foot slip. She clamped her hands to her mouth to muffle her scream. Somehow, he managed to cling to the stones, gather himself briefly, and then move upward once more.

Was it her imagination, or had the clearing become brighter? Were faint shadows visible for the first time, stretching across the worn grass? Were the shapes of the men waiting at the magazine's base more defined? She had to move then, if only to relieve her cramped muscles. The sound of her footsteps on the tinder-dry ground cover made a racket to her ears. She leaned against a nearby tree, rubbing her tired eyes. She turned her cheek against the trunk's cool, solid roughness and swallowed hard against the bile that rose in her throat.

The night was so still. Where were the background sounds she was so accustomed to hearing, the tree frogs' chorus, the common night-bird's call, the hand of the wind clapping through the large-leafed sea-grape? The silence weighed down on her. It isolated and magnified every small sound. She could hear the scrape of Jeremy's shoes against the stone, the muffled American and Bermudian accents of the wait-ing men, and, far off below, the distant slap of the waves striking the shore.

Eugénie knew that she was one of four lookouts posted at the mag-azine. Her position was on the path that ran along the ridge above the bay. From that vantage point, she could keep an eye on both the path and Jeremy's dark shape as he was slowly making his way to the roof of the building. When a twig snapped just behind her, Eugénie wheeled around, her heart in her throat, her eyes straining to pierce the dark shadows. The rustling that followed stretched her nerves to the break-ing point. Should she sound the alarm? A squeak, a snuffling noise, and a small nocturnal animal broke cover, scampered across the clear-ing, and darted into a new hiding place. Eugénie almost laughed with relief.

She turned back to measure Jeremy's progress and was relieved to see that he was finally pulling himself up onto the roof. Wasting no time, he began to cut through the stone block. The seconds seemed like hours, and the sound of the rasping blade was deafening to her ears. At last, he put the tool down and lifted the piece of roofing, laying it aside. He uncoiled the rope that was tied at his waist and threw the other end down to the outstretched hands of a burly American, who began gathering up the slack until it was taut. Then Jeremy lowered himself down through the hole, as the American slowly fed the rope out, hand over hand. Even after Jeremy disappeared from sight, the rope kept moving up and over the wall of the building.

The hand on her arm caught Eugénie by surprise. She gasped and whirled around.

"Qu'est-ce que c'est que ça?" a voice came out of the dark.

O, mon Dieu, un soldat français! her mind screamed, seeing the man's French uniform. Her initial shock turned to alarm.

The soldier, just as startled as Eugénie, dropped her arm and demanded in English, his accent thick, "What have we here?" Paralyzed, Eugénie could only stare up into the stranger's face.

"Monsieur," she began.

"Ah, vous êtes un Français, un déserteur, je pense!" the soldier exclaimed, making a grab for her. His words brought Eugénie out of her trance. She moved quickly, dodging around him, drawing him down the path and away from the magazine. Her sudden movement caught him off guard and gave her the headstart she needed. Too soon, she heard his footsteps closing the gap between them. At the last minute, she saw the ditch that cut across the path and turned sharply to avoid it, crashing into the underbrush. The soldier, running full tilt, was not as fortunate and fell headlong into the ravine. Eugénie stood up and brushed herself off. Cautiously, she approached the edge of the ditch and looked down, half expecting the stranger to leap up and grab her. When he failed to stir after a few moments, she climbed down beside him.

"Monsieur, monsieur," she whispered urgently. But he remained silent and still. She reached out gingerly and felt below his jaw for a pulse. Nothing. Shuddering, she sank back on her haunches, bowed her head, and took a deep breath. There was no time to lose. With one last look at the still form, she scrambled to her feet and climbed out of the

ravine. She took only a moment to catch her breath and then dashed back along the path toward the magazine. She kept looking back over her shoulder, fearing to see one of his fellow soldiers emerge from the woods.

When she arrived at the magazine, the clearing was alive with activity. A steady stream of men were carrying barrels down the path to the bay, passing others returning for another load. She ran to the nearest guard posted along the path and breathlessly told him what had happened.

"We must retrieve the body at once and get it out of sight!" the guard said, starting to move down the path.

"No! No!" Eugénie cried, grabbing his sleeve. "You can't leave your post. Remain here on watch in case others from his company come. I'll dispose of the body." Eugénie did not wait to hear his response, but went off to put the others on notice. Once everyone was alerted, she went in search of Jeremy.

She finally found him down by the whaling boats, helping to load the small craft. When he saw her deathly pale face in the light of the lanterns, he exclaimed, "Miss Eugénie, what's the matter? Has them governor's men come and found us?"

"No, Jeremy," she replied, trying to make her voice sound calm. "Just quickly. Come with me. There's something we must do at once, so that we can get back in time to leave when the boats are ready." Without giving him a chance to ask any more questions, she tore up the path, relieved to hear him close on her heels.

When they reached the point where the Frenchman had suddenly come through the trees, Eugénie slowed her pace. Still walking quickly, she told Jeremy what had happened. His eyes grew as big as saucers, and for once he was speechless. When she had finished, Jeremy's voice rose in a squeak.

"You mean, you mean he's dead? Holy Mary, Mother of God! And you're sayin,' we's goin' to bury him? Oh, Miss Eugénie, there ain't nothin' on God's green earth, nothin,' that I wouldn't do for you, but I'se plain scar't of dead folk. He's goin' to rise up and haint us. Yes, he's goin' to haint us, sure 'nuf, till the day we die. Pleeease, Miss Eugénie, don't ax me to do this thing!" The young man with nerves of steel and cold water in his veins, who had scaled the wall of the magazine such a short time before, dissolved into a scared little boy.

"Jeremy," Eugénie said sharply, "listen to me! We have no choice. If he's found when they discover the theft of the gunpowder, they won't stop to ask questions about how it happened. You and I both know who they'll go after without a moment's hesitation. You don't want the Colonel held accountable for something that was an accident, something that he had not one thing to do with, do you? Come, this is no time for you to lose your nerve."

By then, they had reached the ravine. Eugénie was thankful that the moon was hidden behind the clouds once more and that the body was just barely visible where it lay sprawled on a blanket of leaves. Finally, Jeremy relented, after Eugénie said that even if the poor man's spirit wandered the earth because of his tragic death, which she doubted, his ghost would hardly travel across the whole Atlantic Ocean just to visit Jeremy.

Once committed to the task, Jeremy moved quickly, with surprising strength, in spite of his size. Together, they managed to drag the body deep into the woods. Using his blade, Jeremy dug a shallow grave in the decomposed undergrowth. Only after they had covered the corpse and arranged dead leaves and branches to disguise the fresh mound, did Eugénie allow herself to collapse against the trunk of a palmetto that stood nearby, a sentry to the Frenchman's grave. Jeremy's voice, jabbering his fears and trepidation, brought her back from her numbed state. Straightening up and taking a deep breath, she put her arm around his slight shoulders and ushered the young boy back along the path.

"Hush, Jeremy, hush," she whispered to him. "The woods have ears. Do you want to attract unwelcome company? Put it all out of your mind now. It's over and done with. Besides, we have no time to waste. We must hasten back to the others. We wouldn't want them to leave us behind, would we?"

Eugénie's last words were all that Jeremy needed to put wings on his feet and as much distance as possible between him and their recent handiwork. He fairly flew along the path and didn't stop until he arrived at the water's edge, where Captain Morgan was directing the departure of the whalers, now laden with the barrels of gunpowder.

"Miss Eugénie," Rorick Hamilton said, arriving at her side, "I've been looking all over for you." Before Eugénie was forced to explain, he continued, "We must make haste now. I have all your belongings. My man and I are ready to leave. We'll carry you and Jeremy out to Captain Goodrich's ship. Come, we must go!"

Happy to let Rorick take charge, Eugénie allowed herself to be helped into the small boat. Spent in body and spirit, she erased everything from her mind and gave herself up to the gentle motion of the little vessel as it moved swiftly away from Tobacco Bay. She looked back once toward the shore. In the dim light, the men and boats appeared like forms without substance, wraiths moving against a shadowy background. Shivering, she turned away.

But for the one near-disaster, she thought, Colonel Tucker's plan had gone smoothly and quickly. The plan painstakingly framed over long months, days, and hours was now over in the flash of a gnat's eye. With a sigh, she relinquished the fear that had been her companion since she and Marie had departed from France for the colonies so many months ago. Her mission was over. Barring mishap, shortly she would be on her way home. Home! The word washed over her and she felt her spirits lift.

"Miss Eugénie," Jeremy, fully recovered, called out. "Look! The ship!" Lost in her thoughts, Eugénie had been oblivious to the sounds and the sight of the sloop that now lay just a short distance off the bow of the whaler. As she watched, a rope ladder was flung over the side. In the few minutes that remained, she made her farewells to Rorick, extending to him an open invitation to visit her in France. Holding his emotions in check, the young man resisted clasping her to his breast and begging her to stay.

She saw the wish in his eyes and said softly, "You've been a true friend to me, Rorick. I'll treasure you and your friendship, always." She brushed his cheek with her lips and turned to follow Jeremy. Even laden with all Eugénie's satchels, the young boy still managed to scamper up the ladder with the ease of a practiced sailor. Her ascent was somewhat less agile, but soon she, too, had the solid deck beneath her feet and Bridger at her side as she looked down to wave to the whaler below. Rorick gave her a gallant salute in return as he and the whaler disappeared into the darkness.

XLIII

❧❧❧

They shared the last few hours, before dawn pushed back the dark sky and the French ship came to carry her home. The words had long since been said between them. The past was theirs, carved by a blade held jointly. The future was theirs in memories revisited. And the present was theirs in the immediacy of the wind's kiss, in the flight of a longtail soaring on the edge of the horizon, in the sound of the ship's prow smacking against the ocean. They raised their faces together, smelling the tang of the sea air. And over, on, and through it all, the sweet taste of joy upon their lips mingled and sipped. Drunk but unsated. Seconds swollen. Ages captured in a moment. Their present, a lifetime. Their lifetime, in the burst of an instant, over.

Later she stood alone at the rail of the ship that flew the Fleur-de-Lis, the flag of her country. It felt foreign to her. She looked back over the widening wake and saw the island of Bermuda cloaked in mist and darkness.

In her mind's eye, she saw the island as it had first appeared to her, a patch of green, floating on turquoise, under the arching, sun-drenched skies. Had it only been a few short months?

She saw again the vividness of the colors, the cloud formations, ranging along the far horizons. She had come to know they were characteristic of the place. She saw the deep green ridges of the island thrusting up toward the sky, the white, white sand that ringed the inlets and the schools of fish that swam and leapt, flashing in the light. She remembered the first time she waded in that water and stepped barefooted onto the sand, her shock at the texture of it, so soft, featherlight, as fine as the finest face powder, and so white.

She saw again the houses as she had seen them then, placed by an indiscriminate hand, sprinkled along the shoreline or tucked into the ridges in defiance of storm and wind. How small and plain they had seemed to her, in contrast with the great manor houses and châteaux of France. They were simple in their architecture, bonneted with the gleaming white roofs. She had come to realize that the size and style of the houses had suited the nature and contour of the island, whose width and breadth could fit within the borders of her holdings in France.

Bermuda was a spare and stingy island, offering in abundance only native cedar and the fish life, rich and teeming, in its waters. The softness of its sands was not bred into these people. Instead, Bermuda's threadbare earth demanded a ruggedness in body and spirit. Only the enterprising, the resilient, and the fiercely independent could wrest a livelihood from this tight-fisted island.

When the early hurricanes swept the cedar houses away like tinder, this hardy lot replaced them with structures built of sterner stuff. When they found the shallow soil could only support meager crops, they turned to the sea and to shipping to seek their fortune. Through it all, their pragmatic, nimble wit prevailed, more often than not aimed at themselves. The kindness of the island's climate, except in storm season, was reflected in the kindness of its people. Their hospitality, like the welcoming arms common to their architecture, embraced stranger and friend alike. She had never met their match for openness and generosity.

This people, this island, and this night had played a role in the destiny of Bermuda's sister colonies on the mainland. How large or how small a role remained to be seen. When she undertook her mission, she had thought to hold herself apart, to act simply as an observer, a conduit of information back to France. When had she become engaged?

The answer eluded her, but it really did not matter. She looked up at the stars that dimmed with the approach of dawn and realized how much she had changed since she had arrived in Virginia. And how much more was at stake than she had thought. She remembered her parents' prophecy. Her role in Virginia and Bermuda, as well as the Bermudians' act of treason that night, were a part of a greater plan. Yes, their prophecy had come true. These Americans were on a course to redefine the balance of power amongst people. They would invent a political order in which supreme power would be vested in all the people, and in which freedom with responsibility would be entrusted in equal measure to all from the highest to the lowest.

She looked east and saw a sliver of brightness on the horizon.

Her mission was over. She was going home.

APPENDIX

Often the weaving of the fictitious and the factual in a historical novel blurs the line between what is real and what is the author's imagination. It is my hope that the following list of the real people, places, and events will help you distinguish between the two and whet your appetite to learn more about these people, their times, and the places where they lived. They are listed in order of appearance.

The People

St. George Tucker, nicknamed "Sammy," was the youngest offspring of Anne Butterfield Tucker and Colonel Henry Tucker. He studied the law at the College of William and Mary in Williamsburg, Virginia, became a member of the Virginia bar, and lived out his life there. During his career, he was made a judge and a professor of law at William and Mary. You can visit his house in Williamsburg, Virginia.

Bridger Goodrich was the fifth of six sons of merchant shipper John Goodrich. His father had a ferry service and owned several plantations along the James River. Although the family originally took up the cause of the patriots, through the series of events described in this book, the family became loyalists. When their former comrades learned about their change of allegiance, the Goodrich property was confiscated and they were driven out of Virginia. Bridger, his father, and his brothers then became privateers under the British flag. Bridger, by reputation, was the most daring and notorious of the lot. He won the eternal wrath and animosity of Colonel Henry Tucker and other Bermudian shippers when he preyed on their vessels. Ironically, he met and married Beth Tucker, a cousin of the Colonel Tucker family. She was the young woman in the story who attended the wedding at the Tucker's house and bore such a striking resemblance to Eugénie. In the narrative, I have taken license with some of the events in Bridger Goodrich's life, but records confirm that he cut quite a dashing figure in history, that he was an extraordinary sailor, and that he lived out his life in Bermuda. Upon his death, he was buried there in St. Peter's church, in St. George's.

Edward Goodrich was the sixth son of John Goodrich.

Silas Deane was from the Connecticut colony and acted as an agent for the American cause, carrying secrets back and forth from the colonies to Europe, specifically France. He is credited by some with enlisting the aid of Lafayette, Baron Friedrich Wilhelm von Steuben, and Kazimierz Pulaski in the Americans' cause. He traveled to Bermuda to determine the state of affairs there. He then informed both the American patriots and the French of the importance of Bermuda's strategic position. Later, Henry Lee, Benjamin Franklin, and he were sent to France on behalf of the Americans to negotiate an alliance. While he was in France, there were rumors of misconduct on his part and charges of embezzlement by Henry Lee. He was recalled to defend himself. He died under a cloud of suspicion before the allegations could be confirmed or refuted.

Thomas Jefferson was a member of the Continental Congress (not the first one), was the Chairman of the Declaration of Independence committee, and wrote and presented the first draft of the declaration to the Congress. He was both a governor of Virginia and a minister to France. He proposed the decimal coinage system to the young republic. He was a secretary of state, a secretary of the treasury, and the third president of the United States. He was instrumental in founding the University of Virginia. Jefferson was a noted naturalist, scholar, and architect, to mention just a few of his other avocations. He did not serve in the American forces fighting the British in the Revolutionary War.

Henry Lee was a member of one of the many related Lee families, a large and distinguished Virginian clan. His brilliance as a cavalry commander in the Revolutionary War earned him the nickname "Light-Horse Harry." He eulogized George Washington with the now-famous words, "First in war, first in peace, and first in the hearts of his countrymen." Robert Edward Lee, the General-in-Chief of the Confederate army, was his son.

John Murray, the Earl of Dunmore, was the governor of Virginia from 1771 to 1776. He was driven from Williamsburg by the revolutionaries and was forced to govern as best he could from a man-of-war offshore.

Patrick Henry was a Virginian backwoodsman, a lawyer, and an orator and amongst the radical group of patriots. He was a Virginia delegate to the Continental Congresses and an early governor of Virginia. He turned down invitations to be a member of George Washington's cabinet, ambassador to France, and chief justice of the Supreme Court. He was adamantly opposed to the ratification of the United States Constitution and was instrumental in bringing about the adoption of the first ten amendments to the Constitution, the Bill of Rights.

Peyton Randolph was a very popular and highly respected Virginian lawyer and politician. He was a delegate to the first Continental Congress and the first president of that body.

Benjamin Church was a doctor. He was born in Rhode Island and moved to Massachusetts. He was a very influential member of the inner circles of the revolutionaries. When it was discovered that he was a spy for the British, he was court-martialed and deported to the West Indies. His ship was lost at sea.

John Adams from Massachusetts was a delegate to the Continental Congresses, a member of the committee charged with drafting the Declaration of Independence, a staunch rival of Thomas Jefferson,

and the second president of the United States. He was a cousin of
Samuel Adams.

Samuel Adams was an early revolutionary and agitator. He led the
opposition to the Stamp Act, amongst other things, and was one of
the leaders who organized the Boston Tea Party.

The Family of Colonel Henry and Anne Tucker

Colonel Henry Tucker was one of the long line of the illustrious
Tucker family in Bermuda. He was a merchant shipper and an
influential leader on the island. His life and activities were well documented in the correspondence between him and his sons, St.
George Tucker in Virginia and Harry Tucker in St. George's, Bermuda. He recognized the importance of the trade between the
American colonies and Bermuda and was determined to continue
it. He is believed to have been the ringleader of the Gunpowder
Theft, but it was never proved.

Anne Tucker, born Anne Butterfield, was a descendent of one of the
early Bermuda families. Her family boasted many lawyers and merchants. Her father was General Butterfield.

Henry Tucker, nicknamed "Harry," was the oldest child of Colonel
Henry and Anne Tucker. He married Frances May Bruère, nicknamed "Fanny," who was the daughter of Bermuda's governor,
George James Bruère. They had many children: by some reports six,
by others ten. Their oldest was named Henry St. George Tucker.
Ultimately, all of the children left Bermuda to go into service in the
British empire. His father-in-law, Governor Bruère, showed his
fondness for and trust in Harry when he appointed him to the position of public treasurer and to the Council on which Harry served
both as secretary and later as president. The governor also made him
his executor. All of this the governor did in spite of his animosity
toward and suspicions about Harry's father, the Colonel.

Thomas Tudor Tucker, often called "Tommy" or "Tudor," was the
second Tucker son. Before going abroad, he served as clerk to the
Bermuda House of Assembly. He completed his medical training at

Edinburgh, Scotland, and set up practice in Charleston, South Carolina. He later moved to New York. He was a member of the first United States Congress and later was treasurer of the United States. He lost his wife and eventually his children to smallpox.

Nathaniel "Natty" Tucker was the third Tucker son. Before he went abroad, he served as clerk of the Council. He gained his medical degree in Edinburgh, Scotland, and lived in Yorkshire, England. He considered himself a poet. The author learned about some of the flowers, bushes, and trees planted at the Tucker family home, The Grove, from one of his poems.

Elizabeth Tucker, called "Eliza," was one of the two Tucker daughters. She never married and was considered to be plain. She was known as the letter writer in the family, corresponding with all of the family members wherever they happened to be.

Frances Tucker, called "Fanny," was the other Tucker daughter. She married her cousin, Henry Tucker of Somerset, and lived with him at Bridge House, "The Hermitage."

Other Tucker Relatives

Henry Tucker of Somerset, also referred to as Henry Tucker of the Bridge (for the location of his home), together with his relatives Richard and John Jennings, owned and operated one of the most successful shipping businesses in Bermuda at that time. He was deeply involved in Colonel Tucker's political activities. The lookout on top of his house, "The Hermitage," was used to keep an eye out for customs agents, "Searchers," and other comings and goings of interest to the Tuckers and their colleagues. The lookout was not replaced when it was damaged during a storm.

Captain John Tucker was one of the sea captains who regularly traded with the American colonies before, during, and after the American embargo of Bermuda. On one of his trips, he brought Silas Deane to Bermuda.

Elizabeth Tucker, called "Beth," of the Paget parish Tuckers was a cousin of Colonel Tucker's family. She incurred the wrath of many of her Tucker relatives when she married Bridger Goodrich in 1778. She met Bridger at Government House in St. George's, not at the fictitious wedding of Colonel Tucker's cousin as described in the narrative.

James Tucker owned Bellevue in Paget, an outstanding example of Bermudian architecture that still stands today. He was a member of Colonel Tucker's group and signed the letter sent to the Continental Congress petitioning that body to lift the trade embargo. He did go to his grandfather, Joseph Jennings, at Flatts to request the use of boats and men for the evening of August 14, 1775. His grandfather turned down his request.

George James Bruère was the much beleaguered governor of Bermuda, caught between the Tucker contingent and the ministers at Whitehall. He was Harry Tucker's father-in-law. At his death, his son by the same name served temporarily as the lieutenant governor of Bermuda. This same son let it be known that he felt his father died prematurely because of his constant battling with the Tucker contingent and the Whitehall ministers.

Other Bermudian Surnames of the Period Mentioned in the Narrative
Jennings, Dill, Smith, Trimingham, Harvey, Darrell, and Butterfield: The author took some license with certain Christian names in these families—for example, "Jack" Darrell and "Andrew" Harvey. To her knowledge, there were no such members of those families. Some leeway was also taken with the words and behavior of these historical figures to enrich the text and should not be confused with direct quotations and historically based behavior, with the exception of Patrick Henry's speech.

THE PLACES

Governor's Palace stands today, magnificently renovated during the restoration of Colonial Williamsburg, Virginia, by the Rockefeller Foundation.

Chowning's Tavern, in Williamsburg, Virginia, was a tavern of the colonial period.

The Grove, in Southampton, Bermuda, was the home of Colonel Henry and Anne Tucker and their family. What remained of the house was torn down recently when the Port Royal Golf Course was built.

Bridge House, "The Hermitage," was the home of Henry Tucker of Somerset and Frances Tucker. It is still standing today, keeping watch over Ely's Harbor and the Great Sound. Originally, it had a lookout tower on the roof, which was struck by lightning in the 1790s. Because a person was killed when that happened, the lookout was never rebuilt. The house overlooks Somerset Bridge, whose "trap door" is still in use. When raised, the bridge allows large vessels to sail through from Ely's Harbor into the Great Sound. It is claimed to be the first "drawbridge" on record.

FACTS AND EVENTS OF NOTE

"Wreckers": During Bermuda's early history and during the period of the narrative, the existence of "wreckers" was well documented.

Privateers and privateering: Privateering was a lucrative source of income for audacious merchant seamen. The activities of these seamen were "legitimized" by letters of marque issued by their governments, which allowed these men to prey on ships flying the flags of "enemy" countries.

The Frenchman at the magazine: In the late 1800s, when foundations were being dug for a "new" St. Peter's church in St. George's, Bermuda, a skeleton dressed in a French military uniform was unearthed. This discovery solved the hundred-year-old mystery of what had happened to a French officer out on parole in St. George's on the night that the gunpowder disappeared from the government magazine. How he met his death was never determined, and the "new" St. Peter's church was never completed. The partial building stands today and is called the "Unfinished Church."

The Gunpowder Theft: On the night of August 14, 1775, the government magazine in St. George's, Bermuda, was breached and some 1,800 pounds (approximately 100 barrels) of gunpowder were removed. That much is clear. Rumors abounded at the time about the circumstances of the theft. One rendition was that Bermudians had broken into the magazine and carried the barrels down to their small boats waiting in Tobacco Bay. From there, the barrels made their way up to the west end of Bermuda and were off-loaded onto the American brigantine *Retaliation,* anchored near Mangrove Bay, which then transported the powder to the city of Philadelphia in the colony of Pennsylvania. Another version was much the same, except that the Bermudians stood guard while American sailors carried the barrels from the magazine to the small boats waiting in Tobacco Bay and thence to the west end of the island and away. Other variations on the theme suggested that the small boats in Tobacco Bay carried the gunpowder directly to two American ships, the *Lady Catherine* and the *Charleston and Savannah Pacquet,* which hovered offshore near Tobacco Bay. These ships then, according to this version, sailed the powder to Philadelphia. The facts remain sketchy to this day. The mystery surrounding the Gunpowder Theft/Plot was never solved, although there were strong suspicions that Colonel Tucker and his cohorts were responsible. In spite of Governor Bruère's best efforts, no one was ever accused, arrested, convicted, or punished for the crime. Given the fact that Great Britain was at war with the Americans, and that Bermuda was a colony of Britain, any Bermudian who was party to the theft of the gunpowder was committing an act of treason. There is no doubt that the gunpowder that was spirited away from Bermuda's government magazine that night found its way to Philadelphia aboard Captain George Orde's *Lady Catherine,* for it is stated in the minutes of a meeting of the Pennsylvania Committee of Safety dated August 26, 1775, that "A letter was this day received by [way] of Captain Orde of the 'Lady Catherine' from Henry Tucker, Chairman of the Deputies of the several parishes of Bermuda enclosing an account for 1,182 pound of gunpowder shipped by him aboard said vessel with an account of eight half bars [100 barrels] of powder."

To this day, no conclusive evidence has come to light detailing who was responsible for the theft or how it was carried out. Sources record that the Americans used the Bermudian gunpowder in the momentous battle that General George Washington waged with the British after he crossed the Delaware River. The Americans were victorious in that battle. In November 1776, more than a year after the gunpowder was removed from the Bermuda magazine and transported to Philadelphia, the Americans lifted the trade embargo against Bermuda.